CHANCEY MOVES

CHANCEY MOVES

10

KAY DEW SHOSTAK

August South
PUBLISHING

ISBN: 978-1-7350991-5-6

SOUTHERN FICTION: Women's Fiction / Southern Fiction / Railroad / Bed & Breakfast / Mountains / Georgia / Family Fiction/ Small Town Fiction

Text Layout and Cover Design by Roseanna White Designs
Cover Images from www.Shutterstock.com

Author photo by Susan Eason with www.EasonGallery.com

Published by August South Publishing. You may contact the publisher at:

AugustSouthPublisher@gmail.com

Dedicated to two professionals that have become friends.
They enhance this writing journey, and my life,
in so many ways.
My editor, Jessica Hatch,
and
my cover artist, Roseanna White.

CHARACTER LIST

Jackson and Carolina Jessup – Moved to Chancey one year ago. Operate Crossings, a bed-and-breakfast for railfans in their home. They have three children: Will, 22; Savannah, 16; Bryan, 13. Will married Anna after the move and they have a new daughter, Frances. Carolina also runs the bookstore side of Blooming Books.

Jackson's family – Mother Etta lives at the beach in South Carolina. Father Hank is married to Shelby and lives in Kentucky. Two brothers, Emerson and Colt. Emerson is the oldest, and he and his wife have three daughters and live in Virginia. Colt is the youngest, is single, and moved to Chancey with his girlfriend Phoenix.

Carolina's family – Parents Goldie and Jack live in Tennessee. Carolina is an only child.

Missus Bedwell – Lifelong resident of Chancey. Recently widowed.

Peter Bedwell, 45 - lives two doors down from his mother.

Laney and Shaw Conner – Both from Chancey. Shaw owns an automotive dealership. Laney partners with Carolina in the B&B. They have three children: twins Angie and Jenna, 17; Cayden, 8 months.

Susan and Griffin Lyles – Susan is sister to Laney and manages the Lake Park. Griffin and Susan are currently separated. They have three children: Leslie, 19; Susie Mae, 15; Grant, 13. Laney and Susan's mother is Gladys Troutman.

Gertie Samson – She has one child: Patty, 28, married to Andy Taylor. Gertie was raised in Chancey and returned after her daughter, Patty, settled there. She owns a lot of property in town. She lives in the house she, Patty, and Andy run their businesses out of.

Ruby Harden – Owns and runs Ruby's Café on the town square. Lifelong Chancey resident.

Libby Stone – Works with Ruby at the café and is married to Bill Stone. Daughter is Cathy.

Cathy Stone Cross – Libby and Bill's daughter is married to Stephen Cross, a teacher at the high school. They have a young son, Forrest.

Kendrick family – Moved to town for father Kyle to open new Dollar Store where he hired Anna Jessup as Assistant Manager. Wife Kimmy and their four children live in Chancey. Kyle's daughter, Zoe, from a previous marriage lives with Kimmy and cares for the younger three children.

Shannon Chilton – Operates florist part of Blooming Books. Lifelong Chancey resident. She's 30 and recently ended a relationship with Peter Bedwell.

Bonnie Cuneo – Works in Blooming Books. Retired teacher who lives in Laurel Cove with husband, Cal.

Alex Carrera – Opening new restaurant on Main Street called AC's. He and his girlfriend, Angie Conner, live above it.

WHEREAS, a special election for mayor of Chancey was held on March 2nd; and

WHEREAS, Shermania Cogdill Bedwell won the election; and

WHEREAS, communication about the town of Chancey is critical as we go forward; and

WHEREAS, our new mayor is gifted in communication.

NOW, THEREFORE, I, Shermania Cogdill Bedwell, Mayor of the City of Chancey, do hereby proclaim this book shall begin with a message from your mayor.

Let me officially thank you for your devotion to our beloved town of Chancey, Georgia. Let me also state that whether you live in the vaunted boundaries of our town, in nearby environs, or wholly outside these ancient mountains we call home, you are considered a part of Chancey. I will do my best to honor your wishes and desires while always upholding the highest ideas of governance I find to be the best path forward.

Mayor S.C. Bedwell
City of Chancey, Georgia

Dear friends,

I must say I'm finding the issuing of proclamations exhilarating and believe it is a most efficient means of communication. None of that timewasting and confusing back-and-forth of common conversations. I will be speaking to Carolina about my taking over the duty of opening letters in all forthcoming books, or instead of letters, let's just call them proclamations from here on out.

Now, let me get this update out of the way as I have a very full schedule today, as I do every day. First: I won the mayoral election fair and square, despite any falsehoods you might've heard about the final count. Besides, Laney Conner has moved on to another folly of hers, something called Ladies of the Club. I'll save you from stopping in there. It's basically chairs and tables in the middle of a flea market. Well, that's what it'll be once it opens. I'm sure of it. So that'll last all of a week.

Now, next topic.

Allow me to address the many questions I've been hearing. Yes, my son, Peter Bedwell, did marry Delaney LaMotte in a quiet, private ceremony on Valentine's weekend in my home. I'll cover how beautiful and stately it all was later... if I have room in this proclamation. I'm sure you'd rather hear about your beloved town of Chancey than all that social fodder.

Although I've only been mayor a few weeks, I've created a buzzing atmosphere in our downtown. AC's is a welcome addition with its delightful menu and setting. Alex Carrera and Angie Conner are able managers—with Peter's oversight. They've already expanded their hours and have catered several high-profile events, including Peter's wedding reception, though it was hampered by a late-night snowfall of over six inches. Several guests had to cancel, but it was a wonderful evening anyway. Now, back to town news.

The dance studio and smoothie bar are proving quite popular. Phoenix and Chancey's head football coach, Colt Jessup, are as solid as ever. The rumors of her being seen about town with other men have been found to be completely untrue. The other new couple in town, Danny Kinnock and Shannon Chilton, is equally happy. Or, I'm sorry, is Shannon's last name Kinnock? They were married, but then they weren't? Either way they've finally admitted they have a child on the way. There have been rumors of its due date being in July, but that's impossible. People who don't even know if they're married can't be counted on to be able to figure out a due date correctly. Oh, and the flower shop is doing fine under my mayoral leadership.

The book festival is coming up next weekend, and I've made sure Chancey and Carolina's store, Blooming Books, are featured prominently. I'm finding one of the hardest parts of being mayor is setting events up beautifully, then having to turn them over to others to run, but delegation is part of the job. We'll just have to let Carolina fly or fail. It's out of my hands.

On a more personal note, Savannah has chosen where to attend college, and I'm happy for the family that she'll be close by at a very nice public college where she'll get a perfectly adequate education, I'm sure. Of course it's not as prestigious or historical as the private college my grandson Gregory attends, but then, everyone can't have the Bedwell-LaMotte bloodlines. As needs be when a superior, upper-level education is being sought, Gregory didn't stay long in Chancey. I doubt anyone outside our close-knit family will see much of him, so no reason for curiosity there.

I must be closing and moving on to the important matters of my incredibly busy day. Thank you for your unwavering support of my candidacy and my leadership in the many years to come.

Mayor S.C. Bedwell
City of Chancey, Georgia

Chapter 1

"Do I look like I care about your spring break right now?" I demand of my daughter, who is sitting in the front window of Blooming Books. Sitting. Oh, and talking, though you might also call it whining.

"You should. It is my senior spring break. It's got to be epic." She has on red leggings, a cut-off gray sweatshirt, and is barefoot. "Everyone is booking their trips. Cruises and trips to Miami or the islands." She pulls her feet up in front of her in the window, signaling that she's going to keep talking. And sitting. And whining.

"You're supposed to be helping me. That's what I'm paying you for, right?"

I turn away from her. Maybe if I'm not there for her to talk to, she'll finish up the front window. The shop has been closed for half an hour, and the chamber of commerce meeting begins in an hour—if I can clear some space for people to sit. The North Georgia Book Festival is this upcoming weekend, and I have a mile-long to-do list to get through. Boxes of books have been delivered for the authors who will be signing autographs in our shop. I hired Savannah to help me get ready for the event. All I need her to do is open boxes and stack one of each of the books in the window for Danny to work his magic tomorrow.

Yes, you heard that right. "Danny" and "magic" in the same sentence. The boy, I mean, young man, is a whiz with books. He reads everything. He still drives me crazy in a lot of ways, but I'm learning to put up with him because he has Bonnie's flair for decorating, with an even better understanding of the books. Don't tell Bonnie!

But you know what? She's fine with it. Her decorating business has taken off, so she'll happily play second fiddle to Danny Kinnock. She's in the middle of completely redecorating Peter and Delaney and Missus's home. Once the wedding was over and all the fabric, flowers, and rented furniture were removed, Peter didn't move much of the old stuff back in. He basically handed Bonnie a blank check and told her to start from scratch, and then he and Delaney left for their honeymoon in Greece.

Missus's apartment, in the area she and FM renovated for Will and Anna right after they got married, is not to be touched by Bonnie, but the rest of the house has been fair game. Bonnie worked around the clock, with money as no object, to get things somewhat normal for when the newlyweds returned this past Saturday. Needless to say, I've not seen much of my manager for the last two weeks, so with Shannon being such a grouch and sick to boot, Danny and I formed an alliance. He and Shannon had an obstetrician appointment this afternoon, though, and were going out to dinner afterward, so I hired a relative and that's working out just as it usually does. I grab the heavy metal dolly and wheel it to a newly arrived stack of boxes. I shove it under that stack and struggle to tip it back.

"Mom, we're running out of time!" she squeals behind me.

I jump at her high pitch yelp, and my fingers lose their grip of the dolly. It jolts forward, and the stack of boxes falls in slow motion. Luckily only the top box is open, but even so, books scatter all over the floor.

I sigh and raise my eyes to the heavens. "Pick these up," I tell her. "Don't let the pages get bent."

We gather books while she tells me again about her friends' spring break plans.

"Savannah, stop it. Those are your Marietta and Atlanta friends. It's a different world there. The rest of the normal world doesn't think spring break has to cost thousands of dollars and involve air travel."

"Well, maybe they should. It is my senior year."

I stop, rest my hands on my hips, and take a breath.

"I know. But we can't afford a big trip. Your dad is working like crazy to get the construction business off the ground. I'm up to my eyeballs in this book festival and trying to run this place while Bonnie gets her business going. We don't live in the Atlanta suburbs anymore. You say you like living here? Well, this is part of living here. Spring break is just a week off school, that's it. The church youth group is going to do some fun stuff, right?"

She shakes her head at me. "Whatever. Am I done here?" she asks as she slouches away, returning to the front of the store.

"No, you're not. You could be done. You should be done. But you're not done. If we don't finish in the next ten minutes, we can't get dinner at AC's before the chamber meeting. So it's up to you whether you eat there or at home *and* whether you get paid."

I promised her dinner next door and twenty dollars, so she had better finish if she really wants to afford the senior spring fling dress she has her eye on.

Besides, I'm starving.

CHAPTER 2

"If I get one more proclamation notice from her majesty, I'm going to put Ex-Lax in her next cup of coffee," Ruby grumbles from her seat in front of me at the meeting. Phoenix, sitting a couple seats down from Ruby, snorts a laugh. The chamber of commerce meeting hasn't started yet, but most of us are in our seats.

Ruby raises one eyebrow at me, then turns to talk over her other shoulder, closer to me and farther from Phoenix. "I don't know what Red is laughing about. She's had a starring role in a couple of the proclamations I've seen... and not in a good way."

I scoot up to the edge of my seat and tip my head toward her. "Seriously. It's like Missus is making all these proclamations to try and clean up for Peter's behavior."

It's Ruby's turn to snort-laugh. "They remind me of a Monty Python skit." She adopts a deep voice with an English accent: "No, do not look over here. Do not look at my son. He is fine. Yes, that son. The one you're not looking at." She dissolves into snickering behind her hand as she straightens up and looks forward to where Retta is calling the meeting to order.

I'm still hunched forward, my eyebrows pinched, my mouth opened. Ruby's a Monty Python fan? Who knew?

"Hey, is that my seat?" Jackson says from where he standing in the aisle.

I scoot back and let him by.

He frowns at my furrowed brow and open mouth. "Are you okay?"

"Ruby just quoted, well, I don't know that she was quoting, but she just did Monty Python, an English accent and all," I whisper to him.

He chuckles. "I love Monty Python."

"But Ruby…"

I'm turned completely toward him, but he stops me with a look and a tip of his head toward the front of the room.

"Carolina?" Retta is staring at me. She has on a pink plaid suit. Honestly I'm surprised they made it in her size, but I'm not surprised she's wearing it. "You wanted to go first, you told me. I'm trying to be responsive to the business owners of our town, but if you won't pay attention, I can move on."

I jump up. "Oh, yes! I do. I mean, thank you. So the book festival is this weekend, and it's going to be great. The North Georgia Tourism group has set up a rotation of authors that begins for us on Friday at four o'clock, with three authors speaking and taking questions. Afterward we're having a wine reception here, to which you are all invited. Saturday is full of the same sort of thing, with AC's as the site of an author luncheon, but those tickets are sold out. We'll have more signings Saturday afternoon, and then Sunday—"

"Excuse me for interrupting, Carolina," Peter says from his seat in the front row. He slowly stands, as though he's addressing the joint chambers of congress, not the Chancey Chamber of Congress. "There's been a slight change in plans for Sunday. A college friend of mine, a well-known author who will be announced later this week, will be in town, and we are hosting an event in her honor at our house on Sunday. She said she'd be honored to sign books here at your store following the champagne brunch."

"Oh, Peter!" Retta gushes. "That sounds delightful! Are tickets still available? Who is it? Can you please just tell us? You know we won't blab!"

Peter frowns and smiles at the same time—you know, the way lawyers can. "Oh, no tickets. Our event is by invitation only. Of course anyone can come here afterward and buy a book to be signed." He turns back toward me. "Thank you, Carolina. I'll be in touch with the particulars and the books you'll want to have on hand." He gives me a royal nod, turns slowly back around, and sits.

And since the rest of my planned announcement, as well as every decent thought which can be said out loud, has left my head, I sink into my chair as well.

Jackson pats my knee. "Well, that sounds exciting! Wonder who the author is?"

"Something's different here," Laney says from her side of the booth. We're sitting in Ruby's after the chamber meeting. "Don't you think so?"

I look around and notice that she's right. Something feels off. "What is it? Everything looks the same." I scoot over for Jackson to slide in beside me. Laney has her side to herself for the moment, but she's huddled in the corner, arms crossed defensively. Her presentation at the chamber meeting went anything but well. As Peter walks past our table, she narrows her eyes and stares him into apologizing on bended knee.

Yeah, right. He walks right on past, laughing with a couple of others from the meeting.

Laney leans over the table and hisses, "He's not even the least bit sorry. He wanted to make me look like a fool. He did that on purpose!"

Jackson nudges my leg under the table. We've talked about

me trying to slow Laney's club idea, but now that the time is perfect…

He widens his eyes at me and jerks his head across the table to tell me to get on with it. I however, pick up my cup of coffee and take a long, long drink. He rolls his eyes, then looks at Laney and asks, "Which of his questions bothered you the most?"

Oh. That's a good question. I could've asked Laney that and not gotten in trouble at all.

She studies my husband for just a moment, then sighs. "It's just the whole way he acted, like I hadn't thought this out properly. I mean, I've thought about nothing else."

I set my cup down kind of hard. "Come on now. You've got a new baby, two daughters graduating high school, you're helping run a restaurant, and you're doing all that publicity stuff with the dealership. Your plate is full. Over full."

"So you think I'm crazy to try and open The Club, too?" Her voice is low and her arms pulled tighter than ever around herself. Even with her face pinched, she looks great, but she'd never show up at chamber meeting not looking like she just stepped off the runway. Her Atlanta shopping trip resulted in a wardrobe that fits her new Southern Belle in Charge persona perfectly. Now if she could only get some sleep, she might be able to pull it all off and actually *be* in charge. Her dark hair is just long enough now to be pulled back into a small, low ponytail, and the style makes her eyes stand out even more. But those eyes look tired, and makeup can only do so many miracles.

"No. I'm excited about The Club," I adamantly state, even though I can hear and feel Jackson's sigh beside me. I kick in his direction and meet his shin, which cuts off his dramatic sigh. "But maybe you should delay the opening a few weeks. Give yourself some time to breathe."

"I can't." The word *can't* stretches out to be a full, run-on sentence, which isn't hard to do for a Southerner in distress. "I have contracts with Rachel Lyles's daughter's contacts for their pop-up shops. And all the ladies in town are really excited about being in The Club. Shoot! Can I even call it a club if Peter won't let me charge for membership?"

"Here's your pie," Kimmy Kendrick announces. "Chocolate Bourbon Pecan for everyone here, right?"

"Yes, ma'am!" Jackson says. "The big piece goes right here in front of me. They got the baby pieces."

"Petite pie is what we call it, Jackson," she says as she places brightly colored plates in front of Laney and me with slivers of pie on them.

Picking up my fork, I slice off a bite. "It's ingenious is what it is. Just enough to not feel left out, but to not feel guilty. Was this your idea?"

Kimmy beams. She's cut off her long, blonde hair, and it looks so cute. It's shorter and styled in layers and waves toward her face, which doesn't look as long or sad lately. Her smile helps, too. She wears flowered aprons when she works here and bright-red Keds. "Sure was my idea! Petite pie for a dollar. You'd be amazed how many people get a couple of different flavors."

Laney holds up a hand to signify she wants to say something when her mouth is empty. We watch her chew, and then she swallows. "What's different here? We can't figure it out, but something is definitely different."

Kimmy glances to both sides, then leans over our table. "I cleaned real good yesterday while we were closed."

We all look around, and when our eyes meet again, we know she's right.

Laney laughs. "It sparkles. Even at night. The windows, the chrome on the tables and stools, the glass display cases. Even the frames on all the ball teams' pictures. I can't believe it made that big of a difference."

Kimmy points downward. "I think it's mainly the floor. But

don't look! Ruby's kind of sensitive about it. I came in on my own time, but then before we opened back up for pie tonight, she handed me two twenties and said she wanted to give me that. I think she was surprised how dirty it had gotten."

"I sure hadn't noticed it was that bad," Laney says, wrinkling her nose. "It feels better, though. Lighter."

"Hey, guys!" Susan says as she approaches our booth. Kimmy moves back for her to slide in beside her sister. "This place looks amazing. Ruby was telling everyone up at the front that you came in all on your own and cleaned."

The creator of petite pie pulls back. "She's telling people?"

Susan winks. "I don't think she had a choice. The change is too noticeable. Everyone up there was talking about it. You've really done great, Kimmy."

Kimmy smiles, but as she begins to blush, she hurries toward the back. Susan turns to Laney. "The other thing everyone is talking about is how good you look in that shade of blue. What a great idea to wear that shawl to show some of the things you'll have for sale in The Club."

She doesn't fool her sister. Laney groans. "It was a stupid idea. I probably won't ever open up. You know how I am. Like Peter said, I never stick with anything!" Tears well up, and Jackson takes that as his cue to quietly move to another table with his half-eaten piece of pie. Laney whimpers, "Why do I always do this?"

Susan scoots a little closer to her. She's so wiry she has one leg bent in the seat and can still get close enough to hug Laney. "Peter is just jealous. You're the one with staying power. How long have you been married? You sure didn't quit on you and Shaw. And you didn't move out of town like Griffin and I did. You have a daughter getting ready to go to your alma mater and one opening up a business in your hometown. You are so grounded that you are free to explore your passions! You'll get The Club opened, and it'll work beautifully. Then, when you're done with it, you can move on to something else. Why, the rest of the world would love to have the ability to try more than one thing. Life is too short to be pigeonholed. And, sister, you know and live that!"

Laney straightens in her seat as her sister talks. Her tears seem to have dried up and her eyebrows have flattened as her mind is racing along the path her sister has led her onto. It's as if once she saw past the cobwebs of self-doubt Peter had draped over her, her vision came back to life. "I don't have to charge a membership to call it a club. I like the name Ladies of the Club, and I think it will make people feel good to be a part of a club, even without memberships." She fans her hands at Susan excitedly. "Let me out. I want to go talk to some people. I know my people!" As she pulls herself along the seat, she laughs. "What in the world was I thinking? Since when did I start listening to anyone else, especially someone like Peter Bedwell? Lord knows he ain't ever had a clue what makes things work. Why would he know jack now?"

Standing at the end of our table, she pulls the beautiful, handmade shawl off her shoulders, hold it out, and elaborately fluffs it. Then she places back around her after she can feel all eyes on her.

"Well, I better be going," she announces as she struts to the front. "I'm expecting another shipment of these beautiful shawls tomorrow along with some other delightful things you'll just have to stop in at Ladies of the Club to see." At the door she stops and turns, saying loudly, "And as Peter said, who knows how long I'll actually be in business. You don't want to wait *too* long. I'll be opening later this week. Stay tuned!" With another flourish of her shawl, she pushes out the shiny, clean door.

Susan leans back and winks at me. "There we go. Fixed her." She waves at Kimmy for a refill of coffee as she gives me a grim side look. "Now let's figure out my train wreck of a life."

Chapter 3

"What's all this?"

I'd planned on parking around back this morning, but as I began to turn right at the corner of AC's, I saw Delaney on the front sidewalk with flats and flats of pansies. This piqued my curiosity, so I pulled into a parking spot across Main Street and left the van there. Approaching the new bride, I spread my hands out in greeting. "I mean, first welcome home, and then, what's all this?"

Delaney unbends, takes off her gardening gloves and meets me beside one rolling rack of pansies. "Thanks. It's good to be home. It's officially home now, I guess." She smiles, then winces. "So... I bought a bunch of pansies to spruce things up for the big book festival weekend."

"I see that." I look past her and up and down the sidewalk. "What are you planting them in?"

She drops her head as she puts her hands on her hips. "I for some reason thought there were window boxes all along here." She looks up suddenly and surveys the sidewalk like I was doing. "And weren't there planters all along the sidewalk?"

"Nope. No planters and the only window boxes are those falling-apart, fake redwood ones in front of Ruby's that I've heard have had the same plastic flowers in them for a decade or so."

We meet eyes, but what begins as a stare-down softens first into small wrinkles at the corners of our eyes and lips, then a chuckle as our shoulders drop. I take a deep breath, shaking my head. It feels good to laugh with Delaney again, especially since she has ignored my every attempt at communication since her wedding. The last time the two of us talked was in the Bedwell library, as she got ready to walk down the aisle. There has been no talk about her shocking all of us with the revelation of her son, Gregory; the reception Jackson and I skipped out on; or even a postcard from her honeymoon. Nothing.

Finally I burst out laughing.

"Uh, you think you might've been a tad delusional about some aspects of Chancey? Seeing planters for flowers when there's really only a couple of old trash cans?"

She laughs, too, and then nods. "Possibly. Yeah, definitely possible." She holds open her arms. "I'm sorry. I mean, not sorry for you know, just this flower mess. I'm sorry for lying to you and making you be in the wedding and not letting you bring Jackson and, oh, so much, but I had everything on the line and I wasn't thinking straight. I was, uh…"

I step close and pull her into a hug. "Delusional?"

We hug, and then as we pull apart, she looks around. "What am I going to do? I had these delivered my attempt to get back in Chancey's good graces. Have there really never been window boxes and planters here on the sidewalk? I was sure there were lots and lots of flowers along here, not just in the park circling the gazebo."

"Nope." Looking around, I lower my face and voice. "It's because it's kind of a thing with the garden club. They can't agree on what any planters should look like. Rustic or elegant? Wood or metal? Big, small, painted, not painted, etcetera. If there is something to argue about concerning flowers on Main Street, they've done it."

"I smell my mother-in-law in that."

24

"Big time. She wants elegant planters that are metal with scrollwork, but they are much more expensive. Wait, let me check on something." I pull out my phone and make a call. "Colt. Are those planters the shop kids made still there? Can you get them downtown today? Perfect!"

I hang up and smile at Delaney. "Colt's shop class made planters and some standing window boxes to give to the town last spring, and that's what started the fight. Or reignited it. They were going to stain them, but then even the ones okay with wooden planters couldn't decide whether to paint or stain. There's always something to argue about. Then school got out for the summer, and they were stored in the football weight room. I only remembered them because Colt complains about the space they take up all the time. He says he has a group of guys loading them right now."

"Are you serious? And he's going to bring them down here?" Delaney's eyes are stretched wide, and she looks like she's about twelve in her jeans, gray hoodie, and old tennis shoes. She's not wearing makeup, and her honey-streaked hair is pulled back into a ponytail. Then those wide eyes fill with tears and her chest heaves with a sob.

"Aw, honey. What's wrong?" I hug her again and pull her over to the door of our shop. "Let's go inside." I tug on the door, but it's not unlocked yet. Before I can dig for my keys, I see Danny loping over to let us in.

"Hey there. Guess I forgot to unlock the door again. Most times folks just knock. Hey, Miss Delaney! You're back... oh no, are you okay?" He hovers over us, ignoring my attempts to bat him away. "Can I get you something? Do you want to sit down? Miss Carolina, what should I do?"

"Go away!" I growl through gritted teeth.

He looks at me like a puppy swatted with a rolled-up newspaper. Then he hunches down into his shoulders and steps away from us.

"I'm sorry, Danny. No, you're right. Can you grab her a bottle of water from the fridge in the back?"

He eagerly nods, then turns to run and fetch—I mean, get—Delaney some water.

With a sniffle and a deep breath, Delaney gets herself under control, and we sit down on the couch. She nods toward the back. "Poor Danny. I think I scared him to death."

"Don't worry about him. The way Shannon has been with crying and then raging, he's used to female distress."

"How is Shannon?" she whispers.

Oh. Shoot, I forgot who I'm talking to. Probably not a safe topic, her new husband's old girlfriend. Pregnant girlfriend. "She's fine. But what's up with you? Oh, thanks, Danny." He gives us both water and then starts to sit down in the chair next to the couch. "Uh, can you give us some privacy? Maybe get to work on the boxes back there for the signings?" He studies our faces for a minute, gives a little nod that says he believes we are okay to be left on our own, and then heads back to work.

Delaney smiles. "He's really kind of cute, isn't he? Kind of like a, a…"

"A puppy," I finish her sentence for her and she smiles in agreement.

She takes a long drink of water, then slowly puts the cap back on. "Ignore me. I was just so nervous about seeing people, especially you, and then for you to be so nice. And for Colt to bring the planters, well, I was afraid I'd ruined everything here. I had a hard time enjoying our honeymoon worrying about what was being said, and thought, back here in Chancey." She lifts her eyes up at me. "So, what are people saying?"

"Honestly not much. Of course everyone was completely shocked at first about, well, everything. But one thing I've figured out, well, kind of figured out, is people aren't as worried about us as we think they are. Maybe worried isn't the right word, but you know, they all have their own concerns, so while we think they are thinking about us, they're usually focused on their own problems."

"Even in a small town like this?"

I shrug. "You weren't here to provide new information or fill in our lack of information, so yeah, things moved on. Of course now that you're home, we all want some details." I give her a big smile and pat her arm as the front door opens and Colt sticks his head in.

"Hey, where do you want these unloaded?"

We both jump up, and Delaney darts around the couch. "Oh, Colt, you are a life saver! I'll show you what I was thinking." At the door she stops and looks back at me. "Thanks, you're a good friend. Let's do lunch or a girl's night, and you can ask all the questions you can think of. The other ladies, too. Okay?"

"Oh yeah, that's more than okay. Plus I want to hear more about this author friend coming to town. Good luck with the flowers!"

She turns back and tilts her head. "Author friend?" However Colt calls her name and she hurries away. Interesting. I don't think she knows she's hosting a brunch Sunday.

Through the front windows, I watch her and Colt direct the high school boys he brought with him on the movement of the wooden boxes, then remember how much work I have to do before the festival begins. Whirling around, I shout, "Danny, I'll finish that. You come work your magic in the front window. It's festival week!"

Chapter 4

"Did you know Margaret Mitchell's original name for Scarlett was Pansy?" Danny asks from his perch. He's on his knees against the front window. He's surrounded by books on this side but has a border of pansies outside the window behind him. I think due to my help Delaney has given our window boxes the brightest and biggest pansies.

A customer stops to look at Danny. "I don't think that could be true. Pansy instead of Scarlett? Those names are like night and day."

"I agree, but I am right. She changed the name just before *Gone with the Wind* went to print. All I can figure is the name Pansy didn't mean the same back then." He jerks his head up quickly. "I don't mean like how it can be used in a bad way, but I mean we just think of it as a sweet flower. Kind of weak, you know. Um, not weak in a bad way, but you know like, um…" The more words he spews, the redder his face turns, but he just keeps spewing.

Shannon yells from her flower table. "We all know you didn't mean anything. Stop talking and let the lady go back to shopping."

Danny gulps at the woman and then drops his head back to his work. The customer gives Shannon the evil eye. "No need to be ugly to the nice young man," she says in a huff as she turns back toward Danny.

I'm hunkered down in the bookshelves and hear her semi-whisper, "Don't you worry about her. I know you were just trying to make conversation and didn't want to offend. She shouldn't be so grouchy with her employees."

Danny smiles at the lady. "Oh, I'm her husband, so that makes it okay."

I bite my lip to keep from laughing out loud as I unfold and walk around to the next bookshelf. I'm consolidating all our books so we can have one bookshelf for the authors that will be on the premises signing books this weekend. Shannon catches my attention and waves me back to her. My business partner normally carries a little extra weight and she's short so it's hard to tell she's pregnant, even though she's five months along now. However when she stretches her back like she is now, I can clearly see her baby bump beneath the loose dress she's wearing. I really need to remember than she needs some extra patience. I smile and rub her arm when I get to her.

"Is he right about that? Scarlett being named Pansy?" she whispers.

"I think so. I think I've heard it before, and he's actually pretty good on book stuff."

She shakes her head and keeps wrapping green tape around the stem of a big, lush flower. I've learned so much about how those beautiful arrangements are made watching Shannon. She's wrapping the long stems with tape to hold a thin piece of wire, which gives the flowers stability. I take a minute to rest as I watch her.

We have soft music playing, which is deceptive, given all the energy bouncing around this place. Bonnie is working on promotional materials for the book festival at her decorating desk. She's frantically stuffing folders while making phone calls about the decorating still being done at Peter and Delaney's home.

It's funny how quickly it's changed in our minds from Missus's home to theirs. Of course she still lives there, but it's like she's lost interest in it. Her home is no longer just that building; it's the whole town. She's everywhere at once, and her opinions, and proclamations, are so thick in the air it's hard to breathe at times. I've kept one ear tuned to the sidewalk today, waiting for the explosion when she sees the wooden planters, unpainted and unvarnished, just bare wood for all the world to see.

Shannon shoves my arm. "You're in my way. Don't you have some work to do?" I move, and she pushes a stack of ging-ham-printed papers in my direction. "I not only have my regular orders but also the arrangements for the luncheon at AC's and the bouquets I'm selling this weekend. Delaney says I should just do daisies and greenery in the gingham wraps, but that seems awful simple, don't you think?"

"I think that sounds charming." She immediately clouds over at my words, so I hastily add, "But you know best. Do whatever you think you should. I gotta get back to those shelves." I stalk toward the front, grumbling as I go. "She'll decide on more difficult arrangements, and then we'll all have to pay when she can't get enough done."

I've suggested she get a local high schooler to help her out this weekend, even someone just to sweep up and help move the flowers around in the cooler, but she growled at me when I did. She and Missus have managed to convince everyone she's carrying Danny's child, even though half the town knows Danny had a vasectomy. Missus, true to her word, is ignoring the baby, her grandchild, until it comes. Shannon is flat-out miserable about it all. She is stuck living a lie, which we all know won't stay in place forever.

But we're all ignoring that part.

My phone rings and I answer it, excited to talk to the director of the book festival, Carlie Ruiz.

"Hi, Carlie. We're working hard here to be ready for Friday—"

I barely get my sentence out before she's shouting at me. Not loud shouting, just forceful shouting. Okay, it's kind of loud.

"Who is this mystery author you are springing on me at the last minute? I do not need this kind of a headache at this late date. You are rather off the beaten path, even for North Georgia, but I included you as a favor to Delaney. Now I find out her husband is holding his own event? With his own author?"

"Carlie, I know as much about it as you. I'm planning on moving forward as we agreed. I don't have any idea who this new author even is!" I'm stumbling over my words and my feet as I pick through the boxes scattered around the back of our shop. Finally I reach the back door and plunge out into the cold afternoon. "The first I heard anything was last night at the chamber meeting. How did you hear?"

"Thank goodness Retta Bainbridge is friends with my mother and told her. I'm livid, and Delaney isn't answering her phone. What is her husband's number?"

I don't even bat an eye. "I'll send you his contact information."

"Good. What's his name?"

I can't help smiling. "Peter. Peter Bedwell."

"Send it now. I'll talk to you later."

She hangs up, and I take a deep breath of the cold air. Peter will be shocked to find out everyone isn't as impressed with him as he is. I can't help but chuckle as I send the information to Carlie.

She didn't even know his name. Sure would love to be listening in when she gives him that call.

Chapter 5

"What's up with those awful planters out there?"

It's a sentiment I'd been expecting, but from an older voice. A meaner voice. This voice coming at me is young and more incredulous than accusatory. I was in a fairly cheerful mood as I hung up my call with Carlie, even though she'd basically yelled at me, because I was happy she was going to yell at Peter. Then I remembered her saying how she only included Blooming Books in the festival as a favor to Delaney. I kick a box out of my way as I plow up front. So who is this young whippersnapper coming in here, thinking she's going to judge the planters I arranged to—

"Oh, hi, Athena."

I stop and swallow. I never had much of an opinion about her before, but Athena Markum is now the nemesis of one of my best friends. I haven't run into her since I found out, on the night of Peter and Delaney's wedding, that Susan's ex-husband, Griffin, is dating Athena.

And that he bought a house across the street from her.

And wants to go on a double date with me and Jackson.

"Carolina, those look atrocious. They can't be here this weekend for the festival. They look like some high school shop class made them!" Athena is young, probably not even thirty-five. She's got a big scarf wrapped around her neck, and is wearing a long, gray jacket, gray pants, and matching boots. Her hair is up in a messy bun, except she's one of those women who can make messy buns look intentional. She also, apparently, is very astute on the abilities of high school shop classes. She unwinds the scarf as she walks toward me.

I suck up my courage and false bravado. "So why are you telling me all this? I've been here inside the store all day."

"Duh? The book festival? I need you to get involved and get them removed immediately. If the festival committee sees them, you'll probably be off the schedule." She drops the end of her soft scarf and lays her hand on my arm. "Chancey needs this festival. *You* need this festival. I'm just trying to help."

All I can work up is a frown as my thoughts try to map out why she's concerned. Finally I step back so her hand falls away. "Why do you care so much?"

With a big sigh and a patient smile—I love when self-important people are so obvious with their patience—she explains. "I'm Carlie's assistant for the festival. Didn't you hear?"

No. No, I did not hear that.

She looks around the shop. "I'm in charge of the aesthetics of the events in the individual stores, and towns, too, I guess. We don't want this coming off as something just thrown together. We are getting a lot of attention from Atlanta booksellers, and some of the authors we're hosting will be planning future book events. We'd love to be thought worthy of their time on those book tours."

She's wandered away from me as she talks. Examining our worthiness, I assume.

"Oh, your window is perfect! It includes all our authors, the colors are tasteful, this is exactly what I'm talking about. But those flowers outside have got to go. I bet from out there you can barely see the books. That is, if you aren't so distracted by those bright colors that you'd never even look into the window."

"I was worried about that," Danny says, coming up behind

us. He's been upstairs for lunch. The days of his and Shannon's more amorous lunch breaks have dwindled to nonexistent as we've gotten busier and she's gotten grouchier. "I tried to match the colors, but…"

"Danny, do you know Athena?"

She turns around and puts her hand out. "I don't believe we've met. You are very talented. I wish the other windows on our festival tour were this creative. Almost everyone else just throws the books up in piles or on some kind of makeshift shelf. Just look at this."

So we do. Andy allows Danny to borrow anything from his junk emporium for use in the decorating our window. An old wicker picnic basket and worn chess board on a pink and green tulip quilt make an appealing picnic scene. Books and chess pieces scattered over the folds of faded fabric look so natural, like the owners just got up to go take a walk in the creek. Who wouldn't want to own those books? Who wouldn't want to shop in this store?

Athena sighs and reaches out to hold his hand as she tilts her head at him. "You are very talented." She finishes off her statement with a wink, and they both knowingly chuckle.

That is, until "Danny!" is shouted from the flower table. He hangs his head and swivels around.

Athena continues walking past the window toward the bookshelves. "I assume this is for your authors?" she asks, pointing at the nearly empty shelf.

"Yes. So you're Carlie's assistant. Congratulations."

"Just for this event. Griffin asked me if I'd step in."

"What's Griffin Lyles have to do with it?" I can't help but bristle. I also can't help but want more information, so I tamp down the bristle and end my question with a curious smile.

"Just looking out for Chancey." She leans close to me and whispers, "We don't quite trust Peter and Delaney Bedwell. You know what I mean?"

I laugh. "Oh, then you're going to love finding out who arranged for the flowers out on the sidewalk."

She stops in the middle of throwing her scarf back around her neck. "Who?"

"Uh, never mind. I have a lot to do. See you later."

I try to escape back into the bookshelves, but the front door opens and I hear my name. The voice is older and meaner this time.

"Carolina Jessup," Missus snaps. "You know how I feel about these hillbilly planters, and yet here they are. Delaney says this was all your idea."

"Just the planters. Just for, well, the weekend." My voice drops to a whimper as Athena stares at me, mouth and eyes wide.

With a deep, heartfelt sigh, she takes her phone out of her pocket. "I hate to do this, Carolina, but I'm going to have to tell Carlie. She has to know."

She and Missus exchange a sad look, punctuated with a roll of their eyes.

Yep, they've done the impossible. They've made me hate this stupid book festival.

CHAPTER 6

"They *are* kind of clunky looking," I say to Jackson as we're setting the table for dinner.

"Those flowerpots?" Savannah chimes in from the living room. "They are horrible. Everyone says so."

Her daddy flashes her a "shut-up" look and speaks over her. "I was downtown today. I thought they looked fine." He shrugs. "I mean, a coat of paint couldn't hurt. See less of the, uh, mistakes."

I can't hold in a groan. "Dinner's ready. Savannah, go get the boys."

She gives us her own groan, but she gets up from the couch and her homework. At the front door she calls out for Bryan and Grant to come in. She'd brought them home after basketball practice, saying Grant needed a ride and his folks knew he was coming here for dinner.

Susan responded to my resulting text, checking those facts with a very curt, "Ask his father!" I texted Griffin, but haven't heard anything.

"Wash your hands. Dinner's ready," I say as the boys barrel into the house. There's no one in the B&B, so they push and jostle down the hallway to that bathroom. They are so big, but half the time, they act like they are still in elementary school.

The only problem with this is that nothing is safe from their long arms and big feet.

I put the toasted hamburger buns in a basket and take them to the table. Tonight's menu is sloppy joes, tater tots, corn, and salad. Savannah and I combine the sloppy joe mix and salad to forego the bun. Or you can have sloppy joe on a bun and a salad, which the boys are doing. Jackson would rather die than dilute his meat mixture with salad. Luckily I made a double portion of sloppy joe mix. Filling up these active boys is a full-time job.

"Grant, I hope you let your dad know you're having dinner here," I say as I serve the plates. "I didn't hear back from him."

"He knows. I mean, he knows I'm somewhere. It's not like when we lived up in Laurel Cove and my folks didn't know everyone. Down here in town they know I'm always with someone they know."

Bryan slides a look at me, and I know there's more to Grant's answer.

Jackson jumps in. "But you did let your dad know where you are, right?"

"Oh, yeah. He's good. I've never had sloppy joe on salad. It's good. Good idea, Savannah."

She manages to not roll her eyes at him, but she gives me a weary look. Bryan's friends are always a little in awe of Savannah, an attitude she wholeheartedly endorses even while acting bored.

When Bryan first entered high school in the fall, he got annoyed with his friends always wanting Savannah to notice them. At some point, though, he gave up caring. Besides, she makes it very clear they don't stand a chance. She's a senior. They are freshmen. Everybody knows their place.

However, adoration *is* adoration.

"So you're liking being back down in town? How's the new house?" I ask our guest.

"I miss the pool, and it's a long way to the golf course, but it's all good. Darien was getting old."

Darien Academy is the private school all the kids in Laurel Cove go to. Bonnie taught there, and while she says it's academically excellent, it's also a tad snobby. When Griffin and the kids first moved back to town, Grant was a little aloof from his town friends. That didn't last long, though. He came back half a foot taller and more confident, two attributes that are sure to set a freshman on the path to success. His biggest fan is Zoe Kendrick, but it seems Grant hasn't noticed, so he and Bryan haven't had to cross that bridge. Bryan has had a crush on Zoe for a while and she basically ignores it. Or maybe Bryan is over Zoe? A mom can only hope.

I must've conjured her because the doorbell rings and Bryan jumps up. "That's Zoe." He dashes to the door, explaining all the way there that they're working on a project but she had to eat dinner at her house.

Savannah's head swivels toward Grant like a cat when a bird lands in its peripheral vision. "The three of you are working on a project together?"

"Yeah."

His slow smile is a little too, uh, slow for my liking. A little too mature. His eyes focus on her, and I swear he almost winks. Grant has his mother's height and his father's charming good looks. Plus that aforementioned helping of newfound confidence.

Savannah stares back at him just a moment too long, so I ask, "Savannah, are you done with dinner? What are you doing tonight?"

"Nothing." She stands and begins clearing her things from the table. Grant watches her, so I throw a hamburger bun at him. Yeah, I'm not above such actions.

"Have another sandwich, Grant." Bryan and Zoe walk in, and I throw a hamburger bun at Bryan and threaten to throw one at Zoe. "Y'all have another sandwich. Tell me about this project." Savannah is not interested in Grant, she's just at loose ends in the world of romance. However, teenagers at loose ends is never good, so a few thrown buns is a cheap distraction.

Zoe pulls out a chair at the end of the table. "No, thank you. I've eaten." She smiles at Grant. "But y'all go on and have more." The boys are already filling their buns.

Jackson watches them for a moment, then nods at me. "Hey, throw me a bun. Want to halve one?"

Shaking my head at him, I throw him the requested bun, then shift to Zoe. "So, your project?"

"Turning old railroad depots into museums. Every other year our science projects are combined with local history or ecology."

"That sounds really interesting." Neither boy is paying her any attention, but my husband is enthralled. "I can help with any railroad history or engineering."

Bryan doesn't stop eating to say, "That's why I got in the group."

Zoe explains, "Most of the other groups are just two people. Grant and I thought this was a good idea since he was so involved in reorganizing the depot before he moved up to Laurel Cove."

Grant doesn't look up from his sandwich, but I see him smile. Maybe he does know that Zoe likes him. Bryan is also not looking up, but he's scowling. He mumbles, "I was the one who worked most at the depot."

Jackson and I meet eyes. He's seeing the same thing I am, our own little love triangle. It's good to have backup for squashing this idea of them working on a school project together.

Then my oh so astute husband opens his mouth. "This is perfect. I have some good ideas about how to better use the museum space to show what the railroad was really like. And I can show y'all how the tracks were laid out—hey! We can even get down in the basement of the depot and explore!"

I sigh and stand up. "I'm done eating. Y'all bring your dishes in when you finish." I can't help rolling my eyes as I walk into the kitchen.

Savannah is in there scrolling on her phone, and she chuckles as I walk in. "Looks like they have four on their team now." She lays her phone down and follows me to the sink. "So about spring break... is it just about the money? If I can find a way to go somewhere cheap, you'll be okay with it?"

"Probably not. But feel free to run it by your daddy and me."

She loads two plates in the dishwasher, then softly fades out of the kitchen so that I don't realize my helper has left.

Kids think parents are so stupid. Whatever. I'd rather be thought stupid than have to talk about her spring break delusions one more minute.

CHAPTER 7

"No. No. No! Not this week!"

I keep saying it. They keep ignoring it.

Missus's lips are so tight they no longer exist. She has on a raspberry wool suit, and her cheeks don't need rouge to match the wool. They are bright and look hot—maybe she's got a fever? Delaney has her head down and is looking up at me through lowered eyelashes. She's sitting on the arm of the sofa in Blooming Books, dressed much as she was yesterday in jeans and a hoodie. But yesterday she was distressed and sad; today she's distressed and panicked. Bonnie's eyes are stretched wider than I've ever seen, and she looks like she's close to tears.

So I say it again. "No. I am not able to host anyone at the B&B this week. I'm already stretched to my breaking point. No." The bell on the door makes us all look up as another distraught woman enters the bookstore.

Athena is holding her phone out toward me. Another extra-long scarf, this one in green, is wound around her neck, its wide ends flying behind her. She marches to me, shoving Carlie, via FaceTime, at me.

Carlie wastes no time demanding, "Carolina. Do it, or you are off the book festival tour and we will not reimburse you for any of your costs. I have to go. Do it."

Athena pulls her phone down and stares at me. "Well?"

"Fine. We'll do it. She can have a room."

Missus snorts. "She and her entourage. There are four of them, but the two assistants will share a room." She takes a breath and starts for the door. "Put the publicist in the Chessie room, the assistants in the Southern Crescent, and Ms. Blankenship in the Orange Blossom Special room." She stops and turns toward Shannon at her worktable. "Put together a large floral arrangement for her room from the town. Deliver it today." She turns, opens the door, and then announces, "Expect a formal proclamation from the mayor's office soon. This is an important event in the life of Chancey." She flings her hand toward the paper she left on the counter. "And post that proclamation prohibiting any future sidewalk enhancements and decorations as soon as possible. I couldn't stop this latest debacle, but I fully intend to hinder future embarrassments." She shakes her head and actually ends with an imperial, "Carry on."

Delaney moans as she stands. "I'm so sorry, Carolina, but there's just nothing else to do. Peter says he thought she'd stay in Atlanta, and when she changed her mind, we thought she could stay with us, but well, the renovations…" She swallows. "So you'll take her up to your house soon?"

I study her. "You didn't even know about her a couple hours ago, did you?"

Delaney catches her breath and blinks her eyes at me. "Not really. We've been kind of busy. She's an old friend of Peter's and called to congratulate us. He thinks it'll be good to have her here for the festival." She licks her lip and whispers, "I'm sorry."

I look around the store. It's still full of boxes, not counting the ones just delivered by special courier: a dozen boxes of hardback books by best-selling author Sally Blankenship, the unknown author friend of Peter's and my newest B&B customer.

I throw up my arms. "I apparently have no choice, right?

She's determined to experience her dear friend Peter's hometown she heard so much about so long ago."

Bonnie hangs her head. "He never told me he was having guests before we tore the other rooms apart."

Delaney pats Bonnie's arm. "It's not your fault. He sprang this on all of us. Believe me, I'm not happy about Sally Blankenship being here, but now that she is? Let's make the best of it, okay? I think she's kind of famous. She takes a deep breath and smiles at me. "Let's go introduce you to her. Have you read any of her books?"

I narrow my eyes at her and spit, "Yes." I jerk my coat off the rack before adding, "And I hate them."

Missus is waiting for us outside the closed door to Ruby's. Her arms are crossed, and her foot is tapping the sidewalk. "Finally." She gives us both the once-over I'm used to. It makes Delaney stop and look down at her clothes.

"Oh my. I hadn't given a thought to what I'm wearing. I should go change, or…" Her voice fades as Missus tells her with only a raised eyebrow that she doesn't have time for that. "Or you can introduce Carolina to Ms. Blankenship?" she asks with a hesitant smile at Missus.

Missus grants her a curt nod. "Completely understandable. You go do whatever you were going to do in your work clothes. Carolina has an excuse for looking like this. It's just who she is. Run along. I'll handle everything." She steps in front of her daughter-in-law and gives me the go-ahead to open the door, muttering as she walks past me, "Don't embarrass me." She strides to a booth near the back. "Ms. Blankenship, I've solved the problem of your accommodations. After all, that is my job as mayor."

I step forward. "Hello. I'm Carolina Jessup, owner of the bookstore and only B&B in town." I smile at the woman sitting on the aisle facing the front and the two sitting across from her, but only give those three a quick nod. They are not the main attraction.

Seated next to her against the wall is the author. She's older than the cover pictures she uses on her books. She has that city hardness, too. Brittle. One corner of her lips lifts as she reaches for her coffee cup. "Bookstore *and* B&B? Are you sure we've not fallen into a Hallmark movie?" She wrinkles her tiny, upturned nose at me, but I'm not calling what she did with her lips a smile.

The assistants across from her let out one "ha" in unison and get a look of approval. Looking past past me and Missus, Ms. Blankenship asks, "Where did Peter's little wife run off to?" But before we either one can answer she shrugs her thin bony shoulders as if to dismiss all thoughts of Delaney and turns to the woman next to her. "Is the car outside? I think we should go see this B&B. Our new home away from home."

That's all it takes for the three women with her to spring into action. They peel out of the booth, and Missus and I back up so as to not get in their way. Ms. Blankenship slides across the seat and then stands. I know she's my age, since she was in college with Peter, but unless you're looking at her face, she seems younger, thanks to her long, straight hair and her clothes. She has on a short, loose sweater with bold designs knit into it and tight, black jeans ending a couple of inches short of her black, high-heel pumps. She's tall and super thin, which exaggerates her lips and cheekbones. She's instructing the woman in front of her as they leave, but I can't hear what she says since her voice is low and husky. I smell tobacco in her wake.

Missus looks at me and rolls her eyes.

Wait, what? Missus sharing an eye roll with me?

Hmm, this might get interesting.

Chapter 8

"Hey, Carolina! Come here," someone yells from behind me as I walk up the sidewalk to the bookstore. Turning, I see Phoenix at the door to her studio and juice bar, waving at me. "I have something I want you to try!"

What the heck? Don't people realize I'm busy? I'm already so far behind, though, so what's another ten minutes?

"Sure. Be right there."

It's a crisp spring afternoon. The sun is bright in a solid, blue sky, and everything feels fresh. Ms. Blankenship and her posse have been delivered to my house. I got out of there relatively unscathed, so things are looking up. I hurry along the sidewalk, then pause to tug on the door to Laney's club, but it's locked and I can't see anything inside, so I move on. Phoenix's door pulls open, and I step into the clean, fresh-smelling dance studio. Wood wax, fruits, and...peanut butter? The floor is polished wood, the walls white with lime green trim and accents of orange and yellow. The colors go perfectly with her juice bar, where she's waiting for me. The white stools have cushions made to look like slices of fruit. I pull a lemon slice stool toward me and rest on it.

Phoenix slides a plastic cup filled with some sort of goop toward me. "It's an energy smoothie," she says, "but it tastes really good. And it doesn't have a ton of calories. Try it!"

I take the cup, but I'm a little nervous. Phoenix is different lately, and I'm not sure about trusting her, her transformation, or the smoothie. Although, on second glance, it doesn't look too bad. "What's in it?"

"Taste it." Her eyes are big and round, not catlike and sly, like she used to make them up with thick eyeliner. I can actually see the freckles on her face through her light powder, and her hair is just plain old hair, not shiny and luxurious. It's still full and red, but honestly, now that I look closer, I see that it's faded to more of a brown. "Go on, take a sip."

I pull the straw to me, and it's like I'm sipping a peanut butter milkshake. "Peanut butter? I love it."

She grins and nods. "I know! I know you like peanut butter, and this has some seeds and other stuff for energy. Its base is low-fat yogurt, and it can have protein powder if you want it next time. Anyway, I know you've got a busy week ahead, so I hope that helps." She jumps off her stool and hurries to the door. "I don't want to hold you up. Enjoy!"

"But I want to pay you."

"Next one. You did me a favor trying it." She waits for me to get closer before she pulls open the big glass door. "Good luck with all the book festival stuff."

I pass her, then turn. "What's up? What's going on with you?"

She smiles, then drops her head to look at the ground. When she looks back up, she's serious. "Let's talk when you're done with the festival, okay? For now, let's just say I've had an epiphany and you helped. Now go. I have a class starting and I need to get ready."

"Okay, but I'm holding you to that talk. Thanks." I hold up the cup. "This is really delicious."

Walking back up the sidewalk, I realize something's missing. Several somethings. Yep, what's missing are the wooden planters with their masses of pansies. The sidewalk looks bare.

Guess Delaney has discovered it doesn't pay to fight city hall, especially when your mother-in-law is city hall.

Wonder where all the pansies went?

"Is it true?" Retta demands before I'm in our door. She's standing beside the front table as if she was watching for me out the big window. "Is Sally Blankenship really the mystery author? She's here? Here in Chancey? Oh, I *have* to get an invite to Peter's brunch. I'll pay anything. Anything at all!"

"Good luck," I say as I blow past her to the coatrack.

She draws in a huge breath and then lets it out in a whoosh. "But you're saying the rumor is true? She is here?" Retta is a dog with a bone when it comes to Sally Blankenship, a dog in a dark jean jacket that hangs almost to her knees. It's embellished with embroidery and jewels. She's wearing about as many big, shiny jewels on her fingers, wrists, and around her neck. Her makeup picks up the jewel colors, as do her fingernails. Her hair is teased a little higher than normal, and in her excitement, her accent is almost too much for me to decipher.

I really wasn't sure anyone else in Chancey would have read Sally Blankenship's books, much less like them. If only I could've been so lucky.

"You'll have to talk to Peter about getting an invite to their brunch. I know nothing about it." I stop at Shannon's table and look at the arrangement she's working on. "Is that for her?"

"Yes. Missus did say just one, right? I don't have time to make them for her assistants."

"Just her. It's really beautiful."

"Thanks. I just had a big delivery of flowers for the festival weekend, and when money's no object, it's amazing what I can pull off." She looks at me and tries to smile, but she's out of practice. She refocuses on her work as Retta barrels up to us.

"Oh, Shannon, that is magnificent. Would you like me to deliver it to Sally? I'd consider it an honor. And after all I am head of the chamber of commerce *and* the book club."

"Sure. Be my guest." Shannon gives the planter a little push as she steps away. "Think I should put a card on it?"

I chuckle. "Oh, you better get Madam Mayor's name on there or she won't pay the bill. She's going to want full credit. Although I'm not sure she'd ever heard of Ms. Blankenship before today. Missus is not a big reader."

Retta draws in an affronted breath. "Of course she's heard of her! I'm assuming everyone has heard of her, right? Let me use your facilities to freshen up, and then I'll take these flowers right over to our visiting author."

As she bustles away, Shannon mumbles, "I've never heard of her." Then she tips her head up to look at me. "But you said you don't like her books? I thought you liked every book ever written. You don't seem very discriminating."

"Hey. I mean, I do like a lot of different books, but not all." I whisper, "Has Danny mentioned if he's read her? He reads a lot."

She shrugs. "He's excited to have an author he's heard of here, but he says he's never read her books. He was looking for a paperback in your shelves to read."

I look around to where he and Bonnie are bent over a card table in the front corner of the store, where they are unpacking and logging in books.

Retta bounces out of the restroom toward us. "Okay. I'm ready to deliver your beautiful arrangement to our famous author." She twitters. "I'm so nervous. A famous author right here in Chancy! Now when are you doing her signing?"

"I'm not sure she's all *that* famous, but after the brunch is what Peter said. I guess I should check in with Peter on the timing." I walk away from Shannon, who is giving directions to Retta on delivering the flowers, and dial Delaney.

She answers, and I skip hello. "Hey, I need to know what time Ms. Blankenship is going to sign books here."

She says, "Okay," then talks to someone, but I can't hear

them. She speaks into the phone. "Come up to Peter's office, and we'll work out the details."

"Details? What details? I just need to know what time. Can't we do it over the phone?" I ask, but she's hung up.

While waiting on her, I had meandered all the way to the back door. With a sigh, I push through it to get a breath of fresh air.

Okay. Now I know where the pansies are.

CHAPTER 9

"Carolina, you coming to see me about the festival?" Charles asks from the top of the flight of stairs, where he has just left the *Vedette* offices.

"No. Isn't that all taken care of?" I climb the last few steps and stop to catch my breath.

"You know, I thought it was, but then I've been googling this new author that just hit town. Seems like she might be kinda newsworthy, you know?"

"I guess. I'm headed down to Peter's office to set up her signing."

"Can't help but notice your tone of voice. Not a fan?" He leans back against the hallway wall and crosses his arms. Charles Spoon is not that old, but his white hair and mustache and the way he really listens and pays attention make him seem old and wise. Also, he's not from Chancey originally, so he has a bit more objectivity than most around here.

"Not really, but I don't have to like her books to sell them, right?" We both laugh a bit, and I roll my shoulders. "I'm just letting it all get to me. So much to do to get ready, and now all this." I wave a hand toward the end of the hall, where Peter's law office is.

Charles unfolds his arms. "One thing I'll say about having Mr. Bedwell around, this stairwell sure looks a lot better. He had Jackson and Colt replace the broken molding and give it all a new paint job. I don't think it had been painted since it was built before World War II. And the rug down below and the carpets in the hallway are all thanks to Miss Bonnie. Also the new light fixtures."

"It does look nice. A lot brighter too."

"Yeah, you know, it makes me want to clean up my offices." Then he winks. "But doesn't make me want it bad enough to actually do it! Now, if you'll excuse me, Miss Carolina, I gotta get over to the high school. The gymnasium's all done up for the basketball tournament, and I promised pictures in the next issue of the *Vedette*." He heads down the stairs with a wave, and I turn down the hall, wondering how Peter's offices will look. Jackson told me all about the renovations they did in the law office, but now that I think about it, well...

I don't think I was listening.

When I arrived, I didn't have to imagine my husband's work any longer. Peter gave me the grand tour, and now I know that there are several small offices on the interior hallway, which ends with his very large office, whose windows overlook the town square.

"I'll leave you ladies to it. I have work to do," Peter says at the door to the office he's shown me into. Delaney is seated on a crimson love seat in front of a highly polished, dark-wood coffee table. She looks up at me and smiles, then turns her smile up a notch as she looks at her new husband.

He smiles back at her, then turns to me. "Thank you for coming up here, Carolina. I've been wanting you to see the place. Jackson and Colt did a remarkable job with the remodel, and as you can see, Bonnie is a real treasure."

My shoulders relax. I hadn't been expecting this praise after the rough time he gave Jackson, Colt, and Bonnie before he hired them.

The suite of offices is different from any of Bonnie's other work. It's luxurious in a rich kind of way. That's the only way I can think to describe it. *Rich*. All the furniture is a deep crimson (Harvard Crimson, I've just been told). The wood accents on the high-back chairs and love seats match the dark wood of the other furniture. The walls are covered in a creamy cloth wallpaper that looks really expensive and, well, rich—not just in a moneyed way, but rich in depth and color and feeling. Of course it smells new, with all the furniture and paint and carpets, but it also smells like a wealth of subtle spices. It feels brand new and old at the same time, and I'm impressed all over again with Bonnie.

I nod at her biggest client. "Yes, I have to agree with you. She's even more of a treasure than I imagined." I swallow and take a breath, releasing it with a heartfelt smile. "Your offices are beautiful. Congratulations."

He dips his head at me as he steps back and pulls the door closed. I turn and spread my hands at the stacks of papers in front of Delaney. "So, is this your office? I know you said you plan to spend a lot of time up here."

She laughs and leans back. I see she's changed since this morning and looks more like the put-together businesswoman I know her to be. "That's the plan. Now I have to get things back in gear. Especially with my clothing, apparently. I got lazy on our honeymoon, I guess. Greece was dreamy, and we ran around looking at the sights in just our casual clothes. Then back here I was so busy with moving in and working on the festival I forgot my mother-in-law's, and society's, expectations." She sits up, and a shadow crosses her face. "It's been a while since I've had to worry about what people thought of how I look. There are a lot of moving pieces in everything we have going on. I've got to pay better attention to everything."

"Don't give Missus the time of day on any of that. No one measures up to her expectations," I say as I perch on the other end of the love seat. "So, what do we need to work out for Ms. Blankenship's signing?"

She cocks her head at me. "What are your obligations for the festival on Sunday?"

"Not much, really. I did promise to be open since we are usually closed on Sundays, but we don't have any events planned here. The official closing event of the festival is Sunday over in Cartersville, but I don't think it's anything special. Why?"

Shuffling her papers, she finds what she's looking for. "Yes, here it is: two p.m. Looks like just what you said, nothing special. Probably patting themselves on the back and setting things up for next year. That'll work."

She drops the paper onto the table and leans back. "The invitation-only brunch for Ms. Blankenship will be at our house at eleven a.m. Of course all the festival bigwigs will be invited. If that messes up their closing plans, so be it, but we know we aren't exactly on the top of their schedule or their minds. Peter wants them to think of Chancey first next year and not treat us like some afterthought." She leans toward me. "I told him how that Carlie keeps threatening to kick you out of the festival. He was apoplectic."

"Well, it was over *his* friend who *he* invited…"

Delaney waves her hand at me. "Whatever. We aim to make Chancey more of a player in events such as this. Not just a player, a mover and shaker in area events. The signing for Ms. Blankenship will begin at one p.m. on Sunday in Blooming Books. That way we don't interfere with anyone's church schedule, and AC's will be open for lunch, so that will kick off their being open at noon on Sundays. Won't it be wonderful to not have to leave the square for lunch after church from now on?"

"Alex and Angie want to open on Sundays for lunch? I thought they were trying to take things slow. Plus, I'm not sure how that's going to go over here. You know, being open on the square. No one seems to mind the china buffet but," I shrug because I don't really understand the difference "...maybe it's because it's out of town?"

Her eyes flick to the door where Peter had stood, and she shakes her head. "A new restaurant can't pass up an opportunity like this." She stands. "Don't worry. We'll handle everything. Now I'm sure you have a lot to do with your piece of the festival puzzle."

"Yeah, I do," I say as I also stand. "You didn't say—so is this your office? Are you moving your photography studio here? Looks like plenty of empty space."

She laughs and walks to the door. "This is much too fancy for a photography studio." She opens the door and walks down the hall. I follow to the front area, where no one is seated at the reception desk. "Are you hiring a receptionist?"

She pulls open the main door and motions me through it. "Oh, Peter has all kinds of plans," she says. "Speaking of plans, we need to plan our girls' night out soon. But first we need to get this festival in the books! Pun intended." She laughs again, until Peter steps out of the small rooms down the hall.

"Girls' night out? What a good idea. Have it at our house. I'll hire Phoenix to cater for you ladies, and you can see Bonnie's work there too." He steps over to reception and looks down at the desk calendar. "De, I can't read your writing here. Pick a day and get it on the schedule for next week. You'll need a break, I'm sure, Carolina." He steps up behind Delaney, slides a hand around her waist, and says, "My lovely receptionist will get invitations out to the other ladies, won't you, dear?"

The shame on my friend's face makes me catch my breath, and I stumble toward the door. With a half smile and half wave,

I look down and hurry out the door, down the hall, and down the stairs.

Part of my brain laments for poor Delaney. Another part tsks, arches an eyebrow, and says, "Be careful what you wish for."

CHAPTER 10

"Shoot. I forgot to ask Delaney what she's going to do with all those pansies and the planters," I say as I push open the heavy front door to Blooming Books.

Danny is stocking the shelves I emptied. "Yeah, we promised easy parking for the authors, and I bought all that bright yellow tape to block off that space back there." He sighs. "Miss Carlie ain't going to be happy."

"I'm about sick to death of Miss Carlie and this whole mess. I'll text Delaney that she has to figure something out by tonight. Where's Shannon?"

I look up from my texting when he doesn't answer.

He's pointing upstairs.

"Is she sick?"

He looks around, then back at me and shakes his head. His lips stay closed.

"Is she taking a nap?"

This time the shake of his head comes quicker.

"For crying out loud. What is it?"

"Shh, Miss Carolina. They'll hear you," he says as he rushes toward me. "They didn't look too happy."

I take a deep breath and speak lower. "They who?"

He blushes. "Her momma and her daddy. I think they've finally realized we ain't actually married."

"But I thought you were taking care of that. Besides, everyone else in town knew. How didn't they?"

His big, brown eyes widen. "My ma always says two things: People do what they want to and people know what they want to." He shrugs. "Reckon they didn't actually want to know."

"Reckon not."

We both stare up toward the apartment for a bit before I rouse myself into action. "Nothing we can do about that," I say with a flourish of a turn toward the shelves he just finished. They're filled with the books for the Saturday authors' signings. "But this looks great! Now, the book signing for Ms. Blankenship is Sunday at one. Wait, where's her latest book?"

I look around, but the festival boxes we've been plagued with for weeks are all gone. Including the boxes a very confused FedEx driver delivered for Ms. Blankenship's last-minute appearance. There's nary a one in sight. "Huh. I know at least two of the boxes she sent were her new book."

"Um, yeah," Danny says as he looks around, rubbing the back of his neck. "Have you read many of her books?"

Checking to make sure no customers have slipped in to the empty store, I shake my head and whisper, "No. I read one of her first ones and then tried with another couple, but they aren't my cup of tea. I guess I should take home one of the new ones and try it. But where are they?"

He brightens up. "Hey, that's a good idea. They're right here. Figured we'd make some kind of big display the day of her signing." He drags two boxes out from underneath a cloth-draped table next to the far wall. He then pulls a book out of one box. I hold my hand out for it, but he strides past me to the counter. "I'll put it under here next to your pocketbook so you don't forget it."

"Danny? What's all the secrecy about? Is there something wrong with the book?"

But before he answers he's summoned from above.

"Danny? I thought you were coming up here when Carolina arrived," Shannon scolds him from halfway down the stairs.

"Oh yeah. I forgot." He half smiles at me and then heads to the back. Shannon's scolding drops to a harsh whisper that I can't decipher.

I yell, "Hey, take your time. I'm going to lock up soon anyway. Okay?"

She shouts, "Okay!" and then the apartment door slams.

Thinking on what Danny's mother says, I wonder just how much Shannon's folks really want to know. Right now there's an epidemic of not-wanting-to-know going round this town, but... I don't have time to think about that right now.

There's a little flutter in the back of my mind that says maybe being too busy is just one way we manage to not know stuff, but then I dismiss the flutter. I have too much to do to think about that.

"Then tell them again. I told them we only provided a light breakfast. No dinner. No lunch."

I groan and collapse onto the couch in the store as Jackson begins to explain again that Sally Blankenship's assistants don't understand how there cannot be some kind of food available so they don't have to go out. It's only their first day and they are already a pain.

"Okay," I interrupt him rather loudly. I might have yelled. "Go get them some food then. BBQ or pizza, I don't care. I have at least another hour of work here, so I cannot be involved in this."

It's quiet on his end of the phone. "Jackson? Are you there?"

"Um, yeah, they heard you say you'd bring them pizza in an hour, and so they, like, just went to tell their boss."

"That's not what I said, but whatever. I'll bring home pizza in an hour. But I'm charging them for theirs!"

"Okay, great. I'll get everyone's order and call it in for you to pick up at seven o'clock," he blurts out before hanging up.

Leaning back, I rest for a minute in the darkened store. In spite of ourselves, we're going to be ready for Friday. Bonnie is coming in early tomorrow to finish decorating around the store. She wants to "bring spring into the shop," so I told her everything would be in place and clean by Wednesday morning for her to do her bit and I'm almost done. It's shocking how much I can get done when I'm here alone.

Shannon and Danny left earlier with her parents, and although I didn't see a shotgun, it definitely had a shotgun-wedding kind of feel. Okay, just a little more book arranging, a final sweep, and then pizza.

As I stand, I look at my phone and mutter, "Wonder who all he meant by everyone?"

CHAPTER 11

"See? It's not a good feeling, is it?" Jackson says when I open my door to the van. I'm parked out by the railroad tracks because the driveway, and much of the bridge parking, is full. He's standing in the full light of the streetlamp above us, and I can see when his defiance slides away and his face crumples. "Honestly. I don't know what happened."

I get out, slam my door, and step around to the back van door that is slowly rising to reveal two dozen pizzas. Yep, two dozen. "Is anyone coming to help us carry these?"

"Yeah, but I told them to give me a minute to, uh, talk to you." The front screen door closes with a bang. "That's them now. I'm sorry, I know you're exhausted."

"This. This is why I didn't want any B&B guests this week. What did you do? Invite the whole town? Plan a book festival kickoff pizza party?"

"Hey, Mom, we got this," Bryan says as he, Grant, Zoe, and three other teenagers plunge into the back of the van and emerge with pizza boxes. "Wasn't it nice of Ms. Blankenship to invite all of us and tell us to call our friends? She's awesome!"

A growl is my only answer. I beginning to think this woman, with all her big city attitude, is just an old-fashion, pot stirrer. From insisting on staying here to inviting a bunch of kids to have pizza, it feels like she believes the more drama, the better!

These kids definitely aren't her reading demographic. At least they are not reading them in my house.

I cut my eyes at my husband, and he waves toward the house. "Y'all get these in the kitchen. Everything is set up. Your mom and I will be there in a minute." As he closes the back door, I go back to the front seat to grab my purse and the pizza party lady's latest book. Jackson puts his hands on my shoulders before I shut the door.

"Leave that stuff there. We'll get it in a minute. The moon is almost full out over the river." He pulls me back a step, then puts a comforting arm around my shoulder. "Come on."

The cheer that erupts as the kids deliver the pizzas into the house makes me not struggle too much to go with Jackson. I also notice he has a coat on, so I know he planned this little detour. I appreciate that, so I lean against him a bit and take a step forward. "Sounds like a good idea."

The sun's been down for a good half hour, but there's still dove-blue light outlining the trees. We leave the brightness of the streetlight at the parking area and step onto the bricks leading to the walking bridge.

Years ago, when the train trestle needed replacing, the town convinced the railroad not to tear down the old bridge, but to remove the rails and ties, pave it, and put up hand railings. They also placed decorative, old-fashioned lampposts all along the bridge. They give enough light to walk by, but keep the darkness in place. The new bridge sits still, dark, and quiet until a train barrels off the mountain across the river and flies past. When a train is crossing the river in the other direction, headed uphill, it moves much slower, but it's noisy as it builds up the power to climb the mountain. Either way it's impressive to stand in the middle of the river with a huge train only yards away. There's no train in sight in either direction right now. Believe me, Jackson is looking.

Jackson and his love of trains brought us here to walk this

bridge every autumn when we'd leave our Atlanta suburbs in search of North Georgia apples. It was always a day of beautiful mountain vistas, eating apples, apple pies, apple fritters, and BBQ. Then we'd head back to suburbia, full and happy.

Until I accidentally sold our house at the same time the old house beside the train bridge was available. I laugh and snuggle against my husband as I think of how much I thought I'd hate it in Chancey "Remember how silly I was about moving here?"

He pulls me closer and laughs as we move out farther onto the bridge. It's cold, so I pull my gloves out of my coat pockets and put them on. It may be one of the last times I need them this season. The air is so clean and smells ready. Ready for plants and flowers and life. I can smell the dirt, released from winter's chill, or maybe that's the scent of a river, warming up, moving faster.

He chuckles again, then sighs. "Tonight I saw some of what made you hate it so much. I didn't have any control over what was happening. First her assistants being incredibly pushy about getting food and then Retta and the ladies from the book club showed up."

"What?" I stop and half turn back toward the house. "They're in there?"

He tightens his arm on my shoulders and pulls me on. "Yep. In all their glory, with bags of books to be signed. Apparently the author in residence told Retta when she delivered the flowers earlier to bring the ladies, and their books, back tonight. Wayne's here, too."

"Wayne?" The word might've come out more like a groan. Retta's brother is the manager of the Piggly Wiggly, and they both stayed at the B&B a few months ago when their house was being fumigated. He's a, well, a handful. And not a fun handful.

"Ms. Blankenship is holding court in the living room with her adoring fans. Bryan, Grant, Zoe, and I were working on our—their—project in the basement, and when we came upstairs to get the pizza order, well, she invited everyone to stay, invite their friends, and she offered to pay." He squints at me. "She's hard to read. Definitely high maintenance the way she keeps her assistants jumping. But overall it feels like she's directing some show and the crazier the better!" He sighs. "But I probably should've done more to try and stop her.

Taking a deep breath, I turn into him and hug him. "Been there. Done that. And I want to apologize to you. When I pulled up and saw all those cars—no, when I got to the pizza place and they told me all those pizzas were for me—I was upset. But I did get a better understanding of what you were saying back then when you were working so hard out of town and only coming home on the weekends. When you felt the house was always full and no one was taking you into consideration. I am sorry, but I guess tonight we both got an idea how the other one felt."

We hug for another minute, and then Jackson pulls one arm away and turns us toward the river. "Look there, coming up over the trees."

Clear and cold, the night sky is lit up around the nearly full moon. In contrast, the dark limbs it rose out of look like they've been drawn in black ink. Every single branch stands out, reaching as if they'd personally pushed the moon up onto its trajectory and now want it back. We watch as the water receives its first beams, sparkling back a million fold on the ripples and waves. I shiver, as much from the beauty as the cold, but Jackson pulls me tighter into him, and we step to the railing to bundle against it.

"I don't come out here enough," I whisper. "This is incredible." We watch as the swath of light grows until the whole river dances. Then I shiver again, but this time it's all from the cold.

Jackson gives me another hug. "I'm cold too. Besides, I'm starving. They better have left us some pizza!" He pulls to start walking, but I hold him in place.

"Wait." I look up at him. "I want you to know I'm really happy. Sometimes I forget that, and you know I have a tendency to like to grumble, but I really am happy. I really do love my life."

He smiles and gives me a quick kiss. "I know, and the same goes for me. I really do appreciate you putting up with me working from home and the whole construction business. It's kind of crazy, all the changes."

We begin walking faster as the cold chases us. We get to the van to retrieve my things, and I agree. "It is crazy. Completely crazy, but I'm proud of us for trying to live our dreams, right?"

He closes the van door and tilts his head to look at me. "Oh, is that what we're doing, Mrs. Jessup? Living our dreams? And here I thought we were just careening down a mountain like a runaway train!"

Chapter 12

"My dad did it," Susie Mae says from behind the counter as she puts her backpack away. "Well, he had it done. Last night." She comes out to stand with Bonnie and me as we look out on the sidewalk, where the planters and window boxes are back in place on this Wednesday morning. Bonnie's been here since daybreak decorating, and she says they were already in place when she arrived. We're happy the one in front of our window is lower this time and allows the full window display to be seen.

"Your dad? Why?" I ask, although I'm afraid I know. He did it for his new girlfriend, Athena Markham, since she's assistant to the book festival director, Carlie Ruiz. Athena decided yesterday she liked the flowers and last I heard was trying to get them back on Main Street, so of course Griffin got involved. My stomach does a little flip whenever I think of Griffin and Athena being together and Susan being left out. But then she's the one that moved on from the marriage first with her Silas fling. And now that she wants her marriage back, it may be too late.

Susie Mae shrugs and takes a slurp of her smoothie from Phoenix's juice bar. "Who knows? I'm not really talking to him right now."

Bonnie and I catch eyes, and I give her a nod. She was a

teacher after all. She tips her head in a show of compassion and asks, "Why aren't you talking to your father?"

I mean, I want to hear what the teenager says, but I have to imagine that the fact that Griffin is dating a woman much younger than her mother is of course the reason. I begin to walk away, not too far—like I said, I do want to hear it from her—but maybe she'll talk more if I'm not standing right there.

"He won't let me go on spring break with Savannah and Jenna and their friends."

Wait—what?

"What?" I'm so back in this conversation. "Who says they're going anywhere?"

"They do. Everyone does. Someone's family has a cabin on a lake outside Atlanta, and a bunch of people are going. It's going to be a blast, and he says I can't go. I'm supposed to be staying with him for break, but I'm not going to now. I have a car. I can go if I want."

Now the one backing away is Bonnie. She's raised her kids; she wants no part of this conversation. She won't even meet my eyes as I barrel back in. "Susie Mae, I don't know who told you Savannah is doing this, but she's not. No way."

The girl's eyes are big and bright blue, and now they are flashing fire. "She said all you were concerned about is money, and this isn't going to cost any of us anything. We'll just bring food from home, and it's rent free. See? There's absolutely no reason for y'all to say no!"

I'm surprised at her anger. She's high energy, but usually in a good way. I slow my words and tone. "You need to calm down. We'll talk about this later." I step away from the front window. "We have work to do, and you're only here for an hour this morning, right?"

She takes a breath. "Right."

She's part of the work-study program at the high school. She comes in an occasional hour on Wednesday mornings in addition to the afternoons and Saturdays she works. I want to ask her what her mom says about this spring break trip, but we're not going there. I'll call Susan later. You can also bet I'll also be talking to Savannah about this.

That daughter of mine is single-handedly bringing the Atlanta suburbs' spring break insanity to Chancey.

"Everybody gets a Popsicle!" Alex shouts, coming out of his restaurant. The young man is carrying several plastic grocery bags, and they look like they're filled with Popsicles. That's a lot of popsicles, but then again, there are a lot of kids on the sidewalk.

Around ten thirty this morning, two school buses pulled up in front of the stores, letting kids and teachers out. Athena and a bunch of moms arrived at the same time, and they all came armed with art supplies. By the time we merchants piled out of our doors, the kids were all stationed near the unpainted planters and window boxes. Then the painting began.

"What's going on?" I had asked as Athena made her way down the sidewalk to our door.

Athena looked happy, almost prancing in her jeans and tucked-in shirt. She wasn't sporting one of her big scarfs, but she had a wide leather belt with a big buckle and short leather boots with clunky heels. Her hair fell down her back, straightened and flat. "We needed to make these look like something more than, well, what they looked like." She laughed out loud. "So since the high schoolers made them, we figured the kindergarteners could paint them. We did the phone tree, got permission, and they'll be here for less than an hour. A fun little field trip to help out their town! Isn't it great?" Beaming at everyone in the vicinity, she then took a moment to lean closer to me and whisper, "Let's see those self-important Bedwells move the planters now when the children have worked so hard." She winked and moved away, clapping her hands and yelling, "Let everyone have a turn. We can only stay an hour!"

Now that hour is about up, and it's Popsicle time. As the kids enjoy their treat, I look around, amazed at how great the paint jobs look. The window box and planter near our store is covered with bright flowers and smiley faces, obviously painted by kids, but then I guess that's the idea. The one beside AC's is mostly scenes of, well, I'm not sure, but it's colorful and better than the bare wood. Several of us use the empty grocery bags to collect Popsicle sticks and thank the teachers. It's a clear, early spring day, perfect for an outing like this. The laughter has done a lot to make everything downtown feel better.

"Makes me wish my place was over here on the main sidewalk," Gertie says as she plows through the kids, who are lining up to get back on the buses. "I'd've never believed these clunky things could look this good. Whose idea was this?"

"Athena Markham's, I guess," I answer her. "How are you doing? Haven't seen you much."

The big woman puts her hands on her hips. "I'm sick to death of all this cold weather. Been hibernating over there in the house and moonshine cave. Besides, with Patty happy and busy nesting in her new house, I don't have no need to be bugging you as much. Don't think I mentioned how I appreciate you taking pity on the girl and letting her hang out here at your store when she was feeling down."

"Patty's a friend. She was actually a big help, especially when Francie was around. She loved sitting and holding my granddaughter when I wasn't." I smile at Gertie as I turn to open our door. "You want to come in and have a seat?"

She looks up and down the sidewalk, where things are quickly reverting to normal. "I think I might ought to," she says with a sigh.

Now that doesn't sound good, but I let her in anyway.

"Have a seat on the couch. Can I get you anything?"

"Well, doesn't this look pretty? Why, Bonnie Cuneo, you did all this?"

Our white walls, even up into the white-painted brick, are threaded with vines. They're artificial, but they look real, like they crept in overnight. There are nosegays of flowers tucked in the vines, but also throughout the store, in every little nook and cranny. You wouldn't think they'd stand out in a flower shop, but they do. The most ingenious touch, in my opinion, is the panels of lace draped around the store, over the doors to the flower cooler, then pulled back with pink ribbons above the store entrance, where they move in the breeze from the fan and the door's opening and closing. Bonnie even covered the throw pillows in the lace so their original color shows through. Tucked here and there are also pots of tulips and daffodils, pastel planters with herbs, and decorative birds, their nests full of delicate ceramic eggs.

Bonnie comes toward us. "I've had this in mind since we took down the Christmas decorations. You don't think it's too much? I didn't realize I'd collected so much stuff. Plus, Shannon had things she's used through the years, and she let me spruce them up and use them."

Gertie and I shake our heads as we examine the spring bower we find ourselves in. Gertie says, "Not too much at all. Mind you, I don't have to work here with all this folderol, but it's right nice. Very spring-like. Think I'll take you up on that seat, Carolina." She walks to the couch and lowers herself. "Nothing to drink, though. Can't stay long."

Bonnie and I share a quick smile as I move to sit across from Gertie. Bonnie says, "I'll be in the back if you need me."

Gertie shifts her bulk to lean forward, her forearms resting on her knees. "Carolina, I need your input on something I'm struggling with. You know I don't usually struggle making decisions. That's how folks miss opportunity. How they miss getting in while the getting's good, you got me?"

"Okay," I say when I realize she's waiting for a response.

"So what we've got here now is an old-fashioned power struggle, or a chess game like that one over there on the table." I look toward the chess set Bonnie put on the old table near our older books, most of them from FM's collection. The black and white pieces stand in their places, so I look back at Gertie. She nods at me and clears her throat. "Yep, I'm guessing you know what I'm talking about, right?"

This time she doesn't wait for me, just barrels on. "I'm not about to get caught up in anything, but I'm also not of a mind to get left out. If you're not at the table, you don't get fed. I aim to get fed. You feel the same, I'm sure."

I need to slow this down, so I shake my head and look confused. Is she talking about Peter and Delaney and Missus, or are Athena and Griffin involved? I wrinkle my forehead deeper so she'll see I'm not following, but then I realize she's not looking at me. I follow her gaze and see she's staring at her hands.

Her gravelly voice is serious. "The situation we have here is this author friend of Peter's. Is she for real? Carolina, I'm asking you a question."

I pull my gaze up, but my mind is still focused on her hands. Specifically one hand. One finger. "Oh, I'm sorry. What? Sally Blankenship? Yeah, look there. You can see all her books displayed on that top shelf."

She stares at the shelf and then pushes up on her knees to stand. "Well, there ya go. Then a party it is. She said to let you know she'd like a book display." Gertie pulls a stocking hat out of her pocket and waves it at the display I'd just pointed out to her. "Just bring those. I'll clear a table." She jams the hat on and then heads for the door. "Bring 'em over when you close Saturday. That'll be early enough. I'm thinking I'll close at six."

"The moonshine cave? You're going to close it at six on a

Saturday night?" I ask as I hurry to catch her. She can move pretty fast for a big lady.

"Duh? You just said she's the real deal, and if she wants to pay me to close for a private party, who am I to say no? Besides, she said she's going to invite pretty much anyone who wants to come, so it's like getting paid extra to close. Good advice, Carolina. I never have had the time to get much into books but I knew you'd know what to do." She opens the door, then leans back in. "With this feud going on, the rest of us folks have to stick together, right? I don't aim to be no pawn for these self-made kings and queens!"

The door falls shut as she moves out into the beautiful spring day. This time she didn't wait for a response, which is fine because I didn't have one to give. I whirl around as I hear Shannon and Danny coming downstairs from their lunch break.

"Good, you're back. I'm going out for lunch." I grab my purse out from underneath the counter, decide I don't need a jacket, and rush through the door onto the sidewalk. I pull out my phone and call Laney.

"Where are you?"

"At The Club. Doesn't that sound awesome! I just love saying that. Why?"

"Okay, I'll be there in a minute. Want a smoothie or anything from Phoenix's?"

"No. Susan is bringing us lunch here. You can have some of ours. We didn't invite you because you have the festival this week. Just come straight to The Club." She giggles. "Isn't that awesome?"

"Okay. Even better. See you in a minute."

"Wait!" she screeches.

"What?"

"Say it. Say where you'll see me in a minute."

I can't help but laugh. "Okay. I'll see you at The Club."

Chapter 13

"This really shouldn't work this well," Susan says. "It should feel dark, or closed in. I just don't know how you do it."

We're seated at a table sharing the two banana sandwiches Susan had brought to share with her sister. I don't usually eat my banana sandwiches with mayonnaise like they do. I have to admit, despite my preference for good old bananas and peanut butter, that the mayonnaise adds a little zing.

Laney chews as she looks around. "I don't think I could do it for other people like Bonnie does. I just know what I want a place to feel like and do that." She crumbles up her napkin. "I stop when it feels right."

Holding a baby carrot, I point out the wall across from me. "What is this color? Is it brown or gray or green?"

"Some of all three. I don't remember the name of the paint. I just wanted something that would disappear. Let the merchandise stand out. The chairs are ones I'd seen at the Merchandise Market in Atlanta, and I knew they were sold at one of the big box stores. I started tracking them down and cornered the market. Got a great price—same story with the tables."

Susan and I arrived at the same time, so we oohed and ahhed over The Club as we sat down to eat. If I hadn't already seen Laney's house, I might've been surprised at how comfortable this space is. Laney is so over the top with her fashion personality, it's hard to imagine she puts rooms together like this. The walls do fade pleasantly into the background. Shelves and racks line the walls in little groupings like stalls in a marketplace, and the middle of the room features cozy tables and chairs. The chairs are cushioned, with nice, solid arms made of wood. The fabric is the same color as the walls and the carpet. She has lamps on tall stands, and the overhead lighting is track or can lighting, I'm not sure. There's plenty of light, and yet it doesn't feel bare like this space did before. It feels comfortable. Club-like. Not like a night club; like an old-fashioned ladies' club, but updated.

Laney holds her hands up. "But enough about this place. Carolina, what do you mean Gertie is wearing an engagement ring?"

"That's what it looked like. Maybe it's just a new ring. But I don't remember ever seeing her wearing something like this, and I think I caught her staring at it." With a shrug I finish my last bite of sandwich and mumble, "I just wanted to ask y'all if you've heard anything." They both shake their heads at me, and I sit back. "It threw me off so much that I didn't even get the details on this party Sally Blankenship is throwing at the cave Saturday night."

Susan chuckles. "Forget that. I want to know about this party she threw up at your house last night? Two dozen pizzas?" She sniffs and stretches her neck from side to side. "Grant was there, I assume?"

"Yeah." Laney and I meet eyes when Susan closes hers, still stretching her neck. "Yeah, he was there working on the school project Jackson is helping them with. Grant seems to be doing well moving back to town."

"He does." She talks, eyes still closed while she massages her neck. "He's still working up at the golf course whenever he can, or maybe he's actually at his dad's all that time. Or, for all I know, he's at your house." Her eyes spring open, and they're flooded with tears. "I need to thank you for all the meals you're including him in. Our house was always the one with extra kids at dinner. Now my kids are spread hither and yon in the wind."

Laney gets up, stands behind her sister, and takes over the massage. "They're at that age when it's hard to nail them down, sis. And it's not like you don't know where they are, right?"

I lean forward. "Grant is always welcome at our house. You're right, he has been there often, but then Jackson is totally invested in this depot project. Plus, the adoration Grant's getting from Zoe would be hard to walk away from."

"I've told him he can't lead her on." She scowls at me. "I hate to think we're already into all those games teenagers play with dating. Is he leading her on?"

"Not that I can see. He's his usual confident self. A tad more confident, I think, since his time at Darien Academy, but he might've been like that without Darien." I stand to clean up the table. "But she's got it bad." As I make a trip to the trash can near the back door, I think of how sad Bryan looked watching Zoe moon over Grant last night. Several of their friends showed up for pizza, and one of the girls paid a lot of attention to my son, but did he notice? Nope. I turn and ask, "Hey, speaking of kids, has Susie Mae mentioned this spring break trip to a cabin with Savannah?"

Laney finishes her massage, then reaches down and hugs her sister, saying, "Jenna's going, apparently. At least that's what I was informed of over the weekend. Now Shaw and I are fighting about it. He says no way, and I explained that in a couple months she'll be living across the state in a dorm where we won't know where she's spending her free time." She moves to straighten a set of open shelves near her. "Besides, I told him if you and Jackson are okay with it, then I'm sure it's fine."

"Jackson and I know nothing about it! Nothing at all. First I heard was from Susie Mae this morning at work. I guess Griffin told her no."

Susan swivels in her chair. "Oops. She texted me this morning, just before y'all got here, and I told her it sounded fun." She cringes. "But I'm just trying to stay on my kids' good side, so I'm an idiot. I figured I could say yes since she's at her dad's that week and I don't really get a say."

Laney and I frown at her, and she takes out her phone. "Okay. Bad parenting. I'll text her no, or maybe we'll talk about it?" She looks up at us hopefully, and we both shrug.

I hold out a hand to stop from texting. "Don't say anything. Let me get to the bottom of it all. Find out whose cabin and get the details. Will's last months at home before college are coming back to me. They are on the cusp of adulthood, but still in our houses. It's a fine line: How do we teach them adult responsibilities without ever giving them adult responsibilities?"

I pull one of the lightweight shawls from the display Laney is rearranging. It's a soft peach and looks like spring itself. "I want this one. Are you going to let us run a tab at The Club?"

Laney swings toward me. "Oh, what a great idea! A big ol' ledger book. How fun! Yes, that's a great idea."

Susan is looking at a display of beaded bracelets, and her head snaps up. "Speaking of great ideas, who came up with painting the planters out front? They look amazing, and getting the kids involved was brilliant."

Laney's and my eyes fly to meet, and when they do, they widen. Laney's eyebrows drop and her lips lock together. She's not saying anything. As I turn to Susan, I wrinkle my nose and employ a whimsical smile. "I'm not sure. Maybe just the teachers?"

I'm saved by a savage knocking at the door, but then the person realizes it's not locked and pushes it open. Delaney marches in, plants her hands on her hips, and un-saves me.

"Carolina, what in the world are you trying to do, working with Athena Markham behind my back?"

"I'm not," I declare to the woman near the door in the dark green business suit. Then, with just a slight shift, I declare, "I'm not!" to the woman in the camel sweater and black slacks who just shared her lunch with me. I'm not feeling I can call either of them a friend right now. They then shift to stand next to each other, and Laney from behind me says, "Athena Markham? I do think I remember seeing her out there earlier."

"Thank, Judas," I shoot over my shoulder. I try a small laugh as I advance on the arm-crossed duo. "I'm not working with anyone. I'm just trying to get through this book festival, which I thought, for some strange reason, would be fun."

Delaney frowns. "I told you yesterday I would take care of the planters. That they'd be moved today. Then what do I find when I step outside this morning? There they are, right back in place, and there are hordes of children painting them."

I shake my head at her. "No. You did not tell me anything about the planters. Matter of fact, I remember being mad that I didn't ask you what you planned to do with them since they were taking up our back parking, but I had nothing to do with this. I have enough on my plate. This feud is not my concern."

Susan looks at me, then Delaney, and back at me before asking, "What feud?"

Laney has moved to my right. "Feud? Who's feuding?"

Delaney throws up her hands. "Go on. Tell them, Carolina. Tell Susan how her husband and his new friend have cooked up some imaginary rivalry with Peter and myself. They've gone all *Game of Thrones*. Or maybe Hatfield and McCoy fits better here in the mountains."

"Well..." I lick my lips and realize the more I hesitate, the deeper Susan's frown gets, and Laney's look of amusement has slid into one of confusion. I stammer a bit, trying to make it sound not as feud-y. "Well, for some reason Athena doesn't trust Delaney and Peter and is kind of working behind the scenes to… uh"—I want to say, "Thwart their plans," but that sounds totally like *Game of Thrones*—"to… uh, mess things up."

Susan has pulled the band off her ponytail and is now putting it back up. I've learned it's never a good sign when she starts playing with her ponytail. "Athena has pulled Griffin into all this? Griffin is no longer on the city council. He's too busy with his job and the kids to get wrapped up in all that crazy woman's drama." She pulls her ponytail tighter and darts around me to grab her purse off the table where we ate. "I'll fix this feud. That woman is getting a piece of my mind!"

The remaining three of us step out of her way. We all look like we want to say something, but we don't. We let her fly out the door, on her way to give Athena a piece of her mind.

Delaney sighs, and I sit down in the nearest chair. Laney folds her arms and shakes her head and says, "Well I know one thing about feuds."

We turn to look at her, and she raises her eyebrows while taking a deep breath. "Angry ex-wives rarely help."

CHAPTER 14

"Lemon meringue pie today!" is being yelled behind me on the sidewalk. It makes me turn around on my way from The Club to my shop.

"Hey, Kimmy. Lemon meringue, you say?"

She bounces toward me in her red tennis shoes. "Yep. Doesn't that sound like spring? Ruby said lemon isn't her favorite flavor, but she'd try it. I'm just so ready for spring, aren't you?"

"Yes. I keep looking ahead on my weather app for it to warm up, but it keeps staying cold. At least it's not calling for rain or snow."

"Thank goodness. I couldn't stand one more weekend of keeping the kids inside." She plunges her hands in the front pockets of her jeans. "I guess Zoe's got it bad for Grant Lyles, hasn't she?" When I nod, she echoes it with her own nod. "Yeah, she's always been so mature that we kind of thought she'd never get silly like this over a boy." Leaning a little closer she says, "And if she did, we were really hoping it would be over Bryan. So does Grant like her back, you think?"

"I'm not sure. He's really grown up recently, and I'm just not sure. And I can't ask Bryan."

"No, I guess not. He does still seem to be carrying a torch for her." She shrugs. "Oh well. It's hard being young, isn't it?"

I agree as we head our opposite ways, and then she yells, "But lemon meringue pie can fix most anything!"

With a laugh I wave at her and slow down to a walk in front of our store. The planter on the corner brightens up the old, dark brick. A small tree that's grown up in the strip of dirt between the building and the sidewalk casts a shadow, and I notice there are small, green leaves popping out on it. With a turn toward the park, I see the trees there also have a haze of new green way up in their limbs. It won't be long until the square is shaded. I step into a bright patch of sunshine and pull out my phone. Jackson and Will are working on a house remodel behind the library. Maybe I'll take them some pie this afternoon. I send my text to them and stroll into the store as I rotate my shoulders and take some deep breaths. I'm done stressing about the festival. We're as ready as we can be.

I think.

"I took all of Shannon I could stand. Thank goodness we didn't have many customers this afternoon so I could get out of there." I'm sitting in the gazebo in the square with my granddaughter in my arms. Jackson, Will, and Anna are seated around me, and they are busy eating lemon meringue pie. The guys said it was too pretty to eat inside and Anna said she'd love to join us, so I picked up three slices of pie. Anna brought us each a bottle of water and this bundle of pinkness on my lap. Francie's warm in a soft, pink fleece blanket sleeper and is enjoying her afternoon nap outdoors.

Kimmy actually gave us the pie on plates with real forks and everything, all on a tray to carry over here. Anna slides the meringue off her pie to the side of her plate. "Sorry, I'm just not a fan of meringue. So what's up with Shannon being so mean to y'all? I mean, I know she's pregnant and all, but no need to take it out on everybody else."

"No, but…" I pause as I wonder if Anna realizes Shannon's baby is going to be related to her. Anna was busy with her own pregnancy and Francie's first weeks when all the drama with Peter and Shannon was happening. Also, with Anna and Will living out of town in the cabin this winter, they've kind of been out of the loop. I decide to tread lightly near that topic. "But Shannon's got other issues. Like her folks found out she and Danny aren't married yet. Apparently that's getting worked out, but she's also never been a very happy or content person. At least not since I've known her."

Jackson sets his empty plate beside him on the bench and reaches for his water bottle. "Well, except when she was with Peter. They really got along well. It was good for both of them."

Will agrees. "Shame they broke up. I mean, it's not like I don't like Delaney and all, but Peter was a lot nicer then, too." He puts his last bite in his mouth, then speaks around it. "Makes you wonder what'll happen when the baby comes."

Anna frowns at him, her eyebrows scrunched down, but then they lift as she draws in a breath. "Oh, that's right. I completely forgot the baby is, is," she whispers, "Peter's. I mean, so it's my, oh! It's my cousin!" She covers her mouth with her hand. "How did I forget that? No wonder Shannon's being a bear to live with. You know, maybe I should throw her a baby shower."

"Honey," I say, "no." Will and Jackson are also shaking their heads. "Peter doesn't seem to know, or maybe just doesn't want to know, about the baby, and your grandmother is ignoring it until it gets here. That's probably not something you should get involved with."

My sweet daughter-in-law rolls her eyes. "These people! I've been stuck out there in the cabin and just assumed things had worked out. But I guess you should never assume, especially not in Chancey." She stands up. "If y'all are fine here for a minute, I'm going to go talk to Shannon and see if I can help." Then she jogs down the gazebo steps and is hurrying toward the shop.

I look at Will. "Maybe you should go with her?" But as he starts to stand, Jackson puts a hand out, grabbing our son's arm. "Or maybe not," he says. "She said she'll be right back. I think we should all wait here. Now, let me hold my granddaughter." He leans over and I pass her along. Francie wiggles a bit, but he snuggles her on his shoulder and she settles back down.

Will leans back against the railing and pulls out his phone. "Colt's headed to the jobsite. I'll let him know we'll be back there soon." As he texts, he says, "Dad, you know he's hosting a mini football camp next week, so he won't be working on any of our construction projects."

They discuss their work schedule, and I watch the front door of the shop. Maybe Jackson's right. Maybe Will shouldn't have gone with Anna. Maybe I'm so involved in all this mess that I'm making it a bigger problem than it is. Maybe Shannon will appreciate Anna's concern; like she said, they'll be family soon. When the door of Blooming Books opens, I smile to see Anna coming out, but she doesn't look our direction and she's not smiling. She spins to her right and strides down the sidewalk. Before I can interrupt the guys, she's throwing open the door that leads up to the *Vedette* and Peter's law offices.

"Hey, y'all," I start to say, but then I'm interrupted by Bonnie on the sidewalk outside our store, looking in our direction, and pointing down the sidewalk. She's yelling, "Carolina! Anna's headed to, well, you know where."

I stand up and slap Jackson's arm. "Anna has headed to Peter's office, and she didn't look happy. You stay here with the baby."

Hurrying down the gazebo steps, I look back to where my

son still sits. With raised eyebrows he asks, "You good, or do you need me to come with you?"

Jackson answers for me. "Son, you're probably gonna wanna go with your mom."

Chapter 15

"Oh! Hello." I barrel into the outer office door to find myself face to face with none other than Sally Blankenship.

She pulls the door open further and welcomes me with a flourish of her long, thin arm. "Come in, come in! We could hear you coming up the stairs and tromping down the hall, so I thought I'd just go ahead and open the door. The young woman I assume you're chasing went thataway!" Her icy bluish-green eyes are merry, and her prominent cheekbones are dusted in pink. She's either licking her lips or she has some amazing lip gloss, but I guess if I'd spent money to have those lips, I'd pay for the best lip gloss too. She squeals and wrinkles her nose. "Did she say something about a baby? Don't tell me Peter has been a bad boy! Isn't he a newlywed?" She grabs my arm. "And we must talk sometime about that wedding of his. What a shock! A grown son? I hear you were right up front for the whole debacle."

"It was a mess," Will says over my head. "You say Anna is in with Peter?"

The author practically pushes me out of the way. "And I bet you're her, uh, Anna's..." She pauses, looks him over, zeroes in on his wedding band, and then cocks her head. "Her husband? She looks awfully young, but then that is how you people do it down here, isn't it? Not that you're old by any means." She turns to her assistants, particularly the two young ones. "Isn't he delicious? I think the term our Southern friends are partial to is 'cute as a bug's ear.'"

They cackle and make eyes at my son, who is turning red. However, yelling from behind Peter's office door catches all our attention. Will moves forward, and I follow him down the hall. We stop at the closed door, listening, but the shouting has stopped. Will slowly opens the door and says, "Hope we're not interrupting anything," as the two of us enter.

Peter is standing behind his desk and Anna stands in front of it. Delaney is sitting to the side, her elbows on her knees and her chin in her hands. She lifts her eyebrows at me, and I shoot her a smile as I walk forward. "Anna, are you okay?"

Peter laughs. "She's fine. Why not ask about me? I'm the one having my character assassinated. For some reason she wants to pawn Danny Kinnock's child off as mine. Anna, honey, that's just not possible. I'm happily married. Now I have work to get back to." He looks over at Delaney. "Get Sally back in here. Will, take Anna home, but y'all come over for dinner..." He looks down at his desk and shuffles some papers. "Uh, Sunday night. Put that down, Delaney. Let Mother know." He smiles at his niece. "And bring the baby. It'll be a nice family evening." He shares his smile around the room, then says over our heads, "Sally? We're through here. Come on back."

Anna's mouth has yet to close, and she turns around, shaking her head. "Unbelievable."

"Will. Close the door," I say in a gravelly voice. Seeing as he's known me and my serious voice his whole life, my son knows I mean business. "Peter," I say, once I hear the heavy wooden door click shut behind me. "Shannon is carrying your baby. How you think you can simply deny it is beyond me. Beyond everyone."

His shoulders slump, and he leans forward to rest his knuckles on his desk. He stares at its polished surface and takes a couple of deep breaths. Then he looks up, straight at me, and whispers, "Prove it." I gasp, but his face softens, and he comes around the desk to his niece. He holds out his arms, placing his hands on her shoulders and turning her to face him. "Anna, tell me what you want me to do. Until Shannon tells me this is true, I'm at a loss for what you want me to do."

Anna looks at me, and I shrug. I have no idea what Shannon has said or not said to him. I want to be furious with him, with them both, but mainly I just feel hopeless.

Delaney comes to stand behind her husband and also reaches out a hand to my daughter-in-law. "Come to dinner Sunday. We'll talk more, okay?"

Anna pauses, but then takes a step forward and hugs her uncle quickly. She turns to the door, pulls it open, and heads down the hall with Will behind her. I'm left staring at Peter and Delaney. Delaney smiles at me and leans forward to give me a hug. "It'll all be fine. I promise," she says in my ear.

Peter just shrugs and says, "It's all up to Shannon."

"Never a dull moment south of the Mason-Dixon line!" Sally practically shouts as she pushes into the room. "I just knew I'd find some juicy stories for my next book down here."

With my head down, I plow past her and her assistants, but she says, "And the setting of a bed-and-breakfast beside the train tracks is a whole new idea, but I'm loving it for the book I'm working on!"

I get into the hall and pull the door shut behind me, then move on to the entrance area where Will waits alone. "Anna's in the restroom," he explains. "Did Ms. Blankenship just say she's going to put the B&B into her next book?"

"Sounds like it."

He grins. "Well, that'd be awesome, right? She's, like, really famous."

I close my eyes and reach for the door to get out of here, but then I pause and say over my shoulder, "Oh, son, it's exactly what I've been afraid of since the moment I heard she was in town."

I hear Francie's wails before my foot hits the sidewalk. Jackson waits across the road with his bundle. "She's not happy," he says, handing her to me as soon as I reach them.

"Poor thing. Where's her pacifier?"

He shakes his head. "I can't find it."

"Go look in her bag. Anna and Will are right behind me." I give Francie my finger to suck on. She quiets down, but I know it won't last long. Poor thing thinks she's going to starve to death. I can't help but chuckle as she sucks and the stress leaves her face, but then her little eyes flutter open when she realizes there's nothing coming out of my finger. The muscles in her sweet, pink cheeks stop working so hard, and she opens her mouth to make her complaint as I walk with her to the gazebo. I'm laughing at myself as much as anything. How devastating it was when my babies cried like this. How petrified I'd be, so afraid I was damaging them for life, when all they wanted was to be fed and then all will be forgiven.

I hear Anna coming up behind me, and I know hearing her baby cry has wiped all thoughts of Peter out of her head. Babies are good for that.

"Oh, poor thing. I didn't plan on leaving her, so I didn't think to bring a bottle." Just being with her mom gives us a momentary pause in the uproar, and we use it to get Anna and Francie to her car. The clouds have made it too chilly to sit outside any longer, especially for a nursing mother.

She gets settled in the passenger seat, and Will turns on the car and heater for them. Then he gets back out of the car. "She's been saving all the pumped milk for when she goes back to work next week. I think I'll drive them home and we'll get my car later."

We say goodbye to them and watch as they drive away. Our plates, water bottles, and the tray are in the gazebo just as we left them, so we gather everything while I tell Jackson what Peter had to say for himself.

He follows me across the street. "I hate to say it, but Peter's right. If neither he nor Shannon want to admit it, what can anyone do?"

"We'll see. I'll take this back into Kimmy. You're going back to the job, right? So I'll see you at home." He gives me a kiss along with the tray and opens Ruby's door for me.

Ruby's is quiet, and the front lights are turned off. Kimmy had said she'd be here until four thirty for me to return the dishes.

"How was it?" she asks.

"It was delicious. Ruby should include lemon meringue in her regular rotation." I join her behind the counter. "It's weird being in here with just the two of us."

"Isn't it heaven? So quiet and peaceful," she says with a laugh. "Ruby didn't trust me here by myself at first, but now she does, and it's like my sanctuary before I go home to the craziness at my house."

"Things are still good with you and Kyle?"

"They are. Missus put the fear of God into him, and I just wonder when she's going to do the same to her son." She flips around to me. "Not that I think Peter is as bad as Kyle was, but that's how he started. Thinking he was lord and king and that I was going to do everything he said. Of course, that Delaney is a lot more together than I was. Sometimes I think she's giving ol' Peter all this rope so he can hang himself from an even higher tree."

I wipe off the tray and think of how Delaney rolled her eyes at me, or with me, when I first got to Peter's office this afternoon. Why doesn't all this bother her more? Is she playing a different game? One we don't know about? Wouldn't be the first time.

Kimmy shuts the dishwasher and starts it, then flips the remaining light switch off. "We'll go out the front and lock it behind us."

I lead the way through the still, dark restaurant, and at the door, Kimmy chuckles.

"Maybe it's not rope with Miss Delaney. Maybe it's strings."

"Strings?" I ask, stepping into the chilly spring evening.

"Yeah, like puppet strings. Maybe she's actually the one in control."

Thinking back on how Peter has turned his wife into his receptionist makes me doubt she has any control, but then she did maneuver the whole wedding without Peter having a clue. Maybe she's playing a game amateurs like me can't begin to imagine. The lock clicks in place and I look up. "Kimmy, that might be the smartest thing I've heard today."

She winks. "Second smartest. First was that lemon meringue pie will fix most anything."

Chapter 16

"I finally started her book last night," I whisper to Danny when he comes down to the shop in Thursday morning.

We're huddled at the coffee pot, and after he looks at me, he goes back to pouring his coffee. Lifting his cup to take a sip, he says, "Well, I finished it, and it doesn't get any better."

We watch Shannon move from the back cooler to her work-table, and then he and I stroll to the front of the shop. Everything is ready for the book festival, at least on the book end of things. Shannon, however, says she's far from ready but won't let us help, so we've decided to stay out of her way.

I reach for one of Sally Blankenship's earlier books we'd put out on display. "I was afraid it was as bad as the other one I'd read, but its worse. So much worse."

Just then, the front door opens, and Retta Bainbridge hustles in.

"Carolina, there you are," she clucks. "What in the world are we going to do? This book can't be allowed to be sold!" She's waving one of the big, splashy hardbacks I've not had the gall to put on display yet. "I got mine on preorder for my e-reader, but then I ordered a hard copy when I heard Sally was going to be here so she could sign it. I didn't have time to read it until last night after I took her and all her assistants to dinner at AC's. Cost me a fortune and now this!" She tosses the book onto the couch. "I even changed the next book club book to it and since it's new everyone will have to pay full price for garbage. Pure garbage." She looks around, then flops onto the couch beside the book. "What are you going to do about all this?"

Danny has slunk away, and I wish I could, too. "Retta, did you really enjoy her other books?"

She has on a yellow sweater and slacks, both the color of the pie at Ruby's yesterday. Her beads are the same yellow, as are her shoes. It actually isn't a bad look on her. She usually wears so many competing colors and patterns, which emphasizes her size. This monochromatic look is different and kind of chic-looking. Plus, unlike most people, she can actually wear yellow. "By the way, I like your outfit."

"Thanks. Laney suggested it. I bought the jewelry and sweater at The Club." She brightens up for a moment, but then her face crushes into itself. "I haven't actually read her books. I mean, I've picked through them, but they are really hard to get through, and I mean, I guess that's how people act in Atlanta or over on the coast, but here? In someplace like Chancey? Why, land's sake, we don't act like that at all!"

"But at my house the other night you were raving about her books!" I'd gently sat down on the edge of the chair, but now I jump up. "What about the others in the book club? Have they read her books?"

She lifts her eyes to me, looking through the thickly mascaraed lashes. Her multiple colors of eye shadow look like a healing bruise—pink, purple, blue, and a little yellow around the edges. She softly says, "No. I called them all this morning first thing to ask."

"What? Y'all had me thinking I was the crazy one!" I moan as I sit back down. I let all this with Sally Blankenship go so far because I thought it was just my singular opinion. After all, not everyone likes the same books. Who am I to tell people an author, a seemingly popular author, is going to be a problem?

Retta sniffs a couple of times. Her voice is husky as she asks, "Do all northerners feel like she does about us people in the South?"

"No." I pat her back and let out a long sigh. "At least not until they start reading her books." I get up and go to look at the books Danny had put out. Finding the one I tried to read a few years ago, I look through it. Her books are written like they are nonfiction when they are basically a parody of real life. In recent years, shows on television like her books are called "mockumentaries," and she does a good job of mocking her subject—Southerners. She's sarcastic and biting and loves a detailed sex scene. We Southerners are sex-crazed (and not very discriminating in our partners), according to her books. And her latest one is more explicit than ever. We're also stupid and exemplify every stereotype from the last hundred years you've ever heard about anyone from below the Mason-Dixon Line.

And I'm hosting a book signing for her on Sunday.

"Carolina, why didn't you tell me?" Missus demands as she marches to the back of the shop, where I'm seated at Bonnie's desk in her decorating nook. I just shake my head and tell her I'll be right with her as I'm on the phone with Carlie. Apparently lots of people finally looked past the fancy New York author label to take a look at Ms. Blankenship's books last night.

Missus looks like she's about to barrel on, so I hold up one long-suffering finger and put Carlie on speakerphone.

Carlie is apoplectic. "You arranged all this!" her voice blares into Blooming Books. "I've already changed the posters and everything to include her. I felt blindsided in a radio interview this morning when they asked about the twitter outrage and the anger on some readers' website about her books. I don't have time to sit around reading so I had no idea what she was' even talking about! I downloaded her latest book, and it's awful, just awful. Filth and lies, that's all it is; filth and lies. I do not need this headache!" She stops yelling at me to listen to someone talking to her on her end. Then she comes back to me. "Athena is headed to your store. You need to figure this out!"

She hangs up, and I raise my head to Missus.

"Yes, Madam Mayor? How can I help you?"

Missus acts as if my phone call never happened. "You can tell me how I'm supposed to answer these reporters that keep calling. I'm assuming most of them are headed here at this very moment."

"Reporters? Like, how many reporters? From where?"

"Some paper or something. One reporter is one too many as far as I'm concerned. She was rather upset."

I roll my eyes. "Upset? That doesn't sound like a reporter. That sounds like Retta Bainbridge flouting press credentials because she does that rambling thing she calls a column once a month in the *Vedette*."

Missus sniffs. "Well, she does write for the paper." Then she lowers her voice and leans toward me. "Is this woman as bad as Retta says?"

"She's *your* son's friend. He's the one who invited her. I assumed y'all knew what her books were like."

She folds her arms and scolds me. "Carolina. Obscure books that are not found in the classic literature section of the library are not mine or Peter's forte. We depend on your expertise for the popular reading fodder. I'm shocked you assumed we'd read this smut and lies. Why would you assume that?"

I have no answer for her. "I don't know. You're right. I assumed way too and just let it all happen. Peter has a way of bulldozing everything, and everyone, to get his way."

"Don't try to blame Peter."

"He invited her!" I shout, then take a deep breath. "He's not answering anyone's calls. Delaney isn't either. Where are they?"

She turns abruptly, clearly in response to the question, and moves away a few steps.

"Missus? Where are they?" I ask as I leap up and follow her.

She jerks her head back toward me, her silver hair with the blonde highlights bouncing. She fiddles with the collar of her blue suede jacket and swallows. "Skiing in Colorado. They flew out late last night on Delaney's father's jet. When Mr. LaMotte realized what was going on with this Blankenship woman, he told them they had to leave." She shrugs. "So they did."

"But... but what about the luncheon, invite-only, on Sunday at their house? What about, uh, everything?"

She's staring at the table in front of us. She touches a couple of the white chess pieces, then drawing her gloved hand back, blinks at me for a moment before straightening her shoulders. "I'll handle it. I'll handle it all. Like I always do."

CHAPTER 17

"Mom! Where's your phone?" Savannah yells up to me from the edge of the basketball court. She's in her cheerleader uniform, pom-poms in one hand. In her other she's holding up her phone at me. "Missus is texting me to tell you to call her!"

I shake my head at her and yell back, "No. Get off your phone and cheer. I'm watching the game."

Beside me, Susan holds out her hand for a high five, which I slap as I explain, "I didn't even bring my phone with me because I knew I'd be too tempted. It's waiting at home for me. Tonight is about Bryan's game and Bryan's game only!"

The first night of the big basketball tournament is a round-robin of junior varsity teams from the area. Friday night and all day Saturday is for the varsity teams. Bryan is barely on the JV team, so there's no way he might be playing again this weekend. Grant, on the other hand, is sometimes called up to play varsity. He added several inches to his height in the past year, and he's much more coordinated than Bryan. Bryan's talents lend themselves more to the football field.

Jackson looks up at me from three rows below and winks. He's sitting down there because that's where I was sitting originally. We went out for an early dinner by the interstate. As Jackson said, we needed a break from Chancey and the B&B after our insane day. Dinner was done by five thirty, so we got to the game early. Shortly after we arrived, Griffin and Athena showed up and sat beside us. I hate to admit I have a lot more respect for Athena after today. She really did help the Sally Situation (as I'm calling it). Of course when Susan came in, she couldn't sit there with the four of us, so I followed her up a few rows. We're saving the seats in front of us for Laney, and the space beside us we're saving for Anna when she makes it this far. She is still down on the floor talking to some friends she and Will have made at church. I'm diligently saving her room because she is carrying my Francie. I'm trying not to focus on my baby being all bundled up in that blanket. I'm sure she's burning up in in this hot gym. No worries, Grammy will fix it—if she ever gets up here.

"There's Laney," Susan says as she stands and waves.

Laney sees us, turns abruptly, and hands over seven-month-old Cayden to his dad. She has on jeans and a white sweater, with several loops of silver beads swaying on her chest. On both wrists are matching bracelets. I like the look. Apparently I'm not alone as several folks stop her on her way to us. As she shows them the metal beads, I hear Laney say, "You'll find them at The Club. Come on by tomorrow for our grand opening!"

"Whew," she releases as she plops onto the bleacher in front of us. "Finally!" I can tell by the jerk of her head the moment when she spots Jackson, Griffin, and Athena, but she doesn't mention it, only saying, "Thanks for saving me a seat." She leans back against our legs. "Don't let me give in to Shaw when Cayden starts crying. I wanted to get a sitter, but Shaw wanted to bring him to the game. Might as well bring a live raccoon. So what'd I miss?"

"Bryan hasn't played, but Grant's doing real well," I say, but she waves her hand above her head.

"Not about the basketball game. What else is going on? I hear your author friend basically set the town on fire and is giving out marshmallows? Save me one of those books, I'm gonna need to see if the sex is as steamy as I've been told. I bet you're selling them as fast as you can put them on the shelf."

When I don't say anything, Susan pulls back and looks at me. "Carolina? Are you still selling that book? You can't be!"

Laney laughs and turns to look up at us. "Of course she can. It's a book and she owns a book*store*."

"Yeah, I own a bookstore," I say defensively. "What else am I supposed to do?" I frown and drop my shoulders. "You have no idea what my day's been like. Retta, Missus, and Gertie hit me first thing this morning, so I pulled all her books off the shelves. Then wouldn't you know it? The author herself shows up, with a reporter in tow, to document the banning of books in Chancey, Georgia. Of course the three offended musketeers were long gone, and it was up to me and Danny to defend the sanctity of all things Southern. Danny sauntered up, grinned, and pulled out a few 'Aww, shucks, ma'ams,' saying he just hadn't gotten the books put out like Ms. Jessup told him to. That he's a newlywed, and, well, you know how long and tiring nights are for newlyweds."

Susan and Laney are both staring at me with wide eyes, and then Laney starts laughing. "I swear, that boy is becoming one of my most favorite people. I bet she ate it up like cornbread soaked in buttermilk, didn't she? Feeds into every stereotype I hear she holds most dear." She laughs again, then arches an eyebrow and asks, "So, did y'all end up selling out of her books?"

"Pretty much," I mumble.

Susan rolls her eyes. "You think she planned all this? The negative reaction and all the uproar? You've got to imagine her sales in the Atlanta area have gone up with the local news coverage. I'd honestly never heard of her. I mean, the name sounded familiar, but I had no idea what she wrote."

"I believe the term is 'notorious,'" Laney says. "Speaking of notorious, I heard Peter and Delaney skipped town? I've got to say I'm disappointed in Delaney. Peter, I'm not surprised about. He always was the type to pull up his panties and go home when things didn't go his way." She pauses, then drawls, "However... a ski trip on a private jet? I'd've left y'all under the nearest bus, too."

Susan and I slide down to give Anna space to sit as she arrives at the end of our row with her bundle and the bundle's accoutrements. She'll be beside Susan, but I'm still getting my granddaughter first. As I watch Anna's progress down the row I fill in details on the impromptu ski trip. "I finally talked to Delaney this afternoon. Her father painted a much grimmer picture to her when he insisted they leave town last night. Plus she insinuated he'd found out more about Peter's history with Sally Blankenship. Delaney apologized but said she just didn't feel like arguing with her dad and perhaps it's best they are out of the picture until Sally leaves town."

Laney slowly shakes her head. "I sure do want to know more about this Sally and Peter thing."

Anna sits down with the same exhausted plop Laney sat down with earlier. She hands the baby over to me, and I immediately loosen the blanket sleeper. "There's my girl." Her big eyes are busy looking around, and I just make sure her mama isn't in her line of sight. Absorbed in her, I miss that Griffin has come up the bleachers and is standing in front of me until he clears his throat and starts talking.

"I promised Susie Mae I'd talk to you and Jackson about this spring break trip, but Jackson doesn't seem to know much." His white button-down shirt is starched and looks good with the old jeans it's tucked into. He combines the small-town guy with the business guy well and flows between his two worlds flawlessly. Well, flawlessly except for the fact he lost a marriage along the way.

Susan has gone still beside me, while Laney is turned almost completely around on the bleacher and sitting tall to be in the conversation. She flips her head, and her silver beads flash in the light. "Yes, Shaw and I have some questions, too."

I hold up the hand not supporting Francie. "Savannah has all the details, parents' names and all, but it's been a crazy week. As soon as the book festival is over, we're sitting down with her and figuring it all out. We'll fill y'all in as soon as we know more."

Griffin hooks his thumbs in his jean pockets and looks at Susan. "I guess I can wait until then to make a final decision. Is that okay with you?"

She nods and shrugs. We all look around awkwardly, and then Laney groans. "Oh, what is wrong with him?" She's looking down to the gym floor where the double doors lead out to the school's hallway. Shaw and a couple of other men are talking there with a baby on the floor in the middle of them creeping along, trying to crawl. Laney stands up and yells, "Pick that baby up off that filthy floor, Shaw Conner!" Everything comes to a stop, even the game. She looks back at me and Susan, grits her teeth, and then turns back around to glare at her husband. "Bring him to me!" She starts climbing toward her husband and son. With a laugh, Griffin gives his ex-wife a nod before turning to go back to his seat.

Francie puckered up when Laney's scream startled her, and about that time she got a glimpse of her mother, so by the time Laney gets back with her own wiggling armful, my arms are empty.

"Shaw Conner is getting a piece of my mind when we get home," she says. "Letting this baby crawl around on the dirtiest floor this side of Atlanta! Talk fast, Cayden will only be happy here for a minute. So, tell me what's going with Savannah? I mean, aside from the spring break trip. Is she still broken up with Ricky?"

"Why?" I ask, pulling my focus off Francie.

Laney ignores my question. "Is she? I mean, I hadn't heard of them getting back together. They didn't, did they?"

I shake my head. "Not that I know of. No, she's actually wondering about the spring formal and who she'll go with."

"Good." Laney lowers her voice. "He's been seen waiting on one of the waitresses from AC's after her shift. She's older than him, but a good worker. She lives over near you," she says to Susan.

Susan nods, but doesn't say anything.

I shove her with my elbow. "What? You've seen him with her, too?"

"Just his truck. Late. Early. Susie Mae pointed it out to me. Hey, Bryan's in."

We turn to watch the game, but Bryan's time is cut short with a timeout, and when play resumes, he's sitting on the bench. Susan grimaces at me, but I shake my head at her. "He's fine. He just likes being on the team. Believe me, back in Marietta, with over two thousand students at his old school, he wouldn't have been on the basketball *or* the football team."

Anna speaks up. "I don't know, he's pretty good in football."

"Yeah," I agree. "But I'm not sure he's competitive enough for the athletes at his old school. Plus, if you were on one of the varsity teams, that was all you'd do. It's your life, and I just don't think he likes playing all that much."

Laney winks over her shoulder. "Sounds like it was a good thing you found Chancey."

Drawing in a slow breath, I take in Bryan joking with the others on the bench across the court from us, Jackson below us wearing his new work uniform of jeans and a T-shirt, Savannah in a huddle of girls on the end of court, giggling and talking. Then I smile at Anna and Francie who are sharing a sweet moment, face to face. I know I'm blessed to be right where I am. I smile at my friends. "Finding Chancey was the absolute best thing that could've happened to us."

CHAPTER 18

"I don't like the look of that," Laney says as we enter Ruby's after the game. Susan had to park around the corner, so she's not with us yet. Laney divested herself of her son, strapping his tired and cranky body into his car seat with his father. Then, ignoring his howls, she jumped in my car and said, "Gun it!"

Ruby's, with Kimmy's help, is going to be open late every night after the tournament and book festival, and there's a crowd of appreciative folks inside. "Hey, Miss Carolina," Zoe Kendrick says as we slide into a booth, still taking sidelong looks at the troubling table across the way. "I get to waitress tonight. What can I get y'all?"

Laney groans, "Zoe, I don't want you to waitress. I want you to come be my full-time nanny."

Zoe blinks and her face puckers up, but I reach out to pat her arm. "Ignore her. She just misses the best babysitter in the world. You spoiled her, but she's a big girl and she's going to be fine. Sit up straight, Laney."

Laney is halfway lying in the booth. "I'm not going to be fine. I miss you. Can you quit school?"

I roll my eyes, and Zoe tries a little chuckle. "I'll come get y'all's order in a minute."

Shaking my head, I say to my exhausted friend, "Leave the girl alone. You need to just be done with it and hire a full-time nanny. Especially with the shop—sorry, The Club—opening tomorrow."

"I know, but my mother thinks it's a sign of the end times when a daughter of hers hires a full-time nanny. Shaw agrees. End times for his wallet." She pushes to sit up straight. "Remember how hard a baby seemed until they became a toddler? And twins were rough, but that boy is all over the place already, and he can barely creep. What's it going to be like when he's really mobile?"

Susan strides to our booth and slides in across from me, forcing her sister to scoot over. "So—what's up with that?" she asks, looking at the table on the opposite wall, which had also caught our attention before Laney's parenting woes hijacked the conversation.

With all three of us looking in that direction, one of the occupants of the table in question calls my name.

"Carolina, come here," Missus demands.

Then her tablemate, Athena, adds, "Please?" and her other tablemate, Griffin, laughs.

Missus blasts him. "What's funny about this? We are in a crisis, and she won't answer her phone. Carolina!"

Susan looks down at the table as I slide out of our booth and head across the old linoleum to take the chair Griffin pulled out for me and is now standing behind. "Thanks," I say.

He winks at me and sits back down beside Athena. The three of them exchange looks, then focus on me. Aren't these people supposed to be in a feud?

Athena smiles at me, even reaches out a hand toward me on the tabletop. "We think we've come up with a solution to our problem. We wanted to run it by you before we talk to Carlie."

Missus stiffens. "There is no need to talk to that Carlie person. She's not been helpful to this point. I say we handle this ourselves."

Griffin and Athena share another look, but I keep my mouth

shut. I've decided to cancel the book signing on Sunday. That's my only real obligation. Gertie is still holding the private party on Saturday night because Sally convinced her to sign an actual contract. However, the moonshine maven has said she won't have any of "those" books on the premises, so supplying them is off my to-do list. Sally may be able to bring in books from another source, but that's not my deal.

Missus turns to me. "Are you ignoring Carlie's phone calls as you are mine?"

I hold up my hands. "I forgot my phone at home. Bryan had a game."

She sniffs. "I'm constantly confused if your ability to play obtuse is a personality trait or just plain old cowardice."

Griffins smirks. "Or maybe it's just that she doesn't have access to a private plane in order to fly away and avoid her responsibilities."

Missus's head snaps around. "Don't be petty. Jealously isn't attractive in a teenage girl. It's atrocious in a grown man." She focuses on me. "The brunch at my house has been changed to a forum on Southern stereotypes in modern literature. I have invited some highly regarded, extremely articulate individuals who can stand their own against Sally Blankenship."

"Oh, that's a great idea!" I exclaim. "I want to come to that."

Athena tips her head to Missus. "It is a great idea, and as I actually work for Carlie, she has been notified and is on board. However," she drawls as she turns to face me, "she says the book signing at Blooming Books needs to happen. It's been promoted, and, well, they actually sold some spots to a couple of sponsors. Sponsors who are big fans of Ms. Blankenship."

I open my mouth to protest, but she interjects. "Freedom of thought and speech? Just because you sell a book doesn't mean you have to agree with it, right? If I were you, I'd take that viewpoint and run with it."

Griffin adds, "No such thing as bad publicity, right?"

Missus slaps her hands down on the table. "That's all settled. Told you I'd handle everything. Go on back to your table now. Griffin, get me a piece of lemon pie and decaf coffee."

She pulls off her gloves and uses them to shoo me away. I guess I don't have anything to complain about. She did say she would handle everything, and it sounds like she has. I return to my friends to see that Zoe has left a petite piece of chocolate pie at my place.

As I sit down with a deep sigh, Laney lifts her fork and clinks it against mine. "To Chancey. The absolutely best thing that could've happened to you. Right?"

I plunge my fork into the silky chocolate and pick up a huge bite. Leaning forward to get it in without dropping a bit, I fill my mouth. Soaking in the creamy richness, I still manage to mumble, "We'll see about that."

I was the only one in the family, and our house, to go to Ruby's for pie. Jackson and Bryan stayed to watch the games after ours, and Savannah was going to a girlfriend's house when her cheering duties were done. Usually I make sure our guests know of Ruby's erratic schedule. However, I thought this time it would be best if they just didn't know. It's been odd how the four women have stayed closed up in the B&B hall for the most part. Not that I'm complaining...

Two lamps are on in the living room when I quietly enter our house. Based on the empty driveway, it looks like the rest of the family is still out. There were cars parked down at the bridge, but folks often take walks out there on clear nights like tonight. There are no sounds as I take off my coat. Walking into the kitchen, I look through the dining room and see the door leading to the B&B hall is closed. Usually it stays open, even when we have guests, but not with these particular guests. Again, I'm not complaining.

I turn on some classic rock music and enjoy the alone time by straightening up the kitchen. The few dishes in the sink fill up the remaining space in the dishwasher, so I start the machine. Then, as I wipe off the kitchen table, I notice light in the backyard, and I step to the glass doors to look out.

There are our New York ladies.

And it looks like they found them some Georgia boys.

Chapter 19

"Ricky?"

"Oh, hey, Carolina," he shouts as he jumps up from his seat at the bonfire.

But you know, he didn't actually jump. He just stood up and then sauntered toward the deck where I'm standing. He doesn't look embarrassed or guilty at all.

"What's going on here?" I ask. My voice should definitely relay to him that he needs to be acting embarrassed *and* guilty. I meet him at the bottom of the steps, but I stay on the last one so we're eye to eye. This is one of my go-to parenting tips for when your kids start getting too tall to naturally intimidate.

He shrugs and grins. "Your guests invited us to a bonfire. Ran into them down at the Dew Drop. Didn't realize they were staying here. Funny how things work out, ain't it? Come on down and join us." The tilt of his head says he knows I won't, but what he knows wouldn't fill a flea's backpack.

"Sure."

I step off the stair and stride across the yard to where there are what looks like almost a dozen or so people on the stumps and chairs we have around the bonfire. Jackson keeps it ready to light when we have guests, and there's a waterproof bin of kindling, fire-starters, and lighters we keep under the deck for guests to use if they want. I don't think we've ever had guests start their own fire, but then again, our guests have never had Ricky to help them out.

"Hello, everyone," I say. "Nice fire."

Sally Blankenship is actually sitting in a man's lap. Nope, not just a man—Ricky's older brother, Ronnie Troutman. Of course. She couldn't go find her some stranger to fulfill her hillbilly fantasies; she had to corral Laney and Susan's nephew.

Ronnie is only a year older than Ricky, but he's lived a bit more: dropped out of high school, moved in with his girlfriend, then moved out, then moved back in. I think that's the last I heard. Laney and Susan say he's not been around any of the family functions, but his dad and his mom kind of come and go as they please, too. Ronnie manages a gas station out toward the interstate and spends a lot of time at the Dew Drop Inn, a local establishment of the sort you'll find on the outskirts of almost any small town.

"Hey, Miss Carolina," Ronnie drawls as I approach. He's good-looking, and I can see why Sally chose him. He's tall, works out, and has shoulder-length, blond hair. His little brother, Ricky, wears his dark hair cut short, and he looks young here with this crowd. The other four are the typical rough-looking guys that hang out around the Dew Drop. Yes, I'm generalizing, but prove me wrong.

"So y'all managed to get a fire going."

Sally shifts around on Ronnie's lap, and he moans a bit while she says, "Oh, getting fires started is my specialty." That gets a laugh from her audience. She points at Ricky. "Who knew we'd run into someone so familiar with Crossings B&B out at the local pub? Ricky was engaged to your darling Savannah? How interesting!" She turns to ask Ronnie, their faces only inches apart, "Ronnie, do you know Savannah?"

"Oh yeah. We're all friends. I helped paint the B&B rooms, didn't I, Miss Carolina? Also worked on some of the furniture."

He turns his face up to me. "It all still looks real good. The girls here gave us a tour earlier on our way out to the fire."

Ricky might be coming to his senses a bit because he jumps in. "Oh, we didn't stay inside long. I moved everyone right on through."

Sally pulls Ronnie's mouth onto hers, and we all watch them kiss. Ricky steps toward them and swats his brother's shoulder. "Hey. Cut that out." Sally laughs, then leans to the side to take a long drag off her cigarette. Then she drop it into the damp grass.

Ronnie pulls back, but Sally doesn't let him pull very far. "It is kind of cold out here," she purrs. "How about we move this party inside?" It only takes a slight tip of her head for her to catch my eye.

I shake my head at her.

"Not happening. Y'all are welcome to stay out here and have your party. Ricky, you'll be responsible for making sure the fire is out?"

"Yes, ma'am," he says.

Her two young assistants are bundled up with two guys next to the fire. They seem happy to stay outside. However, Sally's publicist looks cold and miserable, so I say to her, "If you want to come get a cup of coffee, I'll put on a pot."

She doesn't even look at her boss; she just stands and starts for the house. I look around the circle once more. There are two other girls, one who I bet is the waitress Laney was telling me about earlier. Ricky was sitting next to her when I came outside. "We require the fire to be out by ten o'clock, so y'all have about another hour." I turn away and move toward the light of the house.

When I get inside, Sally's publicist is already putting on a pot of coffee so I text Jackson to warn him what's going on here. He'll never believe it. I cringe as I walk to look out the dining room windows into the back yard. Sally Blankenship and Ronnie Troutman.

Yikes. She's going to have enough material for a whole new book. Heck, a whole new series!

"The ten o'clock limit on the bonfire was a good idea, but I didn't see you hurrying out there last night to tell them to wrap it up." Jackson says from where he stands looking out the back doors with his first cup of coffee. The sun isn't up yet, but the sky is a soft blue with wisps of yellow, and the first leaves on the trees give our backyard a fuller look. I love how the tree branches seem to be limbering up. Everything is letting go of its winter tightness.

I nestle my shoulder into my husband's chest. "I was too busy to worry about those yahoos in the backyard." I turn and kiss his chin. "Of course the Kahlua in my coffee last night might've helped me not care."

He grins and kisses my nose. "Might've."

By the time Jackson and Bryan got home, I'd worked myself up into a state. I had the 9 and the 1 dialed and was itching to hit another 1 to tell the police there was a mob in our backyard. Didn't help that Sally's publicist used full-strength coffee and not decaf as I intended. She didn't say a word, just kept filling her cup and mine as she worked on her phone and tablet. I moved from window to window, keeping an eye on our guests and mumbling threats. Yeah, I was a hot mess by the time the guys got home.

Bryan went straight up to shower once Jackson informed him he was in no way going out to the bonfire and that outside of the gym he didn't smell that good. Jackson listened to me rave for a minute before he went to pull out the bottle of Kahlua from the kitchen cabinet and, without even asking me, added a couple of big glugs to my coffee cup. By the time I'd drunk that and taken him on a tour of my different window vantages, I'd worn myself out. Sally's publicist had gone back to the B&B rooms and Jackson started turning out the lights.

I told him, again, about the ten o'clock shutdown I'd invented on the spot. He kept saying, "Uh-huh" and nodding, but then he led me to the couch, sat down, and pulled me down close to him. Then we pretended like we were at our own bonfire.

Turning again I look out to where a low fog off the river crawls up the hill and mingles with the bits of smoke coming off the logs from the bonfire. Someone, Ricky I assume, had broken up the fire well the night before, but the big logs still looked like they were steaming. The layer of shiny dew on everything begins picking up the sun's first rays through the riverside trees. Jackson pats my behind and pulls away. "Okay, you've got a busy day. First day of the book festival, so get going. I've got everything here under control."

I'm dressed, and we've heard both kids awake upstairs, so I top off my nonalcoholic coffee and move into the living room to double-check my list for the morning as Jackson begins pulling out lunch items for the kids. Their lunches have always been a team effort for me. I'd make sandwiches, but they chose the actual ingredients for me to use. (Wait, saying like that it doesn't sound that much like a team effort.) Anyway, Jackson has adopted my way of helping prepare lunches. It's really worked out nicely, him working from home. Even the money is working out with the construction business going so well, especially since Will took over the finances for their projects.

"Was Ricky really here last night?" Savannah asks as she comes down the stairs.

"Good morning. Yeah, he was." I reach for my coat on the coatrack and turn toward her. "You look nice."

"Thanks, but uh, you're gonna want to look at his Instagram." She gives me a look of pity and moves into the kitchen. I consider following her to ask what she means, but it's really early and I have a full day ahead. So I pull on my coat, shout, "Goodbye," and leave the house.

Besides, I don't think I do Instagram. Do I?

CHAPTER 20

"Did you know that Delaney had gotten me an ad in all the book festival folderol?" Ruby asks from behind the counter. I'd stopped in to order a basket for the B&B before I made my way to the bookshop.

"No, I didn't. That's great, right?"

Ruby has both hands on her hips and doesn't look or sound like it's great.

"Woulda been if she'd told me. That woman fits right in with that family of vipers she moved in with. They just do what they want and let ya struggle to figure everything out." She flings her arms in the air. "Look at all these people!"

Ruby's is busy, but I'm not sure the book festival ad is to blame. After a scan around me, I say, "But these look like local people. I'd think the book people will be around later in the day."

She huffs in exasperation. "Exactly!" Then she turns around to jerk open an oven.

Libby comes up behind me. "I heard you checking on the B&B order, right? It's all good. Don't mind Ruby, she's binge-reading that Sally woman's books. I think it's got her riled up in more than one way if you catch my drift."

I furrow my brow and give her a confused look, so Libby leans closer.

"You know. Sexual frustration."

"Oh! Oh, okay." I lean back and then take another step away. Libby looks ready to expound on her theory, and I do not want to hear that. "Well, I better get to the shop. Tell Ruby, I, uh... Bye!"

Rushing out of the store, I wonder if what I've been taking for book festival excitement around town could be folks' newly acquired, late-night reading habits. We've been pushing the books of the authors coming to the festival events and we've sold quite a few to folks who don't normally buy our books. I think people like to have actually read a book when they meet the author, I know I do. However, I bet a lot people picking up Sally Blankenship's books are getting more than they expected. I laugh as I hurry down the sidewalk. However, I can't help but wonder if people will actually admit they're reading her books!

The door is unlocked, I smile at what greets me as I push it open. The shop has never looked better. There are Bonnie's spring decorations, the full bookshelves, the flower cooler stuffed with arrangements, and the spring bouquets Shannon's made for customers to pick up for five dollars each. She has metal buckets placed all around the store and some near the door for us to put outside once we open. She has worked really hard on them, and they will not only add a lot to the store, but will be a bright spot for the whole town once they're set up on the sidewalk.

"Good morning," I call out, and Shannon responds from her worktable. After taking off my coat, I head in her direction, which just happens to be in the direction of the coffee pot. "Don't you look pretty in that color? You love purple, but you don't wear much lavender."

"Thanks. I feel good. Really good for the first time in forever. No morning sickness at all!" My partner is smiling at me and then comes around from behind the table, her long, lavender sweater looking soft and warm, but light. She has paired it with tight-legged cream pants, which match the two long strings of pearls around her neck. "Here's you a corsage for your big day! Want me to pin it on you? I didn't make them wrist corsages because I thought that would get in the way while we work." She stands before me, pink carnations in one hand and a long pin in the other.

"Sure." I lean forward and ask, "For the book festival?"

"Yes. I made ones for Bonnie and Susie Mae, too. Is Savannah going to work today? I can make one for her. Danny went all the way over to Dalton to get Krispy Kreme donuts just because I mentioned them in passing last night. But don't worry, he'll be back in plenty of time to open." She steps away from me to look at her handiwork, and gives the carnations a quick pat. "And he's bringing plenty! We figured we might as well treat the early shoppers, right?"

"Sounds like a good idea to me. I guess I better get the coffee going."

"Absolutely!" Shannon goes back to her table, and I marvel at the stages of pregnancy. I remember that time in the middle when everything is wonderful again. The morning sickness fades, you aren't big enough be uncomfortable, and there's that burst of energy that makes everything that was impossible just yesterday completely doable and fun. I wasn't sure Shannon was ever going to reach this point, but looks like we're here. Finally.

Or else it's just that Peter is out of town and out of mind.

Either way, I'm going to enjoy every single minute of it!

And I have enjoyed every single minute of this Friday. It was a little dicey when Susie Mae showed me Ricky's Instagram pictures of the bonfire party, but as she pointed out, all the comments said it looked like a scene out of a Luke Bryan country song. She convinced me that's not a bad thing for my business, so I'm just not worrying about it. Our four festival-approved authors couldn't have been sweeter or more appreciative. All four said they'd love to come back for a signing anytime, and one took the B&B's info so that she and her husband can come stay in the fall. Only one of the four authors is still here as our wine and chat time winds down. He and a couple of his readers are sitting around the table near FM's collection of history books. They've garnered so much attention I took them off sale awhile back. Like reference books at a library, they are for people to look at while they're here.

"You gentlemen need any more wine, coffee, anything?" I ask as I wander over to them. Even though most of the crowd has left, there's such a good feeling in the store as the outside light fades and the candles we've lit shine brighter that I'm in no hurry to close up.

"Is there a spot more of that merlot?" the author asks. He's in his sixties and has a neat, white beard. His wife is enjoying herself looking through some cookbooks with a couple of other women who came out to support them.

"Of course there is. You picked up some new fans today. Everyone really enjoyed your talk and reading." Each author had twenty minutes to talk about their books and do a short reading. Carlie may seem a bit of a control freak, but everyone stuck to her schedule. Authors can be long-winded when talking about their writing, but she apparently put the fear of God into them that if they ever want to be invited back they would keep things flowing.

Savannah helped out this afternoon, but she had to go cheer at the basketball tournament. Susie Mae and Danny have kept the line at the counter moving smoothly, leaving Bonnie and me to restock and talk to the customers. Shannon retired upstairs shortly after the wine reception began. She finally just ran out of juice, but her good mood lasted all day.

Carrying the bottle of merlot and another of chardonnay, I make my way back to the men at the history table and fill their glasses. I then look for others interested in a final top-off. As pleasant as this is, tomorrow is another busy day.

"Are there any more of those sandwich things in the back?" Danny asks as I tell him we'll be closing up soon. We didn't provide anything other than cheese and crackers for the customers, but I ordered a platter of sandwiches for those of us working through dinnertime.

"I believe so. I was going to tell you and Shannon to take them if you want them, but if you're hungry now, go eat something. We're fine up here."

"Think I will. Thanks!"

He dashes off, and I step closer to Susie Mae.

"You've been amazing today. You really are good with people."

She grins. "I'm glad tomorrow's Saturday. This is way more fun than school." She pauses and frowns. Her voice lowers. "And it's definitely more fun than home. Either home."

"Really? I'm sorry," I say as I pat her back.

She tips her head to look sideways at me. "Ya think Silas will ever come back?"

"Silas? Silas Pendersen?"

She rolls her eyes at me. "Never mind. Hi, are you ready to check out?" she asks the lady walking to the counter.

The store is finally empty of customers, and our last author, his wife, and their friends take their leave, promising to see us again soon. I never thought about the book festival being such a boon to Crossings. It'll be fun having authors stay with us. Maybe I'll start a collection of their signed books up at the house. Oh, that's a good idea!

The lights of Susie Mae's car shine on us for a moment as she pulls out of the back parking lot, and then she heads down the road. I didn't get to ask her why she asked about Silas coming back, but I have the rest of the weekend to find out. Bonnie waits as I lock the back door.

"Ooh, it's chilly out here." Though she shivers, she looks happy. "This was a really good day."

"Yes," I agree. "Much better than I hoped. Both in sales and in how smoothly everything went. Tomorrow is going to be a full day with the luncheon and signings. Are you going to Gertie's party tomorrow evening? Al's welcome, too."

Bonnie laughs as she opens her car door. "Saturday night at Gertie's Moonshine Cave? That sounds like Al's worst nightmare, and if I'm honest, given that it's for Sally Blankenship, it's not much higher on my list of fun things to do. See you in the morning."

I let her back out first. We're the only two cars heading out of town, and then I'm on my own as she turns to the left to head up to Laurel Canyon. It's quite a drive for her to get home, but she and Cal have lived up in the mountaintop luxury community for many years. Bonnie hoped they'd travel more in retirement, but that doesn't look like it's going to happen, so I think she's happy traveling off the mountain and interacting with the townsfolk. Plus, it's given her a whole new venture in interior design. All I know is Blooming Books would be nowhere near as successful without Bonnie Cuneo. If it means giving her office space in the back and sharing her with her decorating clients, it's still a win in my book.

The house is lit up but quiet as I pull into the driveway. Jackson had texted me to let me know he and Bryan were home from the tournament and that the New York ladies were home—alone. Savannah was out at that time, but I see her car is now here, along with some of her friends' cars, I believe. She'd mentioned a couple of girls might spend the night. They'll most likely be corralled up in her tower room.

"Hello," I say, pushing open the front door.

"Hey," Jackson greets me as he jumps up from the chair beside the front window. "Look who's here."

A tall man stands from the couch and turns. "Hey, Carolina."

My mouth drops open and I'm frozen in place. Then I shake my head and take a step forward.

"Silas? What are you doing here?"

Chapter 21

"Absolutely not! I've already got them packing their bags," Sally Blankenship says. Then half over her shoulder, she tells the help, which is me, "If you'll get them a set of clean sheets, they'll see that Mr. Pendersen is taken care of."

She moves closer to Silas and places her hand on his arm. "I'm sure you're more used to roughing it, but when I travel to remote locations like this, I always bring additional help. I've learned the hard way that these quaint, quiet places are woefully understaffed."

Silas smiles and nods as he steps back. "I can't kick your assistants out like this. I just stopped in on the chance Carolina and Jackson had a room open. My arrival was rather sudden."

Sally shakes her head. "No, no. This is perfect. They're in the middle of casting the film adaptation of my first book—I've got executive producer credit, you know—and you are on my short list for the leading man. If you showing up like this isn't a sign, what is?" She steps even closer to Silas as her young assistants pile into the room with their bags. She pulls him toward her, practically into her arms, as she makes room. "Here, we'll make room for you to pass."

He pulls away as he and Jackson step forward, offering to carry the women's bags. Both women smile and bat their eyes at the good-looking movie star and instantly drop their bags.

They do not seem in the least bit annoyed to be leaving Chancey for a hotel down the interstate, closer to Atlanta.

"Carolina, did you get those sheets?" Sally demands.

"They are in the hallway closet. I'll take care of the bed," I say, but she calls the girls and points down the B&B hall.

"Follow her. She'll get you the sheets and help you make the room acceptable. I'll help the men with the bags." She begins shooing Jackson and Silas ahead of her out the front door with the bags, and by the time we have the sheets in hand and I've been dismissed from the Southern Crescent room by the assistants, the living room is empty.

I'd barely had time to say hello to Silas before Sally entered the scene. She smelled fresh meat is all I can figure, but she entered with a plan to have Silas set up in the room next to hers, and, as usual, she got her way. She's maintained her hold on the Orange Blossom Special room, her public relations assistant is in the Chessie room, and Silas will move into the Southern Crescent room.

Wonder if Susan knew Silas was coming back? She's not mentioned him lately and I still can't believe Susie Mae asking about his just this afternoon. They have to know something, right? Or maybe Sally is on to something and Silas is interested in a part in her movie.

"Yuck. Now she's going to have a movie?" I mumble as I dart to look out the front window, but before I get there, Jackson comes in the front door.

"She's got him taking a walk out on the bridge. It's cold out there, but I don't think Ms. Blankenship is counting on either one of them getting very cold."

"What is he doing here? Did he mention Susan?"

"Nope," Jackson says as he picks up his empty coffee cup. "He wasn't here more than a half a minute before you. How did your day go?"

"Perfect. But Susie Mae actually asked me today if I thought

Silas would come back." As my husband walks into the kitchen I follow him closely and whisper, "She said things weren't good at either house, Susan's or Griffin's."

He chuckles. "Heck, Savannah would probably say the same about this place."

I open my mouth to disagree, but he's right. Every teenager thinks their house is the worst place to be. "So, how long is he staying?"

"I don't know. You want a beer?" he asks from behind the refrigerator door. "The Georgia game is coming on."

"More basketball? No, thanks. I'm going upstairs to take a shower and get comfortable." I step into the living room, then add over my shoulder, "Well, once Silas gets back inside and I get to chat a bit."

He speaks up, "I'm watching the game in there, you know."

"I know. We won't talk loud. You know he knows nothing about sports and won't care about the game. Hopefully Sally will move along to her room. Maybe I'll suggest she call Ronnie Troutman." I sit on the edge of the chair and have twisted to look out the front window at the side of the curtain when I hear them on the porch. I turn to sit down so they won't know I was watching, but they take forever coming inside. Just as I start to get up and open the front door, it opens and they stumble in, all wrapped up together.

"It's so cold out there! Silas was such a gentleman, helping me stay warm." Sally has her arms around his waist and is pulling him inside with her. "I think my hands are frozen together," she says with a laugh as she maneuvers them to the couch and drops them onto it.

Silas laughs, too, though he just as suddenly stands up and pulls out of her arms. "Jackson promised me a beer. I think I'll go check on that."

Her brow tightens and she frowns, but it passes before he gets to the kitchen door, and she calls to him, "Bring me one.

I'll save your seat!" Then she flips around to glare at me. "You didn't tell me he was coming back here so soon!"

"What? How would I—" But I stop myself from saying I didn't know any more than she did. How does she know he's coming "back" here? And "so soon"? Something is fishy. "Silas knows he's always welcome," I say with a sweet smile.

As the guys come back into the living room, I stand. "Here, Silas, you can have my chair. I'm going up to shower." He winks in appreciation and quickly sits while I take Sally's beer from his hand. "Y'all enjoy the game. I'll be back down in a while. Here's your beer, Sally."

She shoots me a shady look, takes it, and then takes a big swallow. Both guys are focused on the television, and when she tries to engage Silas in conversation, the men start talking over her about the game. I can't help laughing as I climb the stairs. Apparently the only one who knows less about basketball than Silas is Sally. She's not batting an eye at all his talk of touch-downs, penalty kicks, and goals. Jackson sits there grinning, saying "uh-huh" a lot, and enjoying his beer as he watches Sally agree with all of Silas's opinions.

I'd say it's one of Silas Pendersen's best acting performances ever.

CHAPTER 22

"How was the luncheon?" Shannon asks as I fly into the shop Saturday afternoon.

"Amazing! All that's left is for them to give out the door prizes, and then we are going to be busier than ever. Those are some enthusiastic readers next door, and I didn't see most of them in here before the event."

Shannon is putting together more of the small bouquets as fast as she can, and I can see why as I look around at the silver pails. "It looks like the flowers are selling, too!"

"Like water in the Sahara. Danny, Susie Mae, and Savannah have been running their legs off, and you were so right about me hiring someone to help keep up. I called my mom and dad, and they've been wonderful. I sent them upstairs for a break and some lunch."

We both look up as we hear the apartment door closing and footsteps on the stairs.

"Mr. and Mrs. Chilton, I hear you've been a big help." I greet the older couple with a big smile as they walk over.

Shannon's dad winks at me and starts cleaning up the boxes and flower scraps on and under the table. Her mother pats her daughter's back and looks into her face. "Now you promised you'd go upstairs, put your feet up, and eat something. I'll take over here."

"Thanks, Mom. And don't worry, Carolina. Mom taught me everything I know about flower arranging."

"I'm not worried at all," I say, but my confident smile at Mrs. Chilton is met with tight lips and only a quick glance in my direction.

She places her hands on her daughter's shoulders and gently nudges her to the side. "Go on now. Everything is under control." She starts wrapping the stems Shannon had gathered together, and I'm dismissed. I think. The jingle of the door gives me a good excuse to whirl around and get into action. The folks from the luncheon are here and ready to shop!

Missus left halfway through the luncheon, but now she arrives in the shop with a flyer hot off the presses, and she's making sure each shopper gets one. I don't trust her, so I leave the customer I'm helping with a promise to be right back, making a beeline to Her Honor.

"What are those?"

"Something someone should've thought of earlier, but like usual, I took care of it. Here."

On yellow paper there's a list of the other businesses in Chancey, focusing on the ones around the square: Phoenix's juice bar, Andy's junk store with Gertie's Moonshine Cave in the basement, Ruby's, and Laney's Ladies of the Club. Then at the bottom she has a list of the stores out in the shopping center anchored by the Piggly Wiggly.

"This is really a good idea," I say. "Did you make many of them?"

"There are more coming. I left the chief figuring out what's wrong with the copy machine. It quit after these."

"The chief of police?"

She waves a hand at me. "His officers are doing the patrols. Might as well find something for him to do. We all know this isn't a troublesome crowd in town today. Give these out, and I'll make sure you receive more when they're ready." She looks around the store, then pulls me off to the side, near the front window. "I was impressed with that Athena at the luncheon. She's young, but very well spoken and so on top of things." She pauses to give me a queenly nod. "And she very much appreciates my proclamations."

Hiding a quick eye roll, I take a minute to make sure Susie Mae isn't in earshot. I don't need her reporting to her mother what I think about her father's girlfriend. I nod at Missus and add, in a low voice, "She's very impressive and really nice. Easy to work with, too."

Missus purses her mouth and looks over to where Athena is talking to two young moms near the children's area. "I'm considering having her emcee the forum tomorrow with Sally Blankenship. I was going to do it, but, well, it seems a tad beneath my station as mayor."

"Oh! That's a great idea!" I say. Too enthusiastically, apparently, as she shifts her focus onto me.

"Why is it a *great* idea?" She narrows her eyes. "You don't think I'm up to it. Do you think I'm not up to it?" Her chest expands, her jaw drops, and I can practically see her bones hardening into steel. "I'll have you know—"

"I'm afraid Sally wants to embarrass you, you know, uh, because of, uh, her relationship with Peter in college." I hold my breath until I see her deflate a bit.

"Yes. She could hold some old feelings for my son and be willing to spew lies at me to get back at him. Especially since he and his bride left on another honeymoon trip."

I have to turn away from her because I can't keep myself from groaning. Another honeymoon trip? Try running away on Daddy's private jet, but no, whatever keeps Missus off that podium tomorrow. I wouldn't put anything past Sally Blankenship, but I also wouldn't put anything past Missus. The very last thing we need is video clips of our mayor on the national news spouting off about the South rising again.

"Why don't you go talk to Athena now? Looks like I need to help out at the register." I turn back to her and stick my hand out to shake hers. "It's a great idea. Well done." She hesitantly offers me her gloved hand, which I grab, shake, and drop to rush away.

Before I reach the counter, Susie Mae stops me. "Savannah says Silas is staying up at Crossings?"

"Yeah. He surprised us last night. Why did you ask me about him yesterday? Did you know he was coming?"

She looks in my direction, but her blue eyes are unfocused. "No. But why didn't he call my mom? She really misses him, I think."

I put my hands on her upper arms and look into her eyes. "Look at me." She blinks and then gives me her attention. "This is your mom's business. She doesn't want you trying to fix things for her." I try to tease a smile out of her. "You have enough to think about. You're a junior in high school with a busy life. Your mom and dad love you and want you to not worry about them. Grown-ups make mistakes, and they have to figure them out. Your folks do not want you to spend your time trying to fix things for them. Okay?"

She takes a breath and gives me a real smile. "Okay. I get it." Then her head jerks toward the big front window, and she suddenly exclaims, "But what is he doing with *her*?"

I flip around to see Silas striding past the store. His tailored coat and full head of hair are rippling in the wind, and he has one arm wrapped around Sally Blankenship. Sally stops them abruptly at the window and looks in. She gives a big wave at the customers staring at her. Then, squeezing him closer to her, she pulls Silas on down the sidewalk.

There's a buzz in the store as she's recognized. Although I do hear a couple of people wondering who the good-looking guy is and saying that he looks like an actor, I don't think any of our book festival visitors recognized him from his television movies.

Bonnie catches my eye. So does Danny. We all shrug, so, with a sigh, I go ahead and do it. "Everyone, if I can have your attention? Sally Blankenship, who you just saw pass by, will be signing books here tomorrow after the forum on Southern literature at the Bedwell House just down the street. If you buy a book today, you can bring it back tomorrow to be signed."

There's a scurry toward the festival author display, and Danny makes his way over to replenish it.

Hey, a girl's gotta make a buck when she can.

Chapter 23

"This is the last place on the face of the earth I want to be tonight, but..." Laney's voice trails off as she gestures behind us at her sister. Susan is sitting in one of the cozy booths near the front of Gertie's Moonshine Cave. "She called me in a panic saying she needed me to meet her out front so she didn't have to walk in alone. I didn't have the heart to tell her I was exhausted, I hadn't seen Shaw or Cayden all day, and I need to come in early tomorrow to restock The Club."

Laney and I are standing at the bar waiting on drinks. The reason for Susan's panic is also at the bar." At the other end is Sally Blankenship and Silas Pendersen, acting like as much of a couple as a couple can be. They are seated on stools. His hand is around her waist, and her hand is on his thigh. I'm confused at Silas' behavior. He wanted nothing to do with her last night up at our house, but he's been all over town with her today. Is he trying to make Susan jealous? Is he just wanting to a role in Sally's movie? I really don't know. Maybe it's just that I really don't know Silas Penderson at all.

As Gertie passes us our drinks, Laney and I turn to go back to our tables. Jackson, Phoenix, and Colt got here before me and are halfway through their drinks. I go to join them while Laney veers toward Susan.

Jackson stands up as I near him and speaks low. "We can

easily add a couple of chairs if Susan and Laney want to join us. I wanted to check with you before I invited them."

As tired as I am, I can't help but give him a quick kiss. "You are so good to me. I am beyond tired, but I think they'd like the company. Sure, go ask them."

Phoenix pats my chair. "Sit down. You've got to be worn completely out. The bookstore looked to be jumping all day. Everyone that came into the juice bar had a bag from your place. And the flyers were wonderful! I assume those were your idea?"

I take a sip as I shake my head. "Those were all Missus. So easy, and yet even the chamber of commerce didn't think about doing something like that." Now that I'm eye level with Phoenix, I find myself staring at her. She still hasn't gone back to her dramatic makeup and hair color. I'm coming to realize she's even more attractive with a natural look. More genuine, more approachable. Then, looking at her next to Colt, I realize she also looks younger. They look better together. Maybe they are going to work out.

"Hey, thanks for inviting us to sit with y'all. Although I can only do one drink, right, Susan?" Laney says as she herds her sister to sit down beside me. Susan ignores her. She's too busy staring at the bar and you-know-who. "Susan! Sit down and quit staring," Laney hisses.

Seated, the bar at her back, Susan's manners take over, and she acknowledges all of us. Then Gertie calls for everyone's attention as she comes out from behind the bar to stand near the tables.

"Thanks, everyone, for coming here tonight. I know it was originally for some book or something." She cuts her eyes toward Sally. "That all fizzled out, but I decided we'd come together to celebrate anyway, seeing as I got engaged to Bill last weekend!"

She reaches over and pulls on Bill's arm. He's seated with

Patty and Andy, but she forces him to stand. Bill is an older guy from up in the mountains whom Gertie has kept company with since she moved back to Chancey. Apparently they knew each other from her time growing up here. He stands up next to her and kisses her cheek. She laughs out loud. "Yep, he's going to make a somewhat honest woman of me!"

Congratulations and toasts bounce back and forth, and we end with a round of "She's a Jolly Good Woman," which I'm pretty sure Gertie started, and then after a real kiss with her intended, she moves back behind the bar. From there she announces, "No big folderol, just a simple service in the square in the next month or so. Everyone's invited." She scowls at Sally. "Unless you don't live here. Don't mean you, Silas. You can come."

While everyone is looking at that end of the bar, Sally maneuvers to have one boot on the foot railing, and then she plants her other knee on the barstool. She rises up on that knee, balancing herself with her hands on Silas's shoulders. "Oh, Gertie, we're so happy to hear your news. Congratulations to you and to your darling Bill. I'm so delighted we could book this party to help you celebrate. To aid even further in that happy endeavor, Silas and I would like to buy a round for the house!" She grins as she holds her glass high to the whoops and claps around her. Then she performs a three-point dismount and manages to slide off the barstool onto Silas's lap. She kicks up one boot-covered foot and pulls him to her for a quick kiss before slipping off to stand up and parade through all her fans to the restroom.

Laney raises an eyebrow as she turns back to the table. "I swear that New York woman added several syllables to her little speech trying to sound Southern: 'Buy a r-ooound for the h-oouuse.'"

We all laugh, and then Susan lets out a long sigh. "Silas always did like my accent."

That kills all conversation for a bit. Then Laney pushes her chair back. "I have to go home. Susan, you ready to go?"

"I guess." Susan is wearing a dark green turtleneck sweater, and her hair is back in her old ponytail. When I first met her she had a perpetual tan from working in her garden year round. Between her small, unappealing rental house's yard and the amount of paperwork in her new job, she's pale. It doesn't help that she never had a knack for makeup like her sister. I've always identified with her on that. Some women are just born knowing how to blend eye shadow and apply eyeliner without looking like they work on a street corner. Anyway, she looks weak and sad as she pushes her chair back.

"You leaving?" Silas says from behind us.

The blossoming of energy in Laney is palatable, like a Christmas inflatable coming to life on a front lawn. "Why do you care?" she snaps. "Where's your girlfriend? She been reading you snippets of her sexy Southern tall tales to help you go to sleep?"

Silas smiles. "Good to see you, Laney." He nods around the table as he says our names, and then he finally comes to Susan. He could be posing for a movie ad as he looks down at her in the low lighting, his large eyes sincere and concerned. "Susan. How are you?"

She slumps and sighs as she stares up at him. "Tired."

Laney rolls her eyes and reaches down to lift her sister up to her feet. "She's fine. Just fine. We have to go. Here comes your girlfriend." With her forearm jammed under his sister's, Laney hauls her away from our table, marching past Sally as if she isn't there.

Colt and Phoenix have just accepted a new drink from the waitress, but Jackson and I passed on the free drink round and are getting up. Sally plops down in Laney's seat and crosses her legs. Planting an elbow on her knee, she leans forward. "So," I hear her say. "This forum thing Madam Mayor has concocted tomorrow? What do y'all think I should say?"

Jackson groans as I sit back down and answer her. "Say? Why would you ask us what you should say? You're the famous author. You're the expert on all things Southern!"

She laughs. "Carolina, my books are made-up. Fiction, you know?" She reaches out and pats the back of Silas's thigh. "They're flights of fancy. You know as well as I do that I'm not writing about real people!" She shoots a sly look around the table. "However, that is something I'm exploring for my next publishing endeavor. Real stories or real Southern families. Those long talks with Peter in college stirred my interest in all things Southern. It's just, ah, different down here."

While the rest of us digest her comment, I notice Silas steps away from her to stand behind the chair Susan had been sitting in. I focus back on Sally. "But people believe your books. Believe that's how things really are down here."

She laughs again and sits up straighter. "That's not my problem. Besides, when they hear the true, unvarnished stories all this make-believe will pale in comparison. Don't you think? Anyway, the forum should be fun, right?"

Jackson clears his throat as he slips on his jacket. "Fun? I'm not sure that's the idea. It's about Southern stereotypes in literature," he tries to explain.

She wrinkles her nose. "That doesn't sound like much fun, but I don't do things unless they're fun, so"—she grins around the table—"come expecting big fun." Then she leans back and looks up at Silas. "Speaking of big fun, maybe it's time for us to head home." She cackles. "Well, not exactly our home, but your little B&B will do in a pinch. The beds work just fine." She definitely is practicing her drawl with the way she stretched out the word *fine*.

Silas nods but doesn't look at any of us. He looks a little ashamed, but when Sally puts her hand out, he lifts it like a gentleman and pulls her to her feet. With a goodbye directed toward us, she begins flitting around the room, accepting everyone's thanks for the drinks and signing a few books from the guests who didn't get Gertie's memo about the moonshine cave's change of plans.

As I stand, I growl, "She is infuriating. What is all this about real families? You think it's some kind of expose?" No one answers me and I clinch my teeth wondering aloud, "How can Silas stand her?"

Colt and Jackson don't look at me, just shake their heads. Phoenix, however, cocks her head to the side and meets my eyes full on. "I don't think Susan has one thing to worry about. I could see his face the whole time." She wedges her arm under Colt's folded one and confidently says, "I don't think he's that into that Sally woman. He's back here for Susan."

Chapter 24

"Well, I didn't know they were gonna tell God and everybody," Ruby laments, seated in a most unlikely place with a most unlikely sympathizer.

Laney pats her hand as she shakes her head. Then she stands up and opens another box. She's already explained that she can't stop restocking for long since she's opening up The Club soon. On a Sunday. In downtown Chancey. I guess me being here, too, means I've thrown my lot in with the sinners.

"Come on," I encourage them. "Y'all are just tired. This will all blow over tomorrow. Can I get you another coffee, Ruby?" Laney has a really nice machine that uses those coffee pods, and I'm loving trying out the different flavors. I've had a cinnamon-sugar and a cherry-chocolate already, and I'm feeling fine about my store being open on Sunday. I'm feeling fine about everything!

Ruby tips her cup to see that it's still half full and shakes her head at me, giving me a sad puppy dog look. "Well, Carolina, everyone knows you have to be open today because of the festival. Everyone knows that was a requirement of you being a part of it. Everyone knows because I told everyone." She shrugs. "Just covering for you."

Laney drops her head to the side with an incredulous look.

"Yeah, at the same time you were blasting Peter and Delaney for hosting a brunch right during church time. Think I heard you say something like..." Laney drops her voice an octave, raises it a couple decibels, and puts on a horribly fake Southern accent—except it sounds just like Ruby: "'Only books that should be opened that time of a Sunday morning are hymnals and Bibles.'"

Ruby smiles. "Kinda thought that was a good line. But like I said, I didn't think they'd tell God and everybody I was making the muffins for the brunch."

I can't help but chuckle at her woefulness. Luckily the sound of the coffee maker covers it as I prepare to put a lid on my Styrofoam cup. "I'm making this to-go so I can get to the forum. The brunch part should be over," I explain. The brunch at the Bedwell House was invite-only, and a a very small crowd. Much smaller than Delaney originally planned because, once she left town, Missus scaled it way back, canceled the caterer, borrowed a forty-cup coffee maker, ordered muffins from Ruby, and went out to Walmart to buy a bunch of cut-up fruit. Sally Blankenship was insulted and complained at first, but since Silas arrived in town, she's had other fish to fry. I wasn't at the brunch, so I'm not sure if she even attended it. The door to the B&B hall was still closed when I left. I'm not sure she understood the forum was going to be different from the original plan of her taking questions from the audience. If she didn't so rub me the wrong way, I'd appreciate how little concern she has for the Bedwell's.

I pat Ruby's back as I pass her. "Go on home, Ruby. As hard as it may be, take a page from Laney's book: ignore the complainers." At the door I turn around and give her a stern look. "And next time don't be so quick to criticize other people."

"I don't criticize people. I just speak the truth and make muffins." She pushes up from her seat. "I'll walk out with you.

No need to stay here where someone is choosing to be open on a Sunday. Not something you'll see my café ever doing!" Her lamenting is over apparently.

Laney yells at us from near the back of The Club. "I'm telling everyone you about bought me out of stuff this morning. Shopped like a fiend!"

Ruby *pshaws* and swipes her arm back at her while Laney laughs out loud.

"Hey, y'all turn my sign over to 'Open,'" Laney says. "Might as well get the church crowd on their way home!"

On the sidewalk we take a minute to look around at the magnificent day. Sunny warmth is already chasing the chill away and causing the pansies to practically dance in their bright planters. "You want to go to the forum with me?"

Ruby scowls. "Are you crazy? I'm going home."

She shuffles away from me headed toward her café, where she parks her car out back. On the newest batch of flyers, Missus advertised the forum and brunch. It seemed strange to put the invite-only brunch on the flyer, but then I realized it was on the flyer so she could let everyone—and God, according to Ruby—know where the muffins came from. Ruby told us Missus had stipulated to her they be fresh-baked that morning, which the flyer also mentioned.

Mayor, brunch organizer, host of a forum on Southern literature—and Missus still has time to put the screws to her rival.

Small towns are the best.

I am bored beyond belief.

Athena is trying her best to liven things as emcee, but if the gentleman Missus recruited to destroy Sally's ridiculous Southern fantasy has mentioned Reconstruction once, he's mentioned it a dozen times. His constant name-dropping might've impressed an audience in the late 1800s, but so far I'm not impressed. Heck, I'm barely awake.

Sally is up onstage, but she's not said a half-dozen words. One of her assistants is doing all the talking, and she's some kind of expert in feminist literature stuff. I've heard her say what exactly she's an expert in a couple of times, but I still don't understand it. I'm not even sure she understands it.

Sally is dressed in gray slacks and a matching blazer with a black turtleneck underneath, looking very authorly and interested in the discussion. Wait, did I say discussion?

The two experts are not having a discussion. I don't know if anyone told them that was the idea. This is like two football teams playing each other… on different fields. And neither realizing that's a problem. He gives us a rundown of statistics and names, only stopping when Sally's PR person jumps in with her statistics and names. None of which correlates to the other's statistics and names.

Finally I get the nod from Missus, so I leap from my seat, invite everyone to Blooming Books for the book signing—and flee.

Straight to The Club and coffee. "It was awful," I say to Laney as she meets me at her coffee maker. "Not in a shocking way, but in a completely boring way." I choose coconut coffee this time and get it going. "Looks like you've been busy."

She laughs. "Mostly from people that abandoned the forum. It sure worked out for me."

"Worked for Sally and Missus, too. I think at some point they both realized they didn't want or need the kind of publicity potentially headed their way. I just want this book signing to be over, the festival to be behind us, and for life to get back to normal."

Laney leans across a rack of hand-knitted sweaters she's put out since I was here this morning. "Normal? Hmm, normal?" She stands up and straightens the satin-covered hangers. "Naw." She adds with a grin, "Not interested."

Chapter 25

"I don't know when they're leaving," I lament to Jackson. "I'm about ready to make a fake booking and kick them all out! No one seems to have any idea what Sally is still doing here in Chancey. I can't tell if she's here because of Silas or if he's here because of her?"

Jackson's sitting in bed, reading a train magazine. Although I don't think he's actually reading it, since he's not turning pages and he's actually tracking our conversation. "They aren't really bothering me. I was just asking."

I rub lotion on my rough winter feet and then slide on socks. Laney has promised to have a pedicure chair put into The Club, but I can't go with my feet in this shape. The pedicure lady would think she was working on some prehistoric monster. I grumble as I get under the covers, although my lotioned-up feet do feel pretty nice. "Well, they're all bothering me. Even her publicist, who I kind of liked before. All her moaning about wanting to return to civilization and complaining about being here in the boonies! Ever since she spoke at that forum, she's gotten more vocal and more opinionated and harder for me to ignore."

"Do you think Sally is writing when she's holed up in her room all day?" he asks. "Although I can't really tell when she's here or not. Or Silas, for that matter."

"I don't know. And I can't figure out why she's still here. The book festival's been over for almost a week. I've asked to see if they have plane tickets, but I can't even get an answer for that. I keep worrying she's going to come into the shop and demand another signing or something. Except when I see her downtown, she's with Peter or Silas, and they don't even look toward the shop. Delaney isn't saying anything either. I was all excited about things getting back to normal, but that doesn't seem to be happening. Has Silas said anything to you about what he's doing?"

"Not really. I think he's looking at property. Maybe he and Sally really are a couple. Maybe they're looking for property together?"

"I don't want to think about that," I say as I turn out my lamp. "Good night."

He leans over to give me a kiss. "Is it okay if I keep reading for a bit?"

"Sure. I'm so tired I won't even notice the light is on."

"Okay. I've got a work call first thing in the morning, and then we can head down to Ruby's together. Good night."

My eyes pop open. Ruby's? Oh no. Is that tomorrow? Yep. Tomorrow is Thursday. The day we are meeting with all the parents whose kids are going on this spring break disaster our daughter has arranged.

Well, I *was* tired.

"I thought I'd have more information by now," I try to say over the hubbub without actually yelling. There are some people here who are simply trying to enjoy their coffee and muffins. "You've got to understand it's different down there."

Soooo different in the Atlanta suburbs, I'm discovering

once again. Down there your kids going off to a luxury cabin for a week is no big deal. Kids have way more freedom and way more money. No one I contacted this week from down in Marietta even seemed to understand what I was concerned about, and when I got those responses, our life in Marietta came flooding back. Kids go on big trips a lot. Parents foot the bill for extravagance that I don't think I fully appreciated when I lived there. After-prom parties are more elaborate than a lot of weddings I've been to. Luxury hotels are commonplace for dances and after-parties, and of course the kids stay the night there. Of course! Don't be a stick-in-the-mud. Everyone wants their kid to be at the party everyone is talking about on Monday morning.

And underneath it all is the assumption there will be large amounts of alcohol. Boys and girls staying en masse on the property so they won't be driving is accepted as a wise decision. But boys and girls and alcohol? When has that ever been a wise decision?

Now, up here there is also alcohol assumption, but the gatherings are out in someone's field around a bonfire or in a barn, and sanctioning everyone to spend the night together isn't happening. No way, no how. Besides, the dances and parties are less extravagant and feel safer. There are fewer people overall, most of them have known each other their whole lives, and this means fewer new people trying to impress each other. However, thanks to one fairly new person, my daughter, the suburbs are knocking on the door.

Savannah emailed her Chancey friends the website for the lake house. It's amazing. Sleeps nineteen, so the kids have decided that means forty at least. Kids, that is. Forty kids, zero adults.

Savannah's friends at her old school are on spring break the week before Chancey High, so they've reserved it that week and easily covered the cost, so of course the kids here think it should be no problem for them either. Her Marietta friends are saying the cost is greatly reduced because someone knows someone, but I think they're just lying to make their parents think they're getting a deal. The story that it was a friend's cabin and would be free has mysteriously evaporated. The parents down there that I talked to this week didn't have a lot of details. That was another thing I rediscovered: suburban parents trust their kids a lot more than country parents. That might sound good, but we all know trusting teenagers is crazy. But none of them were concerned with the costs, or the place being destroyed. Maybe it's that they aren't worried about covering the costs of several dozen high school kids being unleashed in a house for a week.

Folks there see no problem with that proposal. One of my suburban friends laughed and said, "Oh, we'll be popping in to leave food and check in. You know it'll all be fine."

Folks here upon hearing the no-adult proposal laughed because they knew I was joking. Until they realized I wasn't. Then, with raised eyebrows, they spat, "No. Hell no!"

But the kids here are listening to Savannah who, I'm beginning to agree with Laney, probably needs a spanking.

If only we knew her parents.

One of the dads doing a lot of talking to the group this morning is our insurance guy. He's trying to keep a smile on his face as he explains he just can't imagine how this is a good idea, and yet his son keeps telling him everyone else's parents are fine with it. That elicits a groan and a lot of nodding heads.

"Exactly! That's what they're all saying," one of the moms exclaims. "I just told Laney and Susan I'd been assured they were one hundred percent on board. Now I find out they aren't." She frowns. "Well, not quite on board, right?"

Susan holds up a hand. "I'm getting the feeling we are all being played by our kids. Having this meeting without them was a good idea. I have to remind everyone it was Savannah's parents' idea for us all to get together. Now, let's listen to what Carolina is trying to say."

I give her a grateful look. "Like I said, I thought I'd have more information, but I don't." I hurry before the noise overtakes me again. "However... however, I do think we have enough information to say this is not a good idea and we should not let our kids do it. The costs are not cheap like Savannah had been told. I mean, of course 'cheap' means something different in different places to different people."

"Not that we don't want our children to have the best!" a mom says from a table in the middle of the café. I'm surprised; I didn't think she was with this group. She gets a swell of support, but that is squashed just as quickly with a flood of opinions that hoity-toity parents are spoiling their kids and going into debt to keep up with the Joneses.

Jackson stands up and cuts through the rumble of voices. "I vote no."

He sits down as Griffin shouts, "I vote no, and I need a coffee refill over here." He laughs and raises his cup as Libby heads his way. As she does, others agree with him on the vote and on getting more coffee. One mom tries to argue in favor of the trip, but she has no support, and before long the conversation has moved on and we have saved the town once again.

I take a bite of my pecan and blueberry muffin and find that it tastes even better than it did a few minutes ago. I'm sitting with Jackson and a couple who haven't lived in Chancey long, but who have a very attractive son who plays basketball and was immediately accepted into Savannah's group. His mom breathes a deep sigh of relief. "Oh, I'm so glad this all went that way. We moved out of the suburbs partially for that reason. Too much money and too much permission. It was hard enough with our son who is focused on sports, but with two girls in middle school? We needed to get out while the getting was good."

"How did you find Chancey?" I ask her. Jackson and her husband are talking over some remodeling the couple wants done.

"Our real estate agent. She's located over in Canton and is a friend's sister. We told her last summer what we were looking for. We've lived on the west side of Atlanta for several years, but we wanted to try small-town life."

I smile and nod. "Yeah. A lot of folks do."

She looks around and frowns. "It's taking some getting used to, but so far I think we'll like it. I'm planning on opening a little preschool, or really daycare. Do you think there's much of a need for one?"

"Oh! Yes. There most certainly is," I exclaim as I look to see if Laney is still here. She'll be very interested. I lean close and whisper, "There isn't anything more than just babysitting in people's homes. Where were you thinking of doing it?"

She laughs a little. "Well, our plan is to actually a use a house, but completely remodeled. That's what our husbands are talking about. It's on our property near the road. The house we live in is back at the lake."

Jackson joins our conversation as he stands up. "They bought out past the library where town ends. We're going to take a ride out there and look over some work they want to get done. You want to go with me? Or I can pick you up at the shop later. We probably should've driven separately."

I'm tempted to go with them and see what the plans are, but I don't want to get stuck there if they get into all the details. "I'll stay here in town. Just call when you're ready to go home. I've always got something I can do at the shop."

The three of them leave, and I head toward the back counter. I half sit on a barstool and wait for Ruby to notice me. The café has pretty much cleared out, and it looks like she's moved on to making pies for the afternoon.

Libby comes and perches on the stool next to mine. "A

daycare? Well, now there's something I never thought a place like Chancey would need." When I look surprised at her, she chuckles. "Oh, I hear everything. Maybe a daycare right here in town would help Cathy decide to have another baby. I mean, I don't think it would help their marriage but don't think it could hurt, and I sure would love a little girl to have around. Forrest is just getting so grown."

"Cathy and Stephen are doing well?" That marriage has had more ups and downs than anyone can count. Although their ups and downs are so interesting, we do usually try to keep track, although it's a struggle. "Last I heard they were buying a house? He was working some up at Darien?"

"Yeah, he's doing some tutoring stuff up there and Cathy's still doing the lingerie. I already texted her we're getting a daycare. What're those folks' names? She wants to know."

"Oh, well, it's not going to be ready for a while. Hey, Ruby!" I call out. No need to get the new folks on Cathy Stone's radar by name. "You got a minute?"

Ruby turns and heads toward us. "Libby, the sooner you get those tables out there all cleared, the sooner I can get out of here. What can I do you for, Carolina?"

"I was just wondering if you got any blowback from making the muffins Sunday morning."

She stares at me. Her eyes narrow, then open wider as she smiles.

"Really? So you're worried about me?"

"Yeah, I guess. I mean, I'm just wondering." I try to match her smile, just friends talking. But then her smile stretches even more.

"I don't think so. Let me see. What is it you really want to know about?" She leans on the counter across from me and closes her eyes for a minute. Then she slaps one hand down and straightens up. "Peter and Silas. You want to know what they were in here talking about yesterday."

I start to answer her, but then I realize she didn't ask anything. I shut my mouth and shrug.

She tips her head forward and spills. "Land. Property. Seems you should've warned ol' Silas off of Peter. Although I guess he's a good enough lawyer if you got enough money." She begins to turn back to her pies, but then she stops. "Oh, and yes, he was with that Sally woman, but she looked as serious as the two men. I don't think there's any romance there. Maybe some booty call action, but no real involvement. Now I've got meringue to whip so I can go home and take a nap. Bye, Carolina."

I lower my head as I leave, a little embarrassed at being so transparent in my desire for gossip. On the sidewalk, embarrassment duly shaken off, I take a minute to think about what Ruby said. Property? Land? So maybe Silas *is* moving here. As for Sally Blankenship? I'm going to just assume Ruby doesn't know what a booty call is.

That would be best for all of our peace of mind.

Chapter 26

It takes a few minutes, but I become aware of how quiet everything is on the street outside Ruby's. It's not yet eleven a.m., so there aren't any people out looking for lunch. Matter of fact, the only motion near me is the unlocking of AC's front door from inside. That's how quiet it is: I can hear someone turning the old deadbolt in the big door down the street. The air is still and light, the sky an expectant blue, and the trees stretch to soak in the rays of a buttery yellow sun. And it's so quiet.

Like the trees, I take a moment to let the sunshine warm me, and then I slowly look from AC's and Blooming Books, past the park, across the street, and then down toward Phoenix's dance studio and juice bar. I'm supposed to be off work today, and I'm tired of the bookstore. Even more tired of the flower shop and Shannon's mom, if I'm honest. Hopefully Shannon won't need her help much longer, so I won't have to actually be honest to her face.

Okay, let's go see what Phoenix wanted to talk about once the festival was over.

"Phoenix? Are you here?" The front door pushes open easily, but there's no one in sight. "Phoenix?"

"Back here. Hey, Carolina!" Phoenix says, sticking her head out of a small kitchen behind the juice bar. "Come on back. My next class isn't until lunchtime, so I'm finishing up some meals for tonight."

"Meals for you?"

She laughs. "Hardly. I'll be lucky if I get a PB&J. Sit there." She points me to a small, white table with two white chairs. "So Savannah is back to square one with her spring break plans, I hear."

"Yeah. She won't be happy, but it was ridiculous. Who told you already?"

She squishes up her face. "Colt. Apparently one of the moms who thinks she's the cool mom texted her daughter that the rest of the parents are just no-fun fuddy-duddies.

"Yep. That's us. Can't believe she already told the kids. Did he say they're mad?" I reach for my phone but remember I'd silenced it for the meeting. Good idea. I drop it back in my purse unchecked and still silenced.

"Oh yeah. But he also said they'll get over it." She's got her back to me and is hustling back and forth in the tiny galley kitchen. "Give me just one more minute, and then we can talk. I'm putting the finishing touches on these before I let them cool. Then all they'll need is reheating before eating."

"Can I ask who your customers are? Or is that confidential?" I laugh, but she doesn't.

She shrugs, then turns toward me. "My biggest customers are Peter and Delaney. And while Missus was balking at first, they've had me add on for a third person, so I think she's now eating with them. They like traditional family-style meals." She pulls back and shows me large, square aluminum containers. "Those are for them. They're having chicken fettucine and salad tonight. Gertie has herself, Patty, and Andy on a reduced-calorie meal plan, so they order pretty much every other day. Everyone else is more sporadic. I do have two orders for weekend pots of a cheesy potato soup I advertised, but I expect I'll get more orders for that today."

"Oh, I meant to order one. Can you put us on the list?" She nods at me and scribbles our name down on a pad. "So it sounds like catering meals is going pretty well?"

"Better than I expected. I barely have time to teach any dance classes. I thought I could have both of my dreams, but I might've bit off more than I could chew."

The small room is warm and smells amazing. I look around and find that every surface is covered. This kitchen was not meant to run a catering service. "Have you thought of doing the food at your house?"

"I'd love to do that, but I just got the juice bar going, and I don't want to give up the dance classes. I just have to figure out how to fit it all in." She pauses, her back still to me. "And then there's Colt. That's what I wanted to talk to you about."

"Okay." She works, and I sit waiting.

She finally speaks up. "Just hearing Colt talk about the kids at school today—he's really good with them."

"I agree. I know Bryan is his nephew, but they really have a nice bond."

She nods, still concentrating on her work and letting the silence stretch. "Colt's going to make a wonderful father," she says in a low voice.

"Oh! Oh, Phoenix, are you pregnant?"

There must be something in the water here in Chancey. I get up from my chair and go to her. With a hand on her shoulder, I turn her toward me. That's why she's seemed different, not just the lack of makeup or her dulling hair color. I can't help but chuckle. She looks scared to death. "Sweetie, Colt's going to be thrilled. Absolutely thrilled."

She shakes her head and turns away from me. What? Wait—my mind short-circuits a bit—could she be carrying Peter's child, too? Oh my gosh! This is awful. I don't even have a place to put this in my brain. My voice is heavy and low. "Oh no. So it's, uh, not Colt's?"

Turning to me, her eyes are full of tears, and she shakes her head even harder. Oh, this is a nightmare. "Don't worry, sweetie. I'm here for you. Colt loves you." I pull her to me in a hug, but she firmly pulls away.

"No. I'm not pregnant. That's the problem. I can't. I won't ever be." She takes a deep breath. "I can't have children, and I can't do that to Colt."

The sidewalk is no longer quiet, especially in front of the dance studio. Phoenix's next class is a mommy-and-me group that does lunch and exercise together. She rushed off to get changed, so our conversation was cut short, and now I'm holding the door for a number of moms, kids, and strollers to enter. After Phoenix's news, I look at the toddlers a little sadly. Wonder how hard it is on her to be with all these adorable little ones? I can't imagine it's easy or comfortable. Poor Phoenix. She has got to talk to Colt. I understand her fear of telling him, but she just has to. I'll have to make sure to talk to her again soon.

I let the door close and watch through the glass as she enters the room, laughing and talking while the moms get their babies out of their coats and hats. Poor Phoenix.

The second time a horn honks, I turn around to see what's going on. Jackson is across the street, his head sticking out his truck window. "Is your phone still on silence?" he yells.

Oops. I smile as I dig it out of my purse and start to cross the street, but he waves me back as he gets out and lopes toward me. "I've been trying to call you. Want to do lunch at AC's?"

"Sure. That'd be nice. Kind of like a date," I say with a grin until he grimaces at me.

"Not so much. Uh, it's with some potential customers."

"About the"—I pause and lower my voice as he meets me on the sidewalk—"the daycare?" You never know where Cathy Stone is these days.

"No. Something completely new. It's Silas. He has a new venture."

"Oh, it'll be good to sit down with Silas," I say as we head down the sidewalk. Then I abruptly stop. "And Sally, too, right?"

He grimaces, which tells me I'm right.

I start walking again. "I can't believe we're going to have lunch with the two of them. Susan's going to kill me if—what am I saying, *if?—when* she finds out."

CHAPTER 27

We both slow down as we walk past Blooming Books and look in the windows. Two of the older men I recognize from church are actually playing chess. That's the first time I've seen someone using the board Bonnie set up. It's a nice, heavy set and serves as a nice decoration, but it's even better seeing it being used. Everything else looks good as well—except for Mrs. Chilton glowering at the worktable. Glad I didn't stop in earlier.

We pass on by, and Jackson pulls open AC's heavy oak door. It's still hard to believe we have an honest-to-goodness restaurant like this in Chancey.

Warmth greets us, along with such good smells. Smells of herbs and bread and deep flavors. We're joined by Silas and Sally, and then welcomed by one of the young ladies I remember seeing at the bonfire at our house last weekend. She acts like I'm her long-lost friend while she leads us to our table. "Here you go! See you later, Carolina and Sally!"

Frowning at the young woman as she flits off, Sally says under a spiked eyebrow, "I never was a fan of being called 'ma'am' and 'miss' down here, but being called 'Sally' by that one, like we're equals, makes me miss the veneer of respect and standing. Call me ma'am and chalk one up for the South."

She then drops the high and mighty Atlanta accent to greet Jackson and me. She's all smiles. "It's about time we all got together, isn't it?" She reaches out and rubs the back of Silas's arm. "Strange the four of us live in the same house, and yet we rarely get to talk."

Silas helps with my chair and I'm relieved to see there's only room for us four. I half expected Peter to join us.

We barely get seated before our waiter is there with water and to tell us the specials. After we've ordered and settled in, Silas leans forward. "Have you been to that nursery outside of town? Sits back on the lake? Really pretty and has a huge wholesale business?"

Jackson and I look at each other, then shake our heads. I say, "I think I've seen it, but I've never been to it. What's the name?"

"County Wholesale Nursery." Silas laughs. "How unimaginative is that? I'll be coming up with something much better."

Jackson asks, "So you're buying it?"

"Yep. And I'm going to add a retail business to it. You know, with classes on lawn and plant care and all kinds of neat stuff. It's going to be great. I'm going to need the buildings updated, and that's where you and Colt come in. There's a place I'm going to move into as soon as the deal's done, but I don't really care what shape it's in."

Silas is practically buzzing with excitement as he goes into more detail on the buildings he wants worked on. I chance a look at Sally and see she's watching him also.

"So, Sally, what do you think of Silas's new venture?" I ask as the waiter brings us some warm, seeded flatbread in a basket.

She thanks the waiter, then takes out a piece of bread and pulls it apart. "I'm delighted for him, of course. Actually I'm enjoying my extra time here in Chancey so much I might stay longer." At my look of concern, she chuckles. "Oh, not at the B&B, of course."

As she hands Silas a piece of bread, he says, "She been great with ideas and just overall moral support."

With her piece of bread almost to her mouth, she stops and

looks at him. "Moral support? Is that all? Don't you mean moral and *financial* support?"

Silas frowns and mumbles, "We haven't agreed on that."

She laughs. "Oh, wait until the bills start coming in and the phone is ringing off the wall but you can't afford to hire any more help. We don't want your acting career to suffer, right?" She places a hand on my arm. "Tell him, Carolina. You own a business. You never turn down investment money, right?"

I lift my arm, trying to not visibly shake her hand loose, but I do not want to be a part of anything she's planning. And she is most definitely planning something. "Can you pass the butter, honey?" I ask, reaching for it with my now free arm.

Jackson hands me the butter dish, but he's focused on Silas as he asks, "It's on the lake you were saying? Just out of town? I was just out there looking at another job this morning. Some folks bought the property with that old brick ranch at the highway and the newer house that sits back on the lake."

"Yeah, the nursery is just past there. There's no signage or anything, just a big dirt-and-grass parking area, but past that you can see over the hill, and it's all laid out with the buildings, greenhouses, and my little house, which is actually a trailer permanently set on a concrete slab. But I'm fine with that." He chuckles. "I've spent a lot of time in trailers on movie lots."

Sally shudders a bit and then sniffs. Under her breath, she says, "We'll see about that. A trailer?" She scrunches up her nose, but to the side so Silas doesn't see.

"So, Sally, when do you plan to go back to New York?" I ask loudly. Maybe a bit too loud, as Jackson and Silas stop talking to look at me. "Enquiring minds, and all that," I lamely try to cover for myself.

"Who knows? It's rather interesting here now that Silas has returned, and the streets at home are full of slush right now. I have some other projects I'm working on, one rather promising one over in South Carolina, that you're really be interested in when I'm ready to spill. However, I'm sending the girls all home to handle things there for me. So you'll have that cute little gray room of yours empty tomorrow." She leans over and rubs shoulders with Silas. "Besides, I can write anywhere. Even in a trailer."

Silas swallows and looks uncomfortable, which just makes me mad. He's a grown man. If he doesn't want her insinuating they're a couple, he should stop hanging around with her—or at least stop letting her hang on him. Give me a break.

"Why don't you—" I start, but then Jackson squeezes my thigh under the table while exclaiming, "Here's our food!"

The waiter with the full tray moves past us to a table by the windows.

I squeeze Jackson's hand back in a quick thank-you as I take a breath. Then I smile and say, "I think I'll go to the restroom before our food arrives." I break all girl code: not only do I not invite Sally to tag along, but I get up quickly and never even look at her.

When I get to the restroom, I'm muttering, "Men are so stupid."

I must've said it a little louder once the door closed behind me because from one of the stalls comes an, "Amen, sister!"

"Men are so stupid," I say again as I climb up in Jackson's truck.

He closes his door and gives me a shrug, saying, "I'd agree, but then since I am a man, maybe my opinion is just stupid."

"You know I don't mean you. I mean men in general."

Now he gives me a shrug *and* a look. "But I'd have to agree. In this case. He's got to shake her loose, but sweetie, I also have to defend him. You have no idea how hard it is to get rid of a woman who's after you without looking like a real jerk."

Now it's my turn to give a look. "Excuse me? So who are these women that are after you?"

He's pulled out of the parking spot, and as he puts the truck in drive, he says, "Hello? Shelby? We got married because I couldn't figure out a way to break up with her without crushing her, and, well, as a guy you spend your whole life thinking about women: how to get one, how to keep one. And then she's there and thinks you're great? I mean, well, ya know."

"I know. But he's a grown man. Not some twenty-year-old like you were." I twist to face the side window. The rest of lunch was calm. Mostly because I stopped talking and asking questions. I smile to myself as I stare out at the passing scenery. Jackson never has to carry the conversation with me around, but he did today. It was cute how he kept talking and talking. Turning back toward him, I smile. "Okay. Men aren't stupid. You aren't stupid and Silas isn't stupid."

"And remember, he just got his heart handed to him, along with a rejected engagement ring. He's in a rough spot."

"Sally also mentioned him getting a role in the movie based on her book. Do you think she would have a lot of say in something like that?"

He nods as we stop at the stop sign before heading up the hill toward the house. "She could. I think he'll get tired of her and all her innuendos before long. I think he just needs a friend right now, and she's, well, like I said, she's there and obviously not going away."

I'm momentarily distracted by the triangle of grass filled with flowers. "Look, the daffodils are getting ready to open!" I point to the tall stands of thin, green leaves and stems topped with daffodil buds, some already showing a bit of yellow. They are my favorite flower, and this area being filled with them every spring is one of my favorite things about Chancey.

The truck revs going up the hill, and I speak over it. "You're probably right. He'll most likely get tired of her and she'll go back to New York." But then a sigh slips out. "Or he'll cave, marry her, and we'll be stuck with Sally Blankenship forever."

Jackson doesn't answer.

He's not stupid.

CHAPTER 28

Maybe the last week went by so fast because Savannah wasn't speaking to me. She was blisteringly mad at the beginning of the weekend, after we held the parents' meeting and nixed her spring break plans. She definitely was speaking to, really at, me then, but by Sunday morning, when I still wasn't budging, she was over me. So over me. Her daddy, not so much. She still talked to him, mostly because he didn't realize she was shunning him. He dismissed the very idea with a chuckle, saying, "How could you live with someone and not talk to them?" And he went on about his business.

Not me. I thought about, actually worried, about it. I tried to trick her into talking, left her notes, reasoned, joked, got mad, yelled, all of the above, until she started talking to me again this morning while we finish getting the lunches packed. I'd like to say my strategy worked, but I don't think that was it.

"You're saying Daddy is serious about us going camping over spring break?" Her dark hair is back in a low bun, her arms, in their light yellow sweater, are crossed on her chest, and her mouth is hanging open. Her unpeeled banana matches her sweater. She shakes her head and takes a bite.

"He said you were excited."

She talks around the banana in her mouth. "I thought he was joking! You know, how he says clueless stuff and you just agree?" She swallows and declares, "I'm not going camping. Especially not with my family."

With a shrug I turn away to put my coffee cup in the sink. "I think it'll be fun."

She's suddenly by my side. "You do?" She's stretching around to see my face. "We haven't gone camping since forever. That's for little kids. You aren't serious. Do we even still own a tent? A tent!"

"He says he's borrowing a camper. It'll have beds."

"That would be better, but I'm still not going." She leans her back against the counter. "I have to work. Y'all can take Bryan." After a pause she adds, "I'll be fine here alone."

I can see the wheels turning, so I shut that down. "You are not going to stay here alone. You can stop that train of thought before it leaves the station."

She walks across the kitchen. "I don't care. I'm just not going camping."

She enters the living room. I can hear her keys jingle as she heads for the front door, so I shout, "Did he tell you who we're going with?"

She growls under her breath and comes back my way, sticking her head in the kitchen doorway. "Who?"

"Not sure who all, but it's at the Yeldins."

Her whole body follows her head as she comes near me, still at the sink. "Nathan's family?"

I nod, and her shoulders drop as she thinks about that. The Yeldins are the new family who are opening a daycare after Jackson, Colt, and Will finish the remodeling. They are also the family with the good-looking, basketball-playing high school senior son Savannah appears to be attracted to. As I learned on Thursday, they have a large lake lot of several acres. On one end beside the lake they've parked their camper, and they say there's room for a couple of other campers. Jackson and Eddie Yeldin have hit it off, and the men came up with this plan.

"We'd be near their house, near the lake, and it's only for a couple of days. Then maybe you and I could go somewhere for a night. A girls' night, Atlanta or Chattanooga?" I slip that last bit in there since she seems to be softening. Juxtaposed with camping, maybe it won't seem so bad.

She looks at me, and her eyes are large and dark. She pulls in a deep breath through her nose and nods. "I'd like that." She pauses, then says, "The cabin trip fell through for the Marietta kids, too. The owners found out it was just going to be kids and canceled the whole deal. Kept their deposit, though, so... everybody's mad." She sniffs a couple of times, then clears her throat. "Looks like you were right," she says, looking me straight in the eye.

With a quick lunge, I hug her before she can get away and then let her go when she says she's going to be late for school.

Watching her out the living room window with the spring sunshine, budding flowers, and puffy white clouds, I'm so happy. All is right in the world.

Well, except apparently I'm going camping.

"Good morning," Sally says behind me.

I roll my eyes—even before she's given me a reason. "Good morning. You're up early."

She gives me her own eye roll along with a flourish of the tail of her long robe. "This isn't actually early for me to be up. It's only early for me to be out here. With Silas moving into his property and out of the B&B, there's no reason to lie around in bed of a morning." She smirks at me, daring me to ask what we all still want to know—are they a couple?

Instead I say, "Want some coffee? I don't have to leave for another half hour." I've been wanting a chance to find out more about why she's still here. I just don't trust her.

She pulls her light blue satin robe tighter around her and drops into the rocking chair that looks out the front windows. "I heard Savannah leaving. Are Bryan and Jackson also gone?"

Carrying both cups of coffee, I come back into the living room. "Yes. Jackson took Bryan in on his way out to the day-care he's been working on. The one out near Silas."

"Yes, Carolina, I may not act all that interested, but I'm aware of the daily ins and outs of the Jessup family. I know what the daycare is and where it is." She takes a sip of coffee and rocks back with a sigh. "All the minutia of a middle class family is hard to avoid here."

See? The preemptive eye roll was a good idea. "So. Are you and Silas a couple, or are you just a middle-aged woman pining after a man who's not interested?" I ask as I settle into my end of the couch. The words were not supposed to come out my mouth, but I've had it with her condescension. Apparently I've also had it with the hefty sums she's been paying for her room because I'm sure the next words from her will be, "I'm leaving."

"That's what you think?" she asks.

"What I think?"

"That he's not interested. That Silas is not interested in me as a partner." She waves a hand in frustration. "Not a business partner. That ship has sailed. Apparently he is breaking the stereotype of the broke actor and is in great financial shape. But as a, you know, as a, uh, girlfriend?"

She's still guarded, her head held high, chin tilted up and eyes suspicious, but there's an eagerness there that reminds me of Savannah. A question behind the suspicion, a worry of remaining unseen, and I melt. Well, a little.

"Oh, Sally. I don't know. He's just not—"

"Not like he was with your friend Susan. Not like you've seen him. I kept thinking if I could just get him into bed he would forget her. I mean, she and I are built quite similarly, so how could he not be interested, right?"

Yuck. "I think there's more to it than that."

She waves her hand again and cuts me off. "No, not really. I've studied it. It's all about eye attraction and some other stuff.

Sure, there's chemistry and enjoying the same things, but that can develop later. Of course it can. My last boyfriend learned to love art shows and fashion shows, all built on a physical relationship that was hot. Very hot, let me tell you."

I feign disinterest for, oh, about a minute. "So what happened?"

"Where? With Silas?" She takes a deep breath. "Frankly, he is *obsessed* with that land and moved out to that awful trailer. I would've gone with him, well, at some point, but he never even asked."

"No," I interrupt. "With your last boyfriend."

She stops and blinks at me, then shakes her head. Her straight hair swings toward her face. "He, I—it was just over. You know? Just ended."

"Well, maybe having more in common helps a relationship last. At least a little longer."

She studies the front yard through the window, her jaw set and eyes distant. Then she gives a little huff. "I don't have time for that. I see something I like, or someone I like, and go for it. Always have. It's just who I am. I'm not like you people here, settling for whoever comes your way or who your parents say you should marry." She focuses back on me and shoots me some pity. "After all, *I* have the whole world to choose from. However, I'm not sure I agree with you that all is hopeless with Silas. He'll get lonely out in that trailer of his and I'll be back around."

"Back around here? Around Chancey?"

"I have some friends that are very interested in your little town." She plays with the ends of her belt as she talks. "I'm finding it's a very small world down here which I'm working to make even smaller." She squints at me. "It may look like I'm only chasing Silas, but I have my own interests at work. Peter always talked about his southern roots and I'm glad I finally got to see them up close. Like I said, it's a very small world down here, she drawls, ending with a smirk.

I'm not going to get any answers from her, she's too fond of playing games. I stand up. "Good for you. I have to go finish getting ready for work. And since you asked, no, I don't think Silas is interested in you as more than a friend. Sorry." The *sorry* jumped out all on its own. I did not intend to extend any grace to her.

She shrugs, then settles back into the chair. "Go get ready. I'm going to sit here and finish my coffee, then make plans to leave. This has all grown tiresome suddenly."

In the kitchen I finish putting together my lunch. The only sound from the living room is the rocking of the chair, I try not to disturb her as I come back through. As I put on my jacket, I sneak a quick look at her and see that her face is turned away from me.

Okay. I can be the bigger person. "Sally, I'm glad I got to know you. You're welcome back anytime."

A little laugh bursts out, and she gives me a friendly look. "Sure. As long as I keep my hands off the men, right?"

I chuckle with her and pull open the door. But as I turn back to say goodbye, she speaks up.

"Like I said, I have some other projects in the works that require me to do a bit of traveling. Plus, I have a lot of work to do adding a sappy actor to the plot of my latest book." She lifts her head and raises her eyebrow at me. "I'll be back around for that book's release, you can bet! I'll let you know when so you can make arrangements—though I guess it all depends on if I'm staying here or in a real hotel. Who knows, Silas might find he gets awful lonely out there in the country by himself. Or Peter does have that big old house. Lots of empty rooms I'd imagine. Chancey holds a lot of potential."

Forget saying a polite goodbye—and I want her final payment too much to say "good riddance"—so I settle for a slammed door and gritted teeth.

"'Open a B&B!' they said," I mutter. "'It'll be fun,' they said."

CHAPTER 29

"I need something green to wear. I completely forgot it was St. Patrick's Day," I say as I fling myself into The Club. "And a cinnamon-hearts coffee."

Taking a moment to examine Laney's emerald-green dress and emerald-green pumps, I notice the Celtic fiddle music filling The Club. "Oh, the music is so nice. And what's that smell?"

"Irish coffee, without the extra Irish until this afternoon. Make you one of those while I find you something to wear. How could you forget it's St. Patrick's Day? Especially with Missus' proclamation distributed on green paper about the recognition of the holiday on Friday?"

"Yeah, I distinctly remember ignoring that. And I missed the significance of the green paper. I just assumed she'd depleted the city's supply of white. You know, everyone's calendar doesn't revolve around the holidays and seasons." I pause as I prepare to push the coffee button. "Well, okay, I guess that's wrong because that's exactly what a calendar does, right?"

"My calendar at least. You didn't help me out much wearing that. Please tell me it's two pieces and I can just find you a top. That shade of brown isn't the most attractive on you."

I level a stare at her. "Well, thanks for the compliment. It's Wednesday, my cleaning day at the store, and I have a lot of books to move and shelves to work on. Being attractive wasn't my main goal. And yes, it is two pieces, but I don't want to buy a top. A scarf, a necklace, heck, a beaded bracelet or a pair of earrings would work. Anything to keep from getting pinched all day."

"No one is actually pinching you." Then she looks up from the shelves she's going through. "Are they?"

I frown at her and take a sniff of my coffee. "They might. This town is a little over the top for all the green stuff. Even before Missus' official holiday proclamation, which must've used all the green ink in city hall, reminding us to wear green. "

"Lots of Irish roots here. Plus, we just love a holiday."

She walks toward me with an armful of green items. I grab the small bracelet on top, which I know is less than ten dollars. "This will do." I slide it on and then sit down on the nearest chair. "Guess what I did this morning?"

Laney shakes her head at me. "I should've known this wasn't about the wearing of the green." She perches on the edge of the chair next to me. I don't think her dress will allow her to sit completely down. It's a little tight, but that's nothing new, so I ignore her teetering posture.

"I got rid of Sally Blankenship. She's going home! Or going somewhere. She was very vague."

"That is good news." She stands up. "Whew! I can't breathe sitting like that. So, what did she say about Silas?"

I lower my voice and lean toward her. "I don't think they slept together. I don't think there's any there there at all."

She presses her lips together and turns away with a sharp "hmm" and a weird breathing sound. Her heels click as she hurries away.

I follow her to the back of the store. "What is it? Are you okay? Can you really not breathe?"

"Not well, but that's nothing new. Damn the unforgiving fabric of vintage dresses. I ordered this one online but didn't think about it having no stretch." She stands tall and sucks in air. "I brought a sweater to wear if I have to unzip it some. Here, unzip me, but just to below my bra."

I do as she asks, and she takes a deeper breath, though still only half of one. "Oh, that's better," she sighs. She puts on a cute, white sweater with pearl buttons and models it for me. "How does it look? Can you tell I'm unzipped?"

The sweater is very light and thin, so yes, it's easy to tell her zipper is only halfway up. "Kinda. Plus, I'm not sure the zipper will stay up like that. I'm thinking it will slide on down below the sweater."

She steps over to a full-length mirror and examines the situation herself. "You're right." Leaving me at the back, she sashays to the front counter. Even half-dressed she sashays, which, of course she does. She pulls out her purse and then meets me as I start to the front. "Stay here for a bit. I'll just run home and change and then be right back."

"I can't stay here. I have my own store to run."

"Shannon's there. Her mother is probably there, too, and Bonnie's hanging around, right? Of course you can hang out here. I'll be right back." She's opening the back door by the time I get to her.

"Why didn't you bring another outfit since you knew you couldn't breathe?"

"Oh, Carolina, don't ask silly questions when I'm trying to get out the door. You already said you have things to do. Should I stay here answering all your questions or hurry on my way?" She gives me a sad look, shakes her head at me, and leaves.

I really don't think it was such a silly question, do you? But then, we're not beauty queens, are we?

Sitting back down at the table to enjoy my coffee, I realize I didn't bring my phone with me. It's in the shop in my purse. Shannon's mother was at the front counter talking to one of her friends, and I didn't want to get involved in all that, so I just walked out the front door saying I'd be back in a minute. Well, it'll be more than a minute now.

Shannon's mother—Mrs. Chilton, as I've been told to call her—is making me hate the shop. She babies Shannon, bosses Danny, and annoys the living daylights out of me. Last night Jackson told me I had to either change the situation or stop complaining about it. He's tired of hearing about it. Honestly, I'm tired of hearing about it, too. She's the one that made me want something green to wear. She came in this morning spouting off something about how, unless you were Catholic, there was no reason to be celebrating some saint from another country. Shannon's eyes grew large, and I watched her shrink into her green overshirt. Danny laughed like she was joking, but then as he realized she wasn't, he slunk off into the bookshelves, he and his bright green T-shirt with a large shamrock from last year's celebration in Savannah. Savannah annually holds the biggest St. Patrick's Day celebration in the South. The size of their parade is only behind New York City and Chicago in the whole country.

I jump up from my chair and realize I need more than the green bracelet to wear because when I get back to the shop, I'm going to leave no doubt who's in charge. Well, at least on the book side.

"No, it does not taste like a Shamrock Shake from McDonald's," I say to Phoenix as I set the plastic cup full of green stuff on the table.

"I never said it would. You're the one that jumped to that conclusion. I mean, I'm assuming theirs is like ice cream? This is healthy. A shamrock smoothie. Take another taste."

Laney shouts over the rack she's behind. "Or don't. We can

run out to the interstate and get the real thing for lunch." Then she comes around to where Phoenix and I are. "Although since I had to actually go home and change because my clothes were too tight, a milkshake for lunch probably isn't a good idea. Give me a taste."

Phoenix showed up at The Club just as I was getting ready to leave. She has a pitcher of green shamrock smoothie and a stack of small cups. She's going down the street giving out samples.

I pick up my bag, which has my brown top inside and some things I acquired while I was left alone, supervising Laney's shop. I left her a detailed receipt since I don't have my purse. I have on a cool, tie-dyed scarf in various shades of green. When Laney got back, she pinned it so that it's hanging mainly over one shoulder. It didn't look right over my brown sweatshirt, so I bought and changed into a new, white-and-pink striped shirt. I also have dangly earrings made of colorful stones, mostly in pinks and greens. I changed out the white shoe strings in my tennis shoes for some green ones and found a new pink lipstick perfect for spring.

Before taking a sip of her drink, Laney lifts my handwritten receipt, looks at it, and then crumples it in her hand. "Thanks for your help this morning. Plus, you are a walking, talking advertisement in that outfit." She waves off my objection, screws up her face, and takes a sip. "Hey. Hey, that's kind of good. Minty."

Phoenix beams at her, and I just smile at them as I move on to the front door. "I have to get back to the shop." With a swirl, I turn back to Phoenix. "Are you coming all the way down to Blooming Books?"

"Sure. I have twenty minutes before my next class, but I'll hurry there."

"Great. Bye, Laney. Thanks!"

I feel on top of the world, and my steps are exuberant as I

glide down the sidewalk. I can't actually fire Mrs. Chilton, but I can make sure she doesn't boss Danny around because he's *my* employee. Plus, I can disagree when she acts like her opinion is straight from the mouth of God.

Seriously. Everyone in Chancey knows Missus is the only one here allowed to speak for God.

Chapter 30

"Where have you been?" Mrs. Chilton demands as I breeze in the front of the shop.

"Shopping. I realized I'd forgotten to wear green today." I hurry past her and greet Shannon with a big smile. "Happy St. Patrick's Day! Here, I got you something."

I plunk my bag down on her worktable and pull out a clear plastic bag. Inside are a pair of dangly, spring-colored earrings like the ones I'm wearing. "When I saw them, they reminded me of you, so I bought us each a pair."

She lights up, then, like a quickly changing spring day, clouds over. I can tell by the look in her eyes that her mother is coming up behind me. I grab another little clear bag out and turn around. "And this is for you, Mrs. Chilton."

The bag holds a bracelet made up of several silver wires, with a few ruby-colored stones sliding along them. She stops and reaches for it, her face shifting from disapproval to surprise.

"For me? Oh."

It's hard to not grin at her look of shock. I knew I'd catch her off guard. "To thank you for being so much help during the book festival. We couldn't have done it without you, and I know it's such an inconvenience." I lean a little closer. "Honestly, though, as a mother, aren't you just so proud of all

Shannon has accomplished? I know it was hard for her to ask her parents for help, but you were such troopers to step in. You are leaving us in much better shape. I hope we can call on you in the future when we need help." When she begins to frown, I hurry on. "Like in July when the baby comes. We will most definitely be calling on you then." She softens at the word *baby*, but then her mouth starts to open again, so I motion toward the bracelet. "Speaking of July, this is also a grandmother gift. Ruby, which of course these stones aren't *real* rubies, but that will be your grandbaby's birthstone. Put it on!"

She takes it out of the bag and slides it on her wrist. As she holds it up for the stones to slide and shine, I give her a hug. I've let this woman get under my skin, but as long as Shannon and I are partners she's a part of my world. Might as well try and get her on my side.

"Thank you again for all your help, especially at a time when I'm sure you're so busy getting ready for the grandbaby. Are you going to have a crib at your house? I know we've found that so helpful. Makes it so much easier when we watch sweet little Francie."

"Oh, I hadn't even thought of that." Her eyes mimic her open, rounded mouth, which then straightens into a determined line. "Shannon, we haven't thought of any of this, and the baby will be here before we know it." She looks around as if she's surprised to find herself in Blooming Books. "I have so much to do. So much to think about." She strides to the front counter, saying over her shoulder, "I'm glad I could help. Thank you for the bracelet, Carolina, and of course call on me anytime." She pulls her purse out, then heads back our way, actually smiling at me. "Unless I'm babysitting my new grandson or granddaughter."

She marches past me, and at Shannon's worktable, without breaking stride, she says, "Shannon, walk me to my car so we can discuss what needs to be done first."

They are barely out the back door before Danny's head pops up from deep in the bookshelves like a Whack-a-Mole. "Carolina?"

"No need to thank me, Danny."

"Yeah? Oh, okay, I was just wondering if you brought *me* anything from Laney's."

Jackson reaches for my hand as we walk down the hill in our backyard toward the river. "So you vanquished two dragons today. Sally Blankenship is headed out of town, and Mrs. Chilton is at home planning a nursery. Well done."

"I had time to think at Laney's and realized no one else was going to deal with Mrs. Chilton. She actually reacted better than I had imagined. Yes, it has been a good day, and now look at this."

Patches of bright green clover stand out from the dull green of old weeds and strips of red clay as we get to the row of trees along the riverbank. Echoing the green patches, patches of an impossibly gorgeous blue peep out as the burnished-gold clouds glide overhead. All the colors, the green, the blue, the gold, appear artificial, yet here it all is. Add a slow-flowing river reflecting the blue and gold and a weeping willow swaying in unison with the clouds, and you have something only found in a painting—or our backyard.

Jackson uses his free hand to part the willow branches. "Next week sunset will be an hour later, and we'll be headed for those long summer days."

"I can't wait. I'm so ready for spring. We've not had much snow this year, but it sure seems like it's been colder than usual." He chuckles, and I pull on his arm. "Or do I say that every year? Feels like something I say every year."

"Pretty much. But I agree, I'm ready for warmer days. Not sure I'll like working out in the summer heat, but maybe we'll make sure we have inside remodels for those months—or maybe I'll just set all my conference calls for the heat of the day."

"You're happy with the way it's all working out? Still good with staying part-time?"

"Yeah, I am. I like the balance, and I've decided I'm not ready to give up on engineering altogether. I do like not being on the jobsite so much, though." He stops before we exit the willow's canopy onto the riverbank, and he pulls me into a big bear hug. "I am really liking our life right now. Everything feels right."

I squeeze him and agree. "Let's be sure to enjoy it. Appreciate it."

He pulls back the green-and-gold curtain for me to step closer to the river, and we both stop as the limbs with their tiny leaves fall closed behind us. It's more like a painting than ever, and I drink it in, holding it all close because, as perfect as this moment is, we all know time doesn't stop.

Except in our memories.

Chapter 31

"Doesn't everything seem abnormally quiet?" I ask Bonnie Monday morning as we work on the latest boxes of books Andy bought for us this weekend at a big estate sale down in Atlanta. It's mostly romances and mysteries, but they are all very current and in high demand, so I want to get them on the shelves as soon as possible.

Bonnie lays her hands on the open book in front of her and sighs. "Yes. Getting my business going was so hectic that now it feels strange to just have a couple projects going—simple projects that are not under the thumb of someone like Peter Bedwell. He just makes everything so much harder."

I nod in agreement. "Missus has calmed down on the hourly proclamations, and everybody just seems hunkered down with their own business and businesses." I look up the stairs, where we can hear Shannon and Danny still getting ready for their day. "Shannon and Patty are nesting, and that's normal for pregnant ladies, but it almost feels like everyone else is nesting, too. Laney is almost as enthralled and preoccupied with The Club as she was with getting ready for Cayden. Ruby's Café is puttering along with their new venture of pies in the afternoon and Kimmy's hard work. Phoenix is busy with her catering, the juice bar, and the studio. Even up at Peter's law office, he's been too busy to mess with anyone. But…"

She cocks her head at me, then grins. "But... mentioning Shannon and Patty wasn't incidental. You feel like there's something coming. Something we all need to be ready for?"

"I do!" I exclaim, surprised that she gets it. Jackson was clueless when I tried to explain it to him over the weekend. "I'm not wishing away the calmness, but I feel expectant. Like, get everything ready for..." I sigh and lift another book to label. "I don't know what. Maybe it's Savannah's graduation. Or maybe I've just grown so used to things being in an uproar that I'm afraid to settle down? That would just be sad, wouldn't it? And a waste of the chance to be content."

"That would be sad, so let's decide to be content while we can. I know it won't be long before I'll be right up against a deadline with one of my decorating jobs at the same time things are crazy busy here, and Cal will be letting everything slip at the house because he's living on the golf course. I, we, should enjoy this down time!"

We laugh as I finish the last book. "I'll get these into the computer and onto the shelves. You can go back to your decorating doldrums. Thanks for your help. It was fun to visit and get this done." We both turn toward the stairs. "And just in time to welcome the Kinnocks. Good morning!"

"Good morning," Shannon says as she moves past us toward the cooler. "I have an arrangement Danny's going to take to the hospital this morning if you can spare him. I'll have it done in no time."

"No problem at all. I'll be here most of the day," I say, adding, "Who's in the hospital?"

"One of the Yeldin twins. She had an emergency appendectomy yesterday," Danny says as he stops at the table to look through the books we'd just labeled. "My dad is on the fire squad, and they got a call out to their house."

"Oh no. Wonder if Jackson knows? He was headed out there to work on the daycare this morning." I dial Jackson, and when he doesn't answer, I hang up and text him. "They're the new people out of town by the lake," I explain to Bonnie.

She nods. "I remember you talking about them." She asks Danny, "She's okay, isn't she?"

Danny shrugs. "I guess. The mom called and left Shannon a message last night about the flowers. My dad told me about the call last night when we talked. I like hearing about all the excitement. Maybe I should join the volunteer fire department."

My phone dings, and I read Jackson's text: "On a call, but I'll text Eddie and let you know what he says."

Bonnie asks, "What's his wife's name? I don't think I've heard you mention it."

"Barbara. She's nice, but we didn't really hit it off. Not like the guys. Eddie and Jackson have a great time together. I don't even think I have her phone number."

Shannon pipes up. "Everything must be fine or they wouldn't be sending her flowers. They'd be too upset. Unless it's a funeral, flowers usually come when things are looking up."

Bonnie heads back to her desk. "That's true. Well, there you go, Carolina. You were wanting something exciting to happen."

"But not like that. And I didn't say I wanted anything to happen. Just that I felt it could."

Danny claps his hands. "That sounds like the perfect intro for our announcement. When we came down the stairs you called us the Kinnocks, but that's not really true... yet." He holds his arms out to us. "You are both invited to our wedding this Friday night in the gazebo in the park."

"Really? Congratulations!" Bonnie and I both say. Then I add, "That seems awfully short notice."

Danny rolls his eyes. "Not according to Shannon's momma. She thinks we're pretty late, but I finally got my divorce and it's all good. She wants us married as soon as possible."

Shannon is arranging some pink and red flowers, so she doesn't look up at us as she explains, "My mom demands we get married this weekend, and lucky for us, no churches are available. I've always wanted an outdoor wedding."

"In March in north Georgia?" Bonnie tries, but Shannon shuts her down with a fierce look. Bonnie backs off graciously. "Thank you for the invitation. I will be there, and I'm happy to help however I can." She turns quickly and darts back to her desk.

"So is your mom doing it all?" I ask as I inch back to my table of books.

"It's going to be super simple. But I have to get this done and can't talk right now. Danny, come cut me a piece of ribbon."

He happily shrugs at me and lopes over to help his fiancée.

Looks like being out of town Friday might be a good plan, though maybe not a good idea.

Mondays are usually pretty slow around town, and today is no exception. Danny made the run to the hospital and reported the Yeldin girl to be doing fine and coming home soon. Shannon worked on her side of the shop and I worked on mine while Bonnie held down her decorating desk and made lots of phone calls. Danny only worked in the morning and then left to go do "wedding stuff."

I didn't ask.

Shannon took several phone calls from, I'm assuming, her mother.

Again, I didn't ask.

"Sorry," I say to the customer I'm helping when I can't hold a yawn back. "It always takes me a bit to get used to the time change."

I turn away from her for another yawn and to try and shake myself awake when I see a group coming out of AC's door and heading down the sidewalk. Delaney and Peter and her parents I recognize right off, and then I catch my breath mid-yawn and choke. Which makes me cough like I have a lung on fire. "Excuse me," I say, dashing toward the bathroom on the back wall to get a drink. I motion at Bonnie, who has swiveled around in her chair, to follow me.

As I drink a full paper cup of water and then fill another one, I manage to catch my breath and wheeze to her, "You're not going to believe who I just saw."

"What?" she whispers back.

"Who, not what. Gregory is in town."

She studies me for a moment, then shakes her head. "Who?"

"Gregory Duvall. Peter and Delaney's son."

CHAPTER 32

Laney doesn't even wait for me to finish saying, "Hello" into the phone.

"Are you heading home soon?" she asks. "A lady called wanting a room at Crossings, but she wouldn't give me any details, just said she'd be there at four o'clock. It was all very mysterious, so you have to get the lowdown. I gotta know what's going on."

"Yeah, I am. I mean, heading home soon. Jackson is still on the jobsite, so the house is empty, but I can be there by four. Is it just a room for her?"

"Like I said, no details. She was totally secretive. Hey, I've got to go. It's been hopping over here all day. Can't wait to hear the story. Call me tonight." And she hangs up.

I'm glad Laney's busy, but the bookstore has been super slow. Susie Mae came in after school and Bonnie will be here until she has a decorating appointment at five, so I was preparing to leave soon anyway.

"Hey guys, I'm going to go on home if that's okay with y'all."

Shannon nods and Susie Mae smiles big, looking up from our front table where she's putting away FM's old books. One of our regulars came in and spent a couple of hours looking through them and drinking coffee. He also gave Susie Mae a couple of chess tips. He says it's much nicer here than at the library, where all those kids are running around and where Ida

May won't let him bring in coffee. We all love the old men who visit and feel so comfortable here. Susie Mae treats them like royalty, and Danny has made them his best buddies.

Checking my watch as I leave out the back door, I see that I won't have time to stop by the grocery store if I want to be home by four, so Jackson will have to do it. It's a partly cloudy day with very little sunshine. Our temps are staying in the low fifties, and I'm chilled all the time, though some of that may be because I put away my winter sweaters and thick socks already. Spring really needs to hurry up and get here!

A silver compact car in the driveway tells me our new guest has already arrived. She gets out of her car as I pull in and then takes a suitcase out of the back seat. Closing the car door, she gives me a little nod and a smile as I park.

"Hello! I'm Carolina. Welcome to Crossings. Hope you weren't waiting long."

She shakes her head, then waits as I gather my things. I take a peek at her out of my peripheral vision. She's a little older than me—in her late fifties, maybe? She's not exactly tall and not exactly thin, very normal-sized. She has a short bob of silver hair and a nice, beige trench coat belted in place. As I come near, I think I've seen her somewhere before. That's confirmed when she sticks her hand out and says, "Good to see you again," though I still can't remember where I know her from.

She can tell. "You don't remember me. Augusta Duvall. We met at the wedding."

"Oh, yes! You're Gregory's mo—"

"Aunt," she interjects. "I'm his aunt." She motions up the porch steps. "You have a room available?"

"I do indeed. Let me get the door for you." As I assumed, the front door is unlocked, so I push it open, then move back toward her. "Let me carry your bag."

"No, thank you. I've got it." She easily climbs the stairs, suitcase in one hand and a tidy, black purse over her other shoulder. She passes me as I hold the door, and then I lead her to the kitchen table.

"Have a seat and I'll get your information." I dart to the small office that used to be a laundry room and bring back the registration form. "Laney said she didn't get any of your information. She's opening a new shop and is very busy." I try and put the blame on Laney. Surely this nice woman wasn't as secretive as Laney said.

Ms. Duvall pulls the small clipboard to her. "I didn't give her any information as I would prefer to work with only you. Delaney chose you to attend the wedding, so I must assume that she trusts you, as will I. I don't like everyone knowing my business."

Okay, so I was wrong. She concentrates on filling out the blanks while I put on a pot of coffee and make a couple of attempts at small talk, which all fall flat.

"I don't know my departure date. Is it all right if I leave that open?"

"Let me check." I look at our calendar in my phone. "Yes, we don't have all three rooms booked at the same time until after spring break and Easter, which is the first week of April."

"That should do fine. I'll write you a check for this week, and then we can revisit our arrangement over the upcoming weekend?"

"Sure," I say.

She immediately stands, saying, "Your rooms?"

"Do you have more luggage we can bring in?"

"No." She prompts me again, "Your rooms?"

I reach for her suitcase, but she beats me to it, so I lead her through the dining room and down the hall, telling her about Crossings and our railroad-themed rooms as we go. We look in the Southern Crescent and then the Chessie, but I take her into the Orange Blossom Special. It's the brightest and biggest of our rooms, so I plan on putting her there, but she only stays in it for a minute. She walks back out, crosses the hall, and enters the Chessie room.

She calls to me as I cross the hall behind her. "This is the room I'd like, if that's all right."

"Of course. Wherever you're more comfortable."

"Yes, it's very cozy." She sets her bag down and unties her coat. "I don't make a lot of demands and won't trouble you and your family."

"Okay. But don't hesitate to ask if you need anything." I back out of the room as she takes off her coat and hangs it in the closet. I feel very much as if I'm no longer needed in the room. Some guests want you to stay and chat, fluff the pillows, fix the curtains, show them the closet. Some don't. Plus I'm trying to digest what she's wearing.

"Carolina, I do need to ask you one thing."

"Sure." I step back inside the room as she comes to the door.

"It won't remain a secret for long that I'm here, but I'd prefer it not to be known all over, as is common in small towns such as Chancey."

"Of course. I won't mention it."

She starts to close the door, but I lift my hand to hold it open for a moment.

"If someone calls or comes here to see you...?" I let the question hang in the air between us.

She sighs. "As I said, it's not exactly a secret that I'm here. I just do not like being the subject of small-town gossip right off the bat. Thank you," she finishes as she pushes the door closed and me out of her room.

I release a sigh myself walking down the hallway and follow it with an opinion: "Good luck with not being gossiped about because Laney smells a mystery. Oh, and you're dressed like a nun."

CHAPTER 33

"Didn't you have her fill out the registration form? How can you not know anything about her? At least tell me what her name is!"

It's after dinner, and I roll my eyes at Jackson, who is seated down the couch from me. He gives me a smile as I go back to my phone. "Laney, stop. She requested privacy, and I'm giving it to her. Now, go play with Cayden and Shaw. Sounds like they both need your attention."

"You're right about that. But you know how I can't stand to not know something. It's killing me!" She half moans, half screeches that last line and I laugh.

"It's not killing you. I'm hanging up. Have a good night."

Jackson joins my laughing as he apparently heard her every word and groan. He raises his eyebrows. "I'm tempted to say Laney is one of a kind, except she's pretty common in small towns, Southern or not."

"You know it." I lower my voice. "I mean, if I didn't know who this mystery woman was, I'd be dying to know. Of course I wouldn't be as out in the open as Laney, but you know I'd be working every angle to figure it out."

He lowers his voice too. "She seems like a nice lady who just wants her privacy." He met Augusta when she came out to make a cup of tea. I invited her to eat dinner with us or to take a plate to her room, but she said she brought her food with her. That she eats very simply. She chatted with us about the house and the town for a while, but when her tea was ready, she said good night and went down the hall. I told her I'd close the door to the rest of the house and she'd have complete privacy, as we don't have any more guests until the weekend, an older couple who've stayed with us before.

Jackson peeks down the hall to make sure the door is still closed. Then he says, "When you told me she was dressed like a nun, I wasn't sure what you meant. Like just simple or plain, but short of the whole nun's habit from *The Sound of Music*, she totally looks like a nun. Down to the large cross necklace."

In the trench coat, all I could see were her sensible, black shoes and black stockings. That didn't register as anything unusual, but when she took off her coat, there was her straight, black skirt coming to mid-calf and a high-neck white blouse with a black cardigan over it. Her cross is a good three inches long and on a leather strap. I've tried to remember what she was wearing at the wedding, but I don't. However, I don't remember her being a nun. Do nuns wear fancy clothes for special occasions? Wait, she's not really a nun.

I do remember Delaney telling me she had an aunt who ran away from her father's overbearing family to join a convent even though the family wasn't Catholic. Then later she told me her aunt left the convent to raise Gregory over in South Carolina so Delaney could go back to college and live her life. Apparently the identity of Gregory's mother was only a thinly veiled secret in the family but he'd only found out that Peter is his father the night before Delaney and Peter were wed. Of course, Peter and Missus only found out about Gregory *at* the wedding.

So now Gregory and the woman who raised him are both in town.

Oh, if Laney only knew.

"You walked to town? This morning?"

Augusta is sitting at our kitchen table, a hot cup of tea in front of her and an air of peace about her. "I enjoy a long walk in the mornings. It's really a lovely little town. I bet the camellias were beautiful when they were blooming. I can't wait to go back and wander in that little field's daffodils when they are opened. You know the poem?"

"Wordsworth, right?"

She gives me a sweet smile. "I thought you'd know. 'And then my heart with pleasure fills, and dances with the daffodils.'"

"Oh, I haven't thought of that poem in forever. I know I have it in one of my books here."

She lifts her cup, but before she takes a sip, she says, "You own a bookstore. Tell me about it."

"Oh, it's not much. Mostly used books. It's in with the florist, which actually works quiet well. You'll have to come visit with us."

"I'd like that very much. Maybe later today. Will you be there after lunch?"

"Yes, I will." I stand. "As a matter of fact, I need to get my day started. Please feel free to help yourself to anything in the kitchen."

She sets her cup on the table and stands. "I would like a banana if that's okay. I'll be stocking up a few things at the store later today. I left in quite a hurry coming here yesterday." She frowns as she steps to the counter where the bananas are. "Gregory's plans for his spring break changed suddenly."

"He seems like a wonderful young man. I only met him for a short time at the wedding, but you should be proud."

She gives me a small nod and smile, but I see her chest swell with pride underneath her cross. Then she lets out a breath.

185

"He's a good boy—no, man. I've been honored to get to share so much of his life."

"He's lucky to have been so loved."

She sits and begins peeling her banana while I put together a lunch for myself. I can feel, as well as see, concern building in her. She takes a small bite and chews, then asks, "Can someone be loved too much?"

"Probably not if it's truly love. But so often it seems love gets confused with other things."

Her concern drops away, and she grins at me. I can't help but grin back at her sparkly, dark eyes and red cheeks. She seems almost like a different person this morning. "Oh, I knew we would get along, Carolina. Now, I don't want to hold you back. Go, go take care of all your duties. I will see you later at your shop. I need to go do my devotions." She stands, her cup in one hand, banana in the other. "Is it okay for me to take these to my room?"

"Of course. This is your home while you're here."

"Thank you. I'll finish them, do my devotions, and then I think a nap is in order." She turns to wink at me. "That *was* a long walk!"

CHAPTER 34

As the sun climbed higher in the sky, the less we saw of it. By the time I got to work, the clouds had thickened to a solid gray. However, my weather app says the rain isn't supposed to start until after lunch. Bonnie comes sailing in the front door looking prepared in a cute, hot-pink raincoat.

"Look at you, Miss Fashion Plate!" I say as Danny gives her an exaggerated wolf whistle.

She does a slow turn. "I decided I needed to stop looking like the schoolteacher I was and more like the interior designer I am! This has actually been hanging in my closet for a couple of years. Finally worked up the nerve to wear it." She tenderly hangs it on the coatrack. "Carolina, can I show you something at my desk?"

"Sure," I say, gladly leaving the books Danny and I are rearranging. Seems like that's all we ever do.

Before I get to her desk, Bonnie turns to me, her eyes large and her mouth dropped. "I met Camille and Thompson LaMotte." She's barely speaking above a whisper, so I pull a chair up closer to her desk

"Where?"

"At the Bedwell House. You know those rooms I've been redecorating? The ones past FM's library?" I nod and she takes a breath. "They're for them! There's a bedroom and a sitting room with the bath across the hall. I thought it was a tad different than the rest of the house, but Delaney was so sure of what she wanted, I didn't question her. It's more of a, well, a country home instead of the formal, darker feel of the rest of the house. I like it, but it felt odd. Until today. This is going to be their home away from home. Delaney is giving them free rein to finish the decorating as they wish. She and Peter weren't even there this morning. She called me last night and asked me to be at the house at eight this morning for the final instructions. I had coffee with Camille and Thompson—well, he was busy on his computer, but every so often he threw in an opinion."

"Wow. Wonder what Missus thinks?"

Bonnie shrugs. "No idea. She wasn't anywhere around either."

I lean closer. "Did you see Gregory?"

She nods quickly and her words rush on. "He has a room upstairs near Peter and Delaney's room. It's actually Peter's old room. He told me when I was redecorating it that Delaney wanted it left much like it was, and he thought that was so sweet, her wanting to think of him growing up there." Our wide eyes match as she says, "But she was actually getting it ready for his son!"

We both sit back as she takes a breath and we gather our thoughts. Of course my thoughts center on what it means for Augusta Duvall being at Crossings indefinitely. But I am not, am not, saying anything to Bonnie. Despite how much I want to.

Danny pops his head around the corner, holding my phone. "Hey, your phone was ringing. You laid it over where we were working." He hands it to me and then wanders toward Shannon's worktable, where she's picking out flowers for her wedding. Which is what she's been doing all morning. I'm assuming she has no other orders because if she does, well, I might need to hand out the number to 1-800-FLOWERS.

As my phone comes to life, I see who the call was from. "Oh, it was Missus. Let me call her back." Bonnie nods and turns away to open her notebook on her desk.

"Hi, sorry I missed your call."

"I need to talk to you. I'm headed to Ruby's and have exactly thirty minutes."

"I'll try, but you know—"

"I'm sure Bonnie explained what is going on at my house by now, so quit playing hard to get. You know you're dying to know what I know."

She hangs up, and I look up to see Bonnie grinning. I can't help but grin too. "You could hear her?"

"Yep. Now hurry and get down there. Go!" She shoos me away and I jump up.

I pat Shannon's table as I pass. "I'll be back in about thirty minutes."

Danny and Shannon both acknowledge me with a quick "okay," then return to discussing natural spring flowers versus more formal arrangements. I guess being a florist makes choosing your own wedding flowers difficult, especially with less than a week to do them. All I know is I'm staying far, far away from that worktable this week.

CHAPTER 35

"Someone staying up at your place?" Ruby asks as she slides into the booth across from me.

"Why? And did you bring the coffee with you?" I lift my empty cup at her.

"Shoot!" She looks around, but Libby is busy with a table full of young moms near the front. "Be right back."

I search out the front window. Come on, Missus, hurry up. Ruby will be hard to brush off, but I'd love to know what she knows that's making her curious. No one else this morning has mentioned our guest. Even Laney is lying low, though I assume that's because she's busy doing her own detecting.

Ruby stops to do other refills on her way back, and Missus beats her to our table. Just barely. Madam Mayor takes her seat, and after a quick second glance to register the scowl on Ruby's face, she turns her cup right side up, then looks down at her phone, ignoring Ruby. I've been to this rodeo before and know my wishful thinking that Ruby will ignore Missus and go away is just a waste of brain cells.

Ruby pours the mayor's coffee, and I see her wanting to poke a bear named Missus, but with a grunt she turns to me. "So? Do you have a new guest?"

I push my cup toward her. "Why?"

Her eyes narrow and she smirks. "So you do. Who is he, and

what's he doing out at the break of dawn, looking in windows downtown?"

"There is no man staying with us."

A woman at the table across from us joins the conversation. "There's a peeping tom in town? What have the police said?"

Ruby turns, tops off the woman's cup, and says, "I didn't say peeping tom. He was walking along Main Street here this morning when I got in. Downright creepy, me here by my lonesome at zero-dark-thirty." She turns back to me with raised eyebrows and a lifted chin, challenging me to fill in some details. When I just sip my coffee, she sighs and plows on. "I didn't call the police in case it's some guest of Carolina's and Jackson's. I watched him head that way out of town." She steps back from the table to look into the kitchen area. "Libby, come here. Tell us what you saw."

Great. I look over at Missus, who is still studying her phone, but I can see it's just the home screen, which tells me she's listening and interested. I yell back at Libby, "Might as well bring some muffins when you come."

Ruby looks down at us and our two lonely coffee cups. "Oh, y'all ain't got muffins. I been a mite distracted. And look at Missus, staring at her home screen, acting like she ain't listening." Ruby cackles, then grabs the basket out of Libby's hand as she approaches. She takes on a serious, ominous tone. "Okay, there's your muffins. Tell them, Libby."

Of course the whole restaurant is listening by now—seeing as there's a crazed peeping tom roaming around town. One man hollers, "Talk loud, Libby. We all need to hear this."

Libby wrings her hands, now empty of muffins and coffee pots. "Well, I didn't think much of it until Ruby told me about the peeping tom, but this person was out by the daffodils. Y'all know? The daffodils the city planted out in the triangle going up the hill. They just keep spreading, and I'm thinking we should look into thinning them out. Who here knows if daffodils need to be thinned out?"

Of course there are daffodil experts at Ruby's, so the debate jumps to life. I hope this means we'll forget the peeping tom, but then Ruby does that two-fingers-in-the-mouth whistle and everything stops. "Libby, what was the vagrant doing?"

Even better—now it's a vagrant.

"Well, he was a-looking at the daffodils, and they aren't even fully open. Then straightened up and just stood there looking back toward town. Back this very direction!" she exclaims with a shudder.

The only things missing are a hockey mask and a bloody machete to round out her dramatic retelling.

Okay, I've got to try and rein this in. "So all we know is a person was taking an early morning walk? Right? That's all."

Ruby heaves a sigh. "Carolina, bless your heart, but you're completely missing the point. I didn't know him!" Then she sweeps out her arm, complete with a pointed finger directed toward Libby. "Libby didn't know him!"

She lifts both hands, palms exposed, in surrender to the undebatable fact that the town of Chancey is under attack.

Missus sniffs and slowly shifts in her seat to face Ruby and her concerned citizens. "Thank you, ladies, for your reports. I will handle this with the chief of police as soon as I return to city hall, which will be in exactly eighteen minutes." With a little nod, she dismisses the room and turns back to face me. "Ruby, I'd like that blueberry muffin heated. Thank you. Now, Carolina, to our business."

Ruby grabs the basket of muffins and stomps away.

Missus stares at me. "So you obviously have a guest you're protecting for some reason I will have to think about at another time. Now, tell me what Bonnie told you."

"Why?" Seems that's all I've said this morning.

She opens her mouth, then shuts it, finishing with a small

nod. "You are correct. I don't have time for all your denial and obfuscation. Here's what you need to know. My grandson is in town for the week. His LaMotte grandparents have had the unfair advantage of knowing him his entire life. I have a very limited amount of time to connect with him, and well…" Up to this point she has been her normal, high-handed, condescending self. Then it's like she has a hairball stuck in her throat. She's not exactly gagging but is choking a bit.

Wait! I gasp. "Are you choking?" I lunge forward and try to remember how to give someone the Heimlich, but she glares at me.

"I'm not choking. Quit embarrassing me!" She looks around and sees she's not the center of attention, then clears her throat. "I've noticed you seem to have a way with young people."

"Well, I'm kinda forced to as I birthed a few of them and we can't afford boarding school." Libby drops off two plates with warm muffins, and I sit down after grabbing mine. "But okay. What's that mean for you?"

"I believe it's your lack of standards and willingness to be goofy. However, neither of those devices are in my wheel-house." She takes her muffin, cuts it in half, and applies a tiny bit of butter to each half. "Honestly, neither is in the realm of possibility for me."

Taking a large bite of muffin, I mumble, "Gee, thanks."

"So what I need from you is an introduction to the other young people of Chancey for Gregory. He's barely twenty, so even Savannah and Jenna will do. Then there's Alex and Angie, not exactly role models in their personal lives, but very hard-working and creative. Of course I'd normally hold a function like this at my house, but as you have been made aware, it's now the enemy camp."

I chuckle. "Really? The enemy camp? I thought you got along well with the LaMottes."

She leans forward. "They played me and my son for fools."

Her high-hatted, superior facade drops and she's angry. Really, honestly angry. "And now they've moved into my home. I will not accept this as surrender. I will show Gregory that his Bedwell roots are just as worthy as the LaMotte ones!" The fierceness of her words is echoed in her face, and I'm taken aback.

"Missus, calm down. First thing about kids, they don't like being fought over. They don't want to be pawns in some power struggle. Now, yes, I will host something this week for the kids to meet Gregory—no pressure, though. We'll do pizza or sloppy joes, something easy and nonthreatening. And it will be up to the kids how long it lasts or if they even come." I pull out my phone. "Do you have Gregory's phone number? I'll text him and run it by him."

"Of course I have my grandson's phone number. But I will set it all up." She checks her watch. "I have to go."

I hold my hand out at her. "No. We are not doing it your way. Send me his number or I'm not helping you out."

"Carolina," she says with a sigh. "Please don't be difficult. This is *my* event for *my* grandson. I will arrange the food and all that goes with that. I only need your house."

"And my daughter and her friends. I'm serious that…" Then, over her shoulder, I watch as Augusta Duvall looks in the window and heads to the door. Missus catches me looking and swings around to see what I'm watching.

"What is she doing here?"

We watch as the woman I've come to think of as The Nun smiles at the table of young moms, smiles at the other tables, and then smiles at me.

"Carolina!" she says. "They told me at the bookshop you were here. And Missus! So nice to see you again. May I join you?"

"Hi, Augusta," I say. "Sure, but Missus has to leave. She has important city business that can't wait."

"No. No, I'm fine for a bit longer, but sit there next to Carolina so I can leave in a minute. We were just talking about a little gathering to introduce Gregory to some other young people in Chancey."

"What a great idea! How can I help?" she asks as she slides in next to me. She has on the same outfit as yesterday, but instead of her trench coat, she has on a short, black windbreaker, unzipped so that her high-neck blouse and large crucifix can easily be seen. Missus is blinking at her and probably doing as I had done, trying to remember what she wore to the wedding.

After giving her a once- and then a twice-over, Missus blurts out, "You're a nun?"

Augusta laughs as she takes the cup Libby is offering her, along with a stumbling series of questions. "Can I get you, uh, some coffee, ma'am, uh, or is it sister? I don't think I've ever met a nun. Do you eat muffins?"

"Of course," Augusta says. "I've heard these are the best muffins around. But can I ask for a cup of hot tea instead of coffee?"

Libby just nods and then backs away. I think she's trying to bow or something as she leaves.

Missus mumbles, "That one watches too much television. So you were saying..."

"Oh, um, I was saying I do like muffins?" Her dark eyes are serious, but I think there's a bit of a twinkle in them. Is she messing with Missus? Oh, I'm liking her more and more.

"No, about being a nun?"

"That's right! You asked if I'm a nun. Well, I'm not. Not exactly. I left the order to raise Gregory, but I feel more comfortable serving God as if I'm still a nun. A quiet life of service and devotion." She turns to beam at Libby as she tiptoes up to us. "Oh, thank you so much. The muffins looks wonderful, and that's the brand of tea I use too."

Libby subtly bows her head and backs away.

Missus groans, "Oh, good lord."

"Yes. He is good. Very good," Augusta says with just a bit of side-eye in my direction.

Oh, she is most definitely messing with Missus. I take advantage of the pause. "So I was just telling Missus that if I had Gregory's number, I'd reach out to him and run the idea of a little get-together by him."

"What a great idea." She nods at me and then Missus. "Just like any young person, he doesn't like to be bossed around." Dunking her tea bag a couple of times, then putting it to the side, she grins. "Oh, I know! Tell him you'll be serving chicken bog, and he won't be able to stay away."

Missus recoils, then shudders. "What is that? I wasn't happy with Carolina's suggestion of pizza or sloppy joes, but bog?"

"Oh, it's an old South Carolina dish. Mine and Gregory's favorite."

"I think I've heard of it, but I don't know how to make," I admit.

"Not a thing to worry about. I'll buy everything we need at the store today, and I'll make it. If I can use your kitchen?"

"Of course."

I see the light dawning in Missus's eyes.

"You're staying at Crossings."

"Possibly," Augusta dismisses the question. "Now, Carolina, how many do you think we'll have?"

Missus won't be put off that easily. "Does Gregory know you're in town?"

Augusta gives a little sigh and delays her first sip of tea as she sets her cup back down. "He will as soon as he hears chicken bog is being served."

"Okay. I have to leave. I'm already late as it is." Missus scoots across her seat and at the end says, "So you can give Gregory's number to Carolina?"

"Of course. It was so good to see you again, Missus."

"You as well," Missus says as she stands. "I also look forward to tasting this chicken bog of yours. If my grandson enjoys it, I'm sure I will also."

"But you're not coming." Augusta's flat tone makes it evident she's not asking a question. "It's for the young people. For Gregory. Carolina and I will be there, but only in the kitchen."

Missus sputters, "But it was my idea."

"For Gregory. It's for Gregory, right?"

Maybe it's the steel in her voice or the light hitting the crucifix on Augusta's chest, but Missus finally nods and does her own weird little version of backing away.

Ms. Duvall lifts her steaming tea and blows on it. "I gave up my vocation in the church for the vocation of raising that boy." She takes a sip and swallows, one eyebrow lifted. "I've fought bigger dragons than her."

CHAPTER 36

"Are you the peeping tom?" Ruby asks, arriving at our table before Missus is out the door. She slides in across from us.

Augusta presses her lips together and tilts her head. "Now there is something I've never been called." She sticks her hand out across the table. "Augusta Duvall. You looked very busy this morning as I ambled past, so I didn't want to stop and interrupt you. Besides, I cannot refuse baked goods, so I knew we'd be meeting soon!"

Ruby sticks her skinny arm out to meet Augusta's. "Nice to meet you. Are you some kind of a nun?"

"No. But thanks for asking! Are you Catholic?"

Ruby jerks. "Oh, no, ma'am. Baptist on both sides. Daddy's people were a Primitive Baptist, but Momma took us to the one in town, and I still belong there. Don't rightly know many Catholic folks. So you ain't in Chancey for no church function. What brings ya here?"

"God sent me," Augusta says as solemnly as if she were giving last rites.

Ruby goes still. More still than I've ever seen her. Then she jumps a mile high when Libby yells, "Ruby! Timer going off. These pies ready to come out?"

"Gotta go," she says as she bustles out of the booth, practically tripping herself to get past us.

I turn in my seat to face Augusta. "What are you doing? Last night you told me you didn't want people knowing you were here, and now you're doing everything possible to draw attention to yourself."

She smiles and shrugs. "God did send me. Big push in the back when Gregory told me he'd been instructed to come stay with his family here in Chancey for spring break." She rolls her eyes—just a tiny bit. "Family, my foot. And remember, I said I knew it would get out that I was here. I just wanted to arrive on my own terms. Like right now Missus is trying to decide how my being here benefits her. Should she tell? Should she not?" She scoots out our side of the booth, then claims the spot across from me as she taps on her phone.

"I just sent you Gregory's number. Text him and tell him you want to get some young people together. He remembers you from the wedding." She leans forward. "He said you were the normal one. Be sure and mention you'll be serving chicken bog, but don't mention me."

While I write my text, she finishes her tea. I read it to her and hit send as she slides out again. I look up. "You're leaving?"

"Yes, off to do some exploring, then a trip to the grocery store. I need to expand my list if I'm making chicken bog."

My phone dings and I look at it. "He says that sounds great and suggests tomorrow night."

"Perfect. Tomorrow it is. I'll see you back at Crossings and save my extended trip to your bookshop for another day. Too-dle-oo!"

Ruby's is much quieter than it was when I came in. The moms are gone. The old men are gone. There's a couple at a front table who look like they're in no hurry as they examine a map and a guidebook. They were in Blooming Books earlier, but they didn't buy anything, so I didn't get a chance to talk to them. There are two local ladies working on something, probably for the women's historical society; I saw them talk to

Missus for a moment as she left, and I know they are both high up in that organization. Missus has left all her positions on town clubs—well, not really left them. She declared a temporary emeritus status while she holds the office of mayor. Now Missus gets to tell her clubs what to do, but she doesn't have to do any of the work.

Libby is working on shifting the tables from coffee and muffins to pie for this afternoon Kimmy is still handling everything herself in the afternoons. She hasn't found someone to help out, but I'm not sure she's looking that hard anymore.

It's actually very peaceful, sitting here sipping my coffee.

I don't think I've ever associated Ruby's with peacefulness.

While it's nice and quiet, I text Savannah. Yes, I know she's in school, but she's a senior and she'll want to know first about the party at our house tomorrow. I send another text telling her to invite some of her friends. I also reach out to Anna and Will along with Patty and Andy. Yeah, they're older than Gregory, but I can watch Francie, and the four of them can act as the older young people. Give the group a little maturity. Susan's oldest, Leslie, is closer to Gregory's age, but I don't think she's home on break from the University of Georgia this week.

I start to text Susan and ask about Leslie, but decide to just call her as I walk back to the shop.

"Hey there. You busy? I was just wondering if Leslie is home on break."

"No. It's next week, and she's going to Florida with some friends. Listen, what's this I'm hearing about someone peeping in your windows last night?"

"Just ignore that. I'll tell you about it later. How are you doing?" Laney and I have been a bit worried about Susan. She's acting completely listless, uninterested in everything.

"I'm okay."

"What have you been doing?"

"Just work. Nothing much. Have you seen that British baking show on Netflix? I went back and started at the beginning this weekend. I'm already to season four."

I lean against the outside wall of the shop, around the corner from the front window. "I didn't think you were a big TV person."

"What else is there to do?"

"Have you talked to Silas?"

"No. That's over. It's Griffin or no one. Griffin or hours and hours of television." Her voice gets husky, and I can hear that she's about to cry.

"Have you talked to Griffin lately?"

"Just arguing with him over the kids' spring breaks. He didn't think Leslie should go to Florida, just like he didn't want Susie Mae to go to the cabin with Savannah." She lets out a cynical laugh. "Looks like he was right about that, huh?" She pauses. "Maybe I should make Leslie cancel and just come home. Then she can sit on the couch beside me complaining about how unfair life is, watching television, and eating Cheetos."

"Susan, you don't sound good. Listen, come have dinner with us tonight. Okay? Grant will probably already be there working on their depot project for school. I'll invite Susie Mae when she gets to the shop later. I don't know what we're having yet, but it beats sitting at home watching people in England cooking in a big, white tent."

"Oh, you *have* watched it?"

I push away from the wall and laugh. "Of course. Remember what a sad case I was when I moved here? Nothing like watching strangers make bowls and bowls of buttercream icing to make you feel better."

"Did you know there's a nun in your backyard?" Susan asks.

She came into the house still dressed from work, poured herself a glass of white wine, and is now leaning against the glass doors going onto the back deck.

"Yep. She's staying in the Chessie room. Her name is Augusta."

"Oh!" Susan stands up straight. "Peter's son's mom—or no, aunt, right?"

"Yes. Who told you?"

"Laney. She didn't mention the nun outfit. She's also put out with you, but you probably knew that. Laney doesn't hold silent grudges."

"No, she doesn't. She's notified me several times today that she's not going to tell me any more secrets since I wouldn't tell her who Augusta was."

We both laugh. "As if she could help herself," Susan says. "So, is she nice?"

"Very."

"What's she looking at out there?"

"The garden. She said she's always wanted to garden, but she's not sure if she can." I set the pot of peeled potatoes on the stove to boil, but watch Susan out of the corner of my eye. My friend is studying Augusta, and her posture is slowly straightening.

She sets her wine glass down and puts her hand on the doorknob. "Think I'll go introduce myself."

"Good idea."

I wash my hands and watch them meet through the window over the sink. The garden area hasn't been cleaned up to get ready for planting because, well, because I don't plan on planting anything. The brown stalks are mostly weeds, but Susan is pointing out the row of jumbled, old tomato vines on the front row. Those were planted by and abandoned by Bryan. We really don't eat that many tomatoes.

"Anything I can help with?" Jackson asks, coming up from

the basement. "The kids are playing a video game until we call them for supper. They've about finished their project." He comes to stand behind me and sees what I'm watching. "Hmm, Susan and Augusta. Seems like they might hit it off."

I turn to face him. "Yeah, I thought they might be a good match. Kind of like meat loaf and mashed potatoes."

He kisses my nose, then wraps me in a hug. "Is that what we're having? I love your meat loaf."

"I know you do. Have I told you lately I love having you home to cook for?"

He pulls back and studies me. "No. I don't believe you have said that. Do you mean it?"

I hug him tight and laugh. "Well, I do right now."

CHAPTER 37

"I'll get it," Augusta says, and she's out of her seat before the doorbell has stopped ringing. We're through with dinner and discussing whether to have dessert now or in a bit. Bryan and Grant are the only ones vehemently on the side of having it now.

"Gussie! I knew you'd be here!" We hear a young man say from the living room. Jackson stands up and steps to the dining room's doorway while Savannah, Susie Mae, Susan, and I look at each other, smiles growing. Gregory's here.

"Boys, start cleaning up the table. Maybe we'll go ahead and have dessert," I say, but then I hold a hand out. "Or wait, maybe he'll want some dinner."

"No, ma'am. Thanks, but I've already eaten." Gregory comes into the room, his aunt on his arm.

Without even looking at the newcomer, Bryan speaks up as he hauls off a stack of plates. "Hi, I'm Bryan. My mom made this crazy chocolate cake for dessert. You're gonna want some of that, right?"

Gregory laughs and nods as Jackson shakes his hand. "Welcome. Jackson Jessup. I'm Carolina's husband."

The young man then comes to my side and bends down to hug my shoulders. "Great to see you again. I'm so glad my aunt is here with you." He looks around. "This is a really great house.

And you can walk out on that bridge? Do trains still run by here?"

Augusta laughs. "Always with the questions! I think we'd all love to have you join us, so let me introduce you. This is Susan Lyles and her daughter Susie Mae. Her son, Grant, is the young man who just took a load of dishes to the kitchen with Bryan. That is Savannah, Carolina and Jackson's daughter. She's a senior. Y'all have figured out this is Gregory Duvall, I assume."

Jackson has brought another chair to the table for Gregory, so we all get comfortable as Bryan and Grant finish clearing the table. Finally Bryan calls, "Can we bring in the cake?"

I roll my eyes and groan. "Give me a minute. I'm going to make a pot of decaf coffee. Anyone else want milk? Or hot tea?"

Augusta gets up to join me. "I'm going to make a cup of hot tea. Susan, would you like a cup of that tea I was telling you about?"

"Sure. Can I help?"

"No, no. I'll just get it from my room." She pats her nephew's shoulder as she passes him, asking over her shoulder if I'd put some water on to boil.

In the kitchen I see that the boys have stacked the dishes beside the sink. But that's all they did, so while the coffee brews, I scrape them clean to load the dishwasher and instruct the boys to take the saucers and clean forks to the table. They are anxious for the chocolate cake they smelled baking earlier, so they are very willing workers. Plus, they've heard me call it wacky, so they are intrigued.

Augusta appears at my side. "Susan seems like a very nice lady who is going through a hard time."

"Yes. You're right. So, what's the special tea?"

"Oh, just some chamomile and mint tea I have from a delightful little tea shop near home. It's not really that special, but it helps calm and soothe me, and I sense that she needs to treat herself with care."

We smile at each other, knowing that's exactly what she needs. "Sounds perfect," I say.

"Anything else, Mom? Want me to cut the cake?" Bryan asks as he and Grant come back into the kitchen.

Augusta meets them in the middle of the room. "So this depot you two were talking about at dinner is a real place? Here in town? Is it possible to get a tour?"

Grant laughs. "It's not big enough to need a tour, but it's pretty cool. Peter got us involved. He used to care about the depot, but he's kind of let it go. Now that he thinks he's a big shot, he doesn't think it's as cool as it used to be."

"Oh, Peter Bedwell?" she asks, but I notice she lowers her voice and turns away from the dining room.

"Yeah. He worked on it when he first came back to town, but that was a long time ago," Bryan says. "Coffee's done. I'll take it in. We took everything else in there already."

I wipe my hands and then reach for Susan's cup of tea. Augusta carries her own. She chuckles. "Your son and his friend sure are excited about this cake. It must be delicious."

"I think it's more the name that's got them excited." I motion for her to go ahead of me, and then I set Susan's tea down in front of her. "It's called 'Wacky Cake.'"

Gregory leans back and grins. "Well, now I'm interested."

"Savannah and Susie Mae, y'all make sure everyone has coffee or milk, and I'll serve the cake while I tell you about it. It's from the time of the Depression when folks had a hard time getting eggs, butter, and milk, so this doesn't use any of those. But it does have vinegar in it!"

Savannah wrinkles her nose. "Vinegar, like the stuff we use to dye eggs at Easter? That stuff stinks."

"Yes, but it makes a delicious cake. I promise."

We're all quiet for the initial tastes, then quiet because we're busy eating.

Augusta nods. "I think I've had this but with a chocolate icing. This caramel icing is much better in my opinion. So, girls, you'll be trying my chicken bog tomorrow night, right?"

Both sets of blue eyes swing from her to Gregory, but the mouths below the wide stares stay shut. He laughs out loud. "I already told them about the chicken necks and boiled okra in it. They can't wait!"

I sputter. "What? That's not what…"

"Gregory!" his aunt admonishes him. "You tell these young ladies the truth this minute. One day I'm going to make you eat chicken necks and boiled okra and see how you like it." She narrows her eyes at him, but then smiles. "Girls, it's delicious. You'll love it. Won't they, Gregory? Nothing more than chicken and rice and sausage. You like all three of those, right?"

Susie Mae nods brightly and winks at Gregory. "I knew he was fooling with us. I knew all along." Susie Mae is a little mature for her age and has gotten most of her flirting lessons from her aunt Lacey. I watch that register with Augusta, and it's like seeing her open a notebook and make a note.

Savannah just shrugs and takes another bite of cake. "I'm sure it'll be good. Where are you from in South Carolina, Miss Augusta?"

Gregory interjects, "Oh, she's not from South Carolina. She's very particular about that. She's a Georgia girl. She just moved there to raise me out from under the nose of my grandparents." He stretches his eyebrows high. "And that was before we even knew about Grandmissus."

That stops the conversation faster than chicken necks and boiled okra. Augusta clears her throat. "Well, Gregory, why don't we lay all our dirty laundry out on the table first thing?" She takes a sip of her tea and then give an apologetic grimace. "But of course he only says that because I've said it to him so often. Yes, I'm a Georgia girl. No, more than that, I'm an Atlanta girl. ITP. Inside the Perimeter. I was raised to think nothing good came from outside that circle of asphalt. Beyond it was a barren wilderness of wild animals and barbaric hillbillies." She swallows and takes a deep breath. "But I found out differently."

Jackson saves the conversation, which has been teetering on the edge of awkward. "My mother recently bought a house near Beaufort, South Carolina. She's loving it."

"Oh, that's on the coast. Nice," Gregory says. "I was raised in Aiken, South Carolina, just over the border from Augusta, Georgia. I think Gussie liked being near a town having her name." He lifts his phone off the table. "Sorry, but I've got to go. I told them I just needed some fresh air and didn't mention I was actually coming all the way up here. They like to keep track of me. He laughs and shrugs. "The wacky cake was delicious, and tomorrow will be fun. Nice to meet all y'all."

He gets up and the rest of us do, too. His aunt says she'll walk him to the car, and I notice that during the goodbyes Grant and Bryan quietly slip away. I'm sure they feel they've met their quota of cleanup this evening. "Girls, you go on. Susan and I will finish this up."

"Susie Mae, we're leaving in thirty minutes, okay? I'm sure your brother still has homework."

The girls chatter all the way up the stairs, and I can already hear the topic is, as I expected, Gregory Duvall. I mean, that's what I plan on talking about until Augusta comes back. I quickly say, "I'm surprised how he doesn't seem bothered at his grandparents keeping track of him. He seems like such a level-headed, relaxed young man. So, what do you think?"

Susan sighs. "He's much younger than he acted at the wedding reception. He was buttoned-up and nervous that night. I don't think he cracked a smile once. Of course I wasn't in a great mood either, seeing as Griffin had just told me he was dating Athena."

"He does seem young. Younger than I was thinking," I say.

We carry our loads into the kitchen, and as we sit them

down, she sniffles. "Probably because she's so young. Makes him feel young."

I turn to her confused. "Augusta?"

"Athena. It's like he's a young father again. Did I tell you I found out why he wants Leslie to come home next week? Athena's going to take her to tour the vet school at North Carolina State. It's like the fourth best vet school in the nation, and of course it's Athena's alma mater. She was just there, what, ten years ago? And she knows someone in admissions, so the two of them are supposed to go up there. Can you believe that?" She's practically vibrating in her sadness, like a just plucked guitar string.

"Oh, honey, no." I reach over to pull her into a hug. "No, I can't."

Her sniffles become small sobs as she relaxes just a bit in my arms. "And it's always been Leslie's dream school."

When we hear Augusta come in the front door, Susan pulls away from me and hurries back into the dining room.

Our guest strides into the well-lit kitchen. "Well, apparently Missus decided to not say anything about me being here. He had an early dinner with the LaMottes—my brother and sister-in-law—and I wasn't mentioned. I guess that's not too surprising, as they wouldn't be in on Chancey gossip. How would they have heard? But doesn't it strike you as funny that Peter and Delaney didn't mention it to him at some point during the day? Surely they heard."

I try to shake off Susan's worry and focus on Augusta's. "I don't know. Peter is pretty obtuse about anything that isn't, well, what he's decided is happening. And Delaney is new. I'm kind of her closest confidante, and well, even that is a 'not so much' kind of situation. Were Peter and Delaney at dinner with them?"

"Gregory said no, they weren't invited. It was just him and his grandparents. Thompson and Camille have always liked that best—no icky reminders of unwed parents, half-nun aunts, or paternal relatives having any sort of claim on him. They like things nice and compartmentalized." She dusts her hands together. "Out of sight, out of mind."

I step into the dining room, where Susan has gathered our napkins and is sitting in a chair with her back to the kitchen. "Are you okay?" I ask, laying a hand on her shoulder.

"I'm fine. I texted Griffin that I agree with him. Leslie should go to Raleigh." She sighs and her voice shudders as she says, "With Athena."

Pulling up a chair, I sit down and hold her hands. "It'll be okay. It's just for a few days, right?"

She nods, then holds up her phone to show me a text with a lot of smiley faces and exclamation points. "It's from Leslie. Her dad lost no time in telling her."

"Oh." I read a couple of lines, but it's pretty easy to see she's excited even without the words. "I guess that's good."

"Yeah. I don't remember Leslie ever using an emoji." She lets out a sad chuckle. "She's always so serious, and being a vet is the only thing she's ever wanted." Taking a deep breath, she squeezes my hands and then stands. "But her little brother cares nothing for school, so I need to get my other two children home. Dinner was just wonderful. Exactly what I needed."

"Here's the tea and an extra tea strainer," Augusta says as we come into the kitchen. She holds up a small bag.

"Oh, I don't know how to do that," Susan objects. "Besides, I can't take the tea you brought from home."

"Yes, you can and you are! Google it, how to brew tea. You need to be good to yourself. Little practices like brewing a cup of tea from real leaves is a good start."

Susan takes the bag, then opens the basement door and calls for Grant. I walk to the stairs and call to Susie Mae up in Savannah's room. It doesn't take long before the three Lyles are out the door. Jackson challenges Bryan to a video game, and they take another piece of cake downstairs with them to split. Savannah never left her bedroom, and so, once again, it's only Augusta and me standing in the darkened living room.

She asks, "Is Susan okay? I take it she wants her husband back?"

"Yeah, that's pretty much it. But..."

"But you don't think that's going to happen."

"No. The woman he's with is, well, probably good for him. She seems to really appreciate him, and he's happy with her from what I can see. And honestly, Susan is the one that left him. I don't think he'll get over that."

"Most men wouldn't."

I collapse onto the couch. "I don't think I could. Especially with it being as public as it was."

She walks past me and the couch to perch on the arm of the chair. "But she can't go back and change any of that. She can only go forward."

"Yes." Looking up at her I can see she has something she wants to say. Her foot is swinging, her lips are pursed, and her eyes are focused on her hands, which are lying in her lap. I'm exhausted, so I'm not going to try to guess whatever subject she has in mind for discussion. Except I can't help but do just that. Gregory and Missus? Or Gregory and his father? Susan and Griffin's marriage, or lack thereof? Her brother moving into his own wing at the Bedwell House? Wait, does she even know about that? I'm not sure. I close my eyes to go back over my day and think of who knows which part of what. Then she shifts around and clears her throat. I look up at her and smile, waiting to see which direction we'll be taking.

She smiles back at me and pats her knee a couple of times. "So. Is Savannah dating anyone?"

Chapter 38

"Do I think Susan would want to go with you? Uh, I, uh…" I stutter to a stop. Athena sits beside me at Ruby's counter, waiting for an answer. "With you and Leslie?" I squeak. "To the vet school?"

"Yeah. Griffin says no way, but why not?"

Ruby's huff can be heard from three feet away, where she's ringing up the muffins I'm taking to the bookshop. Ruby knows why not. I know why not. Griffin knows why not. My question is, Why should I have to explain it to Athena? She's a bright woman. "Are those ready, Ruby? I really need to get back."

Ruby brings the white paper bag down the counter to where we are. I have a twenty out ready for her to take, but she ignores it. Sitting like this, directly below her, she appears even more ornery than usual. Her pink T-shirt has strawberries on it, with black, glittery seeds and yellow bow ties on each of them. It advertises a strawberry farm down where her daughter, Jewell, now lives in Florida. I notice the berry's googly eyes are on my eye level and are still swinging back and forth from her sudden stop. When I look up, I see Ruby's eyes aren't swinging back and forth. They are lasered in on the wide, pretty eyes next to me—complete with varied colors of eyeshadow and abnormally long lashes. Along with full makeup, there's another fancy scarf wrapped loosely around Athena's neck, mimicking the messy bun that is a study in putting a whole lot of effort into effortless style.

In her gravelliest voice, with a little sassy neck motion, our local muffin purveyor says, "I have just one question. Will y'all have two beds in that hotel room? One for Susan and her daughter, and one for you and her husband?"

Okay, I *really* have to go now. I grab the bag, drop the twenty on the bar, and leave. I blame this on all those cute movies and books about small towns, which convince people like Athena to move here. They don't tell you about the Rubys. They don't tell you the important stuff.

"I've got muffins!" I announce as I hurry in the shop door.

Danny and Shannon's wedding is in two days, and so decisions have to be made this morning so it's all-hands-on-deck around the worktable. Blood sugar levels seemed to be dropping dangerously when I first got in, so I volunteered to get some muffins. Shannon's mother and her sister, who lives nearby and is pretty spoiled, are at one end of the table. Shannon is in her usual spot at the back. Danny's mother holds down the other end. She clearly does not want to be here but has been shamed into participation in some unknown way. She has no opinion on anything, just sighs a lot and asks who's paying at each addition.

I balked at this being done in public, in our place of business, but Danny pleaded with me to let it happen. He said this was the last chance, and that when these women have gathered in private, nothing has been accomplished except for an increase in the tension between them all. So, since Wednesday mornings are usually quiet, I agreed.

Plus, I'm nosy and wanted to hear. Sue me.

"If you'll remember, I had white roses. All white roses, which are so pure and innocent," Shannon's sister says. "Totally not appropriate for *this* wedding," she declares with a tsk and a side-eye at her sister's growing baby bump. "How about scarlet roses?"

Shannon growls. "I've already said I don't want roses. They are so, so done! And yes, I know you've already promised my nieces they'll have lots of rose petals to throw as flower girls, but that isn't my fault. That has always seemed so messy to me. They'll be carrying sweet little nosegays in purples. Or yellows. Yellow is such a happy spring color, and it's Danny's favorite."

"Oh, honey, don't worry about my favorites. Whatever makes you happy!" Danny says from near the coffee pot, where he's willing it to brew faster.

His mother frowns at the muffin in front of her. "I assume the muffins are on the house? We *are* eating in the florist shop."

"No charge," I say with a grin. "Just enjoy. The caramel nut ones are super moist and sweet, but the tart apple one is so good with coffee. I cut a few into quarters so everyone can try them." I place the plate on the table in front of Mrs. Kinnock.

With a sniff, Mrs. Chilton says, "Perhaps the one carrying the child that has brought us all here should be given first choice. Shannon?"

But she's overridden by her other daughter. "I want a whole caramel nut one. I'm the one who had to dress and feed three kids this morning to get here and make this wedding happen." Shannon's sister is tall and thin, where Shannon is short and thick. She has the same dark hair, but it's cut in a cute style instead of left wild like Shannon's tends to be. Her sister has three girls who are behaved when they are brought into the shop. It's almost like they have to behave because their mother has cornered the market on tantrums and showing out. Every time I'm around her, I end up liking Shannon more.

"For the bride," I say, placing a small plate in front of Shannon. It holds a half of each muffin and a couple of pats of butter. I can see tears welling in her eyes, and when Shannon tries to take a calming breath, it comes out all shuddery. I lean down to put my arm around her shoulders for a quick squeeze.

She says quietly, to just me, "I can't seem to do anything right, and I thought I wanted—needed—their help. But it's not working is it?"

I whisper into her ear, "Not really, and it's not like you to need other people's opinions." Her back stiffens at my words. "You made this shop successful. You know instinctively what a bride wants and how to make it happen. I've seen you do it dozens of times. Here." I turn over the page of the notebook in front of her. "Eat your muffin and write down what the bride you have at your table wants." I nudge her shoulder. "Give it a try."

I wander away from the toxic scene, though I catch Danny standing between his mother and Shannon's sister, who are debating if it will be too late Friday to serve appetizers instead of a full meal. I've never heard of a full meal even being contemplated for Friday, and the look of alarm on my employee's face says he's surprised too.

The bell over the door rings, giving Danny and me excuses to head up front as I call out, "Andy! I've not seen you in a long time when you aren't carrying a box of books for us. What can I help you with?"

"Hey, Carolina," he says with a nod in my direction. Then he walks past me. "Hey, Danny. It's all good, man. Great idea."

Danny puts a long arm across Andy's wide shoulders and propels him toward the table. "Hey, guys, one problem solved!" I follow behind them and watch from around the corner of the flower cooler as Danny jubilantly continues. "I've been looking high and low for a minister to marry us. Well, as y'all know, Andy's dad is a minister over in Cherry Log."

The settled but unhappy looks on the faces around the table show that they do know of Reverend Taylor and they are not fans. Andy's dad's church is very fundamentalist and takes to picketing when things happen that they don't feel the Lord would agree with. Like shops being open on Sunday. That was the first time I met them, when the coffee shop MoonShots opened. But everyone likes Andy, and his dad is a nice guy and an actual preacher and notary, so after a couple of drawn-out sighs, they nod and give Andy and Danny permission to move closer to the table of power.

The mother of the bride finds a smile to stick on her face. "Tell your father we appreciate him stepping in at the last minute. Who could've imagined finding a minister would be so hard? You'd think it was Easter Sunday." Her look around the table tells us how she feels about ministers having plans on Friday nights. "Let us know how much he expects to be paid and we'll figure out who's paying for that."

"Oh, no, ma'am. There'll be no charge."

Mrs. Kinnock raises a hand and gives a bit of praise. "Hallelujah. Finally."

"But it also ain't my dad gonna do it. The ceremony, that is."

Danny's arm falls off Andy's shoulder as he turns to him. "But you said it's all good."

Andy grins and rocks back and forth on his heels, his thumbs hooked proudly in his pants pockets. "Y'all know my mother-in-law is marrying Bill, and then with y'all getting hitched, I saw an opportunity. I've gotten myself ordained. No need to bother ministers with their busy schedules. They do seem to charge quite a bit, don't they? I remember from my own wedding the surprise of getting a bill, and that was my own dad. So I'm running a discount wedding service, and it's all perfectly legal. All above board. Gonna do the first one for y'all for free. Kind of a practice round."

I've stepped out from my cover behind the flower cooler to

share astonished looks with the ladies around the table. No one knows what to say.

Except Danny. He high-fives his friend. "That's awesome, man. Congratulations!" Then his grin drops and he looks around before saying in a whisper, "Do you also get to do funerals?"

Chapter 39

"I may not be able to keep my eyes open very long, but pass up a free, home-cooked meal after a long day back at work? Not happening," Anna says as she hands my granddaughter to me on Wednesday evening. Francie is just a bundle of smiles and coos as she tries so hard to communicate with anyone who'll listen. But I think she *really* wants to talk to her grandma, so I sit at the kitchen table where we can focus on each other.

In a high-pitched voice directed at the baby, I ask, "So, how is it being back at work?"

"Exhausting. Getting myself and a baby out the door is more work than I ever imagined. Will takes the early shift on the jobsites so he can pick her up in the afternoons and get supper going, but it's, well, exhausting. Listen, though—" Augusta joins us in the kitchen, and Anna takes a step back from me. "Hi, Miss Duvall. We met at the wedding."

"Oh, Anna, of course." Augusta gives her a little hug. "I'm so glad you and Will could make it. It's mostly for Gregory to meet the young people of Chancey, but I'm glad I get to know people better here, too. Where's your husband?"

"Oh, there are some folks in the front yard, and he stopped to chat with them." Anna moves toward the stove. "Sure smells good in here."

Augusta watches her, then looks out toward the front. "Is

Gregory out there? I better go see what's going on." She hurries out, wrapping her black cardigan tighter around herself. She's still wearing the black, heavy-duty shoes, black skirt, and sweater over another white blouse.

Anna hurries to my side. "Missus is out there saying she's not allowed in the house, and then Gregory arrived, driven by his parents. They were just getting out when I came inside with the baby. Is Missus really not allowed inside?"

"Oh goodness. Holler down in the basement and tell Jackson to come up here." I lift Francie and walk into the living room to look out the front window. Sure enough, there's a little gathering on the lawn.

Will notices the curtain move. He ducks his head, and with a couple of long strides, he's coming in the door. "Mom. What's going on? You ought to hear the nun lady taking on Missus and Gregory's Atlanta grandparents. She's not yelling, but they sure are having to listen."

"Look. They're getting back in their car. Missus, too!" Anna exclaims. She joins us as we watch another car pull into the side area of the driveway in order to let the big SUV and Missus's Cadillac turn around and leave. "What did she say to them exactly?"

Will shrugs. "She was nice but firm and said that she and Gregory knew what was best, and tonight is just for him to get to know some young people. She then told them she'd made a reservation for the three of them at the Italian Market toward Dalton. That Peter and Delaney would be joining them there and they needed to hurry on to not be late. Then that's when I saw you at the window. I guess they went on to dinner. Hey, Dad."

"Oh, Jackson, sorry we bothered you," I say. "Thought we might have a rumble, but it looks like Augusta has it all handled."

"Good. Now I'll take Miss Francie from you so you can get

back to cooking." That's the deal for the evening. He and Bryan, with Zoe's expert help, will keep the baby downstairs while dinner is going on. We're trying to give Anna and Will a break from their crazy life with a new baby.

"I notice Bryan didn't come upstairs with you," I say, then whisper, "How are things between Bryan and Zoe without Grant around?"

"Fine. Grant got his part done early since Griffin wanted him home for dinner tonight. Don't worry, we're not letting him slack off on the final paper for the project." He walks off, bouncing his granddaughter and completely oblivious to my interest in the trio being a duo. Oh well…

The front door flies open with lots of voices and laughter. Jenna Shaw is in the lead as usual. She has one arm looped through Gregory's, and the other is pulling her current boyfriend along. Savannah comes bounding down the stairs, and I notice Gregory drop Jenna's arm—or was it more that Jenna dropped his arm and pushed him toward the bottom of the staircase? Either way, he's waiting there, and Savannah gives him a hug. Of course she also gives Patty, Andy, Jenna, Jenna's boyfriend, and everyone else there a hug, but I can't help but see the satisfied smile on Augusta's face as she follows the crowd inside. She's looking pretty confident in her matchmaking abilities.

She must feel my gaze as she looks at me and winks. "Carolina, guess we should make sure everything's going well in the kitchen."

When I got home from work, the smells from the kitchen were intoxicating. Augusta had made two pots of luscious chicken broth from two whole chickens she'd boiled with garlic, onions, and celery. She'd deboned the chickens and strained the broth, which were sitting to the side, ready to be used later. Two packages of smoked sausage were sliced and browning in butter. Just as she said they were ready, Will and Anna arrived.

Turning the pots up to high, she'd added half the broth to each pot. Now those pots are starting to boil.

"Time to get the rice going," she says as she measures out four cups of rice into each pot.

"That's going to make a lot of rice. Want me to put the chicken in?"

"Yes, and you're right. I'm making a lot. I hate to run out of food. Just hurts my soul!" she says with a laugh.

"Spoken like a true Southerner." I follow her example of putting the lid on the pot closest to me. "So you made reservations at the Italian Market, I hear."

"Yes. Was there ever any doubt they would all show up? I know that type; they never listen to anyone else, so I made other arrangements they couldn't ignore. Delaney suggested the Italian place as it's far enough away that they would be out of the picture for a while. Thompson and Camille like to bluster, but they don't scare me. I wasn't sure if Missus would fall in line, but Delaney told me to tell her the reservations were under the name 'Mayor Bedwell' in order to get their premier service. She said that would sway her." She rolls her eyes and laughs. "My niece was right. Missus huffed a bit, then left. Plus, what was she going to do when my brother and sister-in-law acquiesced—say no?" Augusta lays a hand on her chest, widens her eyes, and gasps. "The mayor not fulfill her reservation?! The world would surely stop spinning!"

I laugh with her, then nod. "And honestly, it seems they all love Gregory and want him to be happy."

Her eyebrows lift and she dips her head to the side. "Well, they do for now. We'll see how long that lasts when…" Her words trail off as she gives me an exaggerated shrug and laughs. "Let's just say, 'We'll see.'"

Before I can ask what we'll see, she turns back to the stove. "Dinner will be ready in twenty minutes. The carrots are done, and we even have a small pot of fresh peas. Speaking of which,

I met someone that knows you today. Says he's stayed here often."

"Wait, vegetables and stays here. Silas Pendersen? You went out to his place? What's it like?" I look in the pots on the back burners. "He sold you these?"

"Yes, apparently it's wholesale, but the former owner grew some things for his own use in one of the greenhouses. I stopped in to see if they had anything to sell. Silas said he couldn't eat everything he was harvesting, and once he found out it was for your place, he was more than happy to load me up. I love fresh vegetables."

"But you don't garden? Speaking of gardening, did Silas seem to know what he was doing?"

Augusta takes a look under all the pot lids and then moves to the kitchen table. I sit across from her. "He seemed very confident. Very sure of himself, but he didn't feel like a farmer to me." She leans toward me. "First of all, he's entirely too good-looking to be isolated with all that red clay and old buildings. Reminded me of some feel-good made-for-television movie."

I laugh out loud. "Funny you should say that."

"Mom, do we have time to run out to the bridge before we eat?" Savannah asks as she comes into the kitchen. "Hey, Miss Augusta."

"Let me check." The cook jumps up and heads to the stove. Lifting a lid, she says, "Sure. But don't dillydally. Be back here, ready to eat in ten minutes." She studies my daughter. "You look especially pretty in that color of blue, Savannah."

Smoothing her hands down her sweater, Savannah giggles and hurries back to the living room, telling the others they have ten minutes.

Augusta's smile is even more self-satisfied as she practically struts back to her chair beside the table.

I ask, "Okay, what's going on? Looks awfully suspicious, your smile and Savannah giggling."

"Oh nothing, just that I happened to mention last night Gregory's favorite color is blue. That's all." She stretches her hands out in front of her and looks at them. "Oh yes, everything is going perfectly."

CHAPTER 40

"I'm considering it a trial run for mine and my fiancé's nuptials next month."

Gertie Samson is making her presence felt this morning at Blooming Books. She has a fold-out, wooden measuring rod that she keeps extending and therefore blocking us as we try to work or, worse, blocking the customers from shopping. She's talking to a customer now, explaining how she's going to need room for a chocolate fountain. "I saw one of them things in a hotel ad, and I aim to have one for my wedding reception. I've googled it. You can have all kinds of things to dip in that chocolate. Cookies, fruit, marshmallows, even fudge, one list says. Can you even imagine? Chocolate-covered fudge?"

Danny speaks up as he walks over to them. "Is it too late to get one of those for our wedding?"

Gertie doesn't even look at him as she answers, "Yes. Now, pardon me, ma'am, but if you'll step over the measuring thingamabob, I'll let you get back to shopping."

The customer is smiling big as she moves out of the way, kind of shaking her head. If it were me, I'd be looking for the *Candid Camera* crew. "Gertie, can't you do this another time? This is one of our busiest mornings."

"Don't get your panties in a wad, Carolina. I'm through. How are things going with that crew of shrews putting this wedding together? I met with them for about ten minutes before I realized if ever a saying of nuptials should be done on the run, this here was it. Elopement city, I'm telling you."

I look around and pull her toward the table for historical books, which is empty right now. "It's a nightmare. I'm trying to stay out of it, but it's kinda hard. I'm assuming you'll be here for it?"

"Like I been saying all morning, it's my trial run. Be a bit weird for me to not attend, don't ya think?" Since she's said everything else at top volume, I'm intrigued when she looks around, bends down toward me, and whispers. (I didn't realize Gertie could whisper.) "So no word from Peter? Does anyone know if he's figured out this baby is his? Or if he cares?"

With a shrug and a shake of my head, I step away from her. I thought we'd all decided to act like this wasn't a thing. I know Missus has said from the beginning she's waiting until the baby gets here to worry about it, but I'm kind of hoping if we all ignore it she'll forget.

Gertie gives me a cynical look, complete with one arched eyebrow. "Oh, Carolina. You're sweet, acting like this is some monastery up in the Himalayas, where they take vows of silence and honestly work on their relationship with God. This is Small Town, USA—we think God put us here to keep an eye on our neighbor, and we make vows of nosiness."

"Gertie, shhh. Stop it."

She laughs, big and hearty, as she steps to the front door. "Oh, don't worry. I ain't bored enough to stir up that hornet's nest." She pulls the door open, setting the bell to ringing. Then, before it can close behind her, she sticks her head back in. "Yet!"

Delaney sent out texts this morning in the midst of Gertie's reconnaissance mission, inviting me, Susan, Laney, and Beau to lunch at AC's. After many texts back and forth, it finally worked out that if we got there at 11:30 we could have one hour before Beau's standing 12:45 Thursday hair appointment with the choir leader at the Baptist church. That was fine because Susan could only give us one hour of her busy day. However, Laney and I are more flexible, so we're at AC's shortly after the doors open at eleven.

Alex shows us to our table as he and Laney chat. Laney and Shaw get along with Alex and Angie better now that a little time has passed and they've gotten used to them living together above the restaurant. She even hugged Alex when we came in the door. As he walks away, she sighs. "You know, I think he honestly loves her. She's just so young I can't help but think she's gonna regret this. No college, no sowing her wild oats." She looks toward the door, and when she sees the coast is clear, she whispers, "I mean, think of Susan and Griffin. I can't bear thinking of my daughter being as unhappy as my sister is one day."

"But it doesn't always end up that way. You said Susan and Griffin were never truly a match, more like a set pair of salt and pepper shakers. They went together, they looked good together, so they were together. But you just said you think Alex loves her. What about Angie? Do you think she loves him?"

Laney draws in a deep breath and sits back. Her short, dark hair is slicked into a cute bob that's tucked behind her ears, which is a different look for her. I've seen her hair product selection in her bathroom at home, and it's impressive. She can make her hair do more things than most trained pony acts. Her makeup is still sticking to a more subdued range than it was when I first moved here, but her lips are glossy plum to match the plum sweater dress she's wearing. Her large, copper earrings jangle as she shakes her head.

"I don't know," she says. "I can't tell if she understands holding on to a man like Alex often requires us to keep him a little off-kilter. Lord knows she saw that with her daddy and me. I always made sure Shaw knew he had a good thing at home and he better not ever take me for granted. A good-looking, personable man has always got women aiming for him. Or is she just playing around? Anxious to grow up?" She shrugs. Then her face lights up as the front door opens. "There they are!" Beau, Susan, and Delaney come in at the same time and beat the hostess and Alex to our table. After a quick round of hugs, we are settled in. There's a bread basket on the table, and as we pass it around, we try to remember the last time we were all together.

Delaney holds up both hands. "Okay, let's just get it out in the open. It wasn't at my wedding because it was the weirdest event in the history of social gatherings, and as we all know, not everyone was invited."

"Here, here!" Beau says raising her water glass. "I'm still working on forgiving you, but some details about your good-looking son, who I hear is currently in town, will go a long way toward appeasing me. How is he doing with, with everything?"

Laney exclaims, "He looks so much like Peter! I was shocked when he came in the store. But then he acts like—is it you he acts like?"

I turn to fully face Delaney. After being around Gregory so much last night, I want to hear what she has to say about her son. Delaney glances at me and licks her lips. "Not really. Not like me much. But he is so much like my aunt Augusta that I have trouble distinguishing them at times. Don't you agree, Carolina?"

Giving her a nod of agreement, I smile at the others. "She's right. Augusta is staying with us, and she's, uh, different. I don't know how to put it. She's of her own mind, funny, spiritual—"

Laney interrupts with a laugh. "Well, she does think she's a nun."

Beau says, "I heard that. So *is* she a nun?"

"Are you ladies ready to order?" the waitress asks, and we pick up our menus to make quick decisions and place our orders since we are crunched for time.

"So is she a nun?" Beau repeats when we're alone again.

"She was in training at a convent, but she left to raise Gregory. I wasn't ready to have a child, and more importantly, my parents weren't ready for me to have one either." Delaney rubs her fingers on the tablecloth, deep in thought. "I wonder about all that now, but I didn't at the time." She looks up at us, open and honest. "I didn't wonder about it at all. Never even considered that, if my parents could set my aunt up like that, they should have been able to do the same for me. I wasn't a teenager; I was twenty-two. Peter could've been a part of our lives, helped raise his son, and maybe we would've been together eventually. Maybe even had more children. How different things might've been. But it never even occurred to me." After a long sigh, she laughs. "Listen to me. The past is the past. If someone had suggested I keep the baby, I probably would've had a heart attack at the time!"

Beau pats her hand. "Sweetie, enjoy the moment now. That's all you can do. We all have things we wish we would've done differently, but then who knows how *that* would've turned out." She widens her eyes. "So… if she's not a nun, why does she *dress* like a nun?" Her funny delivery makes us all laugh and eases the tension.

Delaney shrugs, and I copy her as we look at each other. I say, "Less luggage? She only has one bag up at the B&B."

Laney leans forward on her elbows. "We need to get her in my shop and see what I can get her to try on. Maybe she's just never seen how good she can look and feel in new clothes."

"Oh, Augusta Duvall LaMotte knows exactly how good she

can look." Delaney brightens up, spreading her hands as she talks. "She was the belle of Atlanta society. Charleston, too, as she was engaged to the son of one of the oldest and richest families there." Delaney takes a sip of her water. "I was enthralled with her and all her gowns and friends."

"Wait! How old is she? I've been thinking she's Missus's age," Laney says as Susan nods alongside her.

"Not as old as Missus, not quite, but..." I trail off in my thoughts.

"She's only in her mid-fifties," Delaney says. "She's eight years older than me. She's my dad's youngest sibling. There's another sister between them, but she was never well and lived in a hospital, or a nursing home. I never saw her."

I unfold my napkin. "Well, I never thought she was that young. She's actually more our age than she is Missus's or your parents'. We do need to bring her into your shop," I say, pointing my fork at Laney, and then I add, "Looks like our food is here." The waitress is efficient and remembered our orders, so it doesn't take long before we are eating.

Picking up part of her club sandwich, Delaney changes the subject. "Enough about me and my drama. What's up with you ladies? I've felt so out of the loop. I just kept waiting for the perfect time to get together and realized that wasn't going to happen. Hence the last-minute text. Susan, you're being awful quiet."

Susan is picking at a small salad, which is all she ordered, and she seems more than willing to lay her fork down. She takes a breath, frowns at me, and says, "You're going to kill me."

I choke on the bite of shrimp salad I just ate. "Me? Why?"

"Athena says you're completely against it, but I'm going to do it. I'm going with her and Leslie to Raleigh."

"I don't care if you go. I just didn't want to get involved." Then I swallow. "But seriously?"

Laney looks from me to her sister. "Athena? *The* Athena? Is this some elaborate plot for you to get her across state lines and kill her? I mean, I understand the thought, but even I probably wouldn't take my daughter along."

"Laney!" Susan growls through clinched teeth. "Shush!"

Beau is bent over her plate laughing, and when she snorts loudly, we all look at her. She lifts her head and pushes red tendrils of hair off her face. The mass of her unnaturally red hair is back in a braid. "I've missed y'all. With five kids, working around the clock, and dealing with my mother and her sisters, I needed this! Okay, I'll be quiet. I have to hear more about this mother-daughter murder plot."

Delaney sticks a hand out. "I need some background. Isn't... I mean, I know... uh, she's..."

Susan sighs. "Yes. Athena is seeing my ex." She pushes the words out like she's speaking in slow motion. I feel rather than actually see Laney's eyebrows jump at her use of the word "seeing." I have a feeling she would've chosen a more colorful term.

I decide to help. "Athena has ties to North Carolina State University, which has an excellent veterinary program and is Leslie's dream vet school. Athena offered to take her up there on spring break next week and introduce her to some important people and get a personalized tour of everything." I pause to see if Susan wants to take back over the story. She doesn't look up from shoving salad greens in her mouth, so I finish. "She asked Susan to go along."

Delaney looks at Susan, then turns to me. "Why does she think you're against it?"

"Well, Athena mentioned it to me yesterday morning in Ruby's, and I was in a hurry, but before I left, well, Ruby made some good points. Like, uh, asking if Griffin is going along."

Laney's eyes are huge. "Is he? If he's going, I'm going. No way are they going to plunk you in the back seat like some extra baggage. I know you've lost all your mojo and you are paying mightily for your indiscretions with Mr. Pendersen, but even the thief on the cross got a little love." She shakes her head and fluffs her collar as she talks. "Oh, no. This is not going down like this!"

"Would y'all just hush! It's me, Athena, and Leslie. That's all. Just a simple trip up one day and back the next." Tears flood her eyes. "I messed up and let my kids down. It's time they got an adult back for their mother. Leslie works hard and deserves this."

Silence settles on the table as we go back to our meals and give her a minute to calm down. Laney is still muttering under her breath as she picks through the remains of her Cobb salad. Beau reaches to pat Susan's hand and give her a wink. Delaney frowns at me, and I remember how she and Athena were at odds during the book festival. Okay, I need to say something.

"I worked with Athena during the book festival, and I have to say I don't think she is being malicious by inviting you. She's"—I give Susan an apologetic look—"she's younger than us, and I don't think they think like us, the younger generation. She's also not from around here, so she doesn't automatically think of you and Griffin being together. She has young children, so it's a struggle for her to leave them, I'm sure. I think she's just trying to help."

Susan nods and takes a couple of deep breaths. "That's what she said. She offered to give me and Leslie the contacts and have us go without her, but we all know it wouldn't be the same. Honestly, she has been good to my kids. And"—she clears her throat—"I think she's good for Griffin."

Laney lets out one, "Over my dead body." Then she throws her napkin onto her plate and gets up. We all watch because we're not sure if she's leaving, going to the bathroom, or handing a gun to Susan.

To our relief, she wraps her in a hug. "I trust you. You need to do what's best for you and your kids." She straightens up, her hand resting on her sister's shoulder. "You go be the nice sister, the sweet mama, the understanding ex. You just know I've always got your back. And weaponry."

Beau chuckles and checks the time on her watch. "Well, I've got to get back to Beulah Land for Miss Judy's weekly style and rinse." She raises her hand and makes a scribbling motion at our waitress. "Thanks, Delaney, for texting this morning. I sure needed this."

Delaney nods at her. "Absolutely. I needed this, too, just to do a reset and laugh and cry and get out of my own head."

Beau agrees and says sweetly, "Yep, but the most important thing I get from meeting up with y'all is an attitude of gratitude." She stands up, money in hand for the approaching waitress as we all nod at her and smile at her sentiment. Then she winks and laughs out loud. "Gratitude I never got married!"

Chapter 41

Beau left, followed shortly by Susan. Delaney waited until Susan was gone to ask me and Laney, "Is Susan okay? I mean, other than what she said today?"

Laney frowns. "I don't think so. Did you see that tiny salad with no meat, no croutons? I think she's gained a little weight, which is shocking. I've always carried every extra pound the Troutman family came across. Mother, Scott, Susan? All skin and bones."

I think back. "You know, I think you're right. That long jacket she had on today wasn't anything I've seen her wear before. It didn't look like her at all. She did say she's been watching a lot of TV lately."

Delaney hesitates, then whispers, "Can I ask? Wasn't she an item with the actor guy? Isn't he back in town?"

"He is," I say as I move back from the table. "And he's not leaving. He bought a business and a home, but he was hanging around Sally Blankenship a lot and she even talked about coming back and staying with him." I pause as I remember Sally's talk of Peter. "Why did Peter invite her here?"

Delaney's shoulders slump and she shakes her head. "He acts like it was all his idea, but she called up out of the blue and invited herself. He wasn't happy about it. Y'all my husband is not as in control of things as he likes to portray."

Laney chuckles. "Hello? We've met his mother. So Sally just got a bee in her bonnet to visit her old boyfriend's hometown? He was her boyfriend, right? Not just a friend?"

Delaney nods. "He didn't even know she wrote books. At first he was kind of flattered, then the more he thought about it, well… Then my father got wind of it and laid out all kinds of possible disasters like only he can do. Peter panicked and agreed getting out of town was a good idea." She shrugs. "So we did."

I lean forward and whisper. "I can't figure out why she stayed here so long after the festival. Was she after Silas? After Peter? Even with her in New York, I don't trust her as far as I can throw her because she all but promised she's coming back."

Delaney frowns. "Peter says she's got some business deal here. She's looked at a lot of property. He was hoping she didn't find anything."

Laney's eyes cut to mine and I know she's thinking what I'm thinking—we don't trust Peter either. . I lean back. "Maybe with Sally out of town, Susan will get back together with Silas, but who knows. I guess all we can do is wait and see how it works out. I need to get back to the store," I say as I stand.

Laney looks up at me. "What about your garden? Maybe she just needs to get back into gardening—and you've got one that needs a lot of work."

"It's no longer a garden. It's a patch of weeds that is going back to lawn. I don't want a garden because I learned last summer that it's just like letting a kid have a puppy. I'm the one that ends up doing all the work, and I have to live with the mess right outside my back window."

Delaney shoves me. "Oh, come on. We'll all work on it together. Kind of like a community garden. It could be fun."

"No, that's what I thought last year. I'm not good at gardening, and I'm not good at waiting for everyone else to weed the jungle it becomes."

Laney stands up. "We should talk to Jackson. He's working from home now. He probably would want to help Susan. I'll talk to him." She smiles and walks to the front door, saying loudly, "Come on. I want to stop in and look at some flowers."

Delaney shrugs at me and follows her. "I'm going to pass on stopping in your shop. I have work to do up in the office. But that is nice, you doing a garden to help your friend. I promise I'll help." Then she laughs. "When it's time to harvest!"

"I'm not doing a garden," I grumble as I catch up with them at the front door.

Alex comes up behind us and pulls the heavy door open for us. "A garden? I'd love to experiment with growing some fresh vegetables and herbs. Your garden is pretty big, Miss Carolina. Think I could have a corner? I'd help with the whole thing."

Laney answers, "Sure! Where are you headed?" she asks as Alex follows us outside.

"I've been summoned next door."

"Our next door? Blooming Books?" I ask.

He pulls our door open and waves Laney and me inside as Delaney moves past us on the sidewalk. She waves goodbye as he says, "Yep. Something about a wedding tomorrow night?"

I groan and Laney hurries up, saying, "Oh, this sounds good! The club can stay closed a little longer."

At the infamous worktable there's the usual wedding gathering: Shannon, her mother, and her mother-in-law. Shannon's sister is missing, but no one's actually missing her as the volume and tension are high.

"Of course my granddaughters are going to be in the wedding!" Danny's mother exclaims as we walk up.

Shannon's mother sniffs. "Then why didn't you say something before now? It's just too late. We already have three flower girls, and that is plenty."

Danny is standing behind Shannon, and he looks sick, and

sounds sick. "I just never thought Alison would let them come and now…"

Shannon reaches up and pats his hand, which is lying on her shoulder. He's pale, and she's flushed. Her hair is actually damp, and I'm glad she's sitting on a stool. Can these two women not see what they're doing to their children?

Alex is backing away, ready for an escape, but Laney grabs his arm and moves forward. "Did someone want to talk to Alex?"

The four at the table obviously have no idea as they stare at him. Then, a woman steps out of the bookshelves to my left. A woman dressed like a nun.

"Hello. I'm Augusta Duvall, and I couldn't help overhearing the problems with your wedding. You're Shannon and Danny, right? And your mothers." She puts an arm through Alex's. "And you were planning on Alex doing some food for your reception, but…"

Shannon whimpers, "But we couldn't decide, so…" She looks up with blinking eyes at Alex. "I'm so embarrassed."

Alex looks appalled. There's a nun attached to him and a crying business owner in front of him. It doesn't help that Laney keeps nudging him closer to the table. He mutters, "No. It's all fine. All fine. I should get back…"

"I have a proposition," Augusta says, taking a step closer to the table and pulling him with her. "Alex, I'm sure there are some easy appetizers you can serve on short notice, correct? We aren't picky, are we?" She completely ignores the mothers. Once she gets a quick nod from Shannon, she moves on. "For, let's say, forty people. Doesn't that sound about right?"

"Well, we've not exactly agreed on the guest list…" Mrs. Chilton starts, but as she opens her mouth to explain, Augusta turns to Alex.

"Forty is doable, right? If there's food left, I'm sure that's no problem, right, Danny? You'll eat the leftovers. And if we run out, well, it's not like anyone coming is going to starve to death, right?" She laughs and rolls her eyes at us. Shannon smiles and actually takes a shaky breath.

Danny laughs. "Extra food is never a problem. Thanks, Alex."

Alex is staring at the woman still holding his arm as he mutters, "Sure. No problem."

"And mothers," she says, stepping closer to the table. "How blessed, extremely blessed, you are to have six grandchildren between you. Oh, to have all that youth at your knee, watching your every move and learning how to love and care for each other." From her black cardigan pocket, she pulls a tissue and sniffles. "It makes me absolutely weepy." Then she laughs. "Oh, have there ever been too many flower girls?"

"No!" Laney exclaims, startling all of us. "Sorry, I just got caught up in it all. I have these adorable, bejeweled fairy crowns the little girls just love at The Club." She claps her hands. "I know! They'll be my wedding gift to you. The girls will all love them. Oh, and there are little matching wands I'll throw in. Oh, Shannon. It will be magical." She grabs Danny. "Come with me and you can bring them back here to show everyone."

"I'll head out with them," Alex says, walking backward and talking in our direction the whole way. "Appetizers for forty tomorrow will be no problem. I'll deliver them at five." He pauses, holding the door that Laney and Danny just left through. "Oh, Carolina, is Savannah still good to serve?"

Before I can answer, Augusta speaks up. "Yes, that's how I was aware there might be a sticking point. And Gregory is excited to help as well. We will handle everything else for the reception."

He nods at her, and his appreciation of her people skills shows. Turning back to the table, I see such relief on my business partner's face that I reach out to squeeze Augusta's arm.

"So we're all good here. Shannon, why don't you go upstairs and have some lunch? Maybe a nap. Everything is set."

Mrs. Chilton draws in a deep breath, and I wonder if she's thought of a new line of battle, but she smiles as she gets off her stool. "Yes, dear. I'll finish up these two arrangements, and then you are through with work until Monday. Go on upstairs and rest up for your big day."

Mrs. Kinnock looks around, then, leaving her stool, reaches out for Augusta. "Nice to meet you. Marge Kinnock. Thank you for your help and, uh, yeah." After the quick handshake, she leaves without saying anything to the rest of us.

I'm grinning from ear to ear. "Augusta, that was amazing."

I follow her back toward the bookshelves.

"These folks were easy. Wait until Thompson and Camille LaMotte discover their grandson is going to be a waiter." She smiles at me, and then her whole face drops into a frown. "However, I do have an issue to discuss with you." After a pause in which my mind runs in circles, she waves her arms at the shelves on either side of us. "I'm rather appalled at the lack of poetry books on your shelves. I'd hoped there was a run on them during the book festival and you hadn't had time to replace them, but as there is not a single one left, I find that hard to believe."

Okay. Hadn't circled that far out. I start to chuckle, but her frown is pretty serious. "Well, Augusta, I'm not sure they'd actually sell very well here. And we are mostly used books and we don't get many poetry books." I wander around the shelves as if I'm double-checking, but I know there aren't any poetry books. I mean, does she know where she is?

"You can quit looking," she says. "We both know there aren't any for you to find. I'll provide you with a list of some to start with before I leave. I had such hope when you recognized Wordsworth." She sighs and walks over to the table where FM's history books are sitting. "I do find this arrangement encouraging." Opening a book up, she points to the bookplate in the front with neat printing. "This Francis Marion Bedwell is Peter's father, correct?"

"Yes. FM, as we called him, had those bookplates in the front of all his books. Peter donated these books to us, and since there was so much interest, we decided to not sell them. Just let people come in and use them."

"Isn't that something a library would be more likely to do?"

"You'd think. But then you've not met our librarian. Oh! You know FM was Gregory's grandfather. He might be interested in the books."

"At least to look through them. I think he'd be more pleased to find them here for people to use. He's not like his grandparents, who like to hoard their treasures and keep them locked away."

I lean against one of the shelves. "You said your brother and his wife wouldn't approve of Gregory working as a waiter tomorrow night. Well, it's only one night, and they probably won't even know. I wouldn't worry."

She puts the big, old book back on the shelf and turns to me. Her smile is crooked, which goes along with the tilt of her head. "Oh, of course they'll know. I'm headed there right now to tell them."

Chapter 42

"I invited Colt to dinner tonight," Jackson says when I answer the phone. "Hope that's okay?"

"Sure. Although I have to stay until closing and I was going to stop by the store on my way home to pick up something easy. Any thoughts on what you'd like? Is it just him? Where's Phoenix?"

"They had a fight or something. Have you seen her?"

Have I seen her? Well, now that I think about it... I haven't seen her since she told me she can't have kids. It's been a busy week with Sally leaving, Gregory showing up, then Augusta showing up. There's Shannon and Danny's wedding tomorrow and the spring break kerfuffle. He brings me back to our conversation by saying, "Did I lose you?"

"Uh, no, I haven't seen Phoenix. Not in a while." Someone in the background shouts his name, and I'm grateful for an easy out. "Sounds like you're busy."

"We're still on the job, so we'll be home for dinner. Me and Colt. Maybe you can talk to Phoenix and find out what's going on. Talk to you later."

He hangs up, and I don't have to think real hard to remember I did not tell him about my conversation with Phoenix. I didn't talk to anyone about it. As a matter of fact, I'm pretty sure I forgot all about it until just this minute.

I'm alone in the shop. Danny's dad took him and a friend out for a beer as a sort of bachelor party. Shannon is at her parents' house for the night. Her mother is doing a bridesmaid brunch tomorrow with some friends from her church, and tonight is a family dinner. They are playing Old-Fashioned Wedding, where the bride isn't pregnant or living with the groom. I'm just glad they will be getting ready there instead of here. Bonnie and I are holding down the ship tomorrow and over the weekend. The Blooming part of Blooming Books is closed until Monday morning. Tomorrow night the newlyweds are heading to a cabin in the Blue Ridge Mountains for a couple of nights, and then life is back to normal. Well, as normal as this whole crazy thing can get.

So, back to Phoenix and Colt. With the time change it is still bright outside. I step out onto the sidewalk to see if I can tell if her studio is still open. I can't remember which nights she has classes.

"Hey, Miss Carolina," Angie says as she comes out the front door of AC's. "I love saying that. Makes you sound like a contestant in the Miss America pageant."

I roll my eyes, but smile. "Yes, it does. How are you? I had lunch at your place today, and it was wonderful."

"I heard. Alex also told me about that wedding meeting. Who is this nun lady? He was impressed by her. Also a little scared. He went to a Catholic school, so he says nuns really get to him."

"She's, uh, you know Gregory? Peter and Delaney's son? She's his aunt and raised him. How are things with you and Alex and the restaurant?"

"Mom ask you to ask me?"

"No. I'm asking for me. I miss you hanging out with the other girls up at the house." I hadn't realized that I did until I said that. She'd gone from being part of the group to owning a restaurant and living downtown in the matter of a few weeks.

She shuffles her feet. "I just stepped out here for a breath of fresh air, so I gotta get back in. But you know, I do kind of miss all that at times. Maybe I'll see what they're up to this weekend, but we close late and then I'm exhausted. I see everyone at school, you know, but it's not the same."

"No. It's not."

Before she reaches her door, she asks me, "What are you doing out here?"

"Thought I'd see if Phoenix is closed yet. I need to talk to her."

"Well, like I said, I have to go back inside. Tell Savannah I said hi and to give me a call this weekend."

"Sure." I watch the young woman, and I remember how unsure and unhappy she seemed when we moved here. Of course, some of that was the thick Goth makeup and her constant war with her sister and mother.

I'm struck by the thought that some people are just not meant to be teenagers. Angie Conner might be one of them.

"Oh, hi. You're there," I say when Phoenix answers the phone. I'd called a couple of times and sent a text, but she hadn't responded. I chuckle. "Of course, it's your cell phone, so I don't exactly know where there is."

"I'm in my car. Just dropped off a meal at Patty's and Andy's. My phone has been on silent, so I missed your calls. What can I do for you?"

"Just a minute." I lay my phone down while I put my groceries in and close the back door to the van. I pick up the phone and go around to the driver's side door. "Sorry. Just needed to get the groceries into the van. First of all, the cheesy potato soup was so good. Let me know when you're making that again. And, uh, Colt's coming for dinner tonight."

She doesn't say anything for a bit. "Okay."

"Um, do you want to come?"

"Not really."

"Why? I mean, are you fighting? No, that's none of my business. But are you—did you tell him? Is that why you're fighting?"

I start the car just as she starts to talk, and our call drops as the phone tries to connect through the car. I groan and try calling her again, but all I get is a fast beeping. I forgot about the phone connecting automatically. I give it a minute, then try again. This time it rings, but that's all it does. Okay, either she's ignoring me or she'll call back. I hang up and pull out of the parking lot.

Oh well, I tried.

"I know just how ya feel," Bryan says to our two dinner guests.

Jackson is at the end of the table, I'm around the corner from him, and Bryan is beside me. Colt is across from me, and Silas Pendersen is across from Bryan. He'd seen Jackson's truck at the Yeldin house, where the Jessup boys are working on what will become a daycare. They are also doing work on the main house, but that's down in the woods near the lake and out of view of the road. Silas's farm and new home is next door to the Yeldins' property, and his entrance is next to the house where the daycare will be. He brought Jackson over some lettuce, beets, and other parts of his early harvest. In return, Jackson invited him to dinner.

"The girl I care for won't have anything to do with me either," Bryan commiserates as he blows on his bowl of soup. It doesn't get much easier than grilled cheese and canned tomato soup, but it also doesn't get much better. However, it does take a lot of that to fill up three men and a hungry teenager, so I keep missing parts of the conversation as I get up to make more sandwiches or refill soup bowls from the pot on the stove. I've never had to open so many cans of soup. Cooking is exhausting.

Colt points his spoon at his nephew. "Zoe? She still mooning over, uh, you like Zoe, right?" I'd kicked him under the table so he doesn't mention Grant. I don't think Bryan has figured it out, or he at least doesn't need to be reminded of it on the one night his two friends aren't hanging out at our house.

Jackson laughs. "Oh, she'll come around."

Silas sighs. "You'd think so, wouldn't you? But not always."

Colt pops the last piece of sandwich in his mouth and says around it, "Sounds like Griffin has moved on. What do you think is holding Susan back? From what I remember, you two were pretty close in the fall." Then looking at me, he asks, "Are there any more sandwiches?"

"Yeah, I just need to flip them over." I awkwardly chuckle as I stand. "Don't say anything interesting while I'm gone." I rush into the kitchen, cursing myself for finishing too fast and telling Jackson I'd get the second, and third, helpings since they are all still eating. I flip the sandwiches and scurry back to the doorway.

Silas looks up at me. "So you're positive Susan is going with Athena and not Griffin on this school tour?"

"Positive. Heard it from her this afternoon. It was Athena's idea. The three of them are going up one day and back the next. Susan's just trying to do the right thing by her kids."

Silas closes his eyes and groans. "I know you're probably

tired of me saying this, but I am so mad at how we handled all that. I was so involved in the movie it just didn't register with me her kids were so young and how—"

Loudly clearing my throat, I interrupt him while jerking my head toward our own kid sitting across from him. "Well. Now you know. Just give her some space. I'll get the sandwiches."

Coming back to the table, I'm greeted by Colt holding up his empty plate, ready for more. "Thanks, these are delicious," he says. "I don't know why I don't make them for myself. Lord knows Phoenix is so busy cooking for everyone else in the world I can't count on meals together. Maybe I should sign up and pay for her to deliver to me."

"Wait, I can just buy meals from her?" Silas asks. "She delivers?"

"Yeah, she's dancing and cooking pretty much 24/7. Doesn't have time for me anymore." Colt sets his elbow on the table and leans over to look at Silas. "Maybe we should just cut our losses. Maybe it's time to find some women who do want to be with us. Surely you know some actresses who wouldn't mind spending time with a couple of good-looking guys like us?"

Silas laughs. "Me? Aren't there some teachers over there at the school who like to have fun?"

Jackson reaches out and rubs my arm. "I'm glad I'm not out there looking anymore."

Bryan swallows a mouthful of hot sandwich, shaking his head. "It's rough out there, Dad."

We all laugh, and the conversation moves on to Silas's new farm venture, but I only half listen as sadness creeps over me. Two of my friends are letting these good guys, whom I think they love, wander away not feeling loved at all. So often that's all it takes, a bit of miscommunication, lack of time, confusion on wants and needs, and a couple loses their way. A couple becomes uncoupled.

Jackson and I found our way to each other, but we've not always protected that like we should. I've got to get through to Susan and Phoenix what is at stake. As for Bryan… maybe he should move on. Isn't that what high school is for?

CHAPTER 43

"It's not fair when the workers are having more fun than the bride and groom," Shannon says as she comes up behind me at her wedding reception Friday evening.

"Oh, Shannon! It was a beautiful ceremony, wasn't it? And you look wonderful. Where did you find this dress?"

She steps back and sways for the full skirt to swish back and forth. The high waist comes to a point below her breasts and then falls to mid-calf. It's a soft, satiny lavender material that looks like it was made by fairies. It lightly shimmers as she moves, and then the small, pearlized sequins on the lacy top catch the light just enough to cause an unexpected sparkle.

"I ordered it online! Isn't that crazy? Saw it and loved it, but never, never thought it would be this great. I think that's why I couldn't make up my mind about anything else. All I knew was I wanted to wear this dress." She fluffs the skirt as she looks around us. "But it is all perfect, isn't it?"

The ceremony as the sun was sliding behind the mountains was covered in its own shade of lavender. The five flower girls in their sparkly halos, carrying wands and baskets of white rose petals, mesmerized us all as they tiptoed and danced up the pathway to the gazebo. They could've been a fairy queen's entourage. Matter of fact, if you squinted your eyes just a bit—they were. Shannon's bouquet of spring flowers, echoed in the headpiece of her veil, added to the illusion that we were peeking into an enchanted meadow. Andy and Danny waited in the gazebo, which was lit with votive candles and adorned simply with baskets of ferns. The ferns, I found out, Laney bought for her house porch earlier than she usually does so they could be used tonight.

Andy did a wonderful job as minister. His flair for the dramatic was tamped down, but not so much that he didn't seem to have a slight Irish accent. Which, again, added to the magical environment. He said with his red hair he'd often thought he was missing an opportunity to have a more interesting accent than North Georgian. Tonight was its trial run, but I bet we hear more of it because he was actually pretty good. Jackson I couldn't help giggling at first, but then it just felt right.

Afterward, as we walked across the street to the shop for the reception, I felt so good, warm and happy. On Jackson's arm, I saw my husband was just as relaxed and I reached up to kiss his cheek. He squeezed my waist and whispered in my ear his plans for later and heat flushed my face. As we walked into the store, I actually checked myself when I thought the wine must be making me feel like that—I hadn't had any yet.

However, this is my second glass in my hand now. Shannon bumps my free arm. "So, like I said, the workers seem to be enjoying themselves rather a lot."

"Yes, they do." We are standing toward the back of the shop, where all the food and drinks are laid out on Shannon's worktable. Behind the table, refilling the trays and glasses, Savannah and Gregory are laughing. No, it's not the laughing as much as the, well, the way they are standing, facing each other. Both are wearing white, long-sleeved dress shirts and black pants. Will loaned the shirt to Gregory because he hadn't brought anything that formal for spring break. He's also wearing a pair of Will's black pants, although they had to be folded up and hemmed with duct tape. He's a couple of inches shorter than

Will. Almost exactly Savannah's height. But it's not only their matching outfits and dark hair that makes them stand out; it's the looks echoed on their faces. Oh yeah. They are definitely having a good time.

"He seems nice." Shannon giggles. "Who would've thought I'd have a *Bedwell* serving at my wedding?"

"His grandparents were not happy to hear about it, but for some reason Augusta thought it was a good idea."

"There's my bride. And my boss!" Danny comes up to us and gives me a hug, then wraps his long arm around his wife's shoulders. "This has been a blast. Look at the girls. They loved being in the wedding, and they get along so great!"

We slightly turn to watch the six little girls who are now in the front window area playing with a set of tiny plush animals. "Where did they get the animals? Those are cute," I ask.

"Gussie gave them to them." Gregory has come up to us holding an open bottle of wine. "She's a master at knowing what will make people happy. Can I top anyone off?"

"I don't believe so, but you're doing a great job," Shannon says, a small smile and narrowed eyes making her next words seem not so innocent. "So I hear your grandparents weren't happy with you working here tonight?"

He laughs, throwing his head back, looking so much like Peter. "Not really, but my days of having to make them happy are over. I'm having a wonderful time. I think working agrees with me." He nods across the room. "Oh, there are some empty glasses being waved in my direction."

Shannon and I turn to make eye contact. "What does all *that* mean?" I ask her. Then I see past her to my daughter, who is straightening napkins but also looking my direction.

"Come here," Savannah mouths.

"Think I'll see how the food is holding up," I say, excusing myself. The mellowness of the ceremony has traveled here, and folks are talking low, laughing, eating, and drinking in a measured, relaxed way.

In other words, not a usual Chancey gathering.

"Hi there," I say to Savannah. "You and Gregory seem to be having a good time."

"Thanks. He's fun. So when is this over? Everyone is going out to Nathan's. I mean, everyone not here. My friends."

"Nathan Yeldin's house? Out at the lake?"

"Yeah, you know, where Dad's been working and where you think we're camping for spring break. Anyway, when can I leave?"

I look around. "Is Gregory going with you?"

She shrugs. "I don't know. If he wants to, I guess."

Staring at her I can't see anything besides her wanting to get out of here. A minute ago I could've sworn she was interested in her work partner, but then, what do I know? "I'd say you should be good to leave in about thirty minutes. Just consolidate the food that's left onto a couple of trays and folks can serve themselves. We're leaving the extras here for Danny and Shannon. They're going to pack up anything that's left and take it to the cabin."

"Okay, thanks." She turns back to face the table, already working on consolidating the food.

"Mommy!" I hear shouted as Danny's girls in the corner leave their friends and new toys and run toward the door. Their mother is picking them up so Danny and Shannon can have a peaceful wedding night and then leave for the cabin in the morning. Alison is a petite blonde. Her long hair hangs in ringlets, and she's wearing a pair of dressy blue jeans, knee-high boots, and a tucked-in blouse. I met Alison Kinnock back around Christmas when I thought she wanted Danny back. She didn't. Since then I've seen her a couple of times as she and Danny have switched off the girls. However, even though

I've met her before, there's a reason I'm staring and willing my mouth to not drop open.

This time she's with my brother-in-law.

"Colt, what are you doing here?" Jackson asks as they walk toward each other.

I make my way out from behind the table, but not before Savannah grabs my arm. "Is he dating her now? She's cute."

"No. I mean, I don't know."

Shannon stares holes in me as I pass her. Apparently she didn't know about this situation either. Anyway, I ignore her and get to my husband's side. "Colt. Good to see you. So you know Alison?"

He looks around like he doesn't want to meet my eyes. "Yeah, she's a teacher at the elementary school. We're on a committee together."

I step closer and whisper, "Are you on a date?"

He frowns. "Not exactly, but hey, I told you Phoenix doesn't have time for me. I gotta go help Alison."

When Danny's three girls greet Colt with high fives and call him "coach," I realize this isn't exactly a new thing. Under my breath, I grumble to Jackson. "Can you believe this?"

He just smiles, but I know from the way his lips are so tight that he's decided to not have an opinion on the matter.

He has chosen wisely.

I have enough opinions for both of us.

Chapter 44

"Anna had to get to work early, but Francie and I aren't missing Granddad's French toast," Will says as he comes in our front door on Saturday morning.

I take the baby carrier from him and haul to the couch.

"There's my girl!" Francie is three months old and I can't get enough of her. When Jackson suggested stopping by the Piggly Wiggly to get supplies for French toast last night after the reception, I texted Will and Anna to invite them over. Of course the real invite was for Francie, but she doesn't have a phone yet.

"There's Miss Fancy Francie," Savannah yells, running down the stairs. Her niece actually squeals at her and raises her arms.

"No, you stay here with Grammy," I say, pulling her closer to my chest. Of course my very persuasive daughter stands over my shoulder, waving and talking until my granddaughter is convinced she should go with Aunty Savannah. "Fine. Take her," I say when that precious, tiny mouth shapes into a pout and those big eyes start to look shiny. Savannah swoops in and turns the pout into giggles in no time.

"She's just a woman who knows what she wants," Savannah explains. As a peace offering, I guess, she comes to sit beside me so I can see the way Francie is babbling to her with such an intent expression on her sweet little face. Bryan leans over the back of the couch and says hello to his niece, but he's barely functioning. His hair is standing on end, there's still sleep in his eyes, and his breath…

"Gross! Get away from us!" Savannah shouts. Francie startles, and I prepare to take her and soothe her back down because Savannah likes a smiling, cooing baby. Crying is not her thing. However, instead of welling up and melting down, Francie mimics Savannah's yell, then follows it with a big belly laugh. Which makes us all laugh. That starts a back-and-forth between the two of them, yelling, then laughing. I notice Will taking a video of them and then see behind him that we've woken our guest.

"Oh, Augusta. I'm sorry we're being so loud this early."

She waves her hands, dismissing my concern as she walks toward us. "I've been up for ages. Walked down to the river and along it up into the woods. I was just back in my room changing my wet shoes. It's very dewy out there this morning. Who is this delightful creature?"

"My name is Savannah, but we've already met," Savannah jokes.

Augusta pats my daughter's dark hair. "But I should be clearer when surrounded by delightful creatures. I assume this is your granddaughter?" she asks, standing to my side, leaning in for a look.

"Yes. This is Francie. Francie, this is Miss Duvall."

Augusta reaches out a hand and Francie grabs her finger. "Ah, what bright eyes! Sweetie, you can call me Gussie."

"Who's ready for French toast?" Jackson calls from the kitchen. "The first batch is ready. Bryan, take the sausage to the table."

Will is pouring juice and directing traffic at the table. I take Francie from Savannah. "Bring me a coffee refill to the table, and I'll hold her while y'all eat."

Augusta steps over to the front window. "That looks like Gregory pulling up."

"He's just in time for breakfast," I say. "When does he head back to school?"

"Tomorrow after lunch at the Bedwell House. Did Missus invite you yet?"

"To lunch? No, is she?"

"I asked her to," she says stiffly as she heads to open the front door. "Don't worry, I'll remind her."

I try to get out of an invitation I haven't even received. "Maybe she only wants family there."

Augusta rolls her eyes. "Of course that's what she wants. But what about what I want? What Gregory wants?" She pulls on the big door. "Good morning! What are you doing out and about so early?"

He gives her a quick hug but looks over her head inside. "Uh, Savannah invited me for her dad's French toast." He comes in, nods to me as he passes, and leaves the two of us watching him find Savannah and give her a hug. A hug not quite as quick as the one for his aunt.

Augusta bends down to talk to Francie, who is watching everything, snug in my arms. "Well, looks like your auntie is making lots of people happy this morning." She tips her head at me, laughs, and then winks.

"She seems awfully bossy for someone not in control of much," Missus says from her position near our shop's front window, acting like a gargoyle watching the reading table from on high. She's never liked FM's books being on display for just anyone to peruse, but she can't figure out a way to stop it. Plus, I think there's a part of her that *does* like it. Likes seeing them displayed in the antique glass-front case and the way people reverently page through them, like the older gentleman at the table now. You'd think having Missus hanging over his reading would make him antsy, but from what I've heard he's known her all his life. For those folks, ignoring her is second-nature.

She folds her arms, pearl-gray gloves barely distinguishable from the pearl-gray pantsuit she's wearing. "Forcing me to invite you and your family to my home for Sunday dinner."

"Gee, thanks. You make it sound so warm and welcoming."

"You know me, Carolina. Events at my home are always warm and welcoming. I pride myself on being a true Southern hostess. Besides…" Missus turns to face away from the table and motions me to her side. Once I'm there, she raises one eyebrow, tightens the fold of her arms, and whispers, "The LaMottes are not as entertaining as you might imagine. Thompson only talks about golf, and Camille is the most self-absorbed person I've ever met. I expected culture and a rich panorama of conversational topics." She sighs and almost smiles. "Time spent with them makes me appreciate muffins at Ruby's." The smile dies with a sniff. "Almost."

I walk away as I ask, "So, your gracious invitation, is it for only Jackson and me?"

She follows, looking back over her shoulder at FM's books. "Bryan is invited, but not expected. Savannah, however, is very much included. You do know she's much too young for my grandson, right?"

What is it that makes me want to argue with someone I agree with just because of their tone of voice? "Two years? Two years is too much of a difference in age for you? Wasn't FM, like, a dozen years older than you?" Although now that I think about it, two years isn't too much at all. I guess it's just that he's in college.

"Oh, don't be silly. Age has to do with more than the simple passing of years. However, I'm sure Augusta feels Savannah will add a youthful touch to dinner, so please bring her." She stops and turns to me, concern in her look and voice. "Anna and Will are invited but can't attend as they are hosting some gathering of their Sunday School class? Hosting in that tiny cabin? What are they thinking? Let me know if you can talk some sense into them. Family should always take precedence is my belief. Besides, you have to wonder what caliber of people would attend dinner at that, that shack on the river of theirs. We must work on finding them a more appropriate home."

Now I don't want to argue with her *just because*. Now she's making me mad. "You mean their friends? Believe me, with the kind of family they have, the more friends, the better!"

I hear it, but not before she's grinning. "Oh, such harsh judgment of Will's family. Tsk, tsk, Carolina, don't be so hard on yourself." She times the jingle of the door to punctuate her line. She waves goodbye through the glass door, then turns to stride down the sidewalk.

Bonnie pops up from where she's been hiding in the bookshelves, grinning. "And people wonder why big old family dinners are a thing of the past."

Chapter 45

"I wish I had on jeans and was going to a picnic," Jackson says as we walk to our car. At the end of the church parking lot, young couples, along with Will and Anna, are corralling their kids and laughing with each other as they pile into their cars. It's an incredible spring day with bright skies and light breezes. Newly unfurled leaves stretch and flutter as daffodils sway along the edges of the parking lot. Will told us that they were hosting their Sunday school class picnic because the creek area behind their cabin is abounding in spring flowers and there's plenty of room for the kids to explore.

Taking in a deep breath and releasing it slowly, I agree with my husband. "I know. Me too. But she doesn't seem to mind too much," I say with a nod toward Savannah and Gregory, who are walking on the sidewalk down the hill toward Missus's house. Gregory is wearing a new pair of khaki pants and a white dress shirt he bought yesterday on a shopping trip to Atlanta. He'd spent the day with Delaney and Peter, a first for the three of them. After their Valentine's wedding, Delaney and Peter ran straight off to Greece for their honeymoon, and Gregory went back to school. This week hasn't afforded them the time together I think Delaney imagined, but she must be used to her parents and aunt taking over as they have. I much prefer Augusta to Thompson and Camille, but she is still someone who seems to get what she wants. As is evinced by where we are all headed in our Sunday finest.

Savannah is wearing a light yellow dress in a princess cut with cap sleeves. It falls at her knees and flutters around her legs as they stroll down the hill. I chuckle as I climb into our car. "I think the preacher was intimidated with a nun sitting in the congregation. He was not only on point, but finished early."

"I bet Missus told him she had company coming for dinner and there would be no long, drawn-out benediction," Jackson says, pulling away from the parking lot. "Any idea what we're having to eat?"

"No. Have you talked to Colt since Friday? I've decided he and Alison are just work friends."

"Works for me. I've talked to him some. Not about what you want to know. He didn't bring it up, so I didn't bring it up. Used to you didn't think Phoenix was good for him."

"I know, but she's kind of grown on me. Besides, I don't think she's leaving Chancey. She's almost more settled here than he is." I judge that we're too close to Missus's for me to tell him what I know about Phoenix's inability to have a baby. It just never seems the time is right. Plus, I'm not sure if she'd want me telling him. What if he tells his brother?

He laughs. "One plus for Alison: Since she was married to Danny, we know she wouldn't think Colt is too immature."

"I don't know. A woman with kids probably needs a little more stability than Colt is working with."

"Hey, that's my brother you're talking about."

"You're right. I just, I can't help but think Phoenix is messing up."

We pull in across the street from Missus's house and park. As we cross the street, I see Savannah and Gregory are just now turning at the corner by the library. They are talking and taking their time. Augusta left church ahead of us, so her car is already parked directly in front of the house. Walking up the sidewalk,

I reach down to brush the blossoming spires of snapdragons along the path. FM loved gardening, and these returning snapdragons in shades of yellow, blush, and white just say spring, and FM, to me.

The front porch still sports its fresh colors from the wedding paint job. Sage and light pink were the colors of the flowers for Delaney and Peter. Camille made them the colors of everything else that stood still that day. The porch, the rented furniture, everything. The door opens as we near it, and Peter steps forward to welcome us.

"I have door duty, it seems. Oh, and there comes the young people." We watch them walk and chat, unaware they're being watched. "He's a fine young man, isn't he?" Peter asks, and in his voice is a genuine question.

"Yes," Jackson and I both assure him.

I add, "I've truly enjoyed getting to know him this week. Hopefully we'll be seeing more of him."

"Doubtful he'll spend much time here. Especially since Delaney's parents are buying a house in Elon for us to spend more time there."

Jackson whistles. "That's a real investment. Didn't they just pay to redo their wing in this house? What does Gregory think of having his family move to college, and everywhere else, with him?"

Peter cocks his head, then shrugs. "I don't know, but I'm sure it's all been well thought out. Thompson doesn't do anything halfway." He looks up as Savannah and Gregory walk up the porch steps. "Isn't that right, Gregory? Your grandfather thinks through every possibility before he makes a decision."

Gregory smiles and sticks his hand out to shake his father's. "Well, at least every possibility *he* can think of. Sometimes there are things he might just miss." He places his hand on Savannah's back and guides our daughter in between us and into the house, saying, "No worries, though. Gussie will catch him up."

"I'm so glad I'm not having a picnic on a creek bed today," Jackson says in a reversal of his early statement. "This was incredible. Probably the best fried chicken I've ever eaten. And I've eaten a lot."

We'd been treated to a full Southern Sunday dinner by none other than Phoenix. Fried chicken, mashed potatoes, fresh lima beans, biscuits, and the best macaroni and cheese I've ever had. But it did feel weird her serving us and then staying in the kitchen while we ate.

As soon as we finish, I get up and excuse myself to the restroom. I hurry there so I can come back and help clean off the table. I just can't sit and let her do that, too. Missus is demanding I sit down, Camille is silently judging me, but Savannah and Delaney jump up and help.

When we push through the swinging door into the kitchen, we catch Phoenix off guard. She's sitting at the kitchen table with a chicken leg in her mouth. "Oh, I'm sorry! I—"

"Hush. Keep eating," Delaney says. "We're just giving you a hand. Feels good to get up and move around after that amazing meal."

"Can you teach me to cook like that?" Savannah asks, making us all turn to look at her. She shrugs. "I mean, that was really, really good." She wanders to the stove. "What's for dessert?"

"Strawberry shortcake made with fresh Florida strawberries."

Our drooling is cut short as Gregory pushes open the door. "Hey, Gussie wants y'all to come on out."

Phoenix shoos us ahead of her. "I'll finish up the table and put on a pot of coffee."

"There you are. Everyone sit. I have an announcement," Augusta says from where she's standing across the table from Jackson's and my seats. She waits while we sit and Phoenix takes the last few dishes off the table.

It takes a while for the room to fall silent after she's back behind the swinging kitchen door.

Thompson looks at his watch, smiles up at his younger sister, then clears his throat.

She smiles back at him, looking younger than usual, I realize. Looking more like Delaney than before. She's wearing her usual clothes, her hair is the same; maybe it's just the idea of going home soon. I know that would make me happy. This is not an easy family to navigate.

She straightens her shoulders, lifts her chin, and her words come out fast. "I had an interesting visitor at my home in the weeks before my visit to Chancey. This woman contacted me by phone at first, and after several long conversations, I invited her to Aiken to spend some time with us. She then, with my full-throated encouragement, went to visit Gregory at school."

All our heads snap to look at Gregory. After a quick look around the table acknowledging us all, he lifts his face back to his great-aunt. Which leaves the rest of us to do the same.

"My visitor said she'd been looking for someone with true Southern heritage, a desire for truth, and the gift of language. Particularly the ability to write well and express their thoughts cogently with a sharp sense of humor." She holds her hands out, palms up, toward her nephew.

This time, as we think about her words, we turn slower to look at Gregory. He reaches down to the floor between him and Savannah to hand her the straw bag she'd carried to church. She'd said it was a change of clothes in case they wanted to go on a walk or something, but she pulls out a handful of identical books and hands them to him. He then passes the thin, dark green books around to the rest of us.

"Oh, darling," Delaney exclaims. "This is amazing. I'm assuming this is your pen name, Greg Aiken? How wise! I'm so proud of you. We all are! What's it about?"

He's blushing as he looks up and shrugs. "Just some short stories. A university press published it. I won a contest at school."

His grandfather laughs and roars, "Of course you did! You're a LaMotte. Well done, son, well done. But I agree using a fake name is wise with all the legal shenanigans out there today."

Peter gets in on the glory. "I've done some writing myself. Did you know my degree at Harvard is in journalism? And to have a publisher visiting you at school? Why, maybe we should have some champagne."

Augusta holds up both hands. "Wait. I didn't say it was a publisher, and you might want to wait on the champagne. However, you do know our visitor quite well, Peter."

He gives her a quizzical look, and as I look from him, past Delaney, back to Augusta, I know. I know who the visitor is. I know who's been tracking across the South putting all this together.

Augusta gives her great-nephew a quizzical look, as though asking permission, and he says, "Yes, tell them."

Please let me be wrong. Please let me be wrong.

She pulls herself to her full height. "Gregory has a contract to write a series of novels based on old Southern families with a very well-known author. Sally Blankenship."

I'm not wrong.

Chapter 46

Thompson and Camille look around the table as it dawns on them that they are the only ones who don't know who this Sally Blankenship person is.

Delaney licks her lips. Jackson's hand squeezes my leg, I think to remind me to breathe. Savannah won't look up at me, so I think she must've known something about all this. Delaney finally smiles and says, "Aunt Gussie, I don't think you know who this woman is." She slides her hand across the table toward her son. "Of course we're so proud of you, Gregory, but this will take so much of your time and take you away from school. It might be good to let your grandfather look into it all."

Her son reaches out and pats her hand. "School won't be a problem."

"Good. That's good, but—"

"Because I'm no longer going to Elon after this semester, and I'm changing from pre-law to creative writing."

Camille gasps, but that's all that gets out before Augusta sharply claps her hands. "Let me finish, please. Yes, Elon has been notified Gregory is leaving after this semester. He will not be returning to Aiken because I will no longer be living there as that house has been sold. Sally scouted out some properties when she was here for the book festival. I'm signing the contract this week on our new home here. By the time Gregory moves to Chancey, his writing studio will be ready. He'll work on his creative writing degree online starting next fall." She finishes by sitting down, picking up her water glass, and taking a long drink.

Thompson, seated at the end of the table and around the corner from her, draws in a deep breath. "I think not. I bought the South Carolina house. You can't just sell it."

She sets her glass down. "Of course I can. Remember, it was all in my name, my newly changed legal name of Duvall, so no one could connect you to us. Believe me. It's all legal and above board."

Gregory speaks up. "Gussie did a great job of raising me, and she's been kind enough to give me a place to start my career." He turns to Peter and Delaney. "I'm close to the age you were when you got pregnant with me. I understand you had little, if anything, to do with how things were arranged. I really want to get to know both of you, and that's one major reason why we are moving here. After spending this week here, I know it's the right place for us."

He quickly turns to his grandparents. "I also understand you did what you thought best, and it did turn out to be the best for me. Now, however, Gussie and I are making our own decisions. I don't want to be a lawyer, and I don't want to live on a campus with a bunch of other well-to-do young people. She and I like small towns. I want to write, and Gussie wants to, well, she's not exactly sure yet, but we're going to do it here." He smiles at Savannah. "I'm finding friends here. I can't wait to live in Chancey."

Missus hasn't said a word all this time. She's sat back in her chair and watched, but now she quickly stands. "Well, I believe I am ready for dessert. You can all retire to the living room. Thompson, feel free to turn on the television for your golf show." She doesn't hesitate as she leaves the table, ignoring Augusta, who is still standing in place with a hand up. Missus throws back at us as she reaches the kitchen door, "Carolina, can you help me in the kitchen?"

I excuse myself as Augusta sits down, and I hurry after Missus. In the kitchen she's standing with both hands bracing her on the kitchen counter. Phoenix makes eye contact with me, blows out a breath from puffed cheeks, and shakes her head. "I'll see what everyone wants to drink with dessert," she says as she darts out the door.

"Did you know any of this?" Missus asks softly as I step closer to her.

"No," I answer. "Nothing."

She turns around to lean against the counter, her face grim. However, as she folds her arms, she smiles. Then her smile grows until her lips open and she's shaking her head, her face full of delight. "Oh, Carolina. First of all, I'm terrified that Blankenship woman wants to do damage to Peter, personally and professionally and even mentally. I think she truly has it out for him. She terrifies me."

I nod, then study her for a minute. "While I agree with you about Sally Blankenship, I've got to say you don't actually look terrified. What are you thinking?"

She closes her eyes and mouth, then opens them to look at me and explain. "My grandson. He's FM all over again. I hadn't noticed it because of how much he looks like Peter, but he doesn't act like Peter ever did." She slumps and shakes her head as her smile softens and her eyes go misty. "FM is back in Chancey."

"There you are," Augusta says, pushing out the half-opened French door from the kitchen onto our deck. It hadn't been closed as we've gone in and out it all afternoon since we got

om our eventful Sunday dinner. We've wandered
doing little bits of yard work, planning new flower
beds, deciding which trees need to be trimmed, and looking
for newly greened branches or pokes of flowers coming back
again. Spring happens fast here once we near the end of March.
Now, however, I'm sitting on the porch with a book while Jackson is messing with the lawnmower on the side of the house.

I close my book and look up at her. "So you finally decided
to come back. You've not been at the Bedwells all this time,
have you?"

"Oh, heavens no. I left shortly after you and Jackson. I wanted to wait and make sure Gregory got out of there without
a scene. He and Savannah changed clothes and went to her
brother's to visit for a bit. I believe he's leaving her there when
he heads back to school."

"Yes, that's what she texted me. She's going to babysit for
Will and Anna this afternoon while they clean up from the
class party and then go grocery shopping."

She takes the seat across from me where Jackson usually
sits. Our chairs face out, looking down the hill to the river. The
sky is a muted blue as the afternoon softens toward evening.
There's no wind. The air is losing its warmth, but there's a gentleness in the shift. "We might need jackets when the sun goes
behind the house, but right now it feels nice," I say. "Can I assume we were there today to provide you a buffer?"

She tilts her head, still watching the river and sky. "Probably
some. But more for a correct, impartial record when people
start talking. And we both know they are going to start talking.
Probably already are!" she says with a laugh. After a moment,
she turns in her seat to face me. "Our story, mine and Gregory's, has from the very start been orchestrated by my brother,
and don't get me wrong, it's worked out well. We had everything we needed and had a very simple, happy life in Aiken.
We've had wonderful friends, a close community, except… no

one really knew us. I was a single mother who had left the convent to raise her child." She sighs and rolls her eyes. "There's enough in that skeleton of a story to keep people from asking too many questions."

"I suppose so. And I'm assuming Thompson and Camille never came to visit? Delaney either?"

"No. It was my request, but they were all happy to oblige. Delaney bore all the weight I'd grown up with from the family. The expectations, the obligations, carrying the name, but she bore it all alone. No older, ambitious brother like I had to take some of the pressure off. She saw Gregory when we visited, but I was his mother. My niece already had too much on her plate. You can see Gregory's not one to meditate on loss or sadness. He was like that even as a toddler and young boy. He has a gift for living in the moment and seeing things for the way they truly are." She wraps her arms around herself. "Brrrr! It's too cold out here for me," she says. "It's been an exhausting day. I believe I'll make a cup of tea, take it to my room, and retire for the night."

"I don't blame you. It has been a full day. So, do you know when you'll be closing on your house?"

She pauses at the door. "Yes. Wednesday morning. Uh, would you like to come do the final walk-through with me on Tuesday?" She chuckles. "That didn't come out right. Would you *please* come do the final walk-through with me? I'd really like your company, and your opinion."

"Absolutely. Now go inside. You're shivering."

She scurries in, closing the door behind her.

I hug myself, trying to ignore the chill, which I'm not sure has only to do with the temperature. So—Gregory lives in the moment and sees things for how they truly are.

That does sound like FM. All afternoon I've been remembering the strong-willed, easy-going man we all loved. His quiet confidence allowed him to love someone like Missus and yet not be steamrolled by her. . He never shied away from hard situations or truths. He met life head on, always knowing good would win. Gregory did remind me of FM when he spoke up at the table today.

Maybe he and Savannah dating isn't such a bad idea.

Chapter 47

"Silas, this is amazing!" I stumble out of my car slack-jawed at all the color and activity surrounding me. "Last time I was here it was mostly empty gravel parking lots and big, empty buildings."

Silas is loping in my direction, his smile as wide as his gait is long. "Isn't it great? Exactly how I imagined it. Jackson is over there." He points to the second row of greenhouses, where Jackson and Will are working with a handful of guys. "They've completely repaired the greenhouses so they're ready to be used, hence the huge delivery of plants. And they've almost finished laying out the plan for the outside beds and walking paths. Come inside, you have to see the whole plan starting from in here."

He strides ahead of me to a building off to one side. "This is going to be the office and market area. Colt said it's in pretty good shape, so he's finished here."

I turn around and around as he rapidly points out things in his plans one after the other: shelves for produce, a seating area for dining, a counter where he wants to serve fruit milkshakes and ice cream. He darts to the side where a table is laid out with large sheets of paper and waves for me to follow him. "Here's the plans. Isn't this going to be great? There's nothing like it in this area until you get up into the apple orchards and farms over around Blue Ridge. We're going to stay away from apples since they are pretty much covered. I'm leaning more toward flowers and berries. Stuff homeowners want to plant. What do you think about a petting zoo?"

Laughing, I sit on a bench near the window, looking out the back of his property down toward the lake. It's a beautiful view on a mild, sunny morning. "Slow down a bit. This is all incredible."

He sinks onto the bench beside me. "Do you really think so? It's happening so fast, but isn't that maybe a sign that it's all going like it should? Couldn't that be it?" He shakes his shaggy head and then drops it onto his hands, his elbows resting on his muddy, jean-covered knees. "Or is it a slippery slope to doom?" He springs back. "No, I can't think negatively. It's all good. It's all good, right?"

He stares at me, his beautiful eyes made even brighter by the long fringe of unkempt hair and the dirt smudges on his movie-star face. I reach out and lay a hand on his arm. With a squeeze, I ask, "Silas, are you happy?"

He sucks in a deep breath. "It's honestly amazing how happy I am. I love acting and I know acting is what has made all this possible, but acting never filled me up like this. This creating from scratch and the smell of the dirt. The ideas and plants." He waves out the window. "Look at all the plants!"

The hillside is full of black pots, paths winding between them, leading to rows of saplings. "How did you even know what to order?"

When he doesn't answer, I turn back to look at him. The brightness is gone, replaced by guilt. "Susan," he mumbles.

"Susan is helping you? My Susan. Susan Lyles?" I smack his arm. "That's fantastic! Don't worry, I won't tell anyone that y'all are back together. I'm just so happy for you both."

"No. It's not like that." He stands up and brushes off his thighs. "I'd be more than happy if I had some great secret like that, but I don't. Susan wants nothing to do with me, so I stole her, our, plan." He walks over to stand beside the window. "This was all our dream. She drew all this out years ago, and she shared it with me. All those days and nights falling in love with not only her, but this dream. A farm. A nursery, even selling fruit milkshakes. Then she got cold feet."

I wait. He's gone still, traveling well-worn paths in his mind that lead to nowhere. As a truck starts backing up outside with its incessant beeping, he comes back to himself. "So she wasn't using her dream, and I needed a new one. Besides, she's through dreaming. She told me that in no uncertain terms the last time we talked. Which was before I came back."

I stand. "Has Susan been out here at all?"

"I don't think so. She'd be welcome anytime. I've made sure she knows that." He sighs. "But like you said the other night, she has her kids on her mind, and that's what she needs to do right now. Let's go walk around a bit. I want to show you the greenhouses."

He pushes open a sliding barn door on the side of the large building, and the morning sunshine spills in. "Up there, that's my house. Not much to look at, but I don't need much." He's pointing over the roof of the first greenhouse to an old mobile home which faces away from us. "It's situated kind of weird, but when you're up there, you can see that it's set so the living room and back patio look out toward the lake. It's small, but really open. I can even see the mountains behind the lake from my bedroom," he says, though his voice trails off. As we're looking that way, we watch a car pull through the parking lot and keep driving toward the house. I feel him tense and look to see his jaw tighten. The car jerks to a stop, and the driver's door opens. A pit opens up in my stomach as he says, "Wonder what Sally's doing back here?"

We answer her wave with our own, then keep watching as she opens the trunk to pull out a suitcase. I decide to wade on in. "So, Silas, did you hear about Sally's book deal with Peter and Delaney's son, Gregory?"

The lack of a quick response tells me enough, but he goes ahead and answers. "Maybe a little. I better go see, what, uh, she, well... you'll find Jackson over there. Talk to you later."

He heads off, gravel crunching under his boots. I head in the other direction, mumbling about how messed up everything seems. I've never been good at playing chess. I know how the pieces move, but that's about it. However, I believe if I had a chessboard with all the Chancey players on it and complete control, I could pull off a win for everyone.

Problem is they're all stupid and won't let me have control.

Maybe I should issue a proclamation.

"I like it!" Laney says. "Now, tell me just how you'd fix everything if they'd let you. What exactly would this proclamation of yours say? I mean, we all know I don't need fixing. I'm all good. But about these other people..." She rolls her hand to encourage more ranting from me.

I stopped in at The Club on the way to the bookstore from Silas's place. My morning opened up as I was in a hurry to get away from the farm before I had to talk to Sally, and then Andy texted to say he was going to be late with our weekly book delivery. With extra time on my hands, I decided I'd see how things are at The Club. Plus, Laney is always good for a rant session—as long as she's not one of the subjects.

One of the other tables at the far end of the room has a group of ladies listening to a book on tape and doing needlework. They are older ladies, one of whom is Laney's mother, so I'm having to keep my voice down talking about Susan. I wait for Laney to carry her own coffee to the table. I already have mine. A cinnamon-sugar combination. I guess it's a little early for shopping, as there's no one looking over the merchandise, so I don't have to worry about eavesdroppers there. "Where's Cayden if your mom is here?"

"Barbara Yeldin. I figured if she's going to open a daycare she must like kids. Due to the remodeling at their house, most of the time she comes over to our house and watches him, so it's even easier for me."

"Really? I didn't realize you'd hired her."

"Her credentials and references are stellar. Otherwise she's just okay. Pretty strict, I think, and kind of scared of everything. You know the sort? But then strict and worried is probably a good mix for working in childcare. So. I need the quick rundown on who you're fixing and how."

With an eye on Laney's mom, who's heading to the restroom, I start talking in a different direction than Susan and Silas. "Did you know Colt and Alison Kinnock might be dating?"

"Oh, so it's Colt. No, I mean, I knew she was dating someone. She's *always* dating someone." She raises a finger at me. "Not like that. She's just cute and has always had a boyfriend. You know, like the girls in school who are about boys like they should be about jobs? Don't quit one until you have a new one? Hmm, Colt and Alison, I bet they look good together." She leans forward. "Does he know she has three daughters?"

"Yep, they call him Coach. But I want him back with Phoenix."

"Why?"

"I just feel sorry for her…" I suddenly remember I can't say why.

"Sorry for her? Have you seen her legs? They go on for miles. She's got two thriving businesses, her own home, and did I mention her legs go on for miles? She's a dancer. In my experience a red-headed dancer don't need no sympathy. Next."

"Bet you didn't know Sally Blankenship is back in town and is going to be here kind of for good."

She leans back and actually rubs her chin in thought. "Hmmm, think that will light a fire under my sister? Make her jealous and get her back on track with Silas? Yeah, we can use that." She lifts her cup up. "How do you know? She check in at the B&B?" she asks, then takes a sip.

"No. I just saw her rolling a suitcase into Silas's mobile home."

She chokes and jumps to keep from spilling coffee onto her blouse. "She's shacking up with Silas? No. Not having it. Can't we catch even a little bit of a break here?"

"Now you see what I'm talking about. These people will just not cooperate."

"I don't feel good about Silas's ability to hold off that, that"— she rolls her lips like she has a particular thing she'd like to call Sally, but she settles for a biting—"*woman*, even one little bit. I thought she was out of the picture at least for a while. Doesn't she live in New York?"

"That's another thing. I've been given permission to spread the word that Augusta is buying a house here, Gregory is moving here after the semester, and he's writing books with"—I pause to nod as her eyes grow big—"none other than Sally Blankenship."

Laney is not often caught without anything to say, but she is for the moment. Before the moment of silence can be fully appreciated, the door opens and Peter steps inside.

"Carolina. I've been looking all over for you. We need to talk."

"Why didn't you just call me?" I ask as I check to make sure my phone is on.

He shuffles around, looking at the rack of purses near him. "I just thought it'd be better to talk in person. Can you? I mean, like, now?"

Laney stands up. "Sure. You can have my seat. I have some things to do in the back."

Peter frowns. "Here? No. Carolina, I'll meet you outside."

He leaves, and after slipping my phone back in my purse, I say, "And another piece from the chessboard shows up. Another unruly, stubborn piece that won't do what he should."

As she gathers our coffee mugs to take them to the little sink next to the coffee maker, she leans toward me for a kind of side hug. "Sweetie, one thing I learned a long, long time ago about board games. Sometimes the only way to win is to flip the board in the air and stomp off."

I can't help but chuckle. "I don't think that can actually be called winning."

She gives me a wink. "Ya gotta learn that when it's your board, it's your rules. If you say it's winning, it's winning. But most of all, friend, a bit of warning: Don't ask for control if you're not going to use it."

Chapter 48

When I step out onto the sidewalk, Peter is nowhere to be seen. I look to my right, past the dance studio and then across the side street to his house. He could be in the shadows of the porch, but I don't believe he had enough time to get all the way there. I look back to my left, all the way past Ruby's, Blooming Books, down to AC's, and still no Peter.

"He can't have just disappeared," I mumble as I dig out my phone to call him. Just as his phone starts to ring, he steps out the door leading up to his office.

"Are you coming?" Then he looks down at his phone. "Why are you calling me?" His look at me is half frown, half pity.

"I didn't know where you were."

"As if I'm going to stand out on the sidewalk. Of course we'll go up to my office to talk." He holds the door for me and then waves me on up the steep staircase to his office. I turn to the left, heading down the hallway to the door at the end. He's right behind me, walking fast, and it feels like I'm being marched to the principal's office. Laney said I shouldn't ask for control if I don't want to use it, so I decide to slow down and be in control of this forced march. Seriously, I'm already short of breath from dashing up that ancient staircase.

"Oops, are you okay? Do you need to rest a minute?" Peter

says as he almost barrels me over. "Do you want me to get you a chair?"

"No, I'm fine. Just, uh, my, I have a rock in my shoe. I'm fine." Once inside the office reception area, I'm able to stop for a moment and breathe, waiting to see which direction he wants to go.

"You know where my office is, right?"

"Oh sure. That's right." I head down the interior hall. Have you ever noticed when you're out of breath you tend to get even more out of breath trying to catch your breath? Pretty soon it's like you just ran a marathon. I stop to let him pass me and open his office door, which apparently wasn't locked, but I how was I supposed to know that? By the time I get in his office and sit down, I'm breathing almost normally, especially when he pauses to read a couple of messages lying on his desk and I get a chance to take a couple of deep breaths.

Then he drops the small pieces of paper and starts. "So I'm going to assume you understand it is not in Gregory's best interest to move here. I hope to appeal to your desire to help the young man make a better decision for his future," he spills out as he sits hard in his big chair behind the desk.

"Why? Maybe it's exactly what he should do. He seemed very sincere in his intent to get to know you and Delaney better."

Peter can't help but smile at that. "Yes, that was very gratifying. I think I would like that." Then he pulls his frown back in place. "But his future is in the hands of his grandparents. His LaMotte grandparents. He's their only grandchild, and they have considerable means and influence. We must help get him back on track. From what Thompson says, Gregory is assured a slot in the law school at Elon, and that's nothing to sneeze at."

I interrupt. "Except he doesn't want to be a lawyer."

"He says that now, but well, he doesn't have to actually practice law. It's about the doors it'll open. Politics and connections, along with the foundation of analytical thinking."

"Peter, honestly, have you ever seen anyone less interested in those things than your son? Except maybe with the exception of..." I slow down and come to a pause to see if he'll make the FM connection. Or to see if his mother has made it for him.

"You can't mean me, right? What are you talking about?"

Nope, clueless. I sit back and decide to just let him talk. And talk he does. While I think of the way he's refusing to see all the things he doesn't want to see, about Shannon and the baby, about Gregory, I feel myself softening and finding a bit of compassion for him. Almost feeling sorry for him. Then... I actually listen to him.

"They, Sally and Gregory, have to know everyone will sue. They can't just go around besmirching the good names of whole families and not expect pushback. I would be first in line to sue them, and he's my son. Can you imagine what strangers will do if they try to hang out important people's dirty, possibly made-up, laundry?"

"You'd sue your own son?"

"To protect my mother? Our name? Of course I would. You have to make them understand. Sally likes you. Maybe she'll listen to you."

"Sally Blankenship is *your* friend. You're the one that brought her here. Also it feels to me like the two of you might have some unfinished business from years gone by?" As his frown deepens, I stand up. "I have to get to the shop. Why don't you just try and talk to Gregory? Talk to Augusta. She'll be at my house until at least Wednesday when she closes on her new home."

He also stands, but he's smirking. "Like that closing is going to happen. It's emblematic of how little she understands the gravity of this situation that she gave her brother a heads-up. He's shut down bigger deals than that in much less time."

"He wouldn't. Besides, I don't think he can or should even want to. Gregory is an adult."

Coming from behind the desk to motion me toward the door, he says, "You don't understand. There is no way Thompson LaMotte is letting his grandson live here and function out of his control. He has a plan."

"And like I said, Gregory's an adult. The LaMottes can't control him and Augusta like that. They'll refuse to go along with it."

"But their bank? Their Realtor? Thompson has a very well-thought-out plan, and he's going to make it happen," he stresses. I angrily pass through the open door but turn around when he calls my name. "Carolina, honestly. You have to admit it's not pretty, but it's what's best for Gregory. I mean, look at Will. Look at what all he gave up to live in a cabin and go to a local college. His wife, my niece, has to work at a junk store to make ends meet. Everyone knows if you'd had the ability to keep Will on the path to law school you'd have done it." He shrugs as he slowly begins to close the door. "That's all that's happening here. Thompson has the fortitude, and resources, to do what you and Jackson couldn't." And the door closes.

Peter's words sting—because he's right.

If I could've kept Will on the path to law school, if I could've kept him from moving to Chancey, if I could've kept him from becoming a father so young and having such a hard first year of marriage—I would have. In a heartbeat.

Walking toward the shop, I keep my head down as I pass Ruby's and even as I push through our front door. I just want to get back to my little table where I mark the new books. I don't want to talk to anyone, and I definitely don't want anyone to talk to me.

But this is Chancey.

Bonnie meets me before I'm past the counter. "Andy put the new books back at the table. There aren't many this week.

Danny is off until noon, and so I told Shannon to not worry about coming down first thing this morning. Let them pretend they're still on their honeymoon," she says with a laugh. "However…" She slows down to get to what she really wants to say, but then actually looks at me.

"Oh, what's wrong? Are you okay?"

"I'm fine. What 'however'?"

Bonnie is a good judge of character, and she judges wisely to not push me on how I am. "I need to go out and look at a potential job this morning if you can handle the shop by yourself for an hour. Danny and Shannon are upstairs if there's an emergency."

Her words are clipped and efficient, and they make me smile. "That sounds fine. I'm sorry. I just had a conversation with Peter, and it was, well, upsetting. Nothing unusual, sadly. Of course I'll be fine here. What's the potential job?"

She follows me to the coffee pot and excitement creeps back into her voice. "Just a neighbor of Patty's and Andy's. I love their neighborhood, and that size of house is perfect for me. Those huge houses up in Laurel Cove are just too much for me at this stage, especially since I don't have any help. They said anytime this morning, so if it's okay with you I'll pop on over there now."

"It's perfect. Good luck." I pour a cup of coffee while she gets her purse and notebook. By the time I'm seated at the card table, she's left. I don't even look in the open box at my feet, just lean on the table with both elbows, holding my warm coffee close to my face. The store settles into quiet and I settle into that.

What if I could've changed everything for Will? What if the power was in my hands? What if I actually had that control I was begging for earlier? Then there would be no Francie. No cabin on the creek with Anna. No business working alongside his father and uncle. I'm stunned at what all I would've dismissed from existence if I'd had my way. If I'd had control of the board of play.

I close my eyes and take a deep breath. "Lord, thank you for... I don't even know. Just thank you."

CHAPTER 49

"So, what do you think of Gregory's plan?" I ask Savannah as she meanders toward the stairs.

Dinner had been late due to everyone going in different directions today: Jackson working at the Yeldin's house. Savannah working at Andy's Place on the online catalog she's putting together for him. Bryan had basketball practice and then a team meeting. We ate and everyone moved off to different areas of the house. Savannah and I are the last ones in the living room: Me sitting down to turn on the television. Her wandering around like she wants to talk.

I've found teens do better if given space and time to talk when they want. Of course there are times you have to force them to open up, but those are never fun and often bloody.

Sure enough, she detours toward the couch. I lower the volume of the television, but leave it on. Another sure conversation killer, letting them think they have your full attention. That's why car talks are so effective.

She sits on the chair near me. "That was crazy at Missus's dinner yesterday, wasn't it?"

"Very. Seemed like you and Gregory had talked beforehand about it all."

"Yeah, but just on the walk from church. He'd asked me a lot about how it was to move here earlier, and so I think he felt we had that in common. Everyone else pretty much has lived their whole life here."

"True. I hadn't thought of you two having that in common."

She sits back in the chair, folding one leg underneath her. "How weird would it be to not really know your mom and dad? I mean, he loves Miss Augusta. A lot." Her voice is low, but the door to the B&B hall is closed and Augusta hasn't come out since she got home right after we had dinner. "But some of it is for her, too. He says she really likes it here and wants to put down roots where people know who she really is. Also he says she's never been comfortable living in South Carolina. You know what she says. She's a Georgia girl." We both chuckle. It's one of Augusta's favorite lines.

"Is he worried about his grandparents interfering?"

"Not really. He's just excited about writing. About working with Ms. Blankenship." She widens her eyes at me and I feel this is what she wants to talk about.

So I ask, "Do you think that's a good idea?"

"I don't know. I mean, you know about, uh, Ronnie and her? Ricky told me about you catching them all out at the fire. At first I was mad at Ricky, but then I realized I'm really over him. But then did you know she and Ronnie were together, like, more?"

I slightly shake my head to keep her flow going.

"They were out a bunch of times when she was here. I mean, she's really older, right?"

"Yeah, she's more my age. She was in college with Peter."

"Right!" Bingo, this is where her mind's been. "What if she's after Gregory like that? I don't think he thinks of her like that, but what if she, like, comes on to him and you know..."

"I know. Did you try to warn him?"

She scrunches up her face. "Some. Just kind of told him about Ronnie and her. Kind of. I didn't want him to think I was gossiping about her. He didn't seem to be bothered, so maybe he's not interested in her like that. He is kind of obsessed with writing."

"That's good. That's real good. Kind of like you and the computer graphic stuff, I guess. How's the catalog going?"

"It's fun, but I'm seeing what all I need to learn. How much I don't know. So much cool stuff that can be done." She worries her lip. "Do you think I should talk to Miss Augusta about all that with Miss Blankenship?"

"How about I mention it to her?"

"Yeah, that's a good idea. I mean, you did see her with Ronnie, so it's not like you just heard it from me." She stands and stretches. From the ease on her face and the relaxed way she's moving, I can tell she's said what she needed to. "It'll be fun having Gregory here, I think. Miss Augusta, too."

"So are you liking him more than as a friend?"

Never hurts to try and slide one more in at the end. Kind of like reporters when the president is leaving the podium.

She stops, one hand on the stair railing, one foot on a step. "Maybe. Not yet of course. He's all the way in North Carolina and this *is* my senior year." She laughs as she heads up the stairs. "I am looking forward to camping at Nathan's for spring break. Might get a spring fling invite while we're hanging out around the bonfire!"

See, sometimes that last question turns up gold.

"Hey, Colt wants to use one of our rooms until Friday. Is that okay?" Jackson's question brings me out of our bathroom with my toothbrush still in my mouth as we get ready for bed.

"Why? Wait," I say as I dart back inside, spit, then rinse. "Why? What's going on?"

Jackson is sitting on the edge of the bed and holds up his

phone. "He just texted me to ask. I've got to say I'm not surprised. He's been sleeping in his office at the school, I found out today. Bryan said something about it the other night, but you know me, I didn't put two and two together. Didn't even think to mention it you. But I guess he can't be dating that Alison and living with Phoenix."

With a sigh I sit on my side of the bed. "Yeah, I didn't even want to think about that. I mean, I was hoping he wasn't actually dating Alison. More of a colleague. A work friend. We do have guests coming in Friday. What's he going to do after that?"

"He's moving back to the apartments. There's one open, but it's being painted. It'll be available Friday." He turns out the lamp on his side. "I guess the two of them are just not meant to be."

Turning out my light I sadly agree, but settling into my pillow and closing my eyes, that chessboard comes to mind. Colt is like a simple checker trying to play in a chess game—he doesn't even know what he doesn't know.

And Queen Phoenix apparently has no intention of changing that.

Chapter 50

"Can Zoe go camping with us for spring break? Her folks already said it's okay. She'll bring her own sleeping bag. Did you give me Doritos for lunch? Who's picking me up from practice?"

All I can do is stand there, gaping at my youngest. I'm still in my robe, I barely slept, they are running late for school, and his sister is still upstairs. Jackson is already downstairs dealing with some work emergency, so there's no help arriving on a white horse.

I shove his lunch bag at him and walk past him to the living room entrance. "Savannah!" I shout. "You need to be leaving!"

My youngest pushes past me like a loaded-down elephant with his size eleven shoes, lunch, books, and unzipped book bag. Then he echoes me, yelling, "Hey, hurry up! Zoe's in the driveway." Then he looks at me, eyebrows raised. "So, practice? Zoe? Doritos?"

"I don't know. I guess. Okay, I'll get you from practice. About Zoe, I'll talk to your dad, and yes, Doritos."

Savannah comes pounding down the stairs. "Hurry up. We're late." She does a quick tour of the kitchen, comes out with a banana, a Little Debbie oatmeal cake, and her lunch bag. As she maneuvers around me, she sniffs. "Nathan asked Holly, who is just a junior and shouldn't even be allowed to go, to senior spring fling last night, so I doubt I'm going on your little camping trip."

She slams the front door behind her, and I am left debating if opening it and telling her to drive carefully would make her more or less angry. Well, we all know the answer to that, so I go back into the kitchen.

When I hear the front door open, I yell, "What did you forget?"

"How much fun teenagers are," comes the answer followed by a laugh. Augusta then walks into the kitchen. "Good morning. I was waiting on the front porch until the coast was clear. I only ever had one kid to get out the door, but that sure brought back memories."

I chuckle. "Good morning. How was your walk?"

"Nice. I love walking down along the riverbank. So many little woodland flowers popping up." She puts on the tea kettle, then sits at the table.

"So you could hear all that out there?"

"I actually was in the living room for some of it. I was going to make my tea to have out there, but decided it was better, and safer, to wait."

"Probably right." I hesitate in the doorway. I need to get dressed, but I also want to warn her about what Peter said. About her brother keeping her house from closing. However, that's what all my dreams were about last night: Should I step in with her, with Phoenix, with Susan, with Colt? When is interfering help, and when is it, well, interfering?

"Tell me," she says. Her voice is quiet and inviting. I look at her and see kind eyes and a peaceful face. Her brother would destroy her dreams in a heartbeat and not give it a second thought. I have to try, don't I?

"Your house..." I begin, but then the tea kettle starts to whistle.

"I'll get that. Please continue."

Her back is to me as I say, "About your house? What if something happens to stop the closing? I mean, your brother doesn't seem to want it to happen."

She chuckles as she finishes with her cup and turns around to carry it to the table. "You're right about that. But I'm not worried."

I slide into the chair at the end of the table. "Really? Why not?"

"Because I closed yesterday morning, first thing."

"But you told me, and well, Peter knew that your closing is tomorrow. Wednesday."

"Yes, but that wasn't the truth. I wanted to give myself a little breathing room. I also wanted to see if Thompson would try anything." She shrugs. "And of course he did, but it was too late. It's all taken care of. I don't have to move out of the Aiken house for a month. The buyer isn't moving there until the summer, so I'm paying them rent. That gives us plenty of time to get our home here ready. You'll still come see it with me today, won't you? Please don't be mad I lied to you."

"Oh, I'm not. I'm happy you got the house. I guess I'm surprised you aren't mad at your brother."

"Oh no, Thompson is a creature of habit. A habit that has served to make him very wealthy, so he's fairly predictable. I can rant and rail against him, but what good would that do? I love my brother and Camille. They are my family. However, that doesn't mean I ignore what I know." She looks at her watch. "You need to get ready for your day. I'll pick you up at your shop at two, okay? Maybe I'll take my tea back out to the front porch. I love your rockers out there."

I'm not sure what I just learned. There was something good there. I'm going to have to think about it.

"I don't even know where her house is. It's all been such a whirlwind I never remember to ask when I'm with her," I say to Shannon and Danny as I look for my ride out the front window. The newlyweds had a great trip to Blue Ridge, and seem to be mostly glad the wedding is behind them.

Danny is dusting the bookshelves behind me. "Well, all I know is having a house is a major headache. All that yard work and the repairs. We have it perfect in our little place upstairs, don't we, Shannon?"

My partner and I meet eyes. Hers are underneath a furrowed brow. Her voice is low and holds a bit of a warning. "For now maybe. We do have a baby on the way."

Danny doesn't miss a beat. "Oh, that's right. But it'll be tiny."

"There she is." Augusta's timing is perfect. Time to leave this conversation. "See y'all tomorrow!"

We back out of the spot she found across the street from the bookstore and head out of town, passing AC's and then the group of camellia bushes that welcome folks to town. At the stop sign, the daffodils are in full bloom. Their yellow heads bounce and sway in the afternoon sunshine. I'm surprised when she doesn't turn to the left toward the Piggly Wiggly, but goes straight across like she's going up the hill to our house.

"Up toward us? Your house is up here?" But she doesn't have time to answer before she turns to the left, right behind the daffodils. There's a drive that I've never really noticed. It goes down the hill, into the woods before ending beside a white brick house. Augusta pulls up beside it and stops the car.

"We're home!"

"I never even knew this was back here." We get out of the car and walk toward the front door. "Is that the river I hear?"

"Yes, your house is farther away from it up on the hill. Wait'll you see the river from my house," she explains.

The front yard is all woods with just a little buffer of moss and ground cover between the sidewalk and the trees. Large bushes surround the house, but I can see a wide window covered by bushes on the outside and curtains on the inside. The front door has just one step up to a brick stoop, and as Augusta unlocks the door, I realize just how quiet it is back here with the river masking all other noises.

"Now it's rather musty. It's been shut up for a while as the previous owner died and the family didn't know what to do with it." She pushes open the dark green door to the musty smell and I follow her in. The house is empty and the front room is large. There's thick green carpet, but I can see where one corner has been pulled up.

"I did that yesterday. The floors look beautiful underneath, so I'm taking out that carpet."

"Which will help tremendously with the mustiness. Oh, I see what you meant about the river." Past the living room is a dining room with another large window that looks onto an open, sloping backyard that ends at the river.

"The door outside is through the kitchen. Come on." Augusta leads me into an old-fashioned kitchen and unlocks a wooden back door. We step down onto a concrete patio, and the river grows even louder. Sunlight filters through the few trees in the backyard, which is much brighter than the front yard. "Isn't it just perfect? I can't wait to have my tea sitting right out here."

"It's absolutely delightful." We just stand and look for a moment. It's interesting seeing the river from such a different vantage point.

She turns to go back inside. "And I have Sally to thank. She found it, tracked down the owners, and cleared up all the little sticking points."

She holds the door open for me to come in behind her.

"Really? That's interesting." Maybe this is a good time to have a chat with her about Ms. Sally Blankenship. She can't be so clear-eyed when it comes to her brother and yet so blind about this storytelling woman from New York, can she?

"And here she is!" Augusta exclaims. "We were just talking about you!"

And there she is, waiting in the green-and-gold kitchen. Sally Blankenship in all her glory.

CHAPTER 51

"Isn't it perfect for Augusta and Gregory?" Sally says, her hands buried in the pockets of her long, tattered, olive-green army jacket. It has that expensive boutique-thrift look, slouchy but pressed, authentically frayed in just the right places. The jacket, boots, and jeans all look so effortless that it's obvious they aren't. But she doesn't give me any longer to critique her outfit as she spins away and heads down the hall. "Have you shown her the office?"

Augusta grins at me and pulls me along behind her. "Not yet. We just got here." We find her again at the end of the hall, in a corner room with another view of the river. It looks to be a den as it's larger and the inside walls are covered in dark wood bookshelves. A bank of windows on the back wall gives a view of the river going away from town.

"Gregory's desk will go here," Sally says, spreading her hands along the window. "I'll have a small desk back here as I work better without a view to distract me."

"Are you going to live here, too?" I add a chuckle to the end to cut some of the sharpness. They both look at me—and they don't chuckle.

Sally's hands go back into her jacket pockets. "Of course not. But we will need to work together at times. I plan to find something to rent here in town." She shrugs. "Or buy if Chancey continues to grow on me as it has. Lots of reasons to stay, I'm finding."

Augusta says nothing, just wanders back to the hall. "Over here is my room." I follow her into a room on the front corner of the house with nice-size windows, light pink walls, and a mauve carpet. "No view of the river, but the trees are lovely, and I'm hoping to bring some of the flower gardens back to life. Our house in Aiken was in a planned community with a small yard that was taken care of by professionals. I was always grateful for Thompson taking care of all that when he chose the place, but I'm quite looking forward to doing things myself for a change." She looks past me. "Sally? Have you talked to Silas?"

Sally steps into the room and walks to the front window. "Of course," she says with a grin at me. "He thought it was a great idea."

They neither one elaborate, so I have to ask. "What's a great idea?"

Augusta laughs. "Oh, classes at his new place. I'm going to need classes on how to do all this. And I'm going to need help. Until Gregory is here lifting bags of dirt and mulch or whatever I'll need, that is. Isn't this so exciting?" She moves out of the room and down the hall. Sally gives me a smile, and I return it as we both stay in the room, quiet for a few minutes.

"So what did *you* think of Silas's place?" she asks. "It's coming together well with your husband's help."

"It's all pretty impressive." I can't help asking. "So are you staying there long?"

"I don't know. This has all happened rather quickly. Finding Gregory and all these connections. You know, Peter and I were quite close for several years so to live in his hometown he talked about is rather enticing. Then there's your bookshop, this house..." She turns to look back out the window. "It's honestly moving faster than I ever imagined, so I'm still figuring out exactly what I want out of it." She laughs, spins, and walks past me. "Except for bestselling books. That I'm sure I want and sure I'll get. Everything else is just icing on the cake. Let's go find Augusta."

"I'm worried about Mom," Leslie Lyles says by way of greeting when I get back to the shop. She's waiting for me on the couch, her laptop opened on the coffee table and papers strewn around her. Susie Mae pointed me in the direction of her big sister as soon as I walked in the door, and I hadn't even said hello before Leslie told me what she was doing here. No surprise that she's such a great student; she has laser focus and doesn't get bogged down in things like saying hello when you've not seen her in a couple months.

I don't tend to be that focused. "Hey there. How was the trip?" I sit in one of the tall wingback chairs and Susie Mae leans on the arm of the couch between her sister and me.

Leslie blinks at me, then shakes her head. "Oh, yeah, NC State is everything I've always heard, and Athena was amazing." She frowns and I can feel her focus shifting, dragging along with her thoughts. "It's really weird. Our folks didn't seem unhappy when we were growing up." She looks up at her sister. "Did they? But then I watch Athena and Dad, and I wonder how we missed it. Scary to think about. How easy it can be to just... not be happy."

Susie Mae nods, her big eyes moving from Leslie to me. She can be a chatterbox, but it's like she's happy to have her sister here to take the lead, so she's keeping her mouth shut.

Leslie leans forward, her voice less strident, more worried. "So, about Mom. She doesn't look so good. I mean, she's always been skinny, so I guess a little weight doesn't hurt, but it's different. She's not herself."

"Have you talked to your aunt Laney or your grandmother?" She rolls her eyes. "Not Grandma. She gets too freaked out about everything. She never wants to know there's a problem. We're having dinner at Aunt Laney's tonight, so I plan on seeing what she thinks, but Susie Mae thought I should talk to you, too."

"Why is that, Susie Mae?" Ol' Blue Eyes is going to have to talk now.

The younger girl shrugs, licks her bottom lip, then folds her arms. "Just because she, Mom, listens to you. Plus... Silas will listen to you. He and Aunt Laney don't really get along."

Leslie's frown deepens. "So what's up with this Silas? I thought we were done with him, but Susie Mae says he's moved here? I never got to know him, and honestly I didn't want to. He's too good-looking, if you know what I mean, and the way he and Mom were acting in the fall was ridiculous." Then she sighs. "But now something's wrong with her. What do *you* think, Miss Carolina?"

Before I saw Sally roll her suitcase into his house this morning I would've been extolling Silas Pendersen's good points, but now? I take a deep breath and let it out slowly. "I don't know what to say. I think he... I just don't know. Listen, talk to your aunt and talk to your mom. I'll also call her. I wanted to see how the trip went anyway. You're right that your mom is unhappy, but she is most worried about doing right for you two and Grant. You three are her main concern."

"We know," Susie Mae groans. "That's all she keeps saying." She stands up. "Ready for me to turn over the 'Closed' sign? We've not had a customer in the last hour. Danny and Shannon went upstairs when Leslie got here. I guess they're tired from their honeymoon and the wedding stuff. How was Miss Augusta's house?"

"Really neat. It's down behind the daffodils beside the river. I didn't even know there was a house down there."

Leslie closes her laptop. "White house down in the woods? I took piano lessons there from a really old lady when I was little. Mrs. McGlasson was her name. I always thought it was spooky back in there. I'm bummed I don't get to meet the famous Gregory, but Susie Mae says his aunt is moving here? That's who you're talking about, right?"

"Yeah," I say as I start closing out the cash register. "Let me know how it goes with Laney tonight. She and I have been talking about how to help your mom, so you girls don't need to worry. She's just trying to get it back together after the divorce and all. I'm just glad the trip with Athena went well."

Leslie hauls her backpack up over her shoulder and opens the front door. "Oh, did you get the impression it went well? I said the school was great and Athena was amazing. I don't think Mom realized Dad was going along, and so it was basically the trip from hell for me."

Susie Mae nods in agreement with my stunned look as she walks past me. Then as she gets to the door she says with a slow, disapproving wag of her head, "Wait'll Aunt Laney hears."

The bell jangles. The door closes. And I quietly echo her last words as I gather my purse and go to turn out the lights.

Griffin Lyles might want to invest in some asbestos earmuffs because Laney's words about him tonight are going to do more than just burn a little.

Chapter 52

"I was so proud of myself and it's blown up in my face," Augusta solemnly greets me Wednesday morning from the dark kitchen.

Before I've had a cup of coffee.

"Oh! You scared me. Why don't you have a light on?"

"I'm working on finding the energy to get up and go for my walk, but so far..." She shrugs but still hasn't turned to look at me. She sitting facing the back doors leading to the deck. The sky is a dull pink and blue as the sun is still far below the trees and hills across the river.

Without asking, I put on a kettle of water for her tea and then fix a pot of coffee to brew. The rest of the house is quiet as no one's alarms have gone off. Mine never went off, as I woke up before five a.m. and couldn't go back to sleep. I slide into the chair beside her so I can watch the sunrise too. "Can I help?"

She leans toward me a bit and smiles. "Not really, but it's nice to have a friend," she says. "Thompson says he will never speak to me again if I do what I have planned. He says I'll be cut off from him and Camille, and while that's painful, he says he'll also cut off Gregory from everything if he follows through on our plan. Everything."

"He's their only grandchild. I'm sure they're just upset and they'll come around."

She shrugs. "Possibly. But not likely. I've scrimped and saved all these years to be able to move out on my own. I thought he might be proud of me. Happy I could take care of myself. I knew he'd not be happy about Gregory, but if he wanted Gregory to be his Mini Me, he should've spent more time with the boy!" The kettle whistles as if to emphasize her words, and she gets up. "I'll get it."

I watch her move around the kitchen and give her a moment before asking, "What if Peter and Delaney are on your side? Maybe they can get him to come around."

She laughs as she sets her cup on the table, then turns to pour me a cup of coffee. "Have you met those two? Peter is completely in awe of Thompson and owes his new law office to his father-in-law's contacts and business. And Delaney, sweet Delaney, has never bucked her parents. At the beginning of all this I tried to talk them all into her raising her child, but no one entertained that thought for a moment. Not a moment."

"You did? Even Delaney?"

"Well, you have to understand. Delaney was fairly catatonic with fear, but she wasn't a child. The girl would be an alcoholic except she decided to dull her pain with her father's approval instead of alcohol. Every atta-girl from him is like a bottle of liquor to her. She starts to dry out, come to her senses, and he plies her with another photography job for one of his friends or companies. Or sends her on a trip somewhere fabulous. He's the one who found Peter for her again and suggested all this." She takes a small sip. "No, if I proceed with my plan, I will be alone and Gregory will be left in their hands."

"Maybe he's stronger than you think."

"He probably is, but he's still no match for his grandfather." We sit in silence as the sun strikes through the tree branches. Around us we hear first Colt's alarm from the Southern Comfort room, then Savannah and Bryan getting up and moving around.

Jackson comes down the stairs, pausing when he sees us sitting, facing the rising sun. "Good morning."

"Good morning," we say, and then Augusta stands up.

"I think I'll walk down the hill to that willow tree and leave y'all to get your day started." She sets her cup in the sink, then pauses. "So today is my last day here with y'all. I don't know if I'll be back to Chancey, but know that you've left a sweet mark on my heart." She draws in a shuddery breath, then hurries out the back door.

"Everything all right?" Jackson asks.

"Not really. Her brother is none too happy with her sleight of hand getting the house papers signed. It's his game, and his rules."

"He does seem like the kind that's used to being large and in charge." He sips his coffee, leaning back against the counter and staring out the back window. Finally he says, "So Colt eventually got in last night."

He'd waited up for his brother. Colt has a key to the house, but his big brother wanted to make sure he was okay since he was going to go by Phoenix's and pick up some things. "According to him, he and Phoenix really finished it last night. He was pretty upset on the one hand, but a lot of it is his pride, I think. She doesn't seem to have a real reason for breaking up."

I can't help it. I feel him staring at me, and after a deep breath, I have to look at him. I have to tell someone. No, not someone. I have to tell him.

"Do you know something?" he asks quietly.

"Morning, all!" Colt booms from the dining room. "It's hump day, even better really since we have Friday off. Yep, downhill headed toward the weekend and spring break!" Instead of giving us a breath to say good morning, he steamrolls ahead. "I've been thinking, you know, I will join in on the camping. Started making a list of things I need to pick up down at the sports store in Canton. Y'all let me know if there's anything you need."

Bryan runs down the stairs, picking up on the camping talk before he's halfway down and joining in with gusto. Lanterns, sleeping bags, cook stoves—camping requires too much preparation in my opinion. I refresh my coffee, give Jackson a kiss and a squeeze, and slip out to go get dressed, leaving the three Jessup men to plan the adventure.

"She's back there in that booth," Ruby says as I enter her front door. "Libby's feeling under the weather, so I'm having to do everything today."

"Oh, okay." I smile at her and, as I ease past, give her a sympathy nod. Although I truly feel sorrier for myself and the rest of her patrons. It's just not good to be here on a Ruby-only day.

Laney rolls her eyes at me as I near the booth. "Dart back there and get us a couple muffins."

"Us too," the two men who are sitting at the table nearest ours say.

"Anything," one says.

Then Eddie Yeldin stands up. "Hey, Carolina," he says. "I'll come with you. I want to see what she's got."

"Hi, Eddie. I didn't realize that was you. Come on, they're back here." As we near the stove area, I point to a couple of baskets. "How about we take one of these with four different kinds and share it?"

"Sounds good to me. My friend isn't picky. Last week I was in here with guy from the county about permitting for the daycare, glad it wasn't 'Help Yourself Day' then."

"How are things going with the daycare? Jackson says your house is coming along great." We reach our tables. "You know Laney, right?"

"Yep. That Cayden is adorable. Barb loves watching him."

He turns to his guest. "This is Mitch McGlasson. He owns the farm across the lake from our property."

Mitch stands to shake my hand and then Laney's. Laney and he already know each other, but as I introduce myself, I recall where I've heard his name. "McGlasson. My friend just bought a house that I believe was owned by a Mrs. McGlasson? Down near the river, behind the daffodils."

"Yes, ma'am. That was my mother's house. Mama died two years ago, but I just couldn't get up the energy to put it on the market at the time. My wife was sick."

Laney asks, "How are you doing, Mitch? Jean had a really long struggle."

He sadly smiles. "That she did. And hard to lose Mama on top of it. But I'm doing pretty good. Thanks for asking."

Ruby comes up behind me and blasts, "Carolina, you're blocking the aisle. I have enough to do without having to dodge everybody lollygagging in my way. Come with me and I'll get you a pot of coffee to fill y'all's cups. I can't do everything!"

I set the basket on our table and roll my eyes as the other three silently grin at me. Ruby mutters the entire time she's filling a carafe for me, so as soon as she's done, I escape the kitchen area. I fill our four cups and then give the carafe to another table that wanted coffee and hurry back to my seat before I'm yelled at again.

In my absence, Laney has cut all four muffins in half and shared them with Eddie and Mitch. She lets me know with facial expressions and mouthed words that she'll fill me in on Mitch McGlasson later, then gets to the topic we're here to discuss.

"So dinner last night was interesting. The girls told me they filled you in on Griffin going on the vet school trip? I flipped my lid, but Susan just sat there. Didn't seem to bother her a bit. She actually said she was happy he was there! Can you believe it?" Laney puts a big chunk of the chocolate muffin in her mouth, then takes a gulp of coffee, which helps her get back to talking quickly. "I always knew there was a bit of the martyr complex in my sister, and boy, was I right. She's just not going to move forward. Just not going to forgive herself." She stops and just stares at her coffee.

She groans and says in a quieter voice, "I'm kicking myself for being so hard on her and Silas, but at the same time if she'd listened to me and just slowed it all down, maybe she wouldn't be taking it so hard now."

I chuckle. "Being on the morally right side isn't as easy as it looks, is it?"

"No, it's not! I feel like I'm getting a taste of my own medicine from all the trouble I caused my folks. Although I always bounced back faster than Susan. Maybe it's because she doesn't have all that 'having to bounce back' experience I do." Laney shakes her shoulders, pulls herself up taller in her seat, and picks up her cup of coffee. "But never mind all that." She takes a sip of coffee, then says, "No worries at all. I have a plan."

"So you'll make sure Silas is home, okay? I'll be sure to get Susan and the girls there. Grant is off doing his own thing these days, mostly up at your house, but she needs to see the girls are okay with her being with Silas. Or at least being friends with him. We have to start somewhere." Laney hasn't stopped talking about her plan since she started talking about it. It's actually rather simple, but she likes the details. We are now stuck on the sidewalk for one more go-round before we head in opposite directions to our shops.

"Okay. I've got it. Thursday afternoon. I've got to go."

"Yeah, me too. Call me when you've talked to Silas. Remember, don't tell—"

"I remember, I remember. Bye!" It's still early, but a half hour of Laney in planning mode makes me want a nap.

And a drink.

CHAPTER 53

"I'm going to kill Thompson LaMotte," Missus declares as she sails into the shop late Wednesday.

I can't help but laugh. "That might be the kind of thing you don't wanna say out loud in public."

She meets me beside the front table where FM's books are being examined by two men. "Oh, but I'd be celebrated near and far for it. He's a brute. He's practically forbidden my grandson from ever stepping foot in Chancey again. And they're all letting him get away with it! Peter, Delaney, Augusta. All just rolling over and letting him have his way." She folds her arms and looks at the men who are ignoring her. Or maybe it's that they are just so engrossed in FM's books. However, it's more likely they don't want to make eye contact with the basilisk named Missus.

"So Augusta didn't have any luck talking to her brother, I take it." I go over to the chairs and motion for her to come with me. "We don't want to disturb their reading."

She gives a sniff of agreement and comes with me. I sit on the end of the couch and she takes the chair, but she's too aggravated to relax into it. "No, she didn't. I'd hoped having everyone sit down to talk it all out might help. I even had Gregory on FaceTime as we began. I thought that would help, but it seemed to enrage Thompson that I thought I could just 'call and interrupt the boy's studies anytime I felt like it, like some needy meemaw'! He said that to me. Actually called me a meemaw. Roared at the poor boy, telling him that his future lies right there at school and in only a handful of years he'll be free to ruin his life however he chose but not until then. Honestly, Carolina, it was downright barbaric. So"—she lifts her gloved hands in surrender—"only resort left is to kill him."

She stares at me and I wait for a crack, a bit of a smile or a sigh, but she's like stone. "Come on. You're not going to kill him. For crying out loud, stop acting like this. So your meeting idea didn't work. I know you and Augusta had big hopes, but, well, I'm sorry."

"She's at her real estate agent's office right now, trying to figure out the best way to back out of the sale without losing all her money. I don't think Thompson cares. He looked very satisfied at the idea of her crawling back to him for help. He offered his attorney and she grudgingly accepted." She wearily leans back. "Worst of all, Peter just sat there. Didn't say a word. He's too tied in with Thompson to go against him." She waves her hand toward the table. "I was so looking forward to telling Gregory about his other grandfather. To watch Gregory here where FM lived, but I don't think Thompson will allow him to ever come here again. He as much as said so. We have to see him at their house in Atlanta or up at his school." She stands up and tugs on her gloves as if to get herself pulled back right. "I've neglected my mayoral duties trying to fix this mess and all for naught." She marches to the front door and I follow her.

"Missus, you did your best. I know Augusta and Gregory appreciate your efforts."

We step outside into a delightful spring day, but we bring our own gray cloud with us. Nothing seems to be working out. Missus sniffles. Her voice is husky and her eyes are damp as she asks, "What's it all for, Carolina? I'm mayor and can make all kinds of improvements and future plans, proclamations on every topic under the sun, but for what exactly?" She swallows, and a tear rolls down her cheek. "For what?"

"One good thing from all this is that Sally Blankenship will have no reason to stick around," I say to Jackson as we settle into the living room after dinner. My phone ringing startles us. "Oh, I need to take this." I jump up, holding the phone up for him to see it's Phoenix calling me.

As I answer, I rush out onto the back deck. "Hi there. You finally called me back." The deck is really cold on my bare feet, so I move back to stand on the rug by the door, but I talk low so no one inside can hear me.

"Well, I've been really busy. What do you need?"

"I need to talk to you about what you're doing. Colt is crushed that you didn't give him some kind of a reason for breaking up."

"You know I can't tell him. I can't stand pity. Especially his."

"You need to be honest with him."

"No. Believe me, this is best. We'll both be fine. But…"

"What?" I ask, sensing a crack I can use to get them back to talking.

"I do need to talk to you."

"Good. How about tomorrow? I'm not working, so I'm really flexible."

"Yeah, I guess it'd be better in person. How about after my Mommy and Me lunch class? Around one?"

"Sure. I'll be there, but—"

She cuts me off. "Okay. Bye."

The fact that she hung up is fine with me because it's too cold to be out here barefoot.

After checking to make sure Colt isn't in the living room, I whisper to Jackson, "We're getting together tomorrow to talk."

"Good. Maybe you can find out what's going on with her. But isn't tomorrow Laney's big plan? You sure you'll have time for anything besides the *big plan*?" His voice is creepy on the words "big plan," and his eyes are wide and crazy before he starts laughing.

We've been laughing all evening at Laney's scheming and machinations. She's working harder at arranging the pieces on this chessboard than I ever imagined was possible.

I wave off his fake concern. "Oh, I'll be fine. Laney's managed to get Susan the afternoon off from work to go shopping with Leslie and Susie Mae. She got Susie Mae permission to take a science test during her lunch break so she can leave school early. She has Barbara Yeldin babysitting Cayden but at the Yeldins' house because she needs picking him up there as an excuse to go that way when they get back in town. Then she'll pull into Silas's, where I'm to make sure he's there. He has promised me he'll meet me there to discuss something about gardening or classes. I wasn't very specific. Anyway, it should all work so that Susan will see the whole setup and Silas on a beautiful spring afternoon. She'll have both her daughters and her sister there giving her and Silas their blessing."

"I still think y'all should clue Silas in on what's happening."

"I kind of did. I mean, he's still pretty suspicious of Laney, but I did mention Susan should see the place and he said he'd really like that. He's pretty savvy, so I think he has a feeling something's going on. That's one reason I was so vague about what I wanted to talk about. Anyway, I'm meeting Phoenix at one and Silas at two. I feel really good about it all."

Jackson rubs my cold feet I've pulled onto the couch. "Good. I can tell you I feel great about the camping trip. You sure you're okay with us going on out there tomorrow night even though we have guests showing up Friday?"

"Absolutely. Savannah is going to help me. Y'all can get out there and get everything set up, and then she and I will join you Sunday afternoon with all new supplies."

He points the remote at the television, and I pull a blanket off the back of the couch to snuggle in for our movie. The guys were all champing at the bit to camp, so Savannah and I worked out our own little plan. We're going to have a girls' weekend here before we join them for only one night in the tent. I still feel so bad for Augusta and Gregory, but I have a good feeling all our plans for Susan and Silas are going to work out and it's going to be a great spring break.

CHAPTER 54

"Where are you?" Laney threatens me through my phone. In her fake, singsongy voice it may not sound like a threat, but it was definitely a threat.

"In town. I had to stop and see Phoenix, but a little girl in her Mommy and Me class fell and busted her forehead. We were dealing with that, waiting on the paramedics. The ambulance is blocking my car in, and I can't leave Phoenix with all this blood everywhere." I turn away from the chaos to whisper, "Are you there?"

The singsongy fakeness is gone as she snaps, "Of course I am. I've basically locked Susan and the girls in my car and told them to stay there while I got out to call you. Where is everyone? This place is deserted. No Silas. No you. You are ruining my plan!"

"Listen, Silas should be there somewhere. I'll call him. Then I'll call you right back."

Of course Phoenix couldn't talk as soon as I got here. Some of the moms and kids from the class were hanging around having smoothies. Just when they were finally ready to leave, the little girl fell off her stool. I knew the mother shouldn't have let her sit up there, but the kid had whined and cried and of course the mom gave in.

I dial Silas while giving Phoenix a thumbs-up. It looks like everyone is ready to move on. The kid has been more calm than the mom, who insisted on calling her husband and waiting for him to get here from Lord knows where. God bless the paramedics. They've dealt with her, patched the little girl up, and are finally looking like they are going to leave. I hang up when Silas doesn't answer and write him a text saying I'm running late and asking where he is. Although, how would I know he's not there if I'm not there? I take off the last part and just let him know I'm running late. Of course before I can hit send, Laney calls me again.

"We're going to go get Cayden and then come back. I'm talking in circles, but Susan is such a sad sack she doesn't seem to even care. Did you get a hold of Silas?"

"No. I'm about ready to leave here, so you go get Cayden and then I'll be there when you get back. See? It's all fine."

She growls at me as she hangs up, but I'm fine with that. "Whew!" I stick my phone in my pocket and approach Phoenix, who sinks onto a stool as the last person leaves the studio. I give her a weak smile. "How are you?"

"Better. I can't believe they were able to fix her up without stitches. There was so much blood."

"The paramedic said it can be like that on the face. He told me that's why plastic surgery works so well on the face, lots of blood supply."

Phoenix holds up a hand. "Stop. I can't take all this blood talk after seeing that." She swivels around to the bar and lays her head on her arms.

I pat her back. "Can I get you some water?"

She just shakes her head, face still buried in her arms, so I keep patting and waiting.

Finally she sits up. "Okay. I have too much to do to be sitting here, and I still want to talk to you."

I sit down on the next stool. "About Colt and you? Right?"

She frowns and shakes her head. "No. That's done. He wants

kids and I can't have them. I'm actually happier than I ever thought I could be, so that's done. It's time for him to move on." She swallows. "Besides, after all that drama just now, I don't think I even want kids. And I've kinda decided to swear off men. So many of them are just creeps. Not Colt, of course. But like that Thompson LaMotte joker. That's what I wanted to talk to you about."

I'd actually slid off my stool to get going as I think she's serious about Colt moving on and I'm tired of talking about it. But I stop and move closer to her. "What? What about him?"

"So I did several meals up there at Missus's house, and I right off was glad I'd stopped with all the glamour makeup and sexy clothes because I knew the moment I met him he was one of those men. Las Vegas was full of them. You know, the older men who like perky showgirls and all that stuff. Anyway, I steered way clear of him."

"Oh, Phoenix. Did he come on to you?"

"No." She looks guilty. "He's not the kind of creep that hits on just any woman; he only goes where he's welcome. And when you're rich, someone is usually putting out a welcome mat."

"Here? In Chancey?" As I try to anticipate what she's going to say, I realize I don't want to know. I just don't want to know. "Listen, Phoenix, I don't think I want to know. I mean, I know too many secrets already."

"Oh, not here. I mean, that's not what I'm talking about. One of my friends in Vegas knows him. Knows him pretty well." Her spiked eyebrows and nod tells me just how well. "She and I still talk fairly often, and I was telling her a couple days ago how folks have been raving about some of my meals. One for the Bedwells was a luxury hamburger with lobster on it that LaMotte requested because he always gets it in some fancy restaurant in Las Vegas. She immediately asked who requested that and she knew him. Can you believe it? It's her guy." She stands up and slips a folded-up paper out of the side pocket of her yoga pants. "Here's her name. I wasn't going to say any-thing, but then Augusta stopped in to tell me goodbye. So I got to thinking: maybe Augusta can use this to get him to let up on her and her plans. It just can't have come through me, you know? Is she still in town?"

I take the paper and look at it as I mumble, "I don't know. She was supposed to leave, but then she said she was going to be at the bookstore this afternoon."

Phoenix walks behind the bar as I consider what's on the paper. Would Augusta really want to do something like this to her brother? Do I want to be a party to it? My phone buzzing gets my attention, and I read Laney's text. She's got Cayden and will be back at Silas's soon.

I stick the paper and my phone in my pocket. "Thanks," I say with a nod to Phoenix. "I mean, I guess, thanks. I have to go."

She waves at me. "He really is a creep. Keep that in mind."

Pulling into the main parking area, I see Laney's car is on down next to Silas's house, but I don't see Silas. I tried him again on my way but still no answer. Three of the doors on Laney's black SUV swing open as I park beside it.

Leslie is out first and headed to the house with Susie Mae right behind her. I catch up to them. "What's going on?"

The older girl stops and turns to me, whispering, "I've had enough. Mom's practically comatose, and I'm supposed to go back to school with her like this? She says nothing, has no opin-ion. It's worse than it was when we were on the trip to North Carolina." The three of us look back at Laney and Susan talking beside the car. Laney's left it running, and we can hear toddler music playing loudly to keep Cayden happy. Leslie huffs and turns to the house. "We're finding Silas and getting this thing between them figured out once and for all. Come on."

"Okay," I say. "Is he here? He still isn't answering his phone."

Susie Mae raises her shoulders at me. "We don't know. Figure it's as good a starting point as any." The front door is at the end of the short sidewalk, and Susie Mae rushes to knock on it. I hang back, then decide to go around to the patio and sliding glass doors there. Maybe he's fallen asleep on the hammock there; he'd mentioned how he'd done that before. That could explain him not answering his phone.

Leslie and Susie Mae yell that he's not answering as I step onto the patio. The hammock is empty, so I turn to knock on the sliding glass door, but before I touch the glass with my knuckles, I see Sally. And she's not dressed in upscale-distress-boutique. She's not dressed in *anything*. However, she is trying to get dressed—in a sheet she's pulling away from the man in the bed beside her. They are backlit from the front bedroom windows, so I mostly only see shapes. Thank goodness.

"Is he back here?" Leslie says, coming around the corner. I turn away just as Sally laughs and waves at me.

"No!" I hurry toward them. "Nobody home."

"Oh, look!" Susie Mae exclaims. "You can see the whole lake from up here." They keep coming even as I try to force them to go back.

"It's beautiful," Leslie says. "Mom should see this. She'd love living here even if it's just basically a glorified trailer. I'm going to go get her," Leslie says as she turns to face me—and the glass doors. "Hey…"

I can see her putting together the scene like I did. I push her to move as I grab her younger sister's arm. "Time to go!" I corral them down the step, but I hear the sliding doors opening behind us. "Hurry up!" I insist as I shepherd them away from the house.

"Hey, what are y'all doing?" Sally calls behind us, dressed in only a sheet, I'm sure. Why can't she just let us get out of here? Of course she wants us all to know she's with Silas. He's all hers. Well, she's right about that. She can have him!

"Nothing!" I yell. "We're leaving."

Leslie resists my pushing. "What is he doing in there?"

"I don't know, but it's time to leave." I'm so mad at myself. Jackson was right. I should've just come out and warned Silas what we were up to. "Laney, get in the car!"

Laney goes from confused to angry in the few steps it takes for us to get to her and for her to see a half-naked Sally. Susan's face, however, just falls from sad to sadder, and she turns to get back in the car. I can't believe we raised her hopes like this, even if she didn't seem hopeful. She had to know what was going on. Yet we didn't fix anything or help at all. We just made things worse. We didn't just flip the chessboard—we set it on fire.

"Get in the car," I demand again, but Leslie stops completely and turns around.

She points back to the patio, but asks me, "Is she sleeping with him?"

I look over my shoulder to see Sally standing at the edge of the patio with only a sheet draped around her. "Apparently. My mistake. Let's go."

Leslie rolls her eyes, but turns around and continues walking. "He's such an embarrassment. Always has been." We take a couple more steps as I think about what she's said.

"What?" I ask, pulling her shoulder to look at me as she begins to follow her sister into Laney's SUV.

She gives me another eye roll as she plops into the back seat. "I mean, she looks good, but she's too old for him. Ronnie is just like his mother," she spits with disgust.

Laney's head jerks up and she looks at me. Cayden's kid music swirls loudly around us. From the driver's seat she mouths at me, "Ronnie?"

I step away from the car and hurry back toward the house. Sally is no longer watching from the patio, but as I get closer a man comes out. Ronnie Troutman. He has on jeans, but his shirt is unbuttoned and flapping. He waves at the car behind me. "Hey, Aunt Laney. Wait a minute—"

But the only answer is the SUV peeling out of the parking lot.

He grimaces, then looks at me. "Hey there, Miss Carolina. Uh, you think you can give me a ride? See, I ran into Miss Sally on my lunch break and accidentally left my car in town."

He grins at me and winks. "We got distracted."

CHAPTER 55

A large truck turns off the highway into the parking lot and comes to a shuddering stop. Ronnie, in my passenger seat, bends forward to look at it. "That's Silas in the work truck. He's waving. I think he wants you to wait."

"I'm sure he does," I say as I stomp on the brake, put the car in park, and jump out. "Where have you been?" I ask Silas.

He meets me between the two vehicles. "Sorry, Carolina. I was down looking at a piece of property and stupidly locked my phone and keys in the truck here. I had to walk out to a phone and then wait for a locksmith. I tried calling you as soon as I could. You want to talk now?" He goes from apologetic to curious as he looks around me. "Is that Ronnie Troutman in your car?"

I blow out a long breath and look around. "Yes. He was up here visiting Sally Blankenship, who is apparently living with you."

He grimaces. "Yeah. She's kind of hard to get rid of."

"We brought Susan out here. With her girls. Me and Laney did it trying to get you two back together. Not just me and Laney, but the girls, too. Susan is miserable and you're miserable."

Immediately he perks up, looking around. "Where is she?"

"Gone. Sally was naked and there was a man with her, so I thought... we thought..."

He chuckles. "That it was me? No. No way." But his eyes narrow and he looks guilty. "Though I have to admit I might've thought she'd get jealous with Sally being out here. That was stupid, too, I guess." He looks up from beneath his long, movie-star eyelashes. "You think she's still with Laney?"

"Maybe." I step over to the van, reach inside to get my phone, and dial her. "I'm here with Silas. He got locked out of his truck with his phone inside. Where are you?" I listen to Laney for a moment, then nod as I disconnect. "They just pulled into Ruby's for pie."

He doesn't hesitate. "Let's go."

As we pull on to the highway with the big truck lumbering behind us, Ronnie grins at me. "I sure could use some pie. I didn't get no lunch."

Lord help me.

Ruby's pie afternoons are pretty busy, so while I manage to find a parking spot, Silas, in the big truck, has to park over near the railroad tracks on the other side of the park. Ronnie is starving as he has said over and over, so we go on in.

Laney looks up and smiles. Then when she sees that Ronnie is the man following me, she clouds up. "Ronnie Troutman, you should be ashamed of yourself. And don't go sitting down at my table without first washing your hands because I know where they've been."

He grins, but turns to amble to the restroom. I sit down at the large table Laney has commandeered in the center of the restaurant. I'm directly across from Susan, and I concentrate on her. "I'm sorry. We were just trying to help."

She looks a little better and actually smiles at me. "Y'all are too funny. It does mean the world to me that my girls, my sister, and you want me to be happy, and please know that I am going to be, eventually. If my kids have forgiven me, then I have to work harder to forgive myself. I have a great job, a great family, and Griffin is happy." She closes her eyes and takes a breath. "That truly is important to me. I blew everything up, but if he can be happy, well..." She lets that hang. Then she adds, "Silas and I will talk at some point. We will, I promise." She pats my hand, which I'd stretched across the table to her. "Now, let's have some pie."

"Amen, Aunt Susan!" Ronnie loudly agrees, striding across the floor toward us. He folds his dripping-wet hands in prayer. "Please, Miss Kimmy, tell me you still have some of that strawberry pie. I'm starving!"

Kimmy laughs. "Yes, there is strawberry pie. I also have buttermilk pie, coconut custard, and old-fashioned chocolate with mile-high homemade meringue."

We start making our selections while I keep an eye on the door. Where is he? Laney is frowning at me and making faces, but I don't have any answers for her. Just as Kimmy is bringing our plates of delicious-looking pie, Laney looks at the door and her eyes grow huge, but not in a happy way.

I try to look without being obvious, and then I see why she's concerned. Coming in the door is her mother with her whole knitting group. She waves at us, but they sit at a table near the front.

"There's Grandma," Leslie says. "I thought she was watching The Club for you this afternoon, Aunt Laney."

Laney sinks her fork into her strawberry pie. "So did I. Although mostly it was to have her out of the way for our little trip up to see Silas. Looks like absolutely nothing worked out like we planned." She puts a big bite in her mouth, drowning her sorrows as she shrugs at me. Guess even our second plan, Plan B didn't work. I'm just glad no one else knew. I believe I'll also drown my sorrows, but in chocolate and meringue.

But as I lift my fork to my lips, Susie Mae jabs me with her elbow. I frown at her, and she uses her eyes to tell me to look at the door again. There, coming in with a huge armful of flowers, is Silas. Following him are Shannon, Danny, and Bonnie. I guess The Club isn't the only shop closed in the middle of the day.

Silas points at me to get Susan to look in his direction.

"Hey, look at the door," I say and watch as her eyes go soft and her cheeks pink. Then Silas steps to the side, bends down, and hugs Mrs. Troutman. The even bigger surprise is that she hugs him back!

"It was sweet of you to stop in at The Club and talk to me," she says loudly. She slides her eyes over to look at her daughters, trying to convey something to Susan with her stare, before turning back to beam at the man with the flowers. He gives her a bouquet of peach roses, and she flutters her eyelashes and twitters at him. I can't help thinking the man is almost too good-looking for his own good. Almost.

Silas finally walks to our table and asks, "Can I join you, all of you, for pie?"

Laney has already gotten out of her seat beside her sister. "We'd love for you to. Sit here."

"Thanks. Susan, is that okay with you? I don't want to make you uncomfortable."

She nods, and he comes around to the chair and pulls it out. As he sits, he holds out the armful of pink roses, purple irises, and tiny daisies. "Here. These are for you. Your favorites." His voice cracks, and so, as she accepts the bouquet, he swallows and turns toward the rest of us. "Now, what kind of pie should I have?"

"I left Augusta in charge of the store," Shannon says when I walk over to their table to see how things are going. "She insisted we come have some pie and see the Silas-Susan reunion. We only had one customer at the time, and she and Augusta were talking books."

"So she is still in town?"

Bonnie nods. "She said she wanted to say goodbye to you."

I look back over at my table and half-finished piece of pie. "Can y'all get that boxed up for me and bring it when you leave? I'll go see her now."

After assurances my pie would not be thrown away, I check my pocket to make sure I still have the piece of paper from Phoenix.

CHAPTER 56

"Gregory says their plan is back on." Savannah is cuddled in a folding chair beside me at the fire. The moon is rising over the lake, and we're alone while the guys have gone to get the makings for s'mores. I told her she could take a quick peek at her phone while her dad isn't here. He's imposed a no-phone zone at the fire. She whispers excitedly, "He says Gussie is moving here next month and he'll be here as soon as the semester ends."

I nod and turn toward her, careful to keep my blanket from falling off my shoulders. "That's great. I'm glad they could work things out."

She doesn't answer as she's making her limited phone time worthwhile, but I'm good with the silence. We had a fun weekend. Savannah and I watched our old favorite movies, added a couple to the rotation, went to Canton to get our nails done, and even did some cooking with Phoenix on Saturday afternoon and evening. I believe I can safely say Savannah is going to be a much better cook than I am. For one thing, she doesn't seem quite so reliant on microwaves or canned goods as I am. Phoenix seems happy, so I'm just going to be happy for her. I have officially retired her from the chessboard.

The sky through the trees is now solid black and the stars are popping out so fast I can't keep track of them, so I give up and just enjoy seeing them through the bare limbs of the trees around us. The fire site is close to the lake, but the tents are on flatter ground up the hill. A couple of other campfires dot the woods around us. We had a communal dinner beside the Yeldins' camper, with everyone bringing food to share. We ate at a picnic table with the Yeldins. Barbara and I got to know each other better, but she is still awfully quiet. Nathan and Savannah are just friends, now that he's invited another girl to the spring fling and she's done trying to maneuver her own invitation. The twins, still in junior high, are too enthralled with Bryan for them to be friends, but he preferred talking football with his dad and uncle anyway.

Neither Susan nor Laney's families are camping. Susan, Griffin, and their two younger kids took Leslie back to school. Griffin came back today, but Susan and the kids are staying on the other side of Atlanta for the first couple days of their spring break.

Laney takes full credit for getting Susan and Silas back together. She says it all worked out just as she planned and refuses to hear anything to the contrary. In fact, she's so happy with her maneuvering that she plopped her own family onto the chessboard and gave it a whirl. She sent Angie and Jenna over-the-top invitations, including a box of chocolates and flowers and live butterflies, to a two-day stay at a spa in downtown Atlanta for an early graduation gift.

She set the stage for an easy exit and willing childcare for herself by going away with Shaw to a car show yesterday up in the mountains. There were other assorted favors she was planning to bestow, but I didn't need all those details. Needless to say, Shaw is happy to take care of Cayden while she and the girls are gone.

As for Alex, she got him on her side by floating a farm-to-table weekend in Asheville, North Carolina, she wanted to give to him and Angie as a gift… if he made her getaway work. She knew Angie wouldn't want to leave him alone dealing with the restaurant, but he also was happy to play his part. Once everything was in place, she sent the amazing invitations. They leave tomorrow for two days.

As for my final chess move? Augusta took the piece of paper with Phoenix's friend's name on it. She listened to what I had to say, then packed up the books she'd bought, and after a last look around Blooming Books, she left. I don't know what she did with the woman's name and I don't want to know. I'm just happy to see how happy Gregory's return makes my daughter, and I'm thrilled to know Augusta is coming back to Chancey. To stay.

The pounding of Bryan's feet running down the hill toward us alerts us it's time for s'mores. He yells, "Mom! We got everything, but Dad says you're the master s'more maker! Here." He piles two full grocery bags in my lap and then drags over a little campstool. "This can be your table." He warns Savannah, "You better put your phone away. Dad's coming."

"I am," she says, locking it and sliding it into the front pocket of her hoodie. "But speaking of being on my phone, little brother," she draws out, "what's all this news about you going to senior spring fling?"

"What?" I say, tearing a chocolate bar wrapper open with my teeth. "You're a freshman. You can't go."

Savannah takes the clip off the bag of marshmallows and takes one out to throw at her brother. "Well, Mom, you know he's dated an older woman before."

"But Brittany is a sophomore. Sophomores can't invite people to the spring fling. That's just for seniors, right?" I deal out a stack of graham cracker squares onto my makeshift table. "I don't know what you heard, but Bryan's not going. Right, Bryan? Who's saying that?"

Savannah answers, "Ainsley Culpepper."

Bryan is poking at the fire, chewing his marshmallow and not saying anything. "Bryan. What's going on?" I ask.

He looks up at me, his face orange from the firelight, and he swallows. "Ainsley's the trainer on the basketball team. She's a friend. And a senior. And she asked me."

He's so nonchalant. Part of me is absolutely not happy about my freshman being invited to the senior dance, but another part is happy that maybe he's over Zoe, who is still completely obsessed with Grant. That triangle of friends is nothing but trouble in the offing, so I'm kind of glad he's moving on, but with a senior?

"What did you tell her?" I ask, concentrating on placing the chocolate squares on the crackers so they're ready when the marshmallows are toasted. You know, that old 'I'm not really paying attention, so bare your soul' game.

His sigh is as old as the mountains surrounding us. "Ainsley is nice and we're friends, but I never thought she liked me like that." He clicks his tongue. "But you know how it is."

I can roll my eyes because I'm looking down and it's dark, so I do. Big time. "No, son, I don't. Won't you tell me how it is?"

"Well, here's what I'm thinking. Grant will want to go to the spring fling thing when he finds out I'm going, so he'll start flirting with some senior girls to get invited. That'll make Zoe mad 'cause, well, nobody knows, but I think she's kind of got a thing for Grant." He reveals this shocking secret to me and his sister, appreciating our incredulous looks, but totally not understanding that we're not incredulous at the revelation, but that he thinks no one knows. He continues, "Zoe will talk to me about it because I'm a good listener. She says that all the time." I look up to see him grinning, and he winks at me. My little boy winked at me! "Then I'll be able to tell Zoe how much fun Grant had at the dance without her. But that I didn't have that much fun. She'll be jealous of Ainsley; she's really kinda pretty and everybody likes her. Then Zoe will figure out that she really wants to date me!" He wraps up with a nod at us, stands, and brushes off his hands on his pants as he reaches to grab the bag of marshmallows from his sister.

Savannah is as speechless as I am. She shakes her head, then pops the marshmallow in her hand into her mouth. I stare at the small table in front of me. I've covered it with rows of graham cracker squares, then placed smaller squares of chocolate on each one. Hmm, a grid of squares, kind of like a chessboard.

Seems like they're everywhere. And everyone is playing.

Sign up for my newsletter and check out all my books at
www.kaydewshostak.com
I love being friends with readers on Facebook.
Thank you for your reviews on Amazon!
The eleventh book in the Chancey series will be coming
next year, but the fifth in the The Southern Beach Mysteries
series releases later this year.

Books by Kay Shostak

The Chancey Books

Next Stop, Chancey
Chancey Family Lies
Derailed in Chancey
Chancey Jobs
Kids Are Chancey
A Chancey Detour
Secrets Are Chancey
Chancey Presents
Chancey Moves

Florida Books

Backwater, Florida
Wish You Were Here

Southern Beach Mysteries

The Manatee Did It
The Sea Turtle Did It
The Shrimp Did It
The Shark Did It

CPSIA information can be obtained
at www.ICGtesting.com
Printed in the USA
LVHW101543210622
721790LV00005B/391